THE WILL TO DEFY

BY

KEN MYLER

Published by ACME Publications, New York
www.acmepublications.com

© Ken Myler, 2006
ISBN 0-9774636-0-5

Cover design © Ken Myler, 2006

How does an ordinary man prevent his own murder with a simple one-page document?

You accidentally kill the daughter of a powerful underworld boss. His threats give you cause to believe that your time is close at hand. What do you do? Ben Pearce finds himself in this situation.

How does an average man protect himself from a force such as Victor Dracken? After days of agonizing and planning his own funeral, Ben stumbles upon a simple plan – a one-page document that will hopefully put fear into the heart of Dracken. But as with most simple plans, his becomes complicated, unleashing a chain of events that one would wish only to find in a nightmare.

To my father from whom I inherited the ability to do things that I never thought possible.

Chapter One

The ceremonious banging of the gavel signified the end of trading on the floor of the New York Stock Exchange. Banks of TV monitors broadcast the daily ritual throughout the office of Aston Cleary and Co., an old-line brokerage firm, as brokers and secretaries scurried about finishing up last second executions. A sigh of relief could be heard as another day of hectic trading came to an end.

Freshly installed carpeting lay buried under discarded order tickets and scraps of paper; patches of its green color and its smell were the only evidence that it rested beneath. The now calm office had been just minutes before a battleground of buying and selling. The yelling of frantic brokers was now down to a murmur. Traders who had had a good day talked cheerfully on the phone; the others wandered aimlessly about the office, shell shocked – at least until happy hour.

Brokers who maintained the window offices that surrounded the huge trading floor of partitioned oak desks loosened their ties as they leaned back in their leather chairs. They were the biggest moneymakers, and their windows were there to remind them that if they didn't produce, they would be out on the floor with the noise and the chaos.

Ben Pearce sat behind his desk on the trading floor logging his trades for the day into his client book. A seasoned broker, the only evidence of the stress being his slightly graying temples that blended into his full head of sun lightened hair. His tanned skin however bore the scars of a sun worshiper. He paused for a moment to look at a picture of his wife and children nearly buried under a mountain of pink and white order tickets.

His partner and best friend Howie Doyle, an immediate commander of respect, towered over the small partition between their desks. He bent his neck hard to the side, cracking the vertebra.

"Married for eleven years and you still can't wait to get home to her can you?"

"You find it so surprising that I still want to be with my family every minute possible?" Ben replied in his mildly raspy voice. "Some day you'll know the joy of a family, Howie."

"Not me buddy, variety is the spice. There's just too many women, and as long as I keep my looks I'm stayin' single. And you know I didn't mean nothin by that. I love Claire and the kids," he said, passing Ben a handful of papers. "You gonna be ready to leave in about a half hour?"

"Yeah, I'll be finished with this soon. Then we can go. Where am I dropping you off, at home or the bar?" Ben asked.

"Just drop me at home. I hate taking taxis from bars at night. You're picking me up tomorrow morning to get my car, right?"

"Yeah, yeah, no problem. When are you getting a new car, Howie?"

"When I can afford it." They looked at each other and laughed, but Howie turned away, his smile leaving him quickly.

"No seriously, that car is ready for the scrap pile. The thing breaks down every week. It's time to let go and besides..." Ben had to word his statement without hurting his friend's feelings. "There comes a time in life when the little red Corvette needs to be exchanged for maybe a Beemer. You're thirty-seven Howie; come on."

Howie nodded his head in recognition and fell back into his chair. Ben stood up. His slender body and the pin-striping in his suit added a couple of inches to his actual height. He rested his arms on the divider.

"You're right Ben, I know. But the car keeps me feelin' young. I guess I'm just tryin' to hold on to my youth. It's easy for you. You have a great wife and kids, you got it all – the perfect life."

"You almost sound jealous. I thought you didn't want to be married with kids. Am I missing something?" Ben asked.

"Nah, forget it. I guess I just know that the car has to go and I'm a little bummed. Let's get done so we can blast outta here."

Ben finished clearing his desk, never leaving a paper out of place before going home. He checked his messages again to make sure that he had returned all his calls, then glanced over at Howie who was flirting with a secretary.

"Hey, you ready to go?" Ben asked, now realizing that maybe he should have waited a couple of more minutes before interrupting.

"Yeah I'm comin'," Howie said, walking back to his desk and snatching his briefcase. "Thanks a lot pal. I told her I didn't have a ride. Thought maybe I'd go home with her. Now I'm stuck with you and I doubt whether you're going to be as much fun as she would have been. Let's go."

"Sorry buddy," Ben said laughing. "Let me just tell Brenda that we're leaving." He walked to a back office where the secretaries had their desks and peeked in. "Brenda, Howie and I are taking off."

"Okay, you're taking Howie home again?" she asked, knowing full well that Howie's car was in the shop again.

"Like always Brenda. Like always," Ben said, pointing at her blouse. "You've got spots on your..."

"I know, I know. Howie squirted me with a water gun."

Ben tried to hold back a smile.

"It's not funny," she snapped. "I swear, I don't know how you two are friends. You're so different. After you met him and realized what a juvenile he was, how did you continue hanging out together?"

"Brenda, I came here from South Dakota when I was thirteen. Howie and I haven't been apart more than a couple days since then. Wouldn't have it any other way."

"Guess you were pretty lucky to get away from South Dakota, huh?"

"I thought so, but now I can't wait to get back," Ben said, nodding while walking away, leaving her with a puzzled look. "See you tomorrow Brenda."

Ben and Howie walked towards the front entrance, first passing through one set of doors into the reception area. "Good night Kelly," Ben said to the girl as he pushed open the glass doors leading into the building's lobby.

They followed a curved marbled hallway leading to the entrance of the parking garage. The smell of exhaust hung heavily in the air. Ben steered Howie in the direction of his truck, but the sound of crashing trash stopped him and he quickly changed direction. Howie stopped as Ben took a pathway out to the side of the structure.

"Ben, where you goin'?"

"I hear Harry."

"Ah c'mon. How much money you gonna give this guy?"

Ben approached a large green Dumpster and knocked on its side. The noise within stopped and the head of a short and very overweight man popped up. His dirty face and long greasy hair gave hint to his last bath.

"Hi Ben," he said, his face lighting up.

"Hi Harry, how's the bottle collecting?"

"Not so good."

"Well, here's a couple bucks to hold you over."

The man looked grateful. He folded the bills and stuffed them into his shirt pocket.

"I'm going to hate to see you go Ben. When are you moving?"

"Soon, Harry. Soon I hope."

"I'm going to come and visit you out there. Always wanted to see the West."

Ben gave a small salute. "You're always welcome."

They approached Ben's freshly washed Toyota Land Cruiser. Admired by all that he shared the road with, the truck in Midnight Blue, his favorite color, stood out like a trophy. The tires and mud flaps were shiny black as though they had just come off the showroom floor. Ben stopped to wipe a smudge off the rear bumper. Howie just watched, shaking his head.

Ben pushed the button on the key chain remote, unlocking all the doors. Howie laid his briefcase on the back seat. Ben looked across the truck at Howie.

"On the floor, not on the seat," he said.

Howie made a face and placed the case upright on the floor. Ben removed his jacket and placed it on a hanger, clipping it behind his seat.

Climbing into the truck, Howie took a deep breath, taking in what he could of the new car smell that still lingered. A hint of pine also accented the air, emanating from an air freshener hanging on the radio volume control. The little green pine tree remained partially in its plastic so as not to overpower the occupants.

The spotless black interior of the vehicle shone and the leather seats were soft from countless saddle soap baths. Howie ran his finger along the top of the dashboard expecting to find a few specks of dust to show Ben, but to his amazement there were none. He reached up and tapped a small silver cross that hung from the rearview mirror, making it swing wildly. This and the garage door opener were the only items that Howie could see that weren't a standard feature of the truck.

"How do you keep this thing so clean?" Howie asked, buckling himself in.

"You know me, I'm Mr. Clean," Ben replied. "I like things neat, I can't help it."

"Yeah I know, Mr. Perfect... perfect life. You just don't know how lucky you are."

"Actually I think I do, but thanks for jinxing me," he said, pulling out of the spot.

A line of cars was already ahead of him attempting to exit the lot. They crept slowly toward the exit as they settled in for the long arduous ride home. Half an hour had past, before the Expressway, which was three miles from the office, was finally in view. The three-lane road resembled a large parking lot as traffic moved at a snail's pace. Ben glanced out his window at the small space between the left lane and the divider. He was both amazed and disgusted at the objects discarded in this narrow lane. Besides old tires and scraps of metal from previous accidents, he saw keys, rags and even the head of a doll. He shook his head and raised his eyes up high to see the large apartment buildings, which towered over both sides of the roadway. This was not where he wanted to be.

"There's the reason we're moving so slow," Howie said, pointing to a car that had overheated.

"I better call Claire to let her know I'm on my way and that I'm going to be late."

Howie shook his head. "You really are whipped."

"You're just jealous that I'm happy," he said, hitting the speed dial. "Hi honey, I'm on my way. Gotta drop Howie off first and then stop at the vet. Jerry next door asked me to stop and grab medicine for the dog."

Howie leaned over and yelled, "Hi honey" into the phone.

"She says hi and wants to know when you're getting a new car," Ben said with a smirk. "Okay, I'll see you in a bit."

"You're just lucky that I gave her up, maybe I shoulda kept her for myself," Howie said.

Ben laughed. "You gave her up? She dumped you and did the smart thing by grabbing me."

"I dumped her and that's the story I'm sticking to," Howie shot back, cracking a smile.

Claire had caught on to Howie's womanizing traits quickly during a short fling back in college. It was a standard joke of Ben and Howie's as to what might have been.

The long drive home proceeded as usual with long lines of traffic, the smell of exhaust and cranky drivers pounding their horns, fighting to get home. Ben couldn't wait to sell his house on Long Island and move out West to South Dakota where his parents still lived. He spent much of his time during the drive home daydreaming about horseback riding and watching his children grow up in a less congested state.

"Hey this is our exit." Howie shouted. "You awake?"

Ben sighed. "Sorry, I was just thinking how nice it'll be to get out of here."

"Oh that again. You riding a white horse into the sunset," Howie said, sounding annoyed.

"Howie, I know you don't want us to leave but it has to be. Can't I change your mind on moving out there?"

"Not my thing. You know that. There's no women out there."

"Yeah but there's lots of sheep," Ben said, giving them both a good laugh.

"I'm really gonna to miss you man," Howie said after a few seconds of reflection. "You realize that we haven't really been far apart for more than a couple of days in the last...what, twenty years?"

"Yeah I thought of that," Ben replied. "Thought of that a lot. Why don't you come out for a while? You don't have to live on a farm. Live in the city and we can work together."

"Yeah, like I want to work in that rinky dink office out there. There's no noise, no yelling. How do you get excited in an atmosphere like that?"

Ben just shrugged his shoulders as they left the Expressway and followed the service road. He turned onto a street known for its junkyards and auto body shops.

"I hate this short cut. More criminals working down here than are in the county jail," Howie remarked.

"Saves a ton of time though."

The area looked desolate, with Dumpsters and rusting cars along the road. As they passed Rockers Junkyard, they slowed.

"How can Connie work with those clowns?" Howie said. "I don't know how her husband lets her work there. My guess is that the money's good."

"Wonder how she's doing?" He thought back to the days when they were an inseparable threesome.

"God, we had some good times back then. Man, you two were like married except without the sex - or did you?" Howie asked.

"No...she just helped me through my aunt and uncle dying. You weren't much help."

"I wasn't much help? You came and lived with me for a year."

"I guess I can't blame you. That was the year that you discovered girls...and they discovered you."

"Ah, good times." Howie said, rolling the window down and spitting.

"You know we have to..." Ben began to say but Howie cut him short.

"Let me guess, we have to give Connie a call and get together. How many times have we said that? Once a week for years."

"That's about right, it's once a week that I have to take you home because of that poor excuse of a car."

Howie had no comeback, just a dumb look. They rolled past the junkyard, which had all the typical features – a high barbed wire fence, car bumpers and fenders stacked high on rusting shelves and heavy chains holding two Dobermans behind a double gate. The dogs were considered docile compared to the men who worked inside. All had lengthy prison records, but one stood out as the worst. Luke Stafford was infamous for raping and beating a teenage girl but getting off on a police technicality. He would play a bigger role in Ben's life than anyone could ever have imagined.

Ben pulled into a small development and wove through the narrow roads until he was in front of Howie's town house.

"You wanna come in for a minute? You gotta check out my new hot tub," Howie said.

"No, I have to get to the vet and home. The kids start to whine if I'm late. Besides I don't need to see the place where you deflower all those young woman."

"If I'm lucky I'll be doing some gardening tonight."

"Good one," Ben said laughing. "I'll pick you up at seven tomorrow; be ready."

"Hi, I'm Ben Pearce. I'm here to pick up medicine for my neighbors' dog. Their last name is Henderson."

"Okay Mr. Pearce. Let me get the chart and see what we have," the receptionist said.

Ben turned when a sobbing family walked huddled around a golden lab toward the waiting room bench. The young boy and girl, both about eight, sat on the floor cuddling the dog and crying. The parents sat, elbows on knees and heads in hands.

"What's going on there?" Ben whispered.

"The dog needs an operation and lots of medication afterwards. They can't afford it, so the dog has to be put down."

"But that dog can't be more than two years old...doesn't seem right. Can't the doctor help them out?"

"Happens a lot. The doctor does what he can, but if he operated for free on every animal where the owners couldn't afford it, he would be out of business."

Ben stared at the distressed family, remembering the dogs he had when he was a young boy. He remembered the pain of losing his faithful companions as he grew up. As each was buried, his father would hold him tight as they cried together. His father's words would always stay with him. "Nothing can reduce a rugged man to a blubbering mess like the death of his beloved dog. There ain't no shame."

Feeling the family's pain, Ben fought back his own tears as more of his father's words came to mind. "If you do well in life, always give something back."

"Mr. Pearce, here's the medication. Mr. Pearce?"

"Oh...yeah, thanks."

He walked over and stood in front of the grieving family. He bent down and patted the dog on the head.

"This is your puppy dog?" he said to the crying girl.

She could only nod. The dog licked Ben's face while her tail wagged like a propeller.

"What's her name?"

"Goldie," the father replied without looking up. "But they have to put her down because we can't... because we can't..." the man couldn't go on.

"I'll pay for it."

The man, still holding his head, froze for an instant, then slowly looked up through tear-filled eyes. His wife stood up.

"What... what did you say?"

"I said I'll pay for it... the operation and whatever else you need to save the dog."

The man and his wife looked confused. The children, having been taught to be wary of strangers, just stared at him.

"Do we know you?" the woman asked. "I mean we can't take that kind of money from you... this is a lot of money."

"Please, I really want to do this."

"Daddy, does this mean Goldie doesn't have to die?" the little boy asked.

The man stood up and reached out his hand, still not knowing whether to believe that another human being could be so kind. "I guess that's what it means. I don't really understand why you're doing this. I don't know how we can ever repay you."

The dog barked as he ran, chasing the laughing children around the room.

"That's payment enough right there."

Ben floated on air, crossing the parking lot.

Man, that feels good. Sometimes money can buy happiness.

Ben snaked his way through the winding roads of Great Neck, an affluent neighborhood on the north shore of Long Island. Only glimpses of the large homes could be seen, hidden in the trees of the estates. At one time, Ben had dreamed of living in one of those homes, but attaining the high six-figure income needed wasn't easy.

His hour and a half commute finally ended when he turned on to his street, which was much more modest than the stately homes he had just driven past. He pulled into the driveway next to Claire's black BMW and stepped down from his truck.

He surveyed the professionally manicured lawn of the small front yard as he passed through the gate, the black rails of which matched the shutters on the white high ranch house. A white real estate sign hung over the fence, partially over the sidewalk. The words "For Sale" stuck out boldly in red.

Claire waited for him at the front door. Looking much like Ben, she stood tall like a model. Her long hair framed her face and offset her bright blue eyes. Many people mistook them as brother and sister rather than husband and wife.

Coming in the front door, Ben kissed his wife as he stepped into the living room.

"Daddy's home," she yelled toward the back of the house.

Two small children came running, screaming "Daaadddy." Michael was three and Sarah two. Both were carbon copies of their parents when they were children. Their platinum blonde hair and piercing blue eyes were the envy of everyone who met them. He hugged and kissed them, wishing that he could spend all of his time with them.

"How was your day?" Claire asked, watching Ben walk like Frankenstein, having a child sitting on each foot.

"Had a great day; couple of dollars closer to the million." He yelled from the bedroom while peeling the children off his legs to change his clothes.

"You and your million dollars." She came into the doorway.

"Anything from the real estate?" he asked.

"No, not today. Maybe on the weekend they'll show it again," she replied with regret.

"I hope so. I really can't take the stress of New York anymore – took me an hour and a half to get home. Anything exciting happen at your office today?"

"What could happen exciting at a dental office?"

"Daddy, come play outside," Michael said, pulling on Ben's sweat pants leg.

"Let Daddy eat dinner, then he can play," Claire said.

"Did they eat yet?"

"Yeah, they ate a while ago," Claire answered. "Take your sister into the living room. I'll put in a tape for you," she said, shooing the youngsters inside.

Claire took the lid off a glass dish and carried it to the table. Ben was already sitting and staring at the small statue of Kokopelli – the mystical flute player that sat atop a shelf. Supposedly the bearer of good luck, it was the centerpiece of the southwestern theme of the kitchen.

She dished out Ben's favorite food – eggplant Parmesan. He ate quickly, knowing that the children were waiting and that there weren't many mild evenings left.

"This is great," he said, the words barely discernible through his full mouth of food.

"You a little hungry, honey?" She refilled his soda glass. "Ben, slow down, you'll choke!"

Almost finished, he stood and carried his plate to the sink, eating the last few bites as he walked.

The children sat on a recliner that was part of an L-shaped couch opposite the kitchen. They could easily see over the wall that separated the two rooms. Ben's walk to the sink was their cue, and they jumped up.

"Come outside Daddy." Michael led Ben down the stairs and out the back door. Sarah tagged close behind carrying a stuffed bear.

Holly, the neighbor's dog, sat on the other side of the fence wagging her tail, looking for a playmate. The children ran over and barked at the cuddly white ball of fur. She laid her head down on her front paws while the hind remained standing. Ben stamped his foot, sending the dog running in circles at top speed to the joy of the children. After twenty laps around the yard, the dog was winded. Ben reached over the fence and petted the dog's head.

"Okay Holly, go get some water. We'll see you later."

Claire flipped through the TV channels, occasionally glancing at the clock. Her hour of solitude was winding down as the children's bedtime neared. She went to the back door and watched as Ben pushed Sarah on the swing while Michael played in the sandbox. She smiled and tucked her hair behind her ear.

"Okay, c'mon, let's go. It's bath time," she announced.

Michael stamped his feet in a tiny tantrum that ended quickly. Sarah, who was less fearful of the tub, ran right in. Ben had a look of disappointment. Playtime for him was therapy after a long day of stress.

Nearing nine o'clock, the children were in bed. Ben and Claire fell back into the couch, exhausted.

"Oh, by the way your mom called while you were outside. She's asking about the house and is it sold yet."

Ben dropped the newspaper into his lap and let his head fall back on the headrest.

"You know what? I'll call her tomorrow. I can't get into this now. She thinks we can sell the place in a heartbeat and be out there in a week."

Claire just laughed.

"Listen, Claire, I know we've been over this a million times, but you're going to be okay moving out there, right?"

She paused for a moment and thought about what it was like – being able to spend time with her parents before they had passed away. As an only child, she had no close relatives in New York and the thought of having Ben's family around her was uplifting.

"Well you're telling me that the kids will do better out there. Can't say that I believe that though. I mean it's the sticks."

"I told you that the governor out there has spent a ton of money on the schools. They're almost all wired to the Internet. It's not like the one-room schools like in the westerns."

She nodded her head. She wasn't totally sold but she wasn't going to be the one to keep Ben from his family and the children from their grandparents.

She crawled across the couch to him and threw his newspaper on the floor. Pinning him back in the recliner, she kissed him, her hair forming a tent around his face.

"I'm going to bed, you coming?" she asked.

He leaned around her and looked at the clock. She turned to see where he was looking.

"I'll be in in a little while," he said with a guilty look. "I have to go on the computer to do some stuff."

"Some stuff and watch "The Wild, Wild West," right?" She gave him a shove.

"Well..."

"Just go. I'll wait for you."

Ben stood up and stretched as he headed for the kitchen. He grabbed a handful of cookies and made a quick right out of the kitchen and down the stairs to his office.

The room was small, originally intended as a laundry room. Two doors led out from it – one, a metal fire door leading to the two-car garage; the other to a back playroom that exited to the yard.

He wheeled the chair out from under the desk and sat. With the remote, he switched on a small portable TV up on the shelf.

Ah, just in time.

The music from his favorite western from his childhood had just started. He opened the top drawer and took out a picture of himself riding a horse at age five. "The Wild, Wild West" brought him back to that time. He pictured his children in his place in that picture.

The next morning Ben picked up Howie and dropped him off at the repair shop. "You want me to follow you to the office just in case it doesn't make it?" Ben said jokingly.

"Very funny." Howie spun around in a circle. "Hey what's the fastest way to the office from here Ben? I'm used to coming here at night on the way home."

"West about three miles..."

"Wait which way is west again?"

"That way," Ben pointed, shaking his head.

"Hey you were the Eagle Scout, not me," Howie said, walking toward the shop.

Ben had his headset on and was talking to a client when Howie walked into the office. Ben watched to see how long before Howie's nose twitched. He rounded the corner toward his desk and stopped. Ben laughed, watching Howie spin around in a circle as the first scent of shoe polish hit him.

"She's over there." Ben pointed to the far back of the office where the Russian shoeshine girl talked to a broker.

"Man, I gotta have her," Howie said, backing into his seat.

"Forget the girl for now and call Charlie Gable. He wants to place a trade on the open. Oh and one of the guys from the other side put that gadget with the wires on your desk."

"Oh good. This is going to drive Brenda nuts. You plug it into the phone and your voice can be changed to sound like anyone – a kid, an old man, even a chick," Howie said.

"Really. Where'd he get it from?"

"They sell 'em at any electronic store."

Howie draped his jacket over the back of his chair as he inspected his new toy.

"Hey Howie, run over to trading and grab the recommended list."

"Right."

Howie came back, flipping through pages. "You wanna buy some Utopia Motors?" Howie asked. "Our top dog analyst just recommended it and there's a big commission in it."

"If there's a big commish in it, you know they're just pushin' it so they can get out. I would never buy a stock just for that reason so why ask?"

"Yeah, I forgot, Mr. Perfect."

"Hey by the way buddy, how's the heap running?"

"Purrin' like a kitten, at least for today," Howie said while knocking on the wooden desktop.

At day's end, Ben walked with Howie in the parking garage. Ben had a look of anguish as they approached Howie's vehicle.

"Okay, let's see if it starts so I can go home," Ben said.

Howie jumped into the '69 Corvette and turned the key. It kicked over immediately. Howie gave Ben a smug look, "See?"

"Yeah, don't jinx yourself though. Please...I'm beggin' – get a new car. It's time."

The drive home started the same as every day, fighting the fumes and frustrated commuters. Ben looked forward to the serene roads of his neighborhood where he could drive more relaxed and not have to worry about being rear-ended.

As he passed the large homes of Great Neck, he wondered: Were the people living there really happy or did they have dreams of being somewhere else as he did? This was a question that he asked himself every day, and as he did every day, he fell into his usual daydream of being out west.

Coming around a sharp bend, his cell phone rang, startling him for a second and quickly jolting him out of his fantasy.

"Hello?"

"Hey, it's Howie...my car died again. I know, don't say it. The flatbed's on the way. Any chance you can come get me?" He asked in a pleading voice.

Ben was now coming around the final part of the bend, paying more attention to the phone conversation than to the road.

"You gotta be kidding me!" he yelled. "I'm almost home."

Just then out of the corner of his eye, Ben saw an orange flash. He jammed the brake pedal to the floor while steering the truck violently to the left. The pedal pulsed under his foot as the antilock brakes kicked in and the airbag blew open in his face. The sound of metal scraping asphalt pierced the air while sparks shot out from under the truck.

Ben was dazed from the impact of the airbag and for a moment didn't realize what had happened. He kept his head still while he moved his eyes back and forth and blinked, trying to clear the fuzziness. He felt his upper lip and brought his index finger close to his eyes. Blood, obviously from his nose, trickled down his finger.

"What did I hit, oh my God what did I hit?" he screamed.

He struggled to get the seatbelt off as it tangled with the deflated airbag. He scrambled to the front and dropped down on all fours. He was horrified to see a young girl, no more than six or seven, pinned under the truck. The orange bicycle she was riding was mangled and entangled in the vehicle undercarriage. He could see that the girl's helmet was cracked and blood was trickling onto the pavement. She wasn't moving. Ben ran around the car frantically screaming for help but the houses were too far for anyone to hear. He began to climb back into the truck with the thought of backing up and off the girl. He decided against it fearing that his weight in the truck may only crush the girl more. He finally composed himself enough to run to the passenger door and find the cell phone, which lay on the floor.

"911, what's your emergency?" the voice asked.

"I hit a girl on a bike! Please send help. Oh my God, I was on my cell phone and she just jumped out in front of me. I couldn't stop," he said in a panicked trembling voice.

He gave the approximate location and threw the phone back into the truck. He leaned under the vehicle again to see if the girl was alive. The pool of blood had grown larger and began to mix with the fluorescent green antifreeze that had leaked from a tear in one of the hoses. He slid under the truck to see if freeing the child was possible. He got close enough to shake the girl's arm and yell for a response but there was none. Looking closer, he could see where the blood was trickling out from the girl's head – it was an actual crack straight through the skull.

Feeling nauseated, Ben backed away and kneeled by the curb. His stomach crushed in on itself and his body convulsed, but nothing came up. Tears came forcefully from his eyes.

Voices came from the house, which was set way back on a hill. He glanced up through blurry eyes and tried to focus, but his truck was in the way. He crawled a few feet where he could see a man and woman running toward him screaming. "Rachel, Rachel."

They reached the car in hysterics. The man who was obviously the girl's father crawled underneath still yelling her name while the mother watched in horror. He wiggled his way back out and screamed at Ben to help.

"We've got to lift the truck off her," the man said in a heavy British accent.

Ben jumped up. "I don't think we can lift it by ourselves."

"Not lift it up, just tip it over on its side. We have to try. Go call 911!" he screamed at his wife.

"I already called," Ben said.

Ben reached under the sides of the truck trying to get a grip. Together they attempted to roll the truck onto its side with no success. Sirens could now be heard approaching in the distance.

"What happened?" yelled the girl's father as he and his wife leaned under the truck.

"I don't know, I was on the phone. I only looked away for a second. She came out of nowhere." Ben replied.

The boy's father stood up and got right into Ben's face.

"You were on the phone? You better hope she's all right."
Ben backed away surprised that this man would take time to
threaten him while his daughter lay dying.

The man knelt back down next to his wife who was sobbing
uncontrollably and calling the girl's name. Two police cars
screeched to a halt behind Ben's truck. Fire rescue could be
heard in the distance. Four officers swarmed the truck, yelling
commands at each other. Within seconds it was decided that
the best way to release the girl was the original plan of tipping
the vehicle over on its side. In one coordinated effort with Ben
and the father helping, the truck was slowly raised onto two
wheels until finally gravity took it crashing on its side. The safety
glass of the truck exploded on impact and thousands of pieces
bounced away from the truck.

The bicycle was still snared in the truck's underside and
hung in the air above the girl. Her one leg was still entangled in
the metal.

Ben backed away and stood near the curb, trembling and
sobbing as he watched the paramedics who had just arrived
carefully tend to the lifeless body. Within seconds they had an
I.V. in her arm and were placing her limp body on a wooden
backboard. One of the officers held the I.V. in the air as they
ran her to the waiting ambulance and raised her inside.

Ben glanced over at the girl's parents who were hugging
each other as they watched in horror. The girl's father looked
very familiar but Ben couldn't quite place him. The mother
broke away and jumped into the ambulance where she grabbed
the girl's hand.

The father attempted to join his wife but was turned away.

"There's not enough room; go with one of the officers,"
one of the paramedics yelled. The rear doors slammed shut
and the ambulance sped off with its siren blaring.

By now a woman and a man, apparently employees of the
girl's parents, looked on. The girl's father ran over to them giving
them instructions. Once finished, he shoved the man towards
the house.

"Move...now!" he yelled. The man ran with the woman close

THE WILL TO DEFY

behind up the hill.

One of the officers motioned to the father to get into one of the police cruisers. The doors slammed and the car sped by. The man leered at Ben, sending a shiver down his spine. He had never seen such sinister eyes.

With all the commotion, Ben hadn't noticed the crowd of neighbors that had gathered. An older couple approached him and began asking him questions, not noticing his tearful eyes. When Ben didn't answer, they realized he was the driver of the truck.

"I'm very sorry," the man said, ushering his wife away.

Three police officers stood huddled together discussing details and pointing to the driveway and then to Ben's truck. A police officer took pictures of the scene while traffic was routed to the far side of the road by orange cones. An officer waved the line of cars to move quickly past the scene but the temptation to stop and look was too much for most of the passing motorists.

Lights from the squad cars still flashed as the first officer approached Ben, who was now sitting on the curb.

"Were you injured at all sir?" the officer asked, opening his pad.

"No, I'm okay. Did the paramedics say if the girl was gonna be okay?" Ben asked.

"I wasn't near enough to hear," he replied. "Sir, I need to ask you some questions. Let's start with your name."

"Ben Pearce, P-e-a-r-c-e."

"Have you been drinking this afternoon sir?"

"No of course not!"

"I'm just doing my job here, sir. Please stand up." Ben complied as the officer checked his eyes, smelled his breath and made him walk a straight line. "Any drugs?"

"No!"

"Where were you coming from and where were you going?"

"From work to my house." The officer continued writing for a minute while another joined him, taking the paper with Ben's name on it.

"I'll run it through the computer," he said, walking back to his squad car.

"Okay, why don't you describe what happened."

Ben described the entire accident, leaving out that he had been on the phone.

"One of the other officers mentioned that one of the neighbors said something about you being on your cell phone. Is that true?"

"Yes."

Ben hung his head realizing that someone must have overheard him tell the girl's father.

"That'll be all for now, Mr. Pearce. Your truck is being impounded for a safety check. I'll have an officer take you home." The officer pointed to a car that would take him.

As he walked toward the squad car, he watched his truck being uprighted by a police tow truck. A flatbed waited right behind and began lowering its ramp to haul off his now smashed prize vehicle.

He felt the eyes of all the neighbors upon him as the officer opened the rear door to the squad car.

"How you feeling, Mr. Pearce?" the officer in the passenger seat turned and asked.

"I've been better. What hospital are they taking her to?"

"North Shore. Let's get you home. Maybe you can relax a bit there." The officer hesitated a moment and looked at his partner while addressing a question to Ben.

"By the way, do you know who the girl's father is?"

"No, but he did look familiar," Ben replied.

The officer gave Ben a concerned look. "That's Victor Dracken. You know him?"

Ben's eyes opened wide. "Yeah... yeah I know who he is."

Chapter Two

Claire waited with the children on the front lawn after Ben's call from the officer's cell phone. He hadn't gone into any detail, only that there was an accident and he was all right. Seeing the squad car coming down the road, she ran through the gate and stood at the curb.

"What happened?" she yelled. "Are you all right?"

"Yeah, I'm fine, I'm fine," he said, reaching over the fence and picking up Sarah. He motioned to Michael to head for the gate.

"Let's go in and I'll explain what happened."

"Where's your truck?" she asked.

"Just let's get inside first," he said, escorting her.

Ben sat her down on the couch. "I'll just come out and tell you. I was on the cell phone and wasn't paying attention. I took my eyes off the road only for a second. I...I ran over a little girl," he broke down in tears.

Claire didn't know what to say. She sat with her hand over her mouth. "Oh my God, is she all right?" She knelt down in front of him.

"I don't know...she didn't look good when they were putting her in the ambulance. She had an IV and she wasn't conscious."

Michael and Sarah had started moaning because Claire was holding them back from their father. Ben waved them up before the moans turned to crying. They climbed on his lap as he continued the story.

"I can still picture her under my truck. My God I pinned her under my truck. They had to flip it over to get her out." He stood up holding both children. "I have to run to the hospital. Let me get changed quick."

"I knew something was wrong when Howie called," she said.

"I forgot about Howie. He was stuck with his car again," he said, ripping his clothes off.

"He kind of sounded funny when I told him that you weren't home yet. But how could he have known? Did you call him?"

"Sort of." He stopped getting dressed and stood in anger. "Howie called me on the cell because his piece of shit car broke down again. I was talking to him when I hit the girl."

"Does he know what happened though?"

"No, I dropped the phone when the airbag hit me. He may have heard me scream."

"He's probably worried. Why don't you call him before you go," she said, handing him his sneakers.

"Do me a favor? Call him; I don't have the time to get into it with him now," he said, rushing around and gathering his things. "I'm ready, I'll see you later. Oh, where's your phone so I can take it with me? Oh, and tell Howie to come over."

"Do you want me to go with you? I could call Gail to baby-sit."

"No, you stay with the kids."

"Call me from the hospital and let me know if she's all right."

"Yeah, okay, as soon as I know what's going on I'll call. I don't know what time I'll be back though."

He bent down and hugged his confused children. This was supposed to be play time, and they couldn't understand what all the rushing was about.

"Ben...do the police know about the cell phone thing?"

"I made the mistake of telling the girl's father. The police know." He walked toward the door, then stopped. Without turning back to her he said, "I think this may be the first time that maybe honesty wasn't the right way to go."

Claire looked confused but didn't ask what that meant.

"I'm sure they know that I didn't do it on purpose, it was an accident. If they don't want me there, I'll leave." He opened the door and walked out.

Claire dialed Howie's number before Ben was out of the driveway with her car.

"Howie, it's Claire."

"What's going on? Everything okay?" he asked.

"Ben hit a young girl on a bike."

"Oh jeez, is she okay?"

"We don't know yet, Ben just left for the hospital."

"I knew something was wrong when we got cut off. I didn't want to say anything to you when I called though. I didn't want to worry you."

"Ben wanted to know if you could come over now. I don't know why...I mean he's not hurt or anything.

"Yeah sure but I don't have a car. I'll have to grab a cab. I'll be there as soon as I can or does he want me to meet him at the hospital?"

"No, he said to come here. Seemed like he wanted to go alone...Howie, I'm really scared. He sounded like the girl was really hurt." She began to choke on her words. "How...how fast can you get here?"

"On my way as soon as I get a cab." He hung up the phone.

Ben hadn't mentioned to Claire who the girl's father was or the possibility of a lawsuit. Trying not to think of further consequences of his mistake, he drove towards the hospital. He turned into the parking lot and pulled into a spot. Three limousines were parked near the emergency room entrance. Two men in suits were smoking cigarettes and pacing around the cars.

He turned the car off and sat for a minute reassuring himself that he was doing the right thing. He grabbed the handle and began opening the door. His heart quickened as he had a flashback of the accident scene. The picture of the girl tangled in the orange metal of her bike, wedged under the truck, was sickening. He laid his head back on the rest while taking a few deep breaths. What would he say to the parents if the girl was dead? And what would the girl's father say to him?

Victor Dracken was a scary individual known for his illegal operations. Drug smuggling and illegal gambling were well hidden within his vast real estate empire. The FBI was constantly watching him, but even with a million-dollar reward for information leading to an arrest, there were no leads.

Ben walked toward the hospital entrance. One of the men that he had noticed before was resting his arm on the top of the biggest limo, allowing Ben to see a black holster holding a silver 9mm pistol. He thought that maybe they were police, but most cops he had known didn't ride in limos.

The automatic doors opened as Ben approached the emergency room. Cool air rushed past him carrying the smell of antiseptic. He stopped for a moment deciding in which direction to look for the girl's family. There were groups of people standing ahead in a long hallway and many more sitting, watching a television atop a bracket mounted on the wall. Some were sleeping on the seats; they had obviously been waiting for quite a while. Their faces all had the same look of misery and pain as they waited for their names to be called.

Ben walked between the rows of seats looking for the Dracken family, but there was no sign of them. He walked to the nurses' station. Not wanting anyone else to hear, he leaned over the counter as far as he could.

"I hit a young girl on a bike earlier today and Id like to know her condition." Ben whispered to one of the three nurses.

"Do you know the girl's name?"

"Last name Dracken."

The nurse looked up at him quickly in surprise. "You're the man that hit her?"

"Yes, do you know how she is?"

"I believe she's been taken to surgery. She wasn't in very good shape when she arrived," she said. Ben fumbled with his keys dropping them onto her desk. He reached to pick them up.

"Can you tell me anything else?" he asked still whispering.

She could see that Ben was anxious and gave him a look of pity. "Let me see what I can find out. Wait here and I'll be right back." She got up and disappeared toward the examining rooms.

Ben paced nervously as he waited for her to return. One of the men that he had seen outside near the limos walked past him and disappeared down the far end of the hall. Ben, not sure if the man was connected to Dracken, watched as he left his sight.

Ben looked back toward the nurses' station but she hadn't returned. People, frustrated by their long wait, continuously approached the counter asking questions. Ben didn't pay attention to their conversations. He grew impatient. He took a step toward the hallway but stopped short upon hearing the name Dracken mentioned at the nurses' station. Ben walked toward the man, hoping he was related to the girl, but before he was able to say a word, the nurse stood up behind the desk.

"Umm sir, Lucy, the nurse you spoke to before, will be right back," she said, slightly raising her eyebrows. As the man she was speaking with turned, she put her index finger up to her lips, motioning to Ben not to speak in front of him.

"Okay," he mouthed, as he watched the man walk away. "Who was that?"

"A reporter asking questions about the Dracken child. I kinda figured that you probably didn't want to talk to him. I was afraid he might start taking pictures of you if he knew who you were," she replied.

"Wow, I really didn't think about the press getting involved with this. The last thing I want is my picture in the paper."

"I don't know how you're going to avoid it."

Ben began to worry, realizing that he should have told Claire about Dracken and debated whether or not to call home and tell her. He decided to wait and find out the status of the girl first and pray that the story hadn't made it to the evening news already.

"Can you check to see where the other nurse went. I need to know what's going on."

"Lucy should be back in a few minutes...wait, here she is."

Ben felt his mouth become dry, bracing himself for the worst. "How is she?"

"She's in surgery. That's all I can tell you," she said without looking Ben directly in the eye. He could see that she wasn't telling him all that she knew.

"Is she going to make it?" Ben asked slowly.

"I can't give you any more information, I'm sorry."

"Please, I need to know," he pleaded but before the nurse could answer, a man speaking loudly could be heard from the far end of the hallway. People in the waiting room stopped and stared as a large man in a dark suit led the reporter who had been asking questions about Dracken, down the hall.

"Let go, I'll leave on my own!" the reporter yelled, but to no avail. The man, obviously one of Dracken's men, looked straight ahead and continued ushering him, not letting go until they were outside. Ben swallowed hard and turned away as the man walked by.

"I wonder if I'll be treated the same way." The nurses looked at each other.

"Maybe you better not try and find out. Why don't you go home and call later," she said.

Ben stood thinking about the reporter being bodily removed.

"You know...I'd still like to apologize to the family if possible."

"Okay, if that's what you want, I'll call down there and let them know," she said, picking up the phone and dialing. "What's your name?" she asked.

"Ben Pearce"

The call lasted only seconds.

"They said they would send someone up to speak with you," she said, still unable to look him in the eye.

"They aren't very happy that I'm here, are they?" he asked.

She just looked at him not knowing what to say.

"Please have a seat Mr. Pearce."

Ben stood watching and waiting for the family's envoy, hoping it wouldn't be the ogre that had escorted the reporter out earlier. Within minutes he could see a large silhouette approaching from the end of the hallway. As he drew closer, Ben could see it was the same man, except now he looked much larger. Ben took a deep breath and walked toward him. As they met, Ben could feel his own legs shake.

"Are you with the Dracken family?" Ben asked looking up at the man.

"Let's just say I'm Mr. Dracken's associate," the man said in a deep voice.

Although intimidated by the bodyguard, Ben remained composed.

"I'm Ben Pearce," he said slowly. "I'm the man who struck the girl."

"Yeah, the nurse told us you were here. What is it you want?"

"I just wanted to find out how the girl is doing and say how sorry I am to the family, that's all."

"Mr. Dracken doesn't want to speak with you. You might want to go home and send a note or something," he said, crossing his arms in front of him.

"Please... I really need to say something to them," Ben pleaded.

"That's not going to happen."

Ben could see there was no room for negotiation and he didn't want to wind up like the reporter so he backed away and took a step toward the door.

"Can you just tell them that I'm really sorry and if there's anything I can do please let me know. Maybe I'll stop back tomorrow."

"Look Mr. Pearce, take my advice and just send them a card," he glanced around and motioned for Ben to come closer. "You really don't want to get Mr. Dracken any more pissed off than he already is," he placed his hand on Ben's shoulder. "Look Mr. Pearce, you seem like a nice guy and I really believe that you're honestly upset, but what you want is for Mr. Dracken to forget your name."

Ben glanced at the man's hand, which was weighing down and covering his entire shoulder. "Thanks for the advice... What did you say your name was?"

"I'm Willie, and believe me it's good advice," he replied, removing his hand from Ben and again crossing his arms across his chest. "Oh and I will deny having this conversation; I'm just trying to help save your life. You have a good day."

Ben reached out his hand but Willie just nodded his head and walked away. Ben looked down at the floor and turned away dejected as he started for the door. Before leaving he stopped at the nurses' station to offer his thanks for their help and to ask Lucy if he could call her later for an update on the girl. She reluctantly agreed under the condition that he not tell anyone that she was feeding him the information. He left feeling a bit better knowing that he was able to keep tabs on the girl's progress thanks to the pity of a caring nurse.

He walked outside oblivious to what was happening around him, his mind filled with the conversations inside and what reaction he was going to receive from Claire.

Reaching his car, he watched two vans bounce over the speed bumps at the hospital entrance. His vision was blocked by a row of bushes and he could only see writing on the sides of the vehicles. He walked a few steps from his car to get into a better line of sight where his worst fears came true. Both vans were equipped with antennas and satellite dishes on the roofs, which meant only one thing – television trucks.

How big is this story going to be?

He jogged back to the car and jumped in. There was no way of knowing if the camera crews were there for Dracken, but Ben figured it was a pretty good bet. He now realized that if the girl died this may be a headline story, but if she lived the whole thing would blow over in a matter of days. He could only pray for the best.

Driving home, he attempted to keep the car at the speed limit but found himself exceeding it every time he glanced at the speedometer. He was half way home when Claire's cell phone rang. This time he pulled over.

"Ben, it's Howie. I've been trying to get you."

"I had the phone off in the hospital. Where are you?"

"I'm at your house."

"Listen to me Howie, don't put the TV on no matter what," he said with his voice getting a little shaky.

"Too late, we already saw it," he replied in a somber tone.

"Damn...damn," he slammed his hand on the steering wheel. "How's Claire taking it?"

"Not real good Ben, she's in the bathroom. I think she's sick."

"All right, listen: tell her I'll be there in a bit." He stared at the phone after flipping it shut. The full realization of what the accident was going to do to his family was sinking in, causing him to break down. Tears rolled down his cheeks as he gazed up toward heaven.

"Why me? I've tried so hard to do everything right in life. Oh God, please don't let the girl die. I've never asked for anything, please don't let her die."

Ben pulled up to his house and for the first time in his marriage, didn't know what to expect from his wife. He had never kept anything from her before, but she would have to understand this.

He opened the front door. Howie was sitting on the couch with the children watching a video. They screamed with joy, tipping off Claire that he was home. She came running from the bedroom crying.

"We were watching the news and saw a story about Victor Dracken's daughter being run over by a truck. Is that the girl you hit? Please tell me it wasn't her." She could see by his face that it was true. "Oh my God, oh my God." she said in a panic. "What are we gonna do?"

"Calm down, please just calm down," he shouted.

Michael, scared by Claire's outburst and Ben's raised voice, started crying. It wasn't long before Sarah joined him.

"Don't tell me to calm down. You just hit the daughter of one of the biggest criminals in the world and your telling me to calm down? Why didn't you tell me who he was?" She came over and picked up Sarah. Ben stood speechless. Claire covered her mouth in embarrassment that she had yelled at him. "Honey,

I'm sorry. I didn't mean to yell but...Ben wh-whats going to happen? How's the girl?"

Ben, now holding Michael, wiped tears from Claire's face.

"She was in surgery when I left and that's all I could find out. I have to call back later."

Howie just sat on the couch shaking his head.

"Dracken's a bad dude, Ben. Take it from me – I know. Well I mean I've heard things," Howie said, giving Ben a quick guilty look. "Did you talk to Dracken?"

"No... he wouldn't see me. They're not exactly thrilled with me."

Michael had calmed. Ben put him down and poured a cup of coffee.

"Ben...do you think we're in trouble with this man? I mean this man scares me," Claire said.

"He scares me too and I can only hope that he realizes that it was an accident."

"What exactly did happen?" Howie asked.

"Well Howie, my good buddy," Ben said sarcastically. "I was on the phone with you because your car broke down...again. I took my eyes off the road for a second and she shot out in front of me. Howie, do us all a favor and get a new car."

Howie didn't know what to say.

"I'm really sorry Ben, whatever I can do to help, just let me know."

"I'm not blaming you Howie."

Claire could see the pain on Ben's face and refrained from asking any questions about the accident. Even Howie quelled his lust for the morbid details.

"Well what do we do now?" she asked.

Ben sat back on the couch. They watched and waited in suspense while Ben stared at the ceiling remembering the non-threatening but persuasive words of Dracken's bodyguard.

"I'll go back to the hospital tomorrow," he said, looking at his coffee mug. "I don't think this coffee's going to be the best thing for me. I'm going to have enough trouble sleeping." He glanced at the clock. "I guess I'll give it another hour before I call the hospital. Howie, you're gonna stick around for a while?"

"Of course, Claire's already set up the guest room. I'll stay with her tomorrow or do you want me to go with you?" Howie knew that Ben would decline his offer.

"Nah, I think it's best if I go alone." He kept his fears hidden the best he could. "No reason to drag you into this."

"Ben, how about if I go with you? Maybe if the family sees us together they'll talk to us," Claire said.

Ben perked up. "You know that's not a bad idea and if we took the kids, he'd see we were a family."

Ben thought for a second and realized that he just agreed to put his cherished family right in the path of Victor Dracken. The last thing he wanted was for Claire to see Dracken up close, especially if he was threatening.

"On second thought maybe that's not a good idea. I don't know how long I'm going to be there and with the kids and all, maybe it's better that I go alone."

"Well, think about it. I really think you should at least take Howie. You shouldn't be alone."

Claire dragged the two squirming children to their bedroom. Not wanting to miss the excitement of Uncle Howie being over, both put up a good fight. Ben waited until Claire was out of earshot.

"Look Howie, you stay with Claire 'cause this could get a little crazy. I was told not to come back to the hospital, but I have to go." He leaned over. "The only problem I have is, am I going back because I care about the girl or because I want to calm the father? If I stay away from Dracken, will he think I'm afraid of him?"

"Well aren't you?" Howie asked.

"Of course I am, but I can't just hide. This was an accident. Now the guy wants to kill me?"

Howie jerked with surprise, spilling coffee in his lap.

"When did he threaten to kill you?"

"Well he didn't in so many words, but he did say something to the effect that I better hope that the girl was okay." The vision of Dracken's eyes sent a chill down his spine. "You know what? Let me call the hospital and see if there's anything new."

Ben dialed the hospital, reaching the main operator.

"I need to get an update on a patient who was brought into emergency a couple of hours ago."

"I'll give you to patient information," the operator said.

"No, wait! Switch me to the nurses' station in the emergency room."

"Emergency," the voice said.

"Can I speak with Lucy? This is Ben Pearce." He started sweating as he waited on hold for over three minutes.

"Hello Mr. Pearce, it's Lucy. Listen I'll check on the girl now, and you can call back once more in a couple hours but that's it. I could get in trouble."

"I understand and I appreciate what you're doing."

"Hold on, let me see what I can find out. This may take a few minutes so just hold on."

"She's checking for me," he said to Howie.

Ben waited on hold while the nurse checked the girl's status. The minutes felt like hours. His body quivered until the nurse came back on the line.

"She'll probably be in surgery for a while longer. I can't get any more information than that for now." She paused for a second. "Look Mr. Pearce, I understand the situation you're in and I do feel for you, but like I said I could get in trouble giving out information."

"Thanks so much. I won't mention that you gave this info out. What time do you think I should call back?"

"Try in a couple hours, all right?"

"Okay, thanks so much," he said, collapsing into the chair. "This is torture, she's still in surgery. I can call back once more tonight in a couple of hours."

Ben went down to his office to watch TV alone. For hours, he switched from channel to channel trying to find something to occupy his mind. He climbed the stairs for a glass of water. Claire and Howie were sitting on the couch.

"I keep reliving over and over the few seconds of the accident... and then the girl underneath." He went to the kitchen counter.

"My God, he looks terrible. I don't even know what to say to him now," Claire said to Howie.

"Hey Ben, when are you going to call again?" Howie asked. Ben looked up at the clock.

"Maybe I'll try now, but if I do, it's my last call tonight."

He dialed the phone. Howie was sitting close enough to Claire to feel her body shaking. He put his arm around her and together they watched Ben pace, waiting for any sign of hope. After all the agonizing, Lucy had no further updates on the girl's condition.

"Nope, still in surgery. What could they be doing for so long?" Ben stood and rubbed his temples. "This doesn't look good. She's been in surgery too long."

"You don't know that. I know it won't be easy, but why don't you try to get some sleep. Maybe think about letting me go with you tomorrow," Howie said, knowing that Ben wouldn't change his mind.

"Nah, stay here with Claire. She'll need the company more than I will."

"Okay."

"C'mon Claire, let's go to bed."

Ben disappeared to the bedroom. Claire stood up.

"Howie, what do I say to him? I can't help him – what do I say?"

"Look, we'll all get through this. Just go and comfort him in whatever way you can." Howie winked.

"Yeah I'm sure he's in the mood for that."

"Maybe the only thing we can all do is pray," Howie said.

Claire opened the bedroom door. Ben was lying on the bed with his hands behind his head watching TV.

"Ben, I don't know how I can help you." She started crying as she reached the foot of the bed. "I mean you sit downstairs and shut me out."

Ben jumped up and held her. "You're right, I'm sorry. I just can't stop thinking about what happened. I wasn't thinking about how it was affecting you."

"Please, just promise me that you won't keep me in the dark. We'll get through this together."

He kissed her on the forehead. "Promise."

* * * * * *

After hours of tossing, Ben sat up. Not knowing if Claire was sleeping, he slid the covers off quietly.

"You can't sleep either?" she asked.

"No...think I'll go for a walk. There's no way I'm sleeping tonight."

Ben walked slowly through his neighborhood, his hands in his jacket pockets. He often walked at night, but never so late. The quiet night air and the choir of crickets relaxed him. It was the only time in New York that he could compare to the peaceful serenity of the South Dakota evenings.

Tonight, more than ever before, the yearning to be away from New York frustrated him – almost to the point of mental rage. He calmed himself by reminiscing back to the past Christmas – his last visit with his family. He pictured his mother playing with her grandchildren – the joy on her face masking the pain of her failing health.

The booming music of a passing car startled him. His fond recollections ended quickly and thoughts of the girl returned. For the first time in his life, Ben was afraid. He had never had a real crisis before and now had no control over the outcome.

It was before eight o'clock the next morning when Ben rolled down the driveway. Claire stood in the front door wearing her white fuzzy robe and slippers. She and the children waved goodbye, she with a look of concern and they with a look of confusion. This was Saturday morning, the day they watched cartoons in bed with their father. Ben was saddened by their expressions. He would much rather stay home with them, but repeated calls to the hospital yielded no clues to the girl's condition. A visit would be the only way.

Not having any idea of how long he would be, Ben had asked Howie to take Claire along to run some errands. Picking up a rental car was a priority, and second was a stop at the police station to retrieve his cell phone, which he had left in his truck.

Ben was apprehensive as he approached the hospital, having no idea what to expect. His stomach churned as he entered the parking lot. There was only one limo parked outside now and no sign of the bodyguards. The two television vans were still there with their antennas raised. There was only one way to find out for sure if they were there for Dracken or not. He pulled up along side one of the trucks and looked around for anyone connected with them. A man with a clipboard was flipping through papers in front of one of the vehicles.

"Hey, what's going on? Any big stories?" Ben asked

The man walked up to Ben's window.

"Victor Dracken's daughter was run over last night."

"Really? Is she all right?"

"No one's telling us anything and we're not going to push too hard. We all have families if you know what I mean." He walked away.

Ben proceeded to the main lot. While searching for a spot, Claire's cell phone rang. Out of habit he picked it up without stopping the car, but before answering realized his mistake and pulled over.

"Ben, a reporter just knocked on the door." Claire said in a shaky voice.

"Are you kidding me? How could they possibly have gotten our address?"

"I don't know... I just closed the door."

"Oh man, I don't believe this. I didn't give a thought that this might happen. Okay, just lock the doors and stay inside, and whatever you do, don't say anything to anybody."

"Stay inside? We have to go out later."

"All right listen. You're going to borrow Gail's car next door right? Just have Howie pull her car into the garage and get in from there. Are there reporters waiting outside?"

"I've looked through the windows from all directions but I didn't see anyone. Maybe he left."

"Well I'm glad Howie is there at least. What time is Gail coming over to baby-sit?"

"She should be here soon and she's letting us use the Jeep."

"Good, just make sure she keeps the front door closed and says nothing, that's all. I'm at the hospital and I'm going to have to turn the phone off, so I'll call you if I hear anything."

"Okay, good luck, Honey."

Ben walked past the emergency room and around to the main entrance to avoid any reporters. He was now concerned that if the reporters had his address then maybe they also had his picture, possibly from the accident scene. He didn't recall any flashes at the scene, but in his state, he may not have noticed.

Oh shit - today's newspaper.

In his haste, he hadn't even looked at the morning paper to see if the story had run. Walking into the gift shop, he picked up the local paper. On the front page was a small headline with Dracken's name. Ben flipped through to the story. To his relief, neither his name nor picture was there. He was still anonymous.

Stuffed animals covered the shelves of the gift shop. He decided on a small teddy bear, figuring it might be a nice gesture. At this point though, he wasn't sure whether the stuffed animal was for the benefit of the girl or to make himself look good.

Ben stepped lightly to the information desk while looking toward the waiting area for a camera crew. In the last row he could see three men wearing baseball caps. One had a portable camera across his lap and was showing it to a small boy. While the three were distracted, Ben walked up to the desk.

"I'd like some information on a patient please." He felt his body begin to shake, knowing his future lay with what the nurse was about to tell him.

"The patient's name?" she asked.

"Dracken."

"She's in the intensive care unit, third floor." Ben let out a sigh of relief; the girl was still alive.

Keeping his back to the camera crew, he headed for the elevator. Upon reaching the floor, he approached the nurses' station.

"I'd like to find out about a patient," he said as his stomach knotted up again.

"What's the name please?" asked the nurse.

"Last name Dracken."

"I can only verify that the patient is here. If you want more information, you'll have to talk to the family."

"And where would I find them?"

"They've set up a special room for the family to help respect their privacy. You're not a reporter, are you?"

"No."

"Go down the hall and make a left," she said, pointing the way.

"Then where?"

She gave him a peculiar look. "Just make the left and you'll find it."

He followed her direction not knowing what she meant by "you'll find it." As he turned the corner he stopped short, realizing what the nurse had meant. The same mountain of a man that had told him that he couldn't see the family the night before was sitting at a desk, a hundred feet down the dimly lit hallway. Ben walked towards him praying that he wasn't about to be torn to shreds.

"Hi, remember me?" Ben asked trying to act friendly. The man looked up from the newspaper that he was reading. "Willie, wasn't it?"

"Yeah that's me and yes I remember you. I only met you last night; please don't mistake my size with stupidity. I do have my suspicions about your intelligence though."

Ben didn't know until now how afraid of another human being he could be until Willie stood up. Ben backed up a few steps.

"I just wanted to tell the family that I was sorry and to see how the girl is."

"Relax, I'm not going to hurt you unless I'm ordered to," Willie said. "I can guarantee that the situation is the same as last night." He became very serious and began talking very slowly and deliberately. "They don't want to see you. Do you really want to piss off Mr. Dracken? I mean think about what you're doing."

Ben sighed deeply. "Can you at least tell me how the girl is?"

"I don't have any answers for you. Now why don't you leave before it's too late."

Ben started to walk away but stopped short and decided that this was his only chance to reason with Dracken and try and make him see that this was an accident. He turned back.

"Look, I have to a least tell them I'm sorry. Will you at least tell them I'm here? I know...I know I did a terrible thing, but it was an accident. Don't you think I feel horrible?" Ben's body trembled and his voice quivered as he fought to get the words out.   "I've got kids too. Please, could you just ask if they'll see me?" he pleaded.

The man stared at Ben for a moment, then turned. "Wait here, but I think you're makin' a huge mistake."

As Dracken's bodyguard opened the door and went inside, Ben could see a large group of people. He had never felt such fear, and the thought of coming face to face with Dracken again almost caused him to lose control of his bladder. He stepped back a little ways from the door as the knob turned and it swung open. Dracken stepped out with Willie right behind. Ben offered to shake his hand but the offer wasn't returned.

Dracken obviously hadn't left the hospital since the accident. He was unshaven and his hair unkempt. His skin and shirt were wet with sweat – the room that he had come out of had many people inside and lacked ventilation.

"Mr. Dracken, I'm so sorry about what happened. You have to know it was an accident."

Ben looked for a glimmer of forgiveness. Instead Dracken's face had a cold stare filled with rage, his breathing fast and heavy.

Dracken came up close to Ben's face. Ben had never seen the color that Dracken's eyes possessed – almost gray like a nasty storm.

"Did you come here expecting forgiveness?" Dracken screamed so closely into Ben's face that he could feel the heat of his breath. His British accent grew more prevalent the louder he yelled. "Did you really expect me to forgive you? My daughter is lying down there, tubes stuck in her. We can only see her for ten minutes an hour. You just came here to save your skin."

Ben was speechless; he had never seen anyone that angry. He began to think the bodyguard was right and maybe he would have been better off letting Dracken forget who he was.

"I... I just wanted to say I'm sorry, that's all," he said, retreating a few steps backward down the hallway.

Dracken just stared and breathed like a charging bull. Ben turned and walked away praying that Dracken wouldn't follow. He turned the corner and leaned with his back against the wall, sliding down until he was sitting on the floor. He took a few deep breaths. Dracken was much more savage than Ben had expected. He now realized that the severity of the situation had just multiplied.

As Ben sat trying to regain his composure, two doctors, looking tired and unkempt, walked past him towards the family's waiting room. They didn't even pay attention to Ben – a grown man in tears sitting on the floor. They had obviously been up all night and from their expressions, it didn't look as though they were delivering good news. Ben peered around the corner and watched as the doctors reached Dracken, who was still in the hall. He listened intently but wasn't close enough to hear. All of a sudden Dracken let out an ear piercing "Nooooooooo," and began sobbing uncontrollably. Ben listened in horror, realizing that the girl was dead. He buried his face in his hands, distraught, knowing that he had killed the child. Without thinking, he stepped out into full view of Dracken who had his forehead to the wall and was pounding the sheet rock with his fists.

Getting a glimpse of Ben's movement out of the corner of his eye, Dracken wiped the tears to see clearer. In a flash he bolted right for Ben, screaming at the top of his lungs. "I'm going to kill you."

Ben froze, stiff with fear as Dracken raced towards him, the bodyguard chasing close behind. Dracken was only feet away with outstretched hands reaching for Ben's throat when Willie grabbed him, knocking him to one knee.

"Boss not here, not here," he yelled. "Boss this is time to be with your family; take care of this later."

Willie raised Dracken, who was kicking and fighting, off the floor. He carried him a few feet back towards the room until he calmed. The two doctors stood with their backs against the opposite wall, fearing that they were next because the girl had died. But to Dracken, Ben was the only person there, and he continued to stare back at him as Willie led him down the hall.

"You're a dead man," he screamed as he gave Ben one last leer. Willie whisked him inside.

Chapter Three

Ben was in a daze as he drove home. *What am I gonna tell Claire? Will this guy really try to kill me?* He only knew the answer to one of the questions. His perfect life was now becoming a nightmare. But even with Dracken's threats, Ben tried to believe that given time, Dracken would calm down and eventually see that this was an accident.

As he pulled up to his house, he noticed two men seated in a sedan directly across the street. Before Ben's car came to a stop, both men jumped out and ran toward him.

Ben stepped out and immediately covered his face as one of the men brought a camera to his eye. The camera motor ran continuously as the reporter fired off picture after picture.

"Excuse me, are you Ben Pearce?" the other reporter asked, holding a pad and pen.

Ben slipped back into the front seat and ducked down low while leaning on the horn to summon Howie.

"Get off my property," Ben yelled, pulling his jacket over his head.

"Mr. Pearce have you met Mr. Dracken yet? What did he say to you?"

Determined to get a better photo, the reporter ran towards the front of the car. He hadn't noticed Howie coming down the walkway, and ran square into his chest, bouncing backwards. A look of fear filled the man's face as Howie, who outweighed the man by a hundred pounds, looked down at him.

"Get the hell away from him."

Backing away from Howie, he bumped into the other reporter and both fell against the car. Howie grabbed both men by the back collar and led them down the driveway. Like two rag dolls, both men went flying into the street.

"I just wanted to ask a few quick questions, that's all."

"No questions." Howie pursued the man with the camera, yanking it from his hands. He flipped open the catch and exposed the film.

"Hey, you can't do that. We could sue you."

"Fuckin' sue me then."

"Gimme my camera back."

Howie shoved the camera back at the man, hitting him below the eye and knocking him backward. Ben, seeing that Howie had exposed the film, hopped out of the car.

"Just leave the guy alone, he's been through enough," Howie said as they stood in the middle of the street.

"We just want to ask some quick questions, then we'll be gone."

"You're gone now," Howie snapped, taking a step forward. Both reporters retreated quickly back to their car.

"Why don't you just tell us what happened and we'll leave you alone," yelled one of the reporters.

Howie joined Ben again by the front steps.

"You know Howie, maybe I should just tell them what happened and get it over with. But no pictures."

"I don't think it's a good idea Buddy, but it's up to you."

Ben motioned for them to come back across the street.

"No pictures and I'll answer some questions."

They rushed back over minus the camera.

"Look, I just killed a young girl and the last thing I need is you guys hounding me, so let's get this over with so I can... "

Howie and the reporters all responded at the same time, "She died?"

Ben realized that not only had he killed the child but had also leaked it to the press, something that should've been reserved for the family when they felt the time was right. If Dracken found out that he had spilled the story, it might be the last nail in his coffin.

Howie rushed Ben inside before he could do any more damage. The reporters yelled questions at them right up until the point of the front door closing. Claire, who had watched the whole incident from the living room window, was waiting right inside the door.

"What happened? How come you're back so soon?" she asked as Howie slammed the door.

"Ben gave out some info that maybe he shouldn't have," Howie replied.

She turned to Ben. "What kind of information?"

Ben just stood, his face pale white, without saying a word. She covered her mouth, realizing by his expression that the girl was dead.

"Oh Ben, I'm so sorry." She stretched her arms out and embraced him.

Gail, who had come to baby-sit, sat on the couch holding the children until Ben was ready to greet them. Howie sat next to her grabbing Michael who began to moan, wanting his father to hold him. Ben lifted his head from Claire's shoulder.

"Oh, hi Gail."

"Hi Ben," Gail replied with a sympathetic look. "Let me take the kids outside."

"Wait, it's okay Gail. Why don't you go home, we can handle them from here," Ben said, taking his squirming son from Howie.

Howie got up off the couch. "Okay, come on Gail, I'll walk you home."

"Wait... Gail, do me a favor. Cut through the back yard to avoid the reporters and Gail please... not a word to anyone," Ben said.

Claire sat beside him. "Ben...do you feel like talking about it?"

He nodded even though he really wasn't up to answering questions.

"I can't believe that she died." He sat silent for a moment. "I even asked God not to let her die, but I guess he didn't hear me."

"Ben, what happened at the hospital?" she asked, placing Sarah on the floor.

"Well...I got to the hospital, waited around for a little while, then they told me that she had died. That's it."

Ben wasn't a good liar and as soon as he finished the sentence he fled to the kitchen. "You want something to drink while I'm in here?"

"Ben, could you please come back in here." He slinked back into the room unable to look her in the eye.

"Ben... did you see Victor Dracken at the hospital?"

He sat back down on the edge of the couch and faced her. "Yes, I saw him."

"Ben, are we in trouble with this guy? I mean do you think that he'll try to hurt us?"

While in the kitchen, he had decided on telling her the truth. He knew that his guilty expression would eventually give him away if he attempted to deceive her further. But now after seeing her teary eyes, he thought better of it.

"He's very angry with me but I think after time he'll realize that it was an accident. He just lost his daughter; you can't expect the man to be rational."

Claire stood up. "What do you mean rational? What did he say to you? He threatened you didn't he?"

She left the room, her hands covering her face. Ben chased after her into the children's room where he found her sitting and hugging them.

"Honey relax, he didn't threaten me. He yelled a lot but he didn't threaten."

"I don't believe you. Do you think he'll hurt the children?" She jumped up. "I'm going to pack our things and take the kids somewhere."

Ben grabbed her and pulled her away from the dresser drawer, which she had already opened. She fell to her knees crying into her hands. He knelt down next to her.

"Now just calm down. Nothing is going to happen to anyone." He took her by the arm and raised her back to her feet. "Everything is going to be fine. Please believe me, I would never let anything happen to you or the kids."

He didn't feel right telling her something that he himself didn't believe, but that's the way it had to be. He would do enough worrying for both of them.

Claire started to calm as she looked into Ben's eyes. "Okay… if you say so. You've never lied to me, and if our children were in danger, you would tell me, right?"

Trying to keep a poker face, he replied, "Absolutely."

When Howie returned from escorting Gail home, they discussed the best way to get Ben the rental car and his cell phone without the reporters trailing them. The first two reporters were gone from the front of the house, but in their place now sat a van with tinted windows. Assuming that the van was also related to the press, they decided that Ben would stand at the front door while Howie and Claire left the house in Gail's Jeep. The plan called for Ben to show his face only for a few seconds to avoid being photographed while Howie and Claire drove off. Hopefully the reporters would be more interested in hounding Ben than Claire.

The plan worked well, confusing the occupants in the van. At first they started the engine and drove a few feet but stopped short thinking that it was a ploy to get them to follow, allowing Ben to leave in Claire's BMW later.

Within an hour, Claire pulled into the garage with the rental, a white Dodge Intrepid. Howie parked Gail's Jeep back in her driveway and walked back to the house, leering at the van.

"Ben, we're back."

"In here," he said.

Howie followed Claire into the children's room where Ben sat on the floor reading a story to the kids. He put his finger up for them to wait as he finished the last paragraph. Claire lifted Sarah who had fallen asleep. Michael ran to Howie who raised him up over his head.

"Any problems while we were gone?" she asked.

"No, our friends didn't ring the bell but they never left. Guess they know I have to go out eventually, but what are they going to do? Chase me around town?" Ben asked.

"Well, we got your phone. Oh, and did you want your briefcase or should they have left it in the truck?" Howie asked.

"Wow...I can't believe that I forgot all about my case...where is it?"

"In the kitchen with your phone." Claire said.

"Did you take the stuff out yourself?" Ben asked.

"No, the cop gave it to us. It was already in the office. I guess they take the valuables out when the cars come in," Howie said.

"I got you a Dodge Intrepid. The keys are with your other stuff inside," Claire said.

They walked into the kitchen. Ben popped his briefcase open.

"Everything's here. I don't see anything missing. Did you see my truck at all?"

"No. I didn't even ask," Howie said. "I didn't think Claire wanted to see it. I did ask when you could get the truck back, but they had no idea. I mentioned that a girl was killed in the accident and they said that usually the safety checks are done quickly when there's a fatality."

As the day progressed, the house became more of a cage than a sanctuary. More reporters had arrived and by early afternoon Howie had punched two of them and had almost been arrested on both occasions.

Torturous hours passed while they waited for the local stations to air the news of the girl's death. It was only a matter of time before the whole world knew. Ben prayed that there was another story that would overshadow the child's death. This time his prayer was answered. Live coverage of a man who had taken his family hostage was being broadcast live on all channels throughout the afternoon.

It wasn't until early evening that the stations began to break away from the hostage story and back into regular news coverage. The accident was the first story featured. They watched intently as the sad news was reported, and were thrilled that there wasn't much fanfare during the surprisingly short segment. There was a quick picture of Dracken but none of his daughter, and Ben's name wasn't mentioned. He leaned back and sunk into the couch. Maybe he wasn't going to be a public figure after all.

"Well that wasn't as bad as we expected, but what I can't understand is why there were so many reporters coming here today if the story wasn't that big?" Ben asked with a puzzled look.

"I don't know," Howie replied shaking his head behind Claire's back. "Hey Claire, got anything to eat?" he asked, wanting her to leave the room.

"I'll make something," she said, leaving for the kitchen.

Howie waited for Claire to exit the room and raised the volume on the television. He whispered to Ben, "The reason the reporters want to speak to you isn't about you hitting the girl. It's about what you think Dracken is going to do to you. That's the story."

Ben thought for a moment. "Yeah you're right...you're absolutely right."

"You gotta keep your face out of the papers for as long as possible. You want Dracken to forget who you are," Howie said in a low tone, trying to keep from alarming Ben.

"You're not making me feel any better you know."

He realized that he had to escape the lenses of the men outside and peeked out to see how many cars were still parked there. "Only two right now." He thought about what Howie had just said and he flashed back to that morning at the hospital. "Howie, I don't think that Dracken's going to forget who I am for a very long time."

Knowing that his best friend was in the worst crisis of his life, Howie decided to stay one more night. In his mind the next morning would be a telling sign of what was in Ben's future.

He had no way to know what Victor Dracken really had planned for Ben. If the morning newspaper had the story on the front page, it might cause Dracken to retaliate even if he had decided against it earlier. If the world knew that someone had killed his daughter, and he did nothing, it might show weakness. The newspaper might be just the thing to push Dracken over the edge.

The next morning, Ben paced the living room floor. Howie, hearing Ben turn the TV on, stumbled into the room, still half asleep.

"Time is it?"

"Six," Ben said. "Only one reporter out there still."

Ben pointed down the block as the newspaper delivery car approached. Before the paper hit the ground, Howie was out of the house. The one determined reporter jumped out of his car and snapped pictures as Howie crossed the lawn.

"You can take all the pictures you want of me...vulture."

Before Howie had one foot in the door, Ben snatched the paper from him.

"Well is it in there?" Claire asked, just coming into the room.

"I gotta find the main section, all these damn ads," Ben said, pulling different parts from the plastic bag.

Finally, after papers were scattered over the coffee table, the elusive section was in hand. All together they scanned the front page. Howie pointed to the top where, in the right corner box, read the headline, "Victor Dracken's daughter killed on bike, page 8." Ben flipped through the paper frantically until he reached the story.

"Here it is; it's only a small article," he said, scouring the two-paragraph story for his name. "Damn...my name is in here...but no address, thank God, and nothing about the cell phone. No picture of me either. It just says that I wouldn't answer any questions and that no charges were filed. Oh, and that my truck was impounded for a safety check...lets see what else...no comment from the Dracken family and that..." Seeing that the papers weren't making a huge deal out of the situation elated him but only clouded the main tragedy.

"Well that's good news," Claire said, sounding relieved.

"Yeah it is." He looked at her with heavy eyes. "I can't believe that I was so worried about me that I didn't even think about the girl's funeral. It's on Monday."

Claire moved closer to Ben, putting her arm around and laying her head on his shoulder.

"Ben, I know you're upset, but it wasn't your fault. You never would've been able to stop even if you weren't on the phone."

"I know that Claire, but that doesn't bring the girl back. It doesn't take the sight of her pinned under my truck out of my mind; nothing ever will." He got up and walked toward the bathroom.

"You thinkin' about going to the funeral?" Howie asked.

"Thought about it, but I think it might be better if I just kept a low profile with the family for now," he said without turning around.

Howie and Claire just looked at each other, knowing they were helpless to console Ben.

"Maybe he'd feel better if we went to Mass," she said, pausing for a second. "Maybe you'll come with us?"

"I don't know Claire, I haven't been to church in...well, a long time. Maybe it's better I stay here. Now that Ben's name is in the paper, the phone may start to ring and who knows who might come to the door. You guys sneak out and I'll stay and watch the kids."

Ben returned to the living room; Claire and Howie stared at him.

"What's the matter?" he asked.

"What do you think about going to Mass while Howie stays and watches the kids? Be kinda nice to be able to go by ourselves for once."

Ben thought for a moment and realized that he would have to show his face in public eventually, so why not do it in church.

"Okay, let's go. You want to call Gail to make sure she's home in case Howie needs help?"

"Okay, start getting ready so we can make the early Mass."
She grabbed the phone and began to dial, then stopped. "Ben?"

"Yeah," he said from the bedroom.

"You going to call your parents?"

"Yeah, I thought of that. I'll do it later."

As they drove to the morning service, Ben tried not to alert
Claire to his nervousness. He looked in his mirrors to see if he
was being followed and tried to assure himself that if Dracken
were to harm him, it wouldn't be in the daytime while he was
with his wife in the car. He felt in his heart that Dracken wouldn't
harm Claire or the kids, but after the threats at the hospital, he
couldn't be positive and would have to stay on his guard
constantly.

The church was to be the first test of how many people
knew about his involvement in the accident. Ben shook hands
with acquaintances outside the church, looking into their eyes
to see if they were uncomfortable speaking with him. There
was no mention of the incident before or after the Mass, giving
Ben a better feeling about the situation.

Later that afternoon, Ben sat watching a Met game, but
found it impossible to concentrate. His only thoughts were of
how his family would continue if he were no longer alive.
Monetarily, they would be well taken care of. He was fairly well
off and his million-dollar life insurance policy invested properly
by Howie would furnish Claire with sufficient income, allowing
her to easily pay the bills and fund the childrens' education.

He sat for hours planning for his death. The more he
thought about the prospect of his children growing up without a
father, the angrier he became. Victor Dracken was going to
destroy the lives of two innocent children because of an accident.
He was getting ahead of himself to the point of planning to kill
Dracken in order to save his own family. He finally laughed out
loud knowing that he wasn't capable of killing another man.

But at the same time he knew that people were known to do strange things when backed into a corner.

I'm sure in time, Dracken will forgive me...but do I really believe that?

He decided to leave nothing to chance, spending time deep in thought planning his own funeral. He sat back in the large recliner and turned down the volume on the television. He grabbed a yellow legal pad and jotted down the details in a letter to Claire that Howie would take possession of and hand over to her at the time of his demise. Ben's decision to hand write the letter had become a bad choice. Correcting mistakes was difficult compared to the computer but the personalization would outweigh the tedious chore of rewriting. The page resembled that of a child's Christmas list, errors crossed out and arrows pointing in different directions. He decided after repeated attempts to decipher some of his own writing that he would continue on the computer and hand write the final copy. Within an hour he had his final draft typed out on the computer downstairs.

Ben read the letter one more time and decided that even though writing was never his forte, the letter didn't sound half-bad. Now that it was finished, he sat back deciding what other loose ends needed to be cleared up. The thought of dying brought to mind his will, which hadn't been updated in quite some time. An appointment with the attorney would be a top priority for any revisions to the will and also for advice on what could be done about Dracken.

Ben called Howie who had taken a cab back home. "Hey it's me."

"Hey how you feelin?"

"Not too good. I'm afraid for my life and I'm planning my funeral."

"C'mon, you don't know that he's really gonna take any action," Howie said in an unconvincing voice.

"You don't believe that yourself...anyway I can't take the chance. I'm going to take a couple days off. There's no way I'll be able to concentrate on work thinking about the girl...God, her face is etched so deep in my mind." He paused for a moment. "Anyway, while I'm off I think I'll go to my attorney and update my will and see what advice he can offer."

"Does Claire know you're doing this?"

"No, she can't find out or she'll lose it. I haven't really told her how afraid I am." Howie didn't know what to say and they both sat on the phone in silence for a moment.

"I won't mention anything to Claire, and remember I'm right here if you need me."

"You going to be there to catch the bullet?" Ben asked.

"C'mon, this'll all blow over...how long you going to be out?" Howie asked, trying to get Ben off the subject of being killed.

"At least a couple days I guess."

"You'll have your cell phone with you, right?"

"Yeah I will. Okay, I'll call you in the morning to see what's happening."

"All right, if you need anything, just holler."

The next morning, Ben parted two of the vertical blind slats. He squinted, hoping there were no lingering reporters. His eyes opened wide as he saw an empty street in front of his house. Just to be sure, he opened the front door and stepped out, checking up and down the street. Confident that there were no reporters hiding, he returned to the children's room and readied Michael for nursery school and Sarah for day care. He had no real qualms about sending them out. He truly believed that Dracken wouldn't touch Claire or the children.

"Claire, you almost ready?" he called, walking into the bathroom.

He put his hands on her shoulders and watched as she put on the final touches of make-up. She already had her long hair up in a bun, which she preferred for work.

"Do me a favor. I'll be ready in a few minutes. Strap Sarah into her seat for me."

A horn blew outside.

"C'mon Dad," Michael said, grabbing his hand and leading him to the front door.

A yellow school van waited. Ben opened the front door and looked both ways. Seeing everything was clear, they walked out, Michael carrying a small schoolbag. Ben kissed him goodbye as the boy climbed the step into the van. Ben walked back inside.

"Sarah, come on sweetheart," he yelled.

The child came running, wearing a tiny red backpack.

"Let's go Daddy," Sarah squeaked.

Ben led her by the hand to the car and strapped her in as Claire came down the stairs and through the gate. She kissed him on the cheek.

"Ben...are you sure you don't want me to stay home with you?"

"No, I need to be alone for a while. Besides, I've got a few errands to run."

"You're not going to the funeral home, right?"

"I would like to but I really don't think it's a good idea. I'll just hang around here and later I'll take a ride to the police station to see when I can get my truck back."

Ben waited until Claire was out of sight. She was a part-time bookkeeper at a dental office and only worked four hours a day, so he had to move fast. If he were home when she got back, there would be less questioning about where he had been. Ben dialed his attorney but wasn't sure of his hours.

"Lawrence Templeton's office," answered the receptionist.

"Oh good, you're there. Yes, I'd like to speak with Lawrence please. This is Ben Pearce."

"I'm sorry Mr. Pearce, he's in with a client and has appointments all day. I can leave a message if you'd like but I can't guarantee that he'll even have time to return your call today."

"No, this is an emergency. I need to speak with him right away."

"Okay...hold on, I'll see if he can take your call."

Ben waited nervously, knowing that he needed to get the will updated immediately.

"Hi Ben. How are you and what's the emergency?"

"Well Lawrence, I've gotten myself into a mess and I need to see you as soon as you can spare the time – before lunch if possible. Gotta do this before Claire gets home."

"Wait now, slow down Ben. Did you say you didn't want your wife to find out...wait never mind. Tell you what...I've got a tight schedule today and let me see... tomorrow's no good either." Lawrence sighed, trying to fit Ben in quickly because of the urgency in his voice.

"Lawrence, this is really important, I've got to see you today. Isn't there any way you can fit me in... please, I'm begging you."

"Hold on," the attorney said as he yelled to his secretary. "Karen, cancel Mr. Thomas at noon. Tell him I had an emergency. See if you can get him right now and let me know."

"Okay Ben, I can hear by your tone that it's important. Be here at noon. I hope you don't mind that I'll be eating lunch while you tell me what you need me to do."

"Lawrence, I can't thank you enough. Want me to bring lunch?"

"No. I brought lunch but thanks. See you at noon."

Ben approached the rental car in his driveway. He knew that Dracken probably hadn't had enough time to orchestrate a murder, especially under the duress of his daughter's death, but he was cautious just the same. He glanced around at the neighbor's houses to see if anyone was outside or near their windows. Satisfied that there was no one to observe him, he quickly fell on his stomach and checked the underside of the car for anything out of the ordinary. He held his breath as he placed the key into the ignition. He exhaled when the car started without a loud explosion. He knew this was just the start of his paranoia and that it would only get worse.

Ben arrived at the police station after a short drive and a constant watch in the rearview mirror. He walked up to the desk sergeant. "I was involved in an accident and my truck was impounded for safety checks. I'd like to find out when I can get it back."

"Give me your name and I'll check it out."

"Ben Pearce, I'm the guy who hit the Dracken girl."

The officer looked startled. "Wait here, I'll find out for you."

"Oh and I'd also like to speak to a detective."

"Yeah sure, I'll see if someone can talk to you. Have a seat over there," the officer said, pointing past Ben to the opposite side of the room.

Ben sat on a hard wooden bench and waited. Metal rails, obviously for handcuffing criminals, were bolted to the walls. The ceiling was peaked and caused an echo even if a pen were dropped. He could only imagine how noisy it must be when shackled criminals talked and yelled while waiting to be processed.

A man in a shirt and tie approached Ben. "Mr. Pearce?" he asked in a gruff voice.

"Yes, that's me," he replied, standing and walking towards the man.

"I'm Detective Casey. Why don't you come in and I'll check on your truck. The sergeant said you had some other questions?" he shook Ben's hand and led him down the hallway.

"Yeah, I don't really know if it's anything but I figured I'd ask your advice."

Ben laughed to himself over Casey's appearance. With the detective's pear shaped body, Ben could only picture the stereotypical cop at the donut shop.

Cubicles lined the wall of the detectives' area – opposite them was one glass-enclosed office draped in light blue vertical blinds.

"Have a seat, Mr. Pearce... Now what can I help you with? Oh, coffee?" he said, pointing to a small coffee maker seated on a shelf in his bookcase.

"No thanks, I'm jittery enough. I take it the sergeant mentioned who I am."

"Yeah, you're the poor bastard who hit Victor Dracken's girl," the detective said with a pitying look. "I know that you didn't mean to hit the girl, but of all the dumb luck...Victor Dracken's daughter." He shook his head.

"You're really not making me feel any safer. I was hoping you would be able to protect me," Ben sighed. "I think I may have a huge problem." He paused as he tried to decide how to explain the situation. "I was at the hospital when the girl died; matter of fact I was about a hundred feet away from Dracken when the doctors broke the news." Ben paused again. "He kind of said some things to me that made me a little nervous."

"Did he threaten you?"

"That's putting it mildly. If his bodyguard wasn't there, he would have killed me right in the hospital."

"Did he hit you?" He asked, starting to take notes.

"No, the guy stopped him just before he got close enough."

"Okay, give me the whole thing from the beginning."

Ben described the altercation right down to the last detail, remembering it as though it had happened five minutes earlier. Casey recorded the pertinent details. Ben was surprised that the detective was taking such an interest in what had happened, almost as though he actually cared.

"Well, what should I do?" Ben asked, hoping for a simple, magical answer that would make his problem just disappear.

"Unfortunately, unless he acts upon his threats, the only thing we can do is issue a restraining order. He won't be allowed to come near you."

"If that's all you can do, why were you taking so many notes...and how many peoples' last words are 'but I had a restraining order'?"

"Just wanted to have the details for my records. If something were to happen to you, we could pull these out and go over them. Believe me, if there were some way of putting Dracken away for this, I'd be on my way to his house." Casey's face became very serious. "Listen, this guy is bad news and you better take his threats seriously. He's murdered before; we know that. We just can't pin anything on him. I want you to keep your eyes open and if he makes contact with you after the restraining order is in place, contact me immediately."

Ben sat and thought about Dracken's outburst at the hospital. "You know, I think we'll forget the order of protection for now. Maybe after time he'll forgive me...I'm starting to think the order of protection may only serve to piss him off."

"Well, it's up to you. The decision doesn't have to be made right now – think it over. I'll be here if you change your mind. Oh, here do me a favor; jot down your name, address, phone and tag numbers. I'll let the patrol officers know the situation.

They all despise Dracken; they'll be more than happy to patrol your neighborhood more frequently if it'll help you sleep better."

"Yeah okay thanks, I appreciate that. Can't hurt to have extra eyes around. Now, when can I get my truck back?" Ben asked as he stood up.

"Let me check into it and I'll give you a call as soon as I know. Because there was a death involved, they'll probably finish pretty quick."

"Great, thanks." Ben shook Casey's hand and took his card.

The next stop was the attorney's office. On his way, Ben went over in his mind what he wanted added to the will. Most of the changes were minor, but Ben wanted to make sure it was set up perfectly. He had decided that the attorney would be entrusted with the responsibility of delivering the letter that he had written for Claire. Howie was his first choice, but realizing that Howie had a tendency to misplace things, he thought better of it.

Arriving early, Ben decided to wait in the car in front of Templeton's office. The building looked out of place – a single story brick structure with a dark blue shingled roof adjacent to a strip mall. People hurried in and out of the stores, which made him uncomfortable. If Dracken were to send an assassin, Ben would have no idea what to look for – and what would it matter? Ben carried no weapon to protect himself. With that thought he sat up straight – why not go back to the detective and see about getting a gun permit? He was not unfamiliar with firearms. Growing up in South Dakota, he was taught how to handle pistols and rifles, and had fired thousands of rounds. Having no enemies and living in a safe area, he never gave owning a gun a second thought, but now maybe it was a necessity.

As Ben daydreamed, the slam of a car door shook him. He had dropped his guard and hadn't noticed that a car had pulled up and parked behind him. He jumped and turned to see who was getting out. The man in a trench coat walked towards him, causing a rush of adrenaline to course through his veins. As the man passed Ben's door he asked, "Do you know you're parked in a fire zone?"

Ben, frozen with fear and unable to say a word, watched as the man walked past the front of his car towards the stores, pointing at the no parking sign. Breathing a sigh of relief, Ben moved the car and decided to wait inside the office.

He approached the receptionist. "I'm Ben Pearce; I have a twelve o'clock appointment."

"You're a little early, please have a seat."

Ben dialed Howie on the cell phone. "Everything okay there?"

"Yeah, everything's fine. Where are you?"

"I'm at the attorney's office...I really don't feel like talking, though. I just wanted to make sure there weren't any problems."

"No, everything's fine; call me later then."

"Okay."

Ben sat down and picked up a magazine. He flipped through pages, but all he could think about was how frightened he had gotten outside. His palms were still a bit sweaty and his hands shaky when the attorney came out of his office with a client. He gave the man some last minute instructions while standing in front of the receptionist. Ben had forgotten what a distinguished man Templeton was. He was in his late fifties with a full head of salt and pepper hair; a blue three-piece pinstriped suit including a gold watch chain emphasized his athletic form.

He threw a file onto the receptionist's desk. "Hey Ben, how are you? Come on in."

"Thanks for seeing me on such short notice." Ben followed him in.

"Well, I only did it because it sounded like a matter of life and death...Now, is it?"

"A matter of life and death? You might say that," Ben replied.

"Okay Ben, have a seat and I'll be right back. Just have to give my secretary some info on my last client."

Ben admired Templeton's office. Dozens of brown leather-bound books sat atop a wall of shelves directly behind the large mahogany desk. A pile of folders was stacked neatly on one side and a box of cigars along with a cigar cutter on the other.

"Okay, lets see what we got," Templeton said. He picked up the top folder on the pile and put on a pair of black reading glasses. He sat back in his chair and flipped through the folder.

"Okay Ben, what's the emergency?" he asked, sitting with his hands clasped and elbows on the desk.

"I don't know if you read the papers. There was an accident where Victor Dracken's daughter was killed... I was the guy who hit her."

Templton sat up straight. His jaw dropped and he was unable to speak for a second. "I saw that, but never really paid attention to the name of the driver. My God Ben, how did it happen?"

Ben let out a deep sigh. "I was on my cell phone and wasn't paying attention. It happened so fast and I don't think I could've stopped even if I had been more alert."

Lawrence got up and walked around the office, realizing what a serious situation this was. "So you're worried about being sued?" he said, gazing out a window.

"That's a possibility but that's not why I'm here. This guy Dracken threatened to kill me...I'm taking him seriously and I want you to update my will."

"I was going to ask if you were worried about retaliation, but I didn't want to bring it up. You told the police about his threats, right?"

"Yeah but all they could do is issue an order of protection which I figured would only piss him off more. I'm kinda hoping that maybe over time he'll forgive me."

"I really don't believe he'll try to kill you. He'd be the first person they'd go to if you turned up dead."

"He's killed others and gotten away with it. I'm sure he wouldn't do it himself."

"No, I would think not." Lawrence sat back down in his seat. "I don't know what to tell you here. This is not your everyday problem."

"I don't think there's much you can do to help. It's my problem. Let's just go over my will and make sure it's up to date. I also want you to take this envelope and make sure that Claire gets it if something happens to me. It's got some of the things that I want at my funeral, so it's got to be delivered quickly if I'm mur...if I die."

The color left Ben's face.

"Ben, you okay?"

"Yeah, it's just that thinking about dying is one thing, but when you think about being murdered...it sounds a lot worse."

"Yes, I guess it does." Lawrence took his glasses off. "I'll make any changes you want immediately. Let's run over what we got here."

They spent the better part of half an hour making slight changes. Lawrence dropped the letter to Claire into the folder.

"I'll call you as soon as it's finished." He walked Ben to the door and shook his hand. "If there's any way I can help, please let me know."

Fear propelled Ben quickly towards home. After being startled in the parking lot, he was now afraid to be out in the open. He kept telling himself that the girl's funeral had probably just ended and that Dracken hadn't had time to even think about him.

As he drove through the local roadways, Ben's mind continued to wander back to the accident. Could he have avoided the child if he had been concentrating on the road? He played it over and over in his mind so many times that he became totally absorbed and found himself driving slowly down the center of the road. He immediately pulled the car over to the curb and looked around to see if anyone had seen what would probably appear to be a drunk driver. Confident that no one had noticed his erratic behavior, he continued going over the accident as he drove on.

There's no way. There's just no way I could've missed her - she was right out in front of me.

Ben, normally a mild mannered man, jammed on the brakes in the middle of the tree-lined residential street and slammed his hands on the steering wheel in rage.

"How can I let this guy, no matter who he is, take control of my life! It wasn't even my fault. I've got to just live my life as usual and whatever happens, happens," he yelled, trying to convince himself that he wasn't going to let Dracken scare him.

Ben still remained stopped in the street. He turned and noticed two young girls watching as he talked to himself. As they made eye contact, the girls hurriedly walked away. Ben could only laugh.

Look at me. I'm parked in the middle of the road talking to myself...I'm really losing it.

He continued on for a few more blocks before stopping again, this time at a stop sign where he made a fateful decision. With his face still hot from the outburst, he decided there was only one way to handle the whole situation.

I've got to go see Dracken again.

Chapter Four

Once back at home, Ben fell onto the living room couch and turned on the financial channel. He reached to the side of the chair and flipped on the vibration option. He reached for the phone.

"Hey Howie, it's me."

"How you feeling, buddy? Where are you?"

"I just got home. I'm feeling okay I guess – it's weird, I had a lot of feelings of guilt but now they seem to be changing. Now it's more anger."

"I can understand the fear part but what's with the anger?"

"I'm pissed off at Dracken for making me have to live like this. I'm tired of looking over my shoulder."

"You'll get over that soon. I'm not convinced that he'll come after you," Howie said, sounding confident.

"Well I've got to know for sure...I can't live like this Howie. I can't believe that I'm going to say this but I've decided to go see Dracken again."

Howie paused. "Do you really think that's a good idea?" He exhaled deeply into the phone.

"Good idea or bad, it's what I have to do. Maybe I can reason with him after he's had time to calm down."

"I think you should let him forget you after he's calmed down. You're only going to remind him of the accident. Ben, I think you're outta your mind."

"I need to know for sure what he's got planned. The cops can't help me, so what do I do?"

"I suggest you just let it go until you have proof that he's going to do something."

"By then it could be too late; I could be dead." The phone line was silent.

"Okay, if you think it's the only way."

"It is the only way. You don't know what it's like to live in fear. I need to know."

Howie laughed. "Believe me, I know fear."

Ben looked at the phone. "What does that mean?"

"Forget it, man."

"Listen, Howie, if anything happens to me, promise that you'll help Claire move the kids out west."

"No problem but nothing's gonna happen. Listen, when are you going to see Dracken?"

"I figured I'd wait 'til next Monday; my guess is that he'll be back to work by then. The last thing I want to do is show up at his house. All I have to do is sneak back and forth to work from Wednesday to Friday and survive the weekend. And I'll be sweatin' that all the way through, knowin' what Monday has in store for me."

"Well...I don't envy you. I'm taking it Claire doesn't know about any of this."

"You kidding? If she found out she'd be a wreck. I'll only tell her when I absolutely have to."

"Right – listen, I got incoming. Call me later."

The next morning, Ben saw Claire and the children off and stretched out on the couch. He had no intention of leaving the house, and decided to surprise Claire by painting the laundry room downstairs. He had put it off for a year but figured that maybe it would help pass the time and get his mind off Dracken. As he set up the drop cloths, the phone rang. He stumbled over a step stool as he ran for the cordless.

"Hello?"

"Is this Ben Pearce?" the voice asked.

"Yes."

"This is Detective Casey. How's everything?"

"Okay I guess."

"No problems since we spoke yesterday?"

"No, why, did you hear something I should know about?" Ben replied, his heart speeding up.

"No, no, relax. I just called to tell you that you can pick up your truck today."

"Oh okay. I take it everything went well with the safety check?"

"Yeah everything checked out safety wise. I haven't actually seen the vehicle, but there was some minor damage to the under carriage and there is some pretty good cosmetic damage to the passenger side from when it was flipped. At least that's what I'm told. Oh and the passenger window is shattered. It's going to spend some time in the shop without a doubt."

"What do you think, should I have it towed or do you think I can drive it?"

"As far as I'm told, it can be driven, but that's up to you."

"Okay, I'll come down and take a look. If I can't drive it, I'll just call the shop for a tow."

"While I've got you, have you given any more thought to the order of protection?"

"Yeah I've thought about it and decided against it for now. Let's see if there's any further contact from Dracken. What I was really thinking about though was a gun permit."

"Famous last words," Casey said loudly. "First of all, you could only get a permit to carry the gun back and forth to the range. If you got caught carrying it at any other time you'd be arrested. Leaving it around the house can only lead to trouble. Ben, please don't go that route."

"How do I protect myself then?"

Ben could hear Casey sigh. "I don't know what to tell you Ben; this isn't an easy situation and there isn't much I can do..."

"'Til he kills me, right?"

"I'm sorry, I wish I could do more to help. I have the patrol cars passing your house more often, but until he does something my hands are tied."

"All right look, forget the gun thing, don't worry about it. I'll be fine. I appreciate all your help. Just give me the address where my truck is and I'll take a run over and see what I have to do."

Casey, a veteran detective, didn't like the way Ben had given up so easily on the gun permit. "Ben, please don't do anything foolish."

Ben didn't dare mention that he planned to confront Dracken. He took all the information on the location of his truck and again thanked the officer for his help. He gave Claire a quick call to let her know where he'd be.

Ben pulled up to the police impound lot and got out without hesitation, but did check to see if he had been followed. He walked toward the office looking through the chain link fence into the lot. Hundreds of cars, most of them mangled and twisted, were scattered across the dirt lot. As he turned his head back toward the office, he caught a glimpse of blue and immediately changed direction. Clutching the fence tightly and standing on tiptoes, he pressed his face against the chain link, staring at his damaged vehicle. From his angle he could only see the front end. Pieces of the plastic grille hung off their brackets, and orange paint highlighted the dented chrome bumper.

Ben remembered the accident vividly and was reluctant to retrieve his truck. He began to have doubts about being able to climb behind the wheel of his favorite toy again. He pulled himself away from the fence and forced himself to the office where an officer stood up as Ben entered.

"Help you?" the officer asked, noticing that Ben looked reluctant to come closer.

"Yes, I need to pick up my truck – well get it towed I guess. Can I use your phone to call my shop to send a truck?" he said, pulling a business card out of his pocket.

Ben stared out a window that overlooked the lot. The officer came around from behind the counter and stood in front of Ben, who was oblivious to his move.

"You're not the first to have a problem coming here," he said, startling Ben. "I'm sorry, I can see you're not with me here. Why don't you give me the shop number and I'll call for you."

"I killed a little girl with that truck, and now I don't know if I can even drive it. I think all I would do is relive the accident over and over," he said, handing the card to the officer.

"No matter how cold this sounds, when you fall off a horse you have to get right back on. You didn't mean to kill the girl and now you have to get on with your life." The officer sounded more like a professional therapist than a cop.

"You sound like you really care," Ben said, sounding baffled.

"I was picked special for this job. I see a lot of people come through here who have to claim cars that their entire families were killed in. I have a degree in psychology and I'm here to help people through this traumatic experience if they need it. My main job with the force is hostage negotiator, but since that service isn't needed every day, I'm here. I'm part of the Governor's new plan for cops to reach out, you know?"

Ben nodded his head in approval. "Not a bad idea."

"C'mon, let me get your paper work started – what was your name?"

"Ben Pearce, I'm the guy who hit the Dracken girl." The officer hid his face behind the counter.

"It's okay, I'm used to that look when I tell people," Ben said almost laughing.

Ben hesitantly walked out into the lot and approached the Land Cruiser, noticing that the passenger doors were crushed in from being rolled on its side by the police. He ran his hand along the front fender as he walked toward the passenger door, bouncing the side view mirror, which was hanging from its power cables, in his hand.

He leaned into the broken window. Glass littered the passenger seat, and client statements that he had been bringing home were thrown on the floor in front of the passenger seat. Avoiding the front end, Ben examined the side slowly, moving toward the back and cringing at the scratched chrome along the entire length.

A light drizzle began to fall as Ben continued to survey the damage, spending a great deal of time on every scratch – anything to keep from having to sit in the driver's seat or look at the front grille.

He lifted the passenger door latch and tugged, but because of the damage it would only yield a two-inch opening. Sticking both hands into the space, he leaned back putting his weight into it and rocked a bit before the door let out an ear-piercing screech like two pieces of nailed wood being separated with a crow bar. The door wouldn't open completely but Ben was able to squeeze in enough to reach the papers. He brushed the glass away and retrieved them.

The police officer from the office came up behind. "Need any help?"

"Actually I need some plastic and tape. I don't want the interior to get ruined any more than it already is."

"Why don't you come inside. The tow truck will be here soon. I'll have someone come right over and cover her up."

"Yeah, okay thanks. I'll be in in a few minutes. Can you take these papers inside for me?" Ben asked, looking skyward as the drizzle turned to a steadier rain.

Ben walked around the back of the truck to get to the driver's door. He stood for a second, took a deep breath and held it as he opened the door. He stepped up on the running board, brushed the seat of glass and slid his legs in, pushing the deflated airbag to one side. His shirt now stuck to his body, soaked through from the rain. Not even the thought of staining the leather kept him from finishing what he really needed to do – just sit behind the wheel for a moment. He sank into the seat and exhaled. He put his hands on the wheel and looked down the long hood, remembering how much he loved the vehicle. Could he ever drive it again without picturing the young girl wedged underneath?

He looked around the interior, picking up a handful of glass pieces and bouncing them off his palm toward the passenger seat. He climbed back out as a man with a roll of duct tape and plastic walked up. Before closing the door, he unclipped the garage door remote from the visor and slipped it into his pocket.

"I'll close it for you. He's waitin' for you inside."

"Thanks," Ben said.

He started walking towards the front of the truck – his mind made up not to look at the damaged front grille. After walking ten feet past it, he stopped. He thought to himself that this was like when milk goes sour – you just have to smell it anyway. He turned back. The bright orange paint from the girl's bike, embedded in the chrome bumper, caught his attention immediately. He walked back toward it.

Ben realized that he had made a mistake. All he could picture was the last vision in life that the young girl had – a plastic grille and huge chrome bumper crashing down upon her. Ben, now on one knee and with one hand on the bumper, began to cry. Within seconds the officer who had been watching him from the office was helping him up.

"C'mon Mr. Pearce, let's get you inside."

The officer handed Ben a towel.

"Guess you didn't listen to the weather report before you went out, huh?"

Ben shook his head. "Too much on my mind."

Ben's cell phone rang. Lawrence Templeton had his revised will complete and it only awaited his signature.

"Thanks for your help," he said to the officer. "Appreciate the compassion."

Ben prayed that he would make it home before Claire. Having stopped at the attorney's office, he was carrying the copy of his revised will. One look into his eyes and she would know that he was guilty of something.

As he drove down his block, he kept one eye in the rearview mirror and one ahead for Claire's car. All was clear in both directions. He pulled in to the driveway and waited for the garage door to open, then sped inside.

Opening the door to his office from the garage, he immediately sliced open the envelope with his copy of the new will. He read quickly and was satisfied with the minor changes.

With that, he stuffed the will into an overfilled firebox under his desk.

He changed out of his wet clothes and sat on the couch. Claire would be coming home anytime, so he needed to make good use of his time alone. Plans had to be made for getting back and forth to work with the least visibility. Thinking that if Dracken were coming after him it would be during something he did routinely, he decided to take different routes to work every day and leave at different times. He now knew how a fugitive felt, always looking over his shoulder.

Claire walked in the front door carrying Sarah. His strategy session would have to be postponed. He jumped up and took Sarah while kissing Claire on the cheek.

"Ben, a police car stopped in front of the house just now and watched me walk inside. What's that all about? Is there a problem that I should know about?" She took off her sweater and waited for an answer.

Ben fussed over Sarah, not wanting to look at Claire.

"What? No, there's no problem."

"And there was a police car on the block this morning."

Ben shrugged his shoulders and made quick eye contact with her. He knew she wasn't buying his lies.

A short while later, the bus dropped Michael off. He came flying into the house upon finding out from his mother that Daddy was home. He searched the top floor as Ben and Sarah hid in the playroom downstairs. Ben would call his name every few minutes until Claire finally gave them up. They remained downstairs until dinner and afterwards returned to the playroom. Ben kept them up past their bedtime, raising Claire's suspicions that he was avoiding her. He used the excuse of wanting to spend as much time with them after hitting the girl – which wasn't far from the truth.

Claire, being a patient woman, didn't question him further. She always found out if something was being kept from her. Ben knew that and had to be extra careful.

* * * * * *

Ben arrived at his office very early the next morning. He felt that he would be more comfortable sitting as coworkers arrived, rather than being the focus of all eyes if he entered later.

Howie had made an attempt to keep Ben's desk straightened, but Howie's idea of neat wasn't the same as Ben's. He sorted through papers stacked in piles and read through messages.

It became more difficult to continue as his coworkers stopped one by one at his desk to offer their condolences. To Ben's surprise, not many asked questions – most just asked how he was doing.

When Howie arrived he popped his head over the partition. "How's it goin?"

"Oh, good. I'm ready to try and get back into the swing of things."

"How'd you make out? I mean with people askin' you questions and stuff," Howie asked.

"No problems, nobody's asked many questions...Did you ask them not to?"

"No not really. I think that they're all just doin' the right thing. I mean they know what you're going through."

"In a way I wish they did ask more about what happened. I want them to know the truth. You know how rumors fly around. The last thing I want is for guys to stop talking if I walk up to a bunch of them," Ben said.

"Hey I know you got a lot of catching up to do, but what do you say we take a long lunch. We really haven't spoken much in the past few days and I know you're going through hell. I wanna hear what's going on in your head."

Ben paused. "You know... that's not a bad idea, but do you really feel safe being out in public with me?"

Howie thought for a moment. "Okay, we'll stay local...By the way, I bought a new car."

"You couldn't have done that last week?" Ben asked and then wished he hadn't. He stood up and looked over at Howie. "I didn't mean anything by that."

"Yeah I know, but don't you think I realize that if I hadn't put off buying a new car, that girl would still be alive right now? What if my car didn't break down? What if I hadn't called you in the car that night?"

"Howie, I've gone over the accident in my head a thousand times. Even if I hadn't been on the phone with you, I still would have hit her. There was no way I could've avoided it so don't blame yourself; it's no one's fault. Let's just get to work and think about where we're going for lunch. By the way, what kind of car did you get?"

"Caddy Eldorado," he said proudly. "Wait 'til you see it. And the best thing is no money down and no payments for a year."

Ben, still standing over the partition, squinted to see a paper on Howie's desk. It had the names of sports teams written on it.

"Howie, what's that?" Ben pointed the paper. "Please tell me you're not gambling again."

Howie gave Ben the same look that Ben gave Claire when he was lying. "No, I told you I was done with that."

Ben sat back in his seat, reliving Howie's last gambling adventure, which didn't turn out well.

As the week went on, Ben felt more at ease. He kept constant vigil wherever he went, but there was no evidence that Dracken was having him followed and there were no threats. Only the backfire of a car once during the week startled him enough to feel that he needed to visit Dracken.

Ben played a scenario over in his mind many times. He put himself in Dracken's place and weighed the pros and cons of revenge. Finally he decided that by now Dracken would have realized that murdering him would solve nothing and would not bring his daughter back. Unfortunately Ben didn't possess the same violent mental characteristics or the killer instinct that Dracken had and that he needed to rule his illicit empire.

By week end he was off the idea of going to see Dracken. The anger he had felt was waning and day by day he felt more secure. The pain of the girl's death still lingered, but he was now dealing with it.

* * * * * *

After spending most of a very rainy weekend at home playing with the children, Ben was looking forward to work on Monday. Now that he had convinced himself that he was safe, the Monday morning drive, which was brutal as always, didn't faze him. Instead of filling his mind with worries of execution, he was able to return to daydreaming about South Dakota. No more churning stomach or stress headaches, just blissful thoughts of rolling hills and horses.

He pulled into the three-story parking garage, running into the usual wall of cars fighting for the closest spots to the building entrance. The cars crept toward the first interior ramp. Ben sat with his left hand outside the window, slapping the door lightly to the beat of a country song on the radio. He followed the line of cars up the incline, which led him onto the one-way lane on the second floor. Out of the corner of his eye Ben caught a glimpse of a shiny black Mercedes approaching in the opposite direction in the next aisle. Seeing the large black car reminded him immediately of the limos at the hospital. He strained to see the vehicle through the parked cars and concrete pillars, which separated the lanes. As the car passed, Ben's jaw hung wide open. He wished that he was dreaming, but unfortunately it was all too real – the driver of the car was Dracken's bodyguard – or at least it looked like him.

Willie!

The cars that were lined up behind Ben, who was now stopped, leaned on their horns as the lane in front of him had opened. He jammed the gas pedal to the floor, spinning the front tires and sending up a cloud of smoke. He sped toward the exit, whipping around the circular ramp and flying toward the main road. There were three different directions that could be taken at the main intersection. Once there, he snapped his head back and forth searching in desperation for the car but to no avail.

He smacked the steering wheel – he had to know for sure if it was the bodyguard. He had a one in three chance of picking the right direction and decided on the most obvious choice –

the road that led to Dracken's office building which was well known. He put the rental car through its paces, weaving in and out of traffic, taking full advantage of opportunities to punch the gas for bursts of speed – anything to find that car.

Red lights became optional, although he wasn't reckless in avoiding them. First stopping then checking for oncoming cars and police, then carefully driving through them. He couldn't believe that he of all people was breaking the law, but this was an emergency.

After five minutes of chasing a car that he couldn't see, Ben was about to give up. Then, driven by the haunting thoughts of the week before, the feeling of not knowing his fate, the uncertainty of Dracken's intentions, he continued the pursuit.

Speeding once again in the possible direction of the phantom car, Ben finally caught a glimpse of what he thought might be his target. He pulled closer.

There it is.

Trailing ten car lengths behind, he watched the Mercedes through the windshields of a car that he kept between them. He still wasn't absolutely sure that this was the right car but it was his only candidate. If the car returned to Dracken's office, Ben would have to confront him.

It became apparent after following for miles that the car was leading to the villainous destination. Ben trailed the car right to the building that was home to Dracken's empire. He pulled into the lot, parking in sight of the black Mercedes. Not quite believing that it wasn't a dream, Ben watched the same man who had held Victor Dracken from strangling him, walk inside. He sat for a while staring at the building. White puffy clouds with a blue-sky background reflected in its façade. He knew what he had to do – there was no other way.

Gathering all his courage, Ben started for the door. With hundreds of people working in the building, he had no fear of Dracken attacking him on the premises. Upon entering, he located the building directory and found that Dracken's offices were on the top floor.

He stood alone in the elevator trying to keep his composure. But how should he act? Forceful and undaunted by Dracken's power or sorrowful and scared, acting as though he should be pitied. He decided to go with whatever came naturally in Dracken's presence, although the forceful idea was quickly fading into a far second place.

The elevator came to a stop. The bell rang and the doors opened out into a hallway. Ben stepped out. He couldn't decide whether he hoped Dracken was in or out.

He noticed a sign for a men's room and took a moment inside to straighten his tie and take a few deep breaths. This was by far the scariest situation Ben had ever been in and right now stalling was his only defense. Unfortunately, he could only remain secure in the bathroom for a short time and decided that this had to be done – now.

The glass doors to Dracken's office suite were massive, stretching from floor to ceiling. He grabbed the silver handle and leaned his weight into opening it, but to his amazement it swung easily on its hinges. He stepped in cautiously and approached the two young secretaries who were seated behind the semi-circular shaped reception desk. Ben leaned his arm atop the wall, which hid the girls from the outside hallway.

"Excuse me," he said, his voice cracking. "I'd like to see Victor Dracken please."

"Is he expecting you, sir?"

"No, but I have to see him," he said.

"Mr. Dracken is very busy," she replied. "Give me your name and I'll check to see if he can see you."

"Ben Pearce," he said, trying his best not to look nervous.

"Will he know who you are?" She asked.

"Yes, I believe he'll know who I am."

She paused. "Okay, please have a seat." She motioned to a couch behind him.

Ben backed up a few steps, then turned and walked to the couch. As he sat, he could hear the secretary whispering in the phone. With Ben acting skittish, she was obviously alarmed. She popped her head up over the front wall of the desk, making eye contact, then quickly dropping back down.

Immediately, two large men emerged from a set of double doors adjacent to the desk and stood talking to the secretaries.

The men nonchalantly glanced at Ben as they conversed with the two girls.

Ben tried his best to look calm and collected, but his legs trembled and got to the point where he had to hold one knee still. Five minutes felt like an eternity as he sat waiting for Dracken's next move. Was Dracken making him wait, maybe watching him through the security cameras that were mounted in the ceiling?

Then – boom. Willie burst through the doors. Upon seeing Ben, he laughed and shook his head. He motioned for the other two men to return inside.

"I'll take care of this," he said to them.

Ben stood up as Willie approached.

"Are you just stupid or what?" Willie said loudly but not quite yelling. "Mr. Dracken doesn't want to see you. What do I have to do to impress this upon you?"

"I'm...I'm not leaving until I see him."

Willie came closer. Now almost in Ben's face, he stated very slowly, "You will leave or I will remove you."

Before Ben realized what he was saying, the words just came out. "Then remove me."

He regretted those words before Willie even was able to comprehend that someone was standing up to him. In an instant Ben was being held by the collar and pushed towards the door. Ben resisted the best he could, but the bodyguard was double his weight.

"I'm not leaving here 'til I see Victor Dracken," he yelled as loud as he could, trying to make a scene.

"Wait," a voice shouted from behind them. "Let him go." It was Victor Dracken. Ben turned and faced him. "You insist on seeing me, why?"

"I tried before to apologize and you threatened me..." Dracken stopped him from continuing.

"Come inside."

They ushered Ben down the hall. Dracken led the way and Willie followed behind. After passing conference rooms and private offices they came to an open area with a lone secretary sitting at a desk. "Hold my calls," Dracken snapped at the girl.

"I'll be right in," he said to Willie.

Willie placed his hand on Ben's back and guided him toward an office door, opening it and giving him a shove inside. Ben looked around in awe, almost forgetting how afraid he was. He was now in Victor Dracken's corner office. Large windows made for a beautiful view of a tree-covered hill not far in the distance.

"Have a seat," Willie said before leaving the room. "And don't touch anything."

Ben was in shock that he was left alone and became panicky realizing that he was inside the office of the man who wanted him dead. He calmed himself, remembering that many people had seen him enter the office. Dracken would never touch him here.

He stood up and looked around at the beautiful office. The glass desk was six feet wide and weighed at least a thousand pounds, the legs pushing deep into the thick white carpet. The artwork that hung on the walls was breathtaking. Ben wasn't a connoisseur of fine art but knew enough to realize that the Monet and Van Gogh paintings weren't replicas. This was a true millionaire's office. Strange, he thought to himself, how bright and colorful an office for a man who was so cruel and ruthless. For some reason the appearance put him at ease, but that would be short lived.

The appearance of Dracken himself was another matter. The ragged looking man that Ben had seen at the hospital was now dressed in a three-thousand-dollar suit with gold cufflinks. His jet-black hair slicked back. Seeing him like this reminded Ben of the many times Dracken had appeared on television after beating yet another murder rap.

Ben bent over slightly to get a better look at a picture framed in silver atop the desk. An eight-by-ten photo of Dracken's daughter stared back at him. His heart sank and he began to breathe heavily. Dracken was going to sit across from him while looking at his dead daughter's picture. What chance did he have to plead his case, with the girl's happy smiling face right there in the frame?

The door opened. Dracken and his bodyguard entered the office, taking Ben by surprise.

"So Mr. Pearce, you insist on seeing me. Here I am, what do you want?" Dracken said loudly from behind him.

Willie stood in front of Ben and waved an electronic wand over the contours of his body.

"What are you doing?" Ben asked. "What is that thing?"

"That's to tell me if you're hiding a wire or any kind of electronic equipment or even a weapon. I'm a very careful man. Please...have a seat, Mr. Pearce." Dracken circled the desk and sat. "We wouldn't want you to tell people that I wasn't a gracious host and you know us Brits - always ready for a social call. Can we get you some coffee...tea?" he said sarcastically.

Ben was at loss for words. All the rehearsing he had done from the minute he had decided to confront Dracken - everything he had planned to say was forgotten. He was face to face with the man who he had to convince to let him live, and nothing would come out.

Dracken leaned back in his chair. "You must have a death wish coming to see me," he said, smiling.

"I'm glad you find that amusing. You know that I never intended to hurt your daughter, yet you threaten to kill me...you send your bodyguard to kill me," Ben said, finally able to speak.

"My bodyguard? To kill you? You must be delusional Mr. Pearce."

"I saw him driving through my building parking lot and I followed him back here," Ben said, looking over his shoulder and pointing at Willie.

"He was delivering papers to a business associate of mine who apparently has his office in your building. You have an uncanny ability for making foolish mistakes. Now the only thing that you've accomplished is to piss me off further."

Dracken leaned forward, placing his hands palm down on the desk, his face turning to stone. "You killed my daughter while talking on your cell phone and I will never forgive you for that. You made the mistake, not I," he said, raising his voice.

"So you intend to kill me for something that you know I didn't intend to do? I have a two children myself."

Before he could say anything else, Dracken jumped up. "And I had a daughter," he screamed. "You took her from me...an eye for an eye."

Dracken picked up the picture of his daughter and leaned over the desk, shoving it in Ben's face.

"This is what you took from me," Dracken yelled with such extreme force that it forced Ben back in the seat. The rage that he had seen at the hospital was now equaled, making his whole body shake. Ben turned to make sure that the bodyguard was still there; without him he felt that Dracken would surely kill him.

"What kind of man are you? Taking me from my children won't bring your daughter back," Ben said, almost coming to tears.

"Mr. Pearce, I think you better leave now." Dracken still clutched his daughter's picture.

"Mr. Dracken...please understand..."

"Get out," he screamed. "You made the fucking mistake, remember that." He faced out the window.

Ben stood up and took two steps toward the door.

"Oh and Mr. Pearce... you can rest assured that no harm will come to your family," Dracken said without turning around.

"Mr. Dracken," He was about to plead for his life but again he was cut short.

"Get out; Willie, get him out of here," he snapped.

Willie dragged Ben by the arm like a mother dragging a child trying to go in another direction.

"One more thing, Mr. Pearce...you'll never know when or where."

The two secretaries at the front desk looked on with pity as Willie pushed Ben through the glass doors. With his eyes teary and his body shaking, Ben waited for the elevator.

Once in the lobby, people watched, as a grown man in a suit cried as he walked towards the front doors. Finding a men's room, he ducked in. He splashed water in his face and looked at himself in the mirror.

Willie wasn't even there for me.

Once back in the parking lot, he wandered aimlessly. He realized that Dracken was probably laughing at him from high above as he searched for the car. It took Ben a few more minutes to realize that he wasn't looking for his truck but for the white rental car, which he soon found.

He left the lot but had no desire to return to his office and it was too early to go home. Claire would still be there. He parked in another lot down the road from Dracken's building.

Ben sat for half an hour. He could feel deep down that there was a way out of this mess. He just couldn't put his finger on it. He had nothing on Dracken to hold against him and no physical power that would rival the villain's but yet he knew there had to be something – something small, as in the movies when tiny bacteria kill the invading aliens. Maybe Howie would have some ideas; he dialed the phone.

"Howie, it's me."

"Where are you? Did you forget we had an important meeting?"

"Howie, I just met Victor Dracken," Ben said, followed by three seconds of silence.

"Wait...what do you mean you met him? You mean you ran into him somewhere?"

"I saw his bodyguard in our parking garage and panicked. I followed him back to Dracken's office and demanded to see him."

"Are you nuts?" Howie could hear that Ben was physically shaken. "Where are you right now?"

"I'm not even sure, let me see," he said looking around. "I'm in the Atrium building parking lot; down the road from Dracken's building."

"Look, meet me at the Parkway Diner. I'll leave right now," Howie said.

"Okay, see you in a bit."

Ben was already inside, nursing a cup of coffee in a corner booth, when Howie walked in. Howie could see that Ben was shaken and waited for him to tell the story.

"I can't believe that he is actually going to kill me, Howie."

"Did he say that?"

"No but close enough; he said I'll never know when or where."

"Look Ben, you gotta go back to the cops and tell 'em you need help, because Ben - you need help. At least get the order of protection."

"What good will that do? That's not going to stop him, and if they have to send a detective to the house, Claire will find out what kind of trouble I'm in."

"Don't you think it's time you told her? I mean after this you really have to."

"How can I tell her? She'll panic and worry constantly." He put his head in his hands. "What am I going to do?" He slowly looked up at Howie. "The only way I'm gonna stay alive is if I kill him first."

"Now there's a good idea," he said sarcastically. "I'll hold him and you beat him to death with a stick."

"Quit clownin', this is serious."

"No it's not. You know you're not gonna kill him. Just go to the police and see what they say to do."

"Yeah, I guess you're right." Ben looked out the window in thought then banged his fist on the table. "There has to be a way out, I know it, I feel it and I'm gonna find it."

"Look, just get to the police station and see what they tell you to do. C'mon, I'll go with you," Howie said, grabbing Ben by the wrist to get his full attention. "Ben, get this taken care of - let's just go right now."

"You're right, you're right, but I'll go alone. I don't want you connected to this in any way. Go back to the office and I'll call you later. You know if something happens to me I'm counting on you to take care of things."

Howie nodded. "You got it."

Ben pulled Detective Casey's card from his wallet and called the station but got bad news.

"Damn, he's out 'til tomorrow. I'll go first thing. Do you mind taking my calls for the rest of the day...and tomorrow morning? I'm not up to work; I need to go somewhere and come up with a plan."

"Do yourself a favor and let the police do the planning, okay?"

"Okay, okay, I'll just head home and try to relax. When Claire gets home, I'll tell her I wasn't feeling well so I came home early."

"Good idea. Call me later and let me know how you're making out."

Ben arrived home and headed straight for the couch, still exhausted from his encounter with Dracken. He still had trouble believing what had happened and felt like a man that had just been told that he was terminally ill and had only two weeks to live.

Ben waited at the front door for Claire to come home. As she pulled up, he remembered that he had left his life insurance policy out on his desk for review. Claire, surprised to see Ben's car, immediately ran inside.

"Ben? Are you all right?" She called out.

"Yeah I'm down here, I'm fine."

"I ran in soon as I saw the car. Let me go back out and get Sarah, I left her in her seat. Why are you home...wait tell me when I get back in," she said from the top of the stairs.

Ben returned upstairs as Claire carried Sarah into the house. He stretched out his arms to hug the baby, but Claire pulled her away.

"You look terrible, what's wrong?" Claire asked.

"Just some stomach cramps, maybe something I ate. I'll be all right."

"Well then don't touch her until we know what you have. Why don't you go lie down and relax? I'll put her down for a nap. Do you want anything?"

"No, just some rest."

Ben made it through the rest of the day without tipping off Claire that there was a problem. Unfortunately he had to stay away from the children to accomplish this. He was better off because holding them and picturing them without a father and how he might never see them grow up brought him tears.

Both children cried continuously to be with their father; Claire did all she could to calm them as Ben watched TV in the bedroom. Their bedtime could not come soon enough but finally there was silence.

He had the plan of faking sleep and keeping his face buried in the pillows to avoid eye contact but Claire walked into the room full of questions.

"How are you feeling now? Any better?"

"Oh yeah, I'm pretty good now," he said, faking a groggy voice.

"Ben...is anything else wrong? You're not acting right. Something with the accident?" she asked, sounding suspicious.

"No I'm fine."

"You would tell me, right? Look at me and tell me everything's okay," she said, kneeling across the bed to look at him closely.

He lifted the pillow and looked at her, trying not to give anything away. "Everything's fine."

"Okay then." She went into the bathroom.

He let out a sigh – how long could he keep this from her? He needed to find a solution and looked forward to meeting with the detective in the morning. The gun permit idea was top on his list even though the detective didn't like it. The detective wasn't the one who was going to be shot at, and he already had a gun.

Claire came back into the room. She looked exhausted, which thrilled Ben. He wasn't going to sleep a wink – better she didn't know about it.

"Turn the TV down, Hon. I'd kiss you goodnight but I don't want to get too close."

Within minutes, she was sound asleep. Ben flipped through the channels, hoping to find a movie or show with the answer to his problem. When that didn't work, he locked his fingers behind his head and stared up at the ceiling. He had to come up with a backup plan if the police couldn't help him. Unfortunately every idea that he had always led back to the sure fire way of solving everything – killing Victor Dracken first. He went over in his mind how to commit the perfect murder but knew deep down that he didn't have the killer instinct. *Maybe I could come back after my death as a ghost and inflict my revenge on Dracken then. Only problem with that theory is I'd already be dead. There has to be a way.* He thought of hiring someone else to kill Dracken, but he knew that he could never get away with that. Even with his mind racing, Ben began to doze off. Not only was he unsafe while awake but now the sanctity of sleep was taken from him as violent dreams snapped him awake. He debated whether or not to take a sleeping pill, but decided against it.

Dozing off once again, he began to dream about Victor Dracken seated with Claire and Howie at the reading of his will. Dracken began to cry. Howie was laughing, pointing his finger at him. It was Howie's words in the dream that opened Ben's eyes wide. He couldn't quite make out the exact lines that Howie spoke but the meaning rang out.

In an instant, every synapse in his brain fired. He sat straight up and slapped his hand on his forehead. He had his plan.

I knew there was a way. The will. The will.

Chapter Five

Ben tossed and turned for most of the night thinking about his newfound strategy. He would have slept better thinking that he was going to die, but this sleepless night was welcomed. With dawn two hours away, his excitement grew like a child on Christmas morning. As with all sleepless nights, he fell fast asleep twenty minutes before his alarm was set to wake him. He reached and slapped the snooze button on the clock radio quieting the morning news headlines. He smiled; it was going to be a great day.

He jumped out of bed on the second sounding of the alarm about ten minutes later and ran to the bathroom. He quickly returned and rummaged through the walk-in closet for a suit.

Get clothes first then go in the shower.

Ben tripped over his own feet fighting to get ready. The only thing he could concentrate on was getting hold of Lawrence Templeton.

Claire had fallen back to sleep after the alarm but was awakened again by Ben's hurried movements and sat up in the bed. "Ben, what's all the noise about?"

"Oh sorry. I didn't mean to wake you," he said cheerfully from the bathroom. He ran around to her side of the bed and kissed her on the forehead.

"Okay what's going on? Last night you were a bear and now you're happy as a clam."

"I had a great night's sleep and I'm feeling better, that's all."

"You must have had a twenty-four-hour stomach bug."

Ben rushed through the morning's rituals. He woke Claire to go into the shower before the children awoke. As soon as he heard the water running, he rushed to the garage with the portable phone. He dialed the attorney's office but got the answering machine; it was too early. There was, however, an emergency beeper number, which he quickly dialed. He rushed back into the bedroom and turned off the phone ringer so Claire wouldn't hear if it rang.

He paced the living room, praying that Lawrence would call before Claire was finished. Within three minutes, the phone rang. Ben ran down the stairs and back into the garage again.

"Lawrence?"

"Yes, who's this?" he asked sleepily.

"Sorry if I woke you. It's Ben Pearce and I need to see you again immediately...right now, today...well as soon as you can. It's really important."

"Okay Ben, I know the situation you're in and if you say it's important...can you meet me in the office in an hour? I'll come in early for you."

"Perfect, I'll be there."

Coming back inside, he could hear Claire calling him.

"I'm coming," he said.

"Where were you? Don't you hear the baby crying?" she called from the bathroom.

Ben grabbed both children and squeezed them as he carried them to the kitchen for breakfast.

"Claire I have to leave soon, can you take care of them?"

"Why so early?"

"I want to catch up on what I missed yesterday."

"Okay, be right there."

Claire came into the kitchen and kissed the children, who had already dumped a box of cereal on the floor. Ben bent to clean it but she stopped him.

"Just get ready, I'll take care of it...oh and I just thought of something. The real estate agent called yesterday and I told her she could start showing the house again. I figured you'd be okay with that, right?"

"Oh yeah that's fine; let's get this place sold and get out of here."

Ben grabbed a quick breakfast, kissed Claire goodbye and jumped into the car. As soon as he was out of sight of the house, he dialed the phone.

"Hey Howie, you up?"

"Yeah, been up for a while, everything okay?"

"Everything is great. Take my calls for a little while when you get in and if Claire calls for some reason, tell her I'm in a meeting."

"Yeah I know, you're going to the police station. You almost sound happy; what's goin' on?"

"The plan's changed. I'm not going to the police; I'm going back to my attorney. I'll tell you the whole thing when I get in later."

"Okay," Howie said, sounding confused. "I can't wait to hear this."

"You're gonna love it. I told you there was a way. See you in a while."

Both Ben and Lawrence pulled up to the attorney's office at the same time.

"Morning Ben, good timing. How are you doing?" he asked as they walked to the office door.

"I'm great, how about you?"

Lawrence had just gotten the door unlocked and began to push it open but stopped and turned.

"You're great? You're not the same person who came here last week. And if you're great, why are we here? What happened, did Dracken forgive you?"

"No, I went and confronted him after seeing his bodyguard in my parking garage yesterday. The bodyguard roughed me up a little in Dracken's office. Then Dracken went into a rage and pretty much told me flat out that he was going to kill me."

"And this makes you happy? I'm confused."

"No, not at all, but I have a solution to my problem. That's where you come in."

Lawrence walked around to his desk. "Sit, sit." He took his glasses off and placed them on the desk. He sat back in his chair and folded his arms. Having been an attorney for many years, he knew Ben was about to ask something of him that was either illegal or immoral.

"Okay, what do you need me to do?"

"Well I had to figure a way, short of killing him, to keep him from killing me. I need you to adjust my will slightly to help protect me."

"How slightly?"

Ben got up and paced the floor as he explained his idea. He wasn't sure that Lawrence would be able to do what he wanted but he at least expected high praise for his inventiveness.

"I figured that the only way to get Dracken to think twice about killing me would be to make him fear for his life. Just verbally threatening him would only make him laugh."

He walked right up to Templeton's desk and leaned toward him.

"I want you to add a rider to my will that states if I'm killed, fifty thousand dollars will be given to a certain person if he kills Victor Dracken."

Lawrence sprang to his feet. "You want me to do what?" he yelled in utter disbelief.

"I know it sounds a little far fetched, but if I can show Dracken that if he harms me, he himself will be hunted, it may just put enough of a scare into him to back off."

Lawrence shook his head. "Ben, what you're asking is illegal...I think. I've never run into anything like this before. After all these years, I'd thought I'd heard it all, but this... this is the strangest request I've ever had." He began to laugh. "How did you come up with this anyway?"

"Sort of in a dream," Ben replied. "Look, I don't need this to be in place forever, just until Dracken sees it and realizes that it would be in his best interest to leave me alone. I've really got nothing to lose."

"He already told me that he is going to kill me, so if this idea gets him madder, what's he going to do - kill me twice?"

"Have you really thought this out? I mean who's going to carry out this deed in case of your demise? Have you already asked someone?"

"I have someone in mind, but he can't know about it unless it happens. This guy is a person who would kill his own mother for a buck."

"I can't believe that I'm still in this conversation, but I can't help asking more questions."

Lawrence put one of the arms of his glasses into his mouth. "Have you given any thought to making up fake papers to trick Dracken into believing that you actually had this done?"

"Yeah, I thought of that. The thing is, after being abused and humiliated by Dracken, I really want to see him dead if he kills me. I'm not a vindictive person, but Dracken deserves death if he goes through with his threats." Ben paused and reflected on the words he just spoke. "I can't believe that I could feel this way but I can't help it. I don't want another person to ever have to go through this. Just hope God will forgive me."

"Okay, let's say you have this 'adjustment' to the will. What happens if the person you picked doesn't want to go through with his end? Dracken still gets away with it."

"Lawrence, the person I've picked wouldn't think twice about killing anyone for fifty thousand bucks. I should have a backup person, but I'll take my chances."

Lawrence had a new question ready before Ben answered the prior one. "Now what happens if you're killed in an accident that Dracken had nothing to do with? You're now having an innocent man executed."

"First of all, no matter what, this is no innocent man. He's a ruthless killer...you can see it in his eyes. No compassion whatsoever, and if I do die in an accident, that's his problem. He started this whole thing, not me. God built into us a survival instinct and I'm just using mine."

"Well, I'm sure there are more problems with this idea than we're touching upon here. Man - if this ever got out to the public, the reporters would have a field day."

"Well, the only way that they would find out is if you or one of your secretaries told them."

"Whoa, back up, I'm only playing devil's advocate here. I'm not going to write this into your will, Ben. I want no part of this."

Ben looked disappointed but wasn't giving up.

"I understand. This kind of puts me back to square one. By the way, what do you think I could get charged with if someone found out I was trying to do this?"

"Well, I don't know. This is not something you hear about every day. I mean you're not hiring for murder until you're dead. I'm not sure, but the lawyer executing the will might have a problem. He has to instruct the beneficiary that in return for a murder he'll receive fifty thousand dollars." Lawrence started to laugh. "I wouldn't dare tell any of my colleagues about this. No one would ever believe me. Ben, seriously, you're going to be hard pressed to find a reputable attorney who's going to do this for you."

Ben perked up upon hearing the sound of the attorney's voice change when he said the word reputable.

"You know someone who will do this for me?" Ben asked, sitting back down in the chair.

Lawrence stared at him for a minute, then reached for a pad and pen. He looked at Ben over the top of his glasses.

"You really want to pursue this, Ben?"

He nodded. Lawrence jotted a name on the pad. "This man may be the one you want. You are not to tell him where you got his name nor that you have spoken to me about this. He may charge you a small fortune to do this but that's up to you. For the record, I am advising you against this."

Ben took the piece of paper. "You know this guy well?"

"Not real well, but I think he'll do what you want. By the way, you can keep the will we just drew up. Just have a rider added." He paused. "Actually, the simplest thing would really be to just have the attorney send out a letter written by you to your killer if you died." He paused again to think about the best way to go about the plan. "No, that won't work. They're going to have to meet in person. That's the only way your guy is going to believe and understand what he's being asked...well, being paid, to do."

"Okay, let's see what he suggests and I'll call you to see if it's okay," Ben said.

"No, don't call me. I don't want to discuss this over the phone. Hell, I don't want to discuss it at all. Also, don't bring any papers from that attorney here - no letterhead, no business cards. I will help you but I'll deny ever giving you any advice on this subject."

"I understand... Let me call this guy and set up an appointment right now. Can I use your phone?" Ben asked without thinking. Lawrence just looked at him, waiting for him to answer his own question. "Oh, sorry, I'll call from outside."

"Now there's a good idea," Lawrence said, causing Ben to laugh at his own stupidity.

"Okay, thanks for your help, Lawrence. I'll call you once it's done."

"Right...and Ben, please be careful with this...and promise me that you'll go to the police and see if they can help. Maybe they can visit Dracken or something. Just go and see."

"Okay, I'll go back to the detective."

Ben left the attorney's office still feeling good about his idea. After all, Lawrence didn't say that it wouldn't work, he just said to be careful. Holding the phone between his chin and shoulder, he dialed.

"Dan Perry please."

"May I tell him who's calling please?" asked the receptionist.

"My name is Ben Pearce. I need to see Mr. Perry as soon as is possible."

"Have you been to see him before?"

"No, I was referred to him by a friend. I need to have some work done on my will."

"Just a minute, I'll check the book to see when he's available."

"I need to see him today if possible. This is very urgent."

"Let me see if Mr. Perry can speak with you for a moment. Please hold."

Within a minute, a voice came on. "This is Dan Perry. How can I help you?"

"My name is Ben Pearce and I need to have a rider added to my will."

Perry paused. "My secretary said this sounded urgent. If it's just a will you need, I'll give you back to her and she'll set you up with an appointment."

"No wait, this is kind of a matter of life and death. I need this done right away."

"A will is a matter of life and death? Have you been diagnosed as terminal?"

"Yeah, something like that," Ben replied.

"Okay, I can't fit you in today, but how about... let's see, tomorrow at five o'clock?"

"That's perfect; I need directions though."

"I'll give you back to the girl and she'll help you with that; see you tomorrow."

Ben got the directions and drove off towards his office. He would have to wait another day to complete the next step in his plan. The final hurdle would be the toughest - showing Victor Dracken the finished copy of the will. He would have an enormous decision to make - whether to mail it to him, tell him about it over the phone or show it to him in person.

Howie had been watching the main entrance to the office for some time, waiting for Ben to come through the doors. He sat in anticipation, desperate for Ben's new plan. Finally the door swung open and Ben appeared.

"Well what's up? I'm dyin' here," Howie said.

"First, any problems with clients or stocks?"

"Well not with clients or stocks but there's one thing that may ruin your morning."

"What's that?"

"Harry died."

"Homeless Harry?"

Howie nodded. "They found him this morning in the parking lot of the building next door. Probably a heart attack or something."

"Ah, that's too bad. Poor guy - really liked him."

"Now tell me what's going on," Howie pleaded.

Ben looked around and decided that there were too many coworkers nearby, so he motioned for Howie to follow him outside. They walked to the parking garage, where Ben felt the safest talking but still had to fear being out in the open. They sat in the rental car.

"Okay, Howie, you're my best friend and I trust you. You gotta swear to never, never, ever tell anyone what I'm about to tell you."

"Geez, do I really want to hear this?"

Ben explained all the details of his plan and his meeting with Lawrence Templeton. Knowing Ben as well as he did, Howie couldn't believe what he was hearing. Ben Pearce wishing someone dead? Even with Dracken's threats, he couldn't fathom Ben conjuring up such a plan. Howie sat dumbfounded.

"How did you ever come up with this?" he asked laughing. "I mean it's beautiful in its simplicity, but where'd you get it...and are you really going to go through with it?"

"This is the only way that I can think of to protect myself. Nobody else had any ideas. Now be honest with me, do you think it'll scare him enough to back off?"

Howie thought for a second, pressing his lips tightly together. He began to nod slowly as a he smiled broadly.

"Yeah...yeah I think it will. Gotta tell you, when we spoke before and you said you had a plan, I knew it had to be something good by the way you sounded and damn - you didn't disappoint." Howie looked at Ben with a serious face. "This is going to make one hell-of-a book someday."

"Let's see if it has a happy ending first, buddy. I'm not out of the woods yet, but I am seeing light at the end."

They both sat in silence, staring out the windshield while each ran through the plan in his head.

"You really should still go back to the cops just to let them know what happened with Dracken," Howie said, breaking the silence.

"I may go to the station again, maybe tomorrow. What can they do though? They couldn't convict him before for murders they knew he committed. How they gonna stop him from having me killed?"

"Just keep the detective up to date on what's happening. You said the guy really seemed to care."

"Yeah, you're right. Look, let's get back in, I'm a little nervous being out here," Ben said, opening the car door.

"Ben...this is definitely one of the craziest things I have ever heard...but I love it. I think it really might have a chance of doing the job."

Back in the office, Ben immediately began going through the messages and papers left on his desk. After having Howie affirm his feelings about the will, he had a hard time concentrating on his work. He thought more about the upcoming meeting with the attorney. He was also waiting for Howie to ask the one question that hadn't been discussed outside. Howie finally leaned over the divider.

"I can't believe that I forgot to ask and I don't even want to whisper it, so here." He reached over a note which read: "Who's the $50000.00 guy?"

Ben crumpled the paper and put it in his pocket and laughed. "Took you long enough to ask, but don't worry, it's not you."

"Oh, I was so hoping. I could use the fifty grand. So who is it?"

"If you had to pick someone, who would it be? Someone who we both know who wouldn't think twice about doing it."

Howie thought about it for a couple of moments. "One of the guys from the junkyard?"

"Bingo, now that wasn't so hard, was it?"

His partner just shook his head. "Beautiful, just beautiful. Now I guess you want me to figure out which guy?"

Ben just looked at him and in an instant Howie uttered, "Luke," and sat down and laughed. "Crazy man, crazy."

* * * * * *

The following day was an eternity for Ben as he watched the clock, waiting for the closing bell. At ten minutes past four, he packed up his desk and got ready to leave.

"Howie, I'm on my way to my appointment. I told Claire that I'm seeing a client."

"Okay, good luck buddy."

Dan Perry's office was about a thirty-minute drive and wouldn't be hard to find. The Motor Vehicle office was the entire first floor of his building, and Ben had been there before. He spent the entire drive playing over all the possible scenarios of his plan – not that he and Howie hadn't gone over them enough. It had consumed them both since its inception and neither could find a flaw. He was confident that the attorney wouldn't be able to throw a wrench into the mix.

The final thought on Ben's mind as he pulled into the parking lot was money. What was the going rate for a service such as this? It wouldn't come cheap, but if he was alive in the future to complain about the amount, it was money well spent.

Ben got out of the car and looked up at the turn of the century brick building. A large gray and white Department of Motor Vehicles sign was mounted over the first floor windows. People rushed past him carrying license plates and paperwork, trying to beat the five o'clock closing time.

Ben shortened his gait as he walked toward the main entrance, trying to kill the extra few minutes that he had before his appointment. He knew that this was his last hope, and he worried that it would take some convincing to have the attorney do what he asked.

He followed a line of people into the building, most of whom turned and headed to the left for the Motor Vehicle Department. Ben continued down the hallway to the building directory. After a quick search, he found it located in the center of a large open area, half way through the building. He ran his finger up and down the board until he found the listing for Dan Perry, Attorney at Law.

His heart quickened at the thought of telling someone he had never met before about his strategy to stop Dracken. If this man denied Ben's wishes, it would be one more person who could reveal his plan to others. For all Ben knew, this man could be a friend of Dracken's. He would have to take the chance.

Ben stood in the hallway in front of Dan Perry's office; taking one more deep breath, he opened the door. He stepped inside and stopped dead. This office was quite different from Lawrence Templeton's. The furniture was old but clean. The walls were in need of a paint job and the carpet was slightly worn. The smell of fresh nail polish filled the room. He approached the secretary who was obviously responsible for the odor and announced himself.

"I'm Ben Pearce here to see Dan Perry."

"Yes Mr. Pearce, he's expecting you. Have a seat, he'll be right with you," she said waving her hand to dry her nails.

Ben sat down and grabbed a magazine. Realizing that it was from two years earlier, he placed it back down. He checked his watch and then the clock on the wall, noticing that it was ten minutes slow. He could do nothing else but laugh, figuring that if he wanted a lawyer who would take on his problem, this was the kind of office he would have. He was afraid to see what the inside office looked like. Maybe the chair had gum on it.

Dan Perry emerged from his office. "Mr. Pearce, how are you?" he said loudly.

Ben stood up and walked toward him with his hand extended. "I'm fine. Thank you for seeing me on short notice."

"No problem, come on in."

As Ben walked through the door, he took in the office surroundings. It was just as has he had pictured, a dumpy office with files piled high and papers scattered around. Perry was the exact opposite of Lawrence Templeton and looked like he would make the perfect department store Santa – just not the kind you would trust. He noticed that Ben looked uneasy.

"Don't mind the mess. I know where everything is and I've yet to lose a file," Perry said, motioning for Ben to sit.

"Everyone's got his own way of taking care of business." Ben searched his brain for the right thing to say in order to butter Perry up for his request. "You come highly recommended."

"Oh yeah? And who recommended me?" Perry asked, pulling a legal pad from a drawer.

"He...he wanted to remain anonymous."

"Oh I see. My guess is that this will is not going to be your average run of the mill last will and testament," he said with a smug look.

Ben shook his head. "No, not quite. In fact, the last attorney refused to write it...and it's not the whole will, just a rider."

"Really, this sounds juicy. Okay spill it...lay it on me."

Ben explained the situation and gave Perry a brief overview of his idea. Perry listened intently and began chewing on the end of a pencil as Ben finished.

"This is..." He got up and sat on the corner of the desk and laughed. "This is the wildest and craziest idea that I've ever heard. What other way to stop an unstoppable man from killing you than by putting the fear of death into his mind?" He sat back in his chair and took a candy bar out of his desk drawer. He bit a piece off. "But will Dracken cave in to this threat?" he mumbled through the mouthful of candy.

"You don't think it'll work?" Ben asked. Perry didn't answer. He just kept chewing and staring into space. After a minute of deep thought Perry perked up.

"No...I didn't say that. On the contrary, I think it will knock him for a loop. I'll bet no one ever turned the tables on him like this before." Perry again stared in thought. "Yeah...yeah, I love this idea, I'll do it. But it's gotta be done right. First, do you have a will now that you're happy with?"

"Yes, I just updated it."

"Good, then we just have to add a rider. Get the other will from your attorney and let your family know that I'm the person to come to in case of your death."

"Well, that's not what I had in mind. I want the will to stay where it is. I just want you to handle this end of it. For my own security, you can't know who the other attorney is."

"Okay you can explain that to me as we go along. You obviously have this figured out down to the last detail. One thing though: this has to be done quickly. I'm leaving on vacation in a week and I'll be gone for three weeks. I'll be unreachable, so let's roll up our sleeves and get it moving right now. I'm guessing you have time now?" Perry asked.

"Yeah, let's do it," Ben said, overjoyed that his idea was about to become a reality.

"First thing," Perry said as he began to pace the floor. "I assume you have a person in mind to take on the dubious deed of killing Dracken or do I have to supply him?" he asked, leaning against his desk directly in front of Ben.

"No, I have a person in mind," Ben replied. Then after thinking about what Perry had just asked him, he had to pose the question. "You could supply someone to do that if I didn't have anyone?" Ben immediately put his hands up in front of his face and turned his head. "Wait, I don't even want to know."

Perry began to pace again. "How do you know this person will carry out your plan and how does he get paid?"

"I'm ninety nine percent sure that the person I've picked will do it. Do you think I should use more than one person?"

"Well the way I figure, the fewer people involved, the better off everyone is. Stick with the ninety nine percent guy." Perry paused. "Now, my main concern is, how do I convey the message that if he kills Dracken, I give him a large sum of your money? If the police were to find out, they might arrest me for hiring an assassin, even though I'm only carrying out part of your last will and testament."

As Perry continued to pace, Ben could see that his new attorney was putting great thought into the scheme. He already felt confident that this plan was actually going to become a reality. Ben had already worked out how he wanted the money to be handled, but he let Perry continue with his ideas, comparing them with his own.

Perry stopped short, waving his index finger in the air. "How about something like this? You give me a sealed envelope to be given to your Mr. X upon your demise. Inside, the letter states the task that you would like him to perform and of course the money amount." He paused as he returned to his desk. "This is all very rough right now, you understand. I'll iron out all the details later; stop me if you have questions. What you want to do is set up an offshore bank account. Don't wire the money or send a check. It'll leave a paper trail. You've gotta get cash into this account and I have someone that can help you with that."

Ben smiled, nodding his head. The strategy that Perry was coming up with was very similar to his own, although his last idea of an associate of his handling the money in an account didn't sit well.

"Wait, I thought you said the fewer people who knew about this the better. Who's this person that's going to help with the money?" Ben asked, sounding suspicious.

"Don't worry, this person won't know anything about your will. Just that a certain amount of money needs to be in a certain account in a certain country. Now, the account will be set up in both your name and Mr. X. Being offshore also keeps Mr. X from accidentally finding the account and emptying it whenever he wants."

Ben began to realize that he was putting a great deal of faith in an attorney whom he barely knew. If Dracken did kill him, what was keeping Perry from contacting Luke, his assassin, and splitting the cash without the plan being executed? For that matter, what was keeping him from contacting Luke in a week or two while Ben was still alive and giving him the bank account info. There would be no way to prove that Perry gave out the info and to whom would he report it – the police?

Perry noticed Ben's uneasiness. "You look troubled; if you have questions please ask."

"Well, I don't want to seem like I don't trust you, but what's keeping you from letting my guy know about this account and splitting it?"

"I do see where you need some guarantee of your money's safety. I'll have to figure out how to put this together so that we're both safe."

"Both of us safe?" Ben asked.

"Yes, you have to realize that if this whole thing does take place and I have to basically issue a death warrant for Dracken, I want to be covered. Your letter of instructions has to be explicit."

"Right, I see."

"The only reason you actually need to put this in a will at all is to protect the messenger of its contents. Otherwise you could just have a friend take care of the whole deal. If it were found out that he knew the contents of a letter that he sent which caused a death, and that he then gave out a bank account number, he could do jail time...at least I think he could. This is complicated," Perry said, scratching his head.

"I understand that. I would never ask a friend to get involved with this," Ben said, standing to stretch his legs. He walked over to a water cooler in the corner of the office, filling a paper cup and then returning to the chair. They both sat in silence for a moment.

"Look, Dan, I think I have a solution that will cover us. I'll give you an envelope with instructions... the name of the assassin and where he can be contacted. I'll have a second attorney hold another letter with the bank account information. If I'm killed, you meet the assassin and explain what he's being requested to do. When he kills Dracken – it'll be all over the news. When the other attorney sees this, he sends you the letter with the banking info.

"That's sounds okay so far," Perry said.

"That still leaves the problem for you though, Dan. By your meeting him and giving the instructions, does that make you an accessory, or are you just carrying out the last will and testament of a client?"

"This would be a complicated matter in court, but I'm willing to take the chance of meeting this man. If I'm ever confronted, I'll deny knowing about the contents of the letter that I handed to Mr. X. I can also say that he is a client, enabling me to invoke the client attorney privilege of confidentiality. This should make you feel safer because you know that I won't tell anyone about this. If I did it could come back to haunt me."

"Right...okay..."

"Now let's talk more about this offshore account," Perry went on. "Where's my proof that the account actually exists? Try this out for a life-ending scenario: I meet Mr. X, give him instructions; he kills Dracken and comes back to collect, only to find out there's no account." Perry threw his hands in the air.

"How many minutes do you think I have to live after that? I need proof this account is actually open, funded and in the correct names. Obviously you don't want my guy to open the account if you don't want me to have the account number." He leaned forward, clasping his hands on his desk, waiting for Ben to come up with a better solution.

"Well..." he had no quick answer. "We've worked out most of the other details, we'll get past this problem." Again, they both sat staring at the ceiling in thought.

Perry tapped a pencil on the desk, making it hard for Ben to concentrate. He stopped when he saw Ben staring at it.

"I can bring in a statement with the account number and country removed so you can't see it. It'll have the names and amount. Would that be enough?" Ben asked.

"Yeah...yeah, I think that'll work - mainly because I trust you. You don't seem like the kind of person who would go against his word. Ha! Here I am trusting a guy who's leaving fifty grand to kill someone else."

"Yeah but you know why..."

"I know, I know, I'm just kidding. The real reason I feel safe doing it this way is that you would never jeopardize your family's safety. If you pulled a stunt like faking the account, you never know what a pissed off killer might do."

"Good point, very good point."

Perry hopped up and shook Ben's hand. "We have the makings of the perfect life insurance plan. We can only hope Dracken will be intimidated by it. Now let's set up a time to meet again tomorrow. I'm going to give this some deep thought tonight to make sure that we didn't leave anything out. If you have any questions or ideas before we meet again, don't call me. I don't want to discuss any of this on the phone - ever."

"Okay, that's a good idea. Can we meet again at five tomorrow?"

"Let me check the calendar." Perry left the room to the receptionist's desk and flipped through the day planner. From the other room Perry yelled, "Five is good for me."

He reentered the office. "Now, before you go, there's one more little thing - my fee. I expect to be paid tomorrow when you hand me the letter."

"Okay, how much?" He asked, knowing the number was going to be astronomical.

"Five grand."

"Five grand, huh?"

"That's the going rate for hiring a hitman if you die. Oh and Ben, make that five thousand cash. I can use some of it in Europe. I can't wait, I'm outta here Saturday morning for three long weeks."

"Good for you, hope you enjoy it. I'll have the cash and the instruction letter for you tomorrow...wait, what happens if I die while you're away?"

"Well, do you care how fast your guy kills Dracken? I mean does he have to kill him the day after you die? If not, then I'll contact him when I get back. I mean there is no other way without involving other people."

"I guess it can wait 'til you're back."

"Good, now one more thing; the money needs to be in that offshore account before this whole thing can take effect. How long will it take you to set that up?"

"I've got plenty of big clients that use the offshores and I'm familiar with the process of setting them up. It usually takes longer than a day, but I know some people who can help me out. I don't have to worry about wiring the money. It can be done so it's practically untraceable."

"Okay Ben, just bring me a copy of the wire receipt with the account numbers blacked out. That'll be enough proof for me that it's done. Remember Ben, if you were to do something foolish like faking the account, it could be detrimental to your family's well being," Perry said slowly and seriously.

"I understand. I'll see you tomorrow with the cash."

As Ben walked to the door, he thought of one more scenario that he forgot to mention.

"Oh...Dan, listen, what insurance do I have that you will contact Mr. X if I die? I mean what's stopping you from taking the five grand and never chancing the meeting with Mr. X at all if I'm killed?"

"You'll just have to trust me, that's all."

Ben stood and after a few seconds, shook his head. "Please don't be insulted, but I need more than that."

Ben walked back to the desk. "Tell you what I'm going to do. I'm going to leave another envelope for the attorney to send. It'll have another five thousand – in a check made out to you. It'll be marked for legal services rendered. You get that if everything goes all the way through."

"Hey, fine by me," Perry said, slapping his hands on his desk.

Ben spent hours the following day setting up the offshore account. He had Howie check every step as it was completed. There were few problems, and by mid-afternoon the funds were under a company name in the Cayman Islands. Because the account wasn't set up under their individual names, Ben had no concern that Dan Perry or Luke would trace the wired funds. They would need the actual company title, which could only be found in the letter that would follow Dracken's death.

Ben opened his briefcase and took out the letter to Luke that Dan Perry would hold. It was simple and to the point. The attorney could answer any questions that Luke would have. Howie leaned over the partition.

"That the letter?"

Ben looked around and held it high enough for Howie to read.

Luke,

You may remember me from high school. I have a job for you. The reasons aren't important, but I'm asking you to kill Victor Dracken. For your services, you will be paid the sum of fifty thousand dollars. The attorney who is seated before you will give you the details.

Ben Pearce

"It sounds good. Did you do that on a typewriter?" Howie asked.

"Yeah, had to blow the dust off it, but I wasn't putting this on my computer. Too easy to bring back up even if I deleted it."

Ben put the letter into an envelope and sealed it with tape. Brenda, their secretary, was passing Ben's desk and reached out for the envelope. "That need to go into the mail?" Ben jerked it away surprising her. "I'm sorry, I just thought I could drop it in the box for you, Ben."

"I'm sorry Brenda, I'm a little on edge today."

"Okay...by the way, what are you two up to?" she asked, not really looking for an answer. She walked away giving Ben a curious look.

Ben set the envelope into his briefcase and began sealing and addressing the next letter, which had the account number, bank name and address. He would attempt to convince Lawrence Templeton to mail that letter to Dan Perry if Dracken was killed. Ben and Howie walked downstairs to the coffee shop, going over the final details.

"You have both letters done, right?" Howie asked.

"Yup, I'm all ready. I'm going to stop off at Lawrence Templeton's office and persuade him to mail the bank info to Perry if Dracken is gone. Told him I'd be there around four fifteen. Hope he'll do it."

"I don't see why not."

"The main letter I'm bringing to Perry's right after. Once I leave there, it's in effect." Ben smiled and shook his head. "It's amazing what a human being will do to survive. I feel pretty good."

"Ben, don't get cocky yet. You're forgetting the most important thing. You still have to tell Dracken or you may still be in his cross hairs."

"Like I forgot that?"

They sat at a table. Ben sipped coffee while Howie opened a bottle of water.

"Okay what else? The account is set up and I got the five grand cash. I got a copy of the offshore account minus the account number and country. That should be it."

"What's the game plan for Dracken?"

"If everything gets done tonight without a hitch, I'll go see him first thing in the morning."

"Have you given any more thought to maybe mailing a letter or just calling him?" Howie asked as he stood, screwing the top on the bottle. He waited for an answer as they walked down the hallway. "Well?"

"Yeah, I thought about that."

Ben looked up and down the hall. He faced Howie and put a hand on each shoulder, pulling him inches away from his face.

"I need to be this close to him. I need to see his eyes when I tell him. I need to see if he flinches just a little."

"Hey c'mon man, there's people. Don't want 'em to think we're in love here. I get your point."

"Oh so now you don't love me?"

They were both able to have a good laugh for the first time in days. Howie gave Ben a shove and they continued down the hall.

"We're almost through this. Soon you'll be able to go back to your thoughts of riding off into the sunset on that white horse."

"Howie...those thoughts never left me."

Ben walked into Lawrence Templeton's office. The attorney stood next to a file cabinet, reading from a folder. He peered over his glasses at Ben but didn't look happy to see him.

"C'mon in," he said, motioning Ben inside. "What are you going to ask me to do? I'm afraid to hear it."

Ben closed the door. "Very simple." He handed the letter across the desk.

"Wait, I'm not taking anything until I know what it is," Lawrence said.

"All that's in here is a letter with an account number and the address of a bank."

"That's it?"

"Yup. What I need you to do is send it out if you hear that Dracken is dead. It's already addressed."

Lawrence reluctantly took the envelope. "If I hear that Dracken is dead? Don't you need to be dead first?"

"Oh yeah – only if I'm dead first."

Lawrence looked at the address. "Guess I was right. Dan Perry was your man."

Ben nodded. "Didn't take much convincing."

"You're sure there's nothing else but an account number and a bank?"

"That's it."

He opened Ben's file and dropped the envelope in. "Okay, it's done."

Ben arrived at Dan Perry's office a few minutes after five o'clock. Dan was sitting in the receptionist's chair with his back towards the entrance. He spun around as Ben pushed open the door.

"Ah, you didn't change your mind, huh?" Perry asked.

"Got no other way out." He handed him an envelope filled with money. "Five thousand cash, count it."

Perry took the envelope and tossed it in a drawer. "I'm sure it's all there; now where's the letter?"

"Got it right here, signed, sealed and let's hope it never has to get delivered."

"Okay, I've got the rider right here. It states that upon your death a sealed envelope from the deceased shall be delivered to Luke Stafford. It also states that I have no knowledge of the contents of the letter and that I'm just the messenger." Perry looked over the document for a second. "Well, that's it; here, take a look and sign it."

Ben read over the document. "Looks good," he said, dropping his head.

Perry lowered his head almost even with his desktop, trying to look into Ben's eyes.

"You having second thoughts about this?"

"Am I having second thoughts? No, I just can't believe that I'm doing this, but what other choice do I have? My back's against a wall. I only hope that Dracken will back off. I just want him to back off."

"I wish you the best of luck Ben. You shouldn't feel guilty about doing this you know. I don't see any other way out either."

Ben nodded. "Thanks for everything."

Ben's spirits were high as he left the office. Unfortunately the high would only last until thoughts of visiting Dracken again haunted him. Fearing Dracken so deeply, he toyed with the notion of not telling him at all. The will would still be in effect, but Ben wouldn't be protected by it.

As he drove home, he realized that fearing Dracken at his office was silly. It was probably the safest place that Ben could be. Willie might toss him around a bit, but Dracken would never have him killed there. Now he only had to stay safe until the next day. He pulled over and dialed Howie.

"Mission accomplished. I'll talk to you after I see Dracken in the morning."

Chapter Six

The next morning came too soon. Ben went through the usual routine while trying to avoid Claire and just get out of the house. His mood did pique her curiosity; she cornered him coming out from their bathroom.

"Ben...everything all right? You're awful quiet this morning."

"Everything's okay."

"Problem with a client?"

She gave him an out.

"Yeah, but I'll have it all fixed by later today."

He faked being cheerful the best he could. Lucky for him that she was still tired and went back to bed. There was no way he could fake eating breakfast, and he couldn't chance forcing food down that might come back up on Dracken's expensive white carpet. Even coffee didn't appeal to him right now.

Ben's main concern while leaving the house was would Dracken be in his office today? The odds were good, but the last thing Ben needed was to stew over the weekend if Dracken didn't show.

He needed a place to sit for a while. It was early and Dracken's secretaries most likely wouldn't be in just yet. His plan was to call and ask if Dracken was in, then continue on to his office when confirmed.

A local donut shop was the answer. It had a payphone and big parking lot where he could wait while he read the paper. Coffee now became a top priority as his body began to crave its morning caffeine. He bought only a small cup and as he came back outside, sat the cup down on the payphone shelf. He figured he'd try a practice run on calling Dracken's office. He took out a small piece of paper and dialed the number on it. He sipped from the coffee cup, not expecting an answer, but after three rings, someone did pick up.

"Dracken Holdings," the voice said.

Ben's eyes opened wide – it was Dracken himself. He slammed the phone down and in his panic dropped his coffee, splattering his shoes. He looked around but no one had seen.

Why is he answering the phone? It's like he knew I was calling. There's no way he could know it was me.

Once back in the car and sipping his second cup of coffee, he realized that the brokers in his office answered the phones if the girls weren't in. Dracken didn't know it was him, he just answered the ringing phone. He placed the cup in the holder and drove off.

Many of the building's workers were arriving as Ben pulled into Dracken's parking lot. He had rehearsed his plan of attack for most of the ride. He parked the car and immediately jumped out and headed for the door. There was no thinking about what to do; he just wanted to get in and get it over with. He quickened his pace as he neared the entrance and almost jogged down the hallway toward the elevators. He found it hard to stand still and paced in a small area in the back of the crowd of people that awaited the elevator. Not realizing that his actions were causing uneasiness among the surrounding people, he was given a wide berth. Just as the doors opened, a woman approached him.

"You're not going to do this again, are you?" she asked in disbelief.

At first he was startled, not expecting anyone to speak to him until he made it to the office. He then realized the woman was a secretary in Dracken's office who apparently had witnessed the last incident.

"Please don't go back in there again."

Ben wasn't really listening as he looked past her at the elevator doors that were just closing. He took one step towards the door but stopped short when he realized he couldn't make it.

"I'm sorry but I have to see him again," he said

"All I can say is you're making a huge mistake."

Ben could see in her expression that she couldn't say any more than that. She hung her head, turned and walked right up to the elevator doors. He walked up behind her.

"I know you think I'm nuts but..." without turning around, she waved her hand in the air.

"I shouldn't be talking to you."

The doors opened and they entered along with several others. She stayed on the opposite side of the car and didn't make eye contact during the ride up.

The elevator came to an abrupt halt at each floor. Ben grew more apprehensive with each approaching level. He kept telling himself that the worst that could happen was a couple of bruises from a bodyguard. Dracken, as in the past meeting, would not lay a hand on him in his own office. Finally reaching the top floor, the doors opened.

"Wish me luck," he said to the secretary.

She didn't answer as she hurriedly left the elevator and entered the office. Ben followed closely behind as she ran up to the desk where one of the receptionists was now sitting

"Look who's here," she said to the other girl as she turned and faced Ben, not realizing that he was so close behind. With an embarrassed look, she placed one hand on her chest and the other over her mouth. She ran into the back.

"Hello again," he said to the receptionist.

She stared at him in disbelief. "I... I can't believe you're back. Please tell me you're just dropping something off."

"No, I'd like to see Mr. Dracken."

"If you insist. I'll let him know you're here. Please have a seat." She picked up the phone.

Ben walked toward the couch but before he reached it, she called to him.

"You can go right in."

"Just like that?"

"Yes, go right in," she repeated and pointed toward the doors leading to Dracken's office.

He hesitated for a moment, bewildered at the ease in which he was invited. As he swung open the door he could see Willie's huge frame waiting at the end of the hall.

Oh shit.

He took a deep breath and walked towards him.

"Hi Willie...how come he's seeing me so easily?"

Without saying a word, Willie checked him for weapons or electronics. He pushed open the door. "Go ahead in."

Dracken sat in his chair facing out the window. "Mr. Pearce, I must tell you that every day...I heal a bit more." He spoke in a very calm voice. "Your coming here again opens a very large wound." Dracken spun his chair around, stood up and approached him. "What could you possibly want?" Dracken's eyes were slightly bloodshot and glassy. He looked nothing like the sharp businessman that Ben had encountered in their last meeting. The look on his face was now almost soft and not that of a villain. He appeared more like a grieving father who had lost a daughter. For an instant, Ben thought that maybe Dracken had reconsidered his threats, and now Ben himself was reconsidering going through with his mission.

"Well Mr. Pearce I'm waiting. What is it that you want?" Dracken asked, raising his voice. Just for an instant, Ben caught a glimmer of the maniac that had attacked him at the hospital, and decided to continue on.

"You threatened," his voice cracked as he began to speak. He cleared his throat and started again. "You threatened to kill me, so I had to take action to protect myself."

"Mr. Pearce, you will notice that I am much more sedate than at our last encounter. My life has been so shattered by you that my doctor has me on medication to relieve my stress."

Dracken walked calmly about the room. Ben turned in place, facing him continuously.

"He informed me that I was so consumed with the death of my daughter that I was prone to a heart attack. I didn't tell him that most of my time was now spent thinking about what I wanted to do to you." He returned to his chair. "So now when I think of what I want to do to you, I do it calmly," he said smiling.

Ben swallowed hard. He could feel his heart pounding faster, which didn't seem possible without an artery rupturing.

"Now, you have taken action to protect yourself," he laughed loudly. "You went to the police?"

"Yes, I did go the police. They told me there wasn't much they could do except issue an order of protection."

Ben was about to expose his strategy. The moment that he had gone over in his mind a million times was at hand. Would Dracken fold or just laugh it off?

"Mr. Dracken, I added a rider to my will that states, if I die, the sum of fifty thousand dollars will be paid to a certain person for killing you."

Dracken sat in silence as he let Ben's idea sink in.

"Very interesting Mr. Pearce, but what happens if you're killed falling in the bathtub or in some other way that I had nothing to do with?"

"Unfortunately, it only states if I die."

Suddenly Ben felt an uplifting. He thought that maybe he detected a slight waver in Dracken's voice and maybe, just maybe, Dracken might actually be frightened by the will. Gaining a bit of confidence, he continued.

"There is no discrimination. If I die in any manner, my attorney will notify the appropriate persons and then you become the hunted."

"Very nice try Mr. Pearce. How hard do you think it will be for me to find out who this person is? The minute you leave here, I'll make a phone call and find out who your attorney is. Trust me, once I speak to him, your will becomes history."

Ben knew that there was no way that Dracken could trace the attorneys. He was too careful. There were no phone records except from his office phone to Lawrence Templeton and none to Dan Perry. Even if Dracken could get Ben's company phone records, it would take years to trace the calls made from his line.

"And what makes you think that your assassin could ever get near me? I have enemies everywhere and none of them has ever even tried."

"First of all, I doubt very much that you could find the attorney I used. He's not anywhere near here and it's not something that he is going to talk to anyone about. Second, your enemies are afraid to try and harm you; my guy won't be."

"Mr. Pearce, you're beginning to bore me. I can't believe I let this conversation get this far - damn medication. Now if you'll excuse me, I have a meeting to attend." He motioned to the bodyguard. "See Mr. Pearce out, Willie."

"If this is the way you want it, Mr. Dracken. Let me guarantee that this is no joke. My will is set up in the way I described. Do you really want to take the chance?" Ben said, almost sounding defiant.

Ben took a step forward and could now see the picture of Dracken's daughter, automatically bringing the images of Michael and Sarah into his mind. The thought of never seeing his children grow up gave him the courage to go on.

"Just think about being hunted after you kill me. And like you said to me - you'll never know where or when."

Dracken looked annoyed. "Get him out of here... oh, and Mr. Pearce, please don't waste my time again."

"That took balls," Willie said quietly, escorting Ben down the hallway. "You're the first to stand up to him in any way."

Ben had to react quickly to the small window of sympathy that Willie had opened. "Do you think I scared him enough to leave me alone?"

"It would make me think twice, but Mr. Dracken isn't easily scared."

They came to the doors at the end of the hallway where Ben stopped, wanting to continue questioning.

"I can't say more than that." Willie turned and walked away.

The two receptionists looked at Ben with pity as he walked past them. Not wanting to taunt Dracken by holding his head high with confidence, he stared at the floor in case he was on the surveillance cameras.

Ben was still shaking slightly as he stepped into the empty elevator. As it descended, he closed his eyes and burned the image of Dracken's face into his mind. Was it the face of a man unnerved or was the medication throwing off his read? There wasn't a clear answer. But there was a man who showed a glimpse of compassion, a man who might hold some answers if Ben could find him separated from Dracken.

Willie.

Ben walked into the office and immediately caught the suspense-filled eyes of Howie, who stood talking on the phone. He abruptly ended his conversation and waited for Ben to get closer.

"Well, how'd it go?"

Ben immediately looked around to see who was in earshot of their conversation. "Keep it down," he snapped.

"Relax, no one knows what we're talking about."

"Sorry, you're right. I'm just a little stressed." He removed his jacket and hung it over the back of his seat. "To tell you the truth, I don't really know how it went." He spun his chair around to sit.

Howie leaned over the partition to hear Ben's low talking.

"He's on tranquilizers or something. Its hard to tell but if I had to bet..." he smiled. "I'd say that it shook him."

"Excellent," Howie yelled.

"Quiet."

"Oh, sorry. Tell me the whole story, man."

Ben described the entire encounter, trying to remember every detail. Howie stood intently, hanging on every word, trying to create the scene in his mind.

"Well... it's kind of hard to tell. He probably took you seriously but the main problem is will he care? This is a man who probably thinks he's invincible." He stopped speaking as another broker walked past them.

"Maybe we should continue this outside," Ben said, sliding his keys into his top drawer. "Let's head downstairs and grab coffee."

"You know what, we're gonna have to finish this later. I have to run to the dentist and do a few little bullshit errands, so I'm not coming back. I'll give you a buzz later," Howie said. "I wish I could stay but I gotta get this tooth fixed; it's killing me."

"Okay," Ben said, sounding disappointed. "Howie listen, we can't talk about this over the phone at all. I have to worry that Dracken is going to have my phone tapped to get my attorney's name."

"Didn't think about that. We'll have to talk about it tomorrow. Sorry to have to run out on you – we're still on for tomorrow, right? Driving range?"

"Yeah, even though I'm not sure how safe I feel...if I start staying home all the time, Claire will get suspicious."

"Right. Okay, I'll see you tomorrow. Listen, Ben, you did it. It took balls but you did it. I really believe it's over. Think about it – Dracken's gotta be worried even if he won't admit it."

"I hope so."

"Go about your normal life. Just be cautious and aware that's all. See you tomorrow, buddy."

Howie patted Ben on the shoulder and left.

Ben picked up the picture of Claire and the children and just stared.

Sunlight flooded the bedroom, waking Ben from a sound sleep. He rolled on his side trying to focus on the clock but was blinded by the rays cutting across his face. Rolling back he realized that Claire was already up and had closed the door, keeping the children out until he awoke. She must have known that he had had a restless night, not falling asleep until the wee hours. The little bit of sleep he did get was filled with dreams of Dracken stalking and chasing him. After playing the encounter with Dracken over in his head thousands of times, he really had no better idea whether he was still to be hunted.

Ben always looked forward to the weekend mornings, the smell of coffee and pancakes, children climbing over him in bed while the cartoons ran for hours. Jumping up and opening the door he could hear the three at the kitchen table.

"Michael...Sarah, I'm waiting," he yelled to them. There was one second of silence then chaos.

"Slow, slow," Claire yelled as the two children fought to reach the bedroom first, screaming with joy as they ran down the hall. As they piled into the bed wrestling and tickling, Ben picked Sarah into the air above him. She giggled with glee as Michael dove onto Ben's chest. Claire appeared in the doorway and leaned with her arms crossed, smiling at the antics of the Saturday morning ritual. "You want to eat breakfast now and then come back in here?" she asked.

"No, I'm really not hungry yet and Bugs Bunny is about to come on."

Michael and Sarah cheered and got comfortable, snuggling against Ben as they waited for the show to start. Claire remained at the door. Her smile was replaced with a serious look. Ben could feel it, but not wanting to look at her, he continued to fuss over the children.

"Ben, we need to talk later - look at me."

"What, everything's fine," he said, trying his best to look and sound convincing.

"Ben, I want to know what's going on. One day you're happy and the next you're in another world. Last night you tossed and turned all night. I've waited all I can for you to open up and tell me what's happening with you...so, what is going on? Is it the girl? Remember, I'll know if you're lying."

"Yeah and that bothers me. How come when you're lying, I never know? It's not fair."

"When do I lie to you?"

"Not lie, but hide things like surprise parties, you know, like that."

She laughed. "That's my secret."

"I swear, if you had an affair, I wouldn't know about it 'til you were married to the other guy."

She still smiled. "Nice try in changing the subject and it almost worked. You let me know when you're ready to talk. Honey, I only want to help." She turned and went back to the kitchen.

Damn, she always knows.

If he could find out if Dracken was scared off, Claire would never have to know. If the threat persisted, she would have to be told. Ben's next plan would have to be finding Willie alone – but how? Maybe Howie would have an idea.

The children had both fallen asleep curled up beside him. He rolled to his side and wiggled his body down to be closer to them, staring into their sleeping faces. Michael breathed deeply through his wide-open mouth and Sarah lay sucking her thumb. Ben grew envious.

How lucky to be a child sleeping. So carefree, so safe.

His peaceful moment was disrupted as he envisioned them growing up in South Dakota without a father. He recalled his own father placing him on a pony for his first ride. The thought of missing theirs was heart wrenching. He flipped on to his stomach, trying to avoid tears, but the pressure was finally too much. With his back now to the children, Ben's body convulsed into a fetal position. He sobbed uncontrollably, pulling the down pillow tightly over his face as he squirmed, entangling himself in the covers. He knew that if Claire came in, it was all over, but he needed this and didn't fight it. After five minutes of non-stop tear flow, he began to calm. Surprisingly, he hadn't woken the children. He freed himself from the sheets and slipped into the bathroom, splashing water into his face. He looked into the mirror.

God, I look like death.

Now more concerned about Claire seeing him in his condition, he blew his nose and squirted drops in his eyes to lose the redness. If she were to catch him like this, she would undoubtedly panic. A confession in his current state would be a thousand times worse than if he were able to sit her down on the couch and explain calmly.

He climbed back into the bed, this time not looking at the children for fear of a recurrence. With his body now drained of energy, Ben slipped back to sleep.

* * * * * *

"Higher daddy, higher," Michael yelled as Ben pushed him on the backyard swing. Ben kept one eye on his watch and the other on Sarah, who sat in the sandbox filling a plastic bucket. Waiting for Howie, who was usually punctual, was an eternity. At two minutes after one, Ben heard a car door slam. Hearing voices from inside the house, he scooped up the children and carried them in.

"Ben, Howie's here," Claire yelled.

"Yeah, I hear. I'm coming," Ben replied, carrying the children up the stairs.

"Uncle Howie's here," he said to the children.

They wiggled wildly until he placed them down. Howie was already flipping through the sports channels as the children attacked him on the couch. Ben walked into the kitchen. Claire sat with her back towards him, flipping the pages of a newspaper.

"What's up, Howie?" he said, leaning over the sink to wash his hands.

"Not much," he replied in a rather meek voice.

With the water still running, Ben turned, spying the uneasiness on Howie's face. He realized that Claire's mood had placed Howie in an awkward position, not knowing if she had been briefed on the Dracken situation.

Ben leaned over Claire from behind and moved her hair away from her face. He attempted to kiss her cheek but she pulled away.

"You get nothing 'til you tell me what you're feeling," she said - not in a nasty way but more playfully concerned.

He whispered in her ear. "I told you everything's fine."

Coming back in the living room, Ben, out of habit, grabbed his keys off the TV.

"Hey, we're takin' my car," Howie said proudly. "This one will get us there and back without breaking down."

"Wow, this is a first. I can't remember a time that we took your car. I'm going to sit back and enjoy being chauffeured for once," Ben said laughing. "How's it running so far?"

"It's a dream come true. I'm not used to a car starting every time."

Ben kissed the children goodbye. Claire continued to read the paper.

"Bye Hon," he said.

"Bye Hon," Howie mimicked.

She smiled. "See you later. Have fun."

Ben walked around the bright red Cadillac Eldorado, admiring the shiny rims and jet-black tires. Howie hit the button on his keychain to unlock the doors. As Ben sat inside, the new leather smell hit him instantly.

"Ah, love that new car smell."

"I don't know anyone who doesn't," Howie replied, starting the engine.

"I still can't believe that it took you so long to buy a new car."

"It feels great, should've done it a long time ago." He gunned the engine and rocketed the high performance car down the road. "Now what just happened inside? Did you tell her? Is that why she's upset? I didn't know what to say."

"She's asking a lot of questions. I don't want to tell her anything unless I have to. I'm hoping you have some ideas on how I can find Willie alone," Ben said.

"Willie?"

"Yeah, I forgot to mention that yesterday. He told me that I had guts to talk to Dracken the way I did. I think I can find out if Dracken is scared by the will. But I gotta get him alone."

"Okay, first tell me the whole thing again and don't leave anything out. Man, I gave what you did a lot of thought last night and I give you a lot of credit. I could never have gone back to Dracken's office."

"If you had children you could. I didn't have any choice. I still can't tell you what I expect. There's a ton of ifs."

"Like what?"

"If Dracken were to contact me and say that he's decided to forgive me, do I believe him? What do I do then, do I change the will and hope he's telling the truth? I gave it a lot of thought last night, and even if he is scared off by the will, I don't think he would give me the satisfaction that I won. At the same time, he would have to consider that I could die in the shower and set the will in motion."

"What would he have to say to you for you to believe he's changed his mind?"

Howie attempted to light a small plastic tipped cigar.

"I just don't know. If I'm not convinced that he's really sincere about giving in and I keep the will in force, what happens if I die? I just killed a man who no longer planned to harm me."

Howie stopped the car. "Ben, are you listening to yourself? You're not the one who started this whole mess. You can't worry about what happens to him." He put his hand on Ben's shoulder. "If I were you, I wouldn't cancel the will no matter what he says. He started this and it's his problem. You tried everything to reach this guy and nothing worked. You did what you had to do to protect yourself and your family, right?"

Ben gazed out the windshield. "You're right..." He nodded his head. "You're absolutely right. Let's go hit some balls."

"Yeah, let's whack a few." He turned up the radio.

The feeling of well-being that Ben had gotten from Howie's pep talk was short lived. The problem still remained – was Dracken intimidated?

"I gotta talk to Willie. He's the only one who will know if Dracken is taking this seriously."

Ben fidgeted in his seat. "You know what I mean?"

"Yeah," Howie replied, deciding to let Ben ramble.

"If there was only a way to show Dracken the ruthlessness of Luke without actually naming him. That..." Ben waved his finger in the air. "That would make him think twice. It's funny; I'm taking for granted that Luke is still as mean and scary looking as he used to be."

"Oh he is... still scary looking." Howie said, his words getting less distinguishable.

Ben looked quickly in Howie's direction. "How do you know?"

Howie paused for a moment. "I ran into him yesterday."

Ben erupted after a moment of disbelief. "You saw Luke...Luke-from-the-will-Luke and you didn't tell me?"

"Look, I didn't want you to think about it, all right?"

"Think about what? Where'd you see him?"

Howie again paused. "At Motor Vehicle when I was turning in my old plates."

Ben looked at Howie with suspicion. "What aren't you telling me?"

"Nothing – I just didn't want you to think about it."

Ben sat in silence as different scenarios played quickly through his mind. "Oh no," he yelled as he reached and grabbed Howie's shirt tightly. "Pull over, pull over!"

"What's the matter? Calm down," Howie yelled as he brought the car to an abrupt halt.

Ben's breathing was slow and heavy, his hand still pulling on Howie's shirt. "Did you see Luke in Motor Vehicles?"

"Ah, No, I saw him leaving the building. I assumed he was at the motor vehicle office. Why, what's the problem?"

"Howie, that's the same building the attorney who fixed the will is in." Ben punched the side window glass with the bottom of his fist. "Damn."

"Easy! Easy!" Howie yelled.

"Did you tell Luke anything?"

"Don't be fuckin' stupid. Of course not...just kinda nodded and kept going." Ben stared out the window. "Ben, what's the problem? It's probably just a coincidence."

Howie became alarmed. Ben wasn't responding and his breathing grew heavier.

"You all right?"

"I never figured on this scenario. I can't believe I never thought of it," Ben mumbled.

"What scenario? What are you talking about?"

"Think about it. The attorney tells Luke about the will. Next, Luke kills me and the will goes into effect. After that he kills Dracken, Luke and the attorney split the money. Everyone will think Dracken killed me, but he'll be dead so they can't question him."

Howie sank into his seat. "Wow, I didn't figure on that possibility either." He opened his mouth to continue but stopped short.

They sat in absolute quiet for a minute until Howie broke the silence. "You know, we don't know that he didn't go to Motor Vehicle."

"Yeah, but we don't know that he didn't get a call from my attorney who I can't even contact because right now he's on a plane to Europe." Ben got out of the car and leaned against the rear fender.

"Ben, c'mon, get back in the car and we'll go somewhere for a drink," Howie said, walking around the car towards Ben. "C'mon, we can't figure this out here. Get back in."

"I don't believe this." He sat back in the car. "Now I have two lunatics that want to kill me. I'm gonna have to find out if Luke was at Motor Vehicle or some place else in that building. I think I know how to find out. C'mon, let's grab a beer."

Chapter Seven

"Give me a pitcher of whatever you have in light beer," Howie called over to the waitress, as he and Ben headed for a corner table. Howie spun his seat around and sat with the chair back against his chest.

A loud cheer from a group of men sitting near them startled Ben. "What was that?"

Howie leaned back to see the screen of the TV that sat on a shelf above their table. "That was a home run. Hold on a second while I hit the men's room."

Before Howie made it to the bathroom, he stopped and looked at a different TV over the bar. He watched as the scores of different games were displayed. Ben couldn't make out what Howie was looking at but he had a pretty good idea.

Ben was reading from a menu when Howie came back. "So what's your plan to find out why Luke was at Motor Vehicle?"

"Well, I don't think you're going to like it, but it's the best I got."

The waitress returned and placed a pitcher and two frosted mugs on the table. Howie reached into his pocket and counted out some bills, laying them on her tray. "Keep it," he said with a wink.

"Ben, it don't matter if I like it or not, I'm in this with you 'til the end. Wait, let me rephrase that to be – 'til this matter is resolved."

"Right. Now, if Luke really does know about this whole thing, he will probably be in contact with Dan Perry."

"I take it that's the attorney?"

"Yup. Now my guess is that Perry will call him at work to find out what's happening. Luke can't call him because he's in Europe."

"Wait a minute. Didn't you tell me before that Perry didn't want you to discuss things on the phone, I mean about the will," Howie said, pouring beer into the glasses.

"Yeah...yeah. Wait, don't kill this idea, it's the only way that I might be able to find out. Perry could call from a payphone or something. That can't be traced back to him."

"Yeah but the calls Luke gets can be traced back to Europe...well anyway, go ahead."

"Look, Howie, if they were going to be that careful, they never would've met face to face at Perry's office."

"That proves they didn't meet right there."

Ben was convinced that they had met and Howie's words went unheard.

"But why would they have met in Perry's office? Any number of people could have seen Luke go into that office," Ben said, contemplating their lack of discretion.

"Ben, will you please listen to me." Howie grabbed him by the arm.

"Maybe they just didn't meet," Howie said, banging his hand on the table with every word, trying to get Ben to snap out of his paranoia-induced trance.

Ben took a long drink of his beer, never taking his eyes off Howie.

"Maybe," he said slowly. "But I have to be sure. I'm gonna have to do the thing that you're not gonna want to hear."

"Okay, let's have it."

"I'll have to talk to Connie. She works with Luke. Maybe she could find out for me."

"Are you nuts? Do you really want to get her involved in this?"

Ben sighed deeply. "You know I don't, but if I do it discreetly no one will get hurt."

"How you gonna do it discreetly? You sure can't call her at work and explain your problem over the phone, unless of course you want to give her a heart attack."

"I could call her at home."

"Ben, you really have to think about this. You're talkin' about upsetting her and possibly putting a woman with a family in danger."

"All I'm going to ask her to do is keep an ear open and see if she notices anything strange, that's all."

"Well, you're right. I don't like the idea but I guess it's a last resort. Just be careful."

"I will."

The pitcher of beer was empty. Howie started to call the waitress for a refill but Ben stopped him.

"You're driving and you know what? If I don't tell Claire that we hit a bucket of balls, she'll ask more questions. Sitting here drinking isn't going to make any of this go away. Let's just go to the range."

"Sure, why not? Maybe after the beer I'll drive the ball a little straighter."

Ben pulled out of his driveway early Monday morning. The rain fell so hard that he needed the windshield wipers on high.

Thank you God.

He had prayed for rain to help conceal him. He unfolded a map that he had printed from the computer and placed it on the passenger seat. Pulling over from time to time, he followed the directions carefully. He rolled down the street, searching for Connie's house among the closely situated homes. He squinted, trying to read the numbers on the houses, which were obscured by the rain.

"Two ten, two fourteen, here it is, two eighteen." Ben shifted the car into reverse and backed up, stopping in front of the house next door to hers. He was at Connie's; she was the only person who could get close enough to Luke without causing suspicion.

Ben sat, trying to muster up the courage to make the call. Considering that the most recent conversation they had had was two years earlier and that they hadn't seen each other in ten, would she feel obligated to help?

What do I say? Hi Connie, can you find out if I'm going to be killed?

Picturing Connie's svelte frame and long auburn hair brought a smile to Ben's face, for they shared a secret. An embarrassing moment many years back still caused Ben to blush. Two teenagers - best friends - together with a bottle of cheap wine and adolescent hormones, had led to a fumbled attempt at sex. Reminiscing about the most awkward ten minutes of his life caused him to burst out in laughter.

All I can do is ask and hope she remembers the good times.

Ben dialed the number scribbled on the bottom of the map. As the phone rang, he closed his eyes tightly, praying that Connie would answer.

"Hello?" the voice said.

"Hello Connie," he replied. "How are you?"

"Who is this?" she asked, trying to place the voice.

"It's Ben."

"Ben? Ben Ben? Oh my God. How are you?" she yelled, her voice changing from excitement to confusion. "And why are calling me so early in the morning? Oh my God, who died?"

"No, no... no one died. Listen I'm kinda in some serious trouble and only you can help me."

"Okay," she said. "I'm not sure I understand how I can help. What kind of trouble are we talking about?"

"Well, I'd really like to talk face to face if it's okay."

"Sure, when do you want to meet? I'd really love to see you."

"That's good because I'm right outside your house." Ben cringed, waiting for her reaction.

"Outside, right now?" He could hear her walking with the phone. "Oh my God, you really are here." She paused a moment. "Well I guess come in. I don't have a lot of time, I'm getting ready for work."

"It won't take long, be right there." Ben snapped the phone shut. He stuck an umbrella out the door and popped it open. He jogged up the walkway and up the stairs where Connie held the door for him. He turned, faced the umbrella out and snapping it open and shut quickly, shedding the water. He backed away from the door still not having made eye contact with her. Connie pulled the door closed, stalling, afraid of the emotional reunion.

"Some rain, huh?" she said, their eyes finally meeting.

Instantly, their bodies pulled together in a tight embrace.

"Oh Ben, it's been so long. It so good to see you." Tears streamed down her cheeks.

"Good to see you too, Connie. Let me look at you." Keeping his hands on her shoulders, he moved her back. "You haven't aged a bit. You look fantastic."

She backed away, fanning her eyes with her hand. With a slight smile, she blushed. "I'm glad I didn't put my makeup on yet. Come in, come in," she said, leading him to the kitchen.

For a brief moment, Ben felt his eyes well up, but the anxiety of what he was about to ask overshadowed the nostalgia.

"So how's Claire and the kids?" she asked, taking out two coffee mugs.

"Good, everyone's good."

"And how's our buddy Howie?" she asked, her back still towards him.

"Horny as ever, Connie. Horny as ever – if you can believe it."

"Oh I believe it."

"Look, I'm really sorry to barge in on you like this but it's really important. Actually it's a matter of life and death and may take a little time to explain."

"Life and death?" She motioned for him to sit.

"Yeah, I got myself into sort of a problem."

Connie handed Ben a cup of coffee and sat across the table.

"Well if it's that important, I'll take the time, but I have to get the kids off to school. They'll be down in a half hour or so."

"Kids, wow, I forgot about your kids. How old are they now?"

"Donna's fourteen and Lisa's eleven," she said, sipping her coffee. She got up and added milk to her cup. "It's been a while since you've seen them."

"Sure has...Connie, I'll understand if you can't help me."

"Ben, I'll help. Just tell me what's going on."

"You better hear what I have to say before you volunteer. What I'm about to tell you may make you think that I've gone nuts but it was the only choice I had."

"All right already, the suspense is killing me. Tell me. Tell me. Wait, hold on," she said, putting her finger up to her mouth. She tiptoed to the hallway and looked up the stairway. "Thought I heard the girls. I don't think I want them to hear this."

"Okay, here goes," Ben said, sighing deeply. "Did you hear about a car accident involving Victor Dracken's daughter?"

"Ben, I never have time to watch TV or read newspapers. Tell me you're involved with Victor Dracken."

"Connie, I ran his girl over while talking on the cell phone; I wasn't paying attention. She died and Dracken threatened to kill me. I tried to reason with him but it didn't work. He still wanted to kill me." He stopped for a moment to let Connie take in what he had said so far. She sat there with her mouth wide open.

"Oh my God Ben, what are you going to do? Did you go to the police?"

"Yeah but they can't do much unless he actually does something. The only thing they suggested was a restraining order, which we all know does absolutely nothing."

"Ben? Where do I fit into this?" she asked cautiously.

"Well wait, this gets better. After weighing all my options and redoing my will, I got the idea that if I threatened him in some way; he'd cave in. To simplify, I set up the will so that if he killed me, another man would be paid to kill him."

"Ya did what?" she yelled. "Oh my God, have you gone nuts?" she quickly covered her mouth, afraid that her yell would be heard by her daughters.

"It gets worse. The guy I picked to kill Dracken if I die may have found out about the will. If he did, this guy may try to kill me in order to set the will into motion. You following this?"

"Yeah...yeah, I think so, but where do I come in?" Ben had a guilty look on his face. She leaned over the table towards him. "Let's have it."

"The guy I picked to..." Connie stopped him in mid sentence. "No way. No way. Please don't tell me you picked someone from the junkyard." Ben's expression of guilt gave her the answer. "Oh Ben, why would you do something so stupid?" She banged her hand on the table, sending a spoon spinning across.

Ben stood up, startled by her reaction. "Shhh," he said, spying around the doorway, checking the stairway for Connie's daughters. "I had to pick someone that I knew would go through with this if I were killed. How did I know that this would happen?" he whispered.

"Which one of the lunatics did you pick?" she asked, already knowing the answer.

"Luke, who else?"

"I knew it," she said with a look of panic. "Ben, you don't know how crazy this guy really is. All he ever talks about is killing things. He's not even supposed to own a gun, but from the way he talks to his friends, I think he's got an arsenal."

"I just need to know if he knows...if my lawyer told him."

"Ben, I spend most of my day trying to avoid him. Now you want me to ask if he's going to kill you?"

"No, no, I don't want you to talk to him about this at all. What I need you to do is just listen around and see if you pick up on anything strange, like my attorney calling him."

"You think your attorney told him about the will? Why would your attorney do that?"

"In a nutshell, if Luke killed me, then killed Dracken, he would collect fifty grand which he would split with my shady lawyer. Get it?"

"Yeah, yeah, I get it," she said. "So all I have to do is keep my ears open; I don't have to ask him any questions?"

"No questions. Don't let on that you know anything and

for God's sake don't tell anyone about this." Connie laughed. "Who would I tell? I mean who would believe me?"

"Will you do it? If you say no, I'll understand."

She locked her hands around her coffee mug. "Ben, you're in trouble. There's no way I could turn my back on you. I'll see what I can find out."

Ben slumped back in the chair. "Thank you. Thank you. You're my last hope."

His concern for Dracken's possible phone taps led to the decision of e-mail communication only. Connie would stay alert for any talk of Ben or the name of Dan Perry. She would attempt to answer the phones more often than usual, hoping to intercept a call from Perry.

"Now remember, delete any e-mails that you send or receive from me," Ben said.

"They're not exactly computer literate there, Ben. That's why I'm there."

"Just want you to be careful. That's all."

"I will. Don't worry." She dropped her head and looked at the floor then back at Ben. "Maybe after all this is all over, we could spend some time together?" she asked.

He reached his hand out and touched her cheek. "I promise. Listen, I'm really sorry for getting you involved and coming here after all this time to ask a favor."

"Don't be sorry. It's great to see you again." She kissed his cheek and embraced him. "It'll all work out."

"Hope so." He stood on his tiptoes, peering out the small glass windows atop the front door. Confident that no one awaited him outside, he sheltered his face with his umbrella and ran back to his car.

Ben sat at his desk, unable to concentrate. Hours had past and there was no communication from Connie. Howie leaned over the divider.

"You all right?"

"Just some heartburn. My stomach is churning because I haven't heard anything."

He opened a desk drawer, overflowing with remedies for common broker ailments. He poked around the drawer, knocking aside the aspirin and upset stomach medication in favor of the bottle of antacid pills. He poured them into his hand, picking out two green tablets and popping them into his mouth.

"Did you expect her to hear Luke talking to the attorney the minute she walked into work? C'mon, this could take days if it happens at all," Howie said.

"Yeah I know. At least she can keep an eye on him and maybe let me know if he's leaving the building for a couple hours or something." Ben motioned for Howie to come closer. "You know, it's funny. The only good thing to come out of this new twist is that I'm so worried about Luke possibly wanting to kill me that I almost forgot that Dracken definitely wants to kill me."

"Ben, you gotta calm down or your heart's gonna explode," Howie said. "Oh and by the way, and I'm not trying to give you any more to think about, but when are going to let Claire in on this whole mess?"

Ben leaned back in his chair. "I have to do it soon. She's really losing patience." Leaning forward again, he propped his elbow on the arm of the chair and rested his cheek in his palm. "We're barely talking and that's not like us. If it were just Dracken, I would tell her now, but I need to know more about Luke first."

He hadn't noticed that Howie's phone had rung and that he was now talking aloud to himself. Frustrated and on edge, Ben decided to e-mail Connie for any kind of information. He quickly formed a two-line, how's-everything type message, and sent it off.

All the while, as Ben worked on the computer researching stocks and gathering information, he kept one eye on the bottom corner of the monitor, waiting for the little e-mail indicator flag to pop up. Finally, thirty minutes after his e-mail to Connie, the flag appeared and the sound of a bell chimed. Ben sat up straight and clicked on it.

"Is that Connie?" Howie asked from the other side.

"Wait, I'm looking. You could hear that over there?" He began to read. Howie stood up and squinted to see.

"It says Luke is acting a bit stranger than usual and is planning a hunting trip to some cabin for the weekend."

He scanned the message as fast as his eyes would take him. "Says that he is going alone to an upstate cabin to hunt."

"That it?" Howie asked.

"She says it's odd because he always goes with friends – never alone." Ben picked up the coffee that Brenda had brought for him earlier, and added a small container of cream. "That's all it says except she's telling me to relax."

"I agree with her. Just relax 'til you have a reason to sweat it."

Ben stared into his coffee as he stirred it, watching the cream swirl and mix. He tried to put meaning to Luke going hunting upstate on his own. He had ideas but didn't share them with Howie.

"Back to work until we hear from her again," Ben said.

Ben checked his e-mail repeatedly for the remainder of the day. He became obsessed. Sounds from around the office began to resemble the chime of the e-mail bell, making him check for mail even though there was no flag on the monitor.

An hour after the closing bell of the market, Ben made one last desperate check of his e-mail, but still nothing. Maybe Connie would send something at night from home, he thought. Maybe she couldn't type anything because there were people around her desk.

Claire waited at the front door with both children as Ben pulled into the driveway. He could see Michael and Sarah's faces light up as they jumped up and down. Claire's face was not as accommodating. It was going to be another cold night, Ben thought as he waved to the children. Claire opened the door, letting the children out for a mad dash to the car.

"Hi, my babies," Ben said, hugging them. He prolonged the embrace, trying desperately to put on a guilt-free face. He walked the children up the stairs, avoiding eye contact with Claire until at the top. She backed away as he attempted to kiss her cheek, instead reaching out and leading each child by the hand.

"There's food here if you want it," she said, her voice so cold that it froze Ben where he stood. He had never seen this side of Claire. By shutting her out, he realized that he had created a breach in their relationship. He now felt isolated, as though she was no longer there for him – a terrible feeling, probably exactly what she had been feeling for recent days. It was time. Telling her would be the most difficult task that he had ever faced, but she deserved to know and Ben deserved her wrath for keeping it from her. The question was, should he mention Luke or just Dracken?

Ben walked past the kitchen without looking in, and tiptoed down the stairs and turned the computer on, hoping that Connie had left a message for him. He sat patiently, waiting for the computer to boot up.

"C'mon, c'mon," he said, putting his hand atop the monitor and shaking it.

Claire walked down the stairs and into the doorway of his office. "Everything all right?" she asked.

"Oh... yeah, I just forgot to check something in a client's account. Wanted to make sure there was no problem or I wouldn't be able to sleep," he said without turning around.

She nodded, remaining in the doorway. Ben was so consumed with checking the e-mail that he didn't notice that Claire had remained, watching him curiously as he continued to shake the computer.

Two long minutes later, the computer was ready, but still no message. He would have to give Claire the Dracken-only version of his ever-expanding debacle.

Ben, in a brief second of lunacy, thought of calling Connie. Immediately coming back to his senses, he shook his head back and forth quickly, still unaware that Claire was watching. She walked up behind him.

"Ben, is everything all right?"

Ben jumped, smashing his knee under the desk. He grabbed it in pain while swinging the chair around, simultaneously scattering a box of paper clips across the floor. He knelt down on the uninjured knee and started picking up the clips. Claire knelt facing him, their eyes meeting for longer than they had in days. Her look was softer, not the cold, stern visage of the past days. Ben thought he saw daylight.

"Ben, is there a problem at work that I should know about?" Claire asked tenderly.

Ben was taken by surprise, detecting pity in her eyes and in her voice. Immediately, he took advantage of her moment of good nature. He had his way out, albeit a short, quick fix, not a remedy.

"Yeah, there's some stuff at work but nothing to worry about. And you know the girl is still in the back of my mind."

They stood up. Claire reached her arms out around his neck and laid her head on his shoulder. He closed his eyes tightly - he had lied to her again. Now had to be the time to confess the situation.

As he held her, he opened his eyes. He was facing a group of oak shelves, atop which sat their wedding pictures. In an instant, Ben reminisced to their wedding day: Claire in all her beauty, speaking the words "for better or worse". This was definitely going to be the worse part of that commitment.

The words, "Claire, we better go and sit down," almost slipped through his lips, but another glance at the wedding photos brought the next line of the vows - 'til death do us part. With his mind changed once again, he decided to wait the extra day, hoping to find out more about Luke.

"You were going to say something?" she asked.

"Just that I'm sorry that I haven't been myself."

"Ben, maybe it's time to see someone, you know, someone," she said, waiting for his reaction as he filled in the blank.

"You mean a psychiatrist?"

She looked at him shyly. "Couldn't hurt could it?"

He kissed her on the forehead. "I'll think about it."

Ben shut the computer down while Claire ran back upstairs to check on the children.

If I told a shrink what I did, he'd have me committed on the spot.

He laughed out loud as the monitor went black, reflecting the silhouette of his head. He stared into the dark screen, contemplating his next move. With Claire temporarily appeased, he could now focus better on a game plan. Knowing his options were few and time was growing short, he would have to make swift decisions. If Luke were stalking him, his family would be in danger. Unlike Dracken, who would never harm the family of an adversary, Luke would have no qualms about burning Ben's house, children included.

"What's up, buddy?" Howie asked, dropping his briefcase on the desk. He leaned over the partition. "Anything new? I feel bad that I can't help you, except here at work."

"Don't worry about it. Nothing new from Connie yet."

Howie leaned closer to see Ben's eyes, which were bloodshot, his eye sockets deep and dark.

"Ben, ya look like shit," he said, leaving his cubicle and walking around to Ben's desk. He squatted next to him.

"Thanks a lot." Ben reached for his coffee cup and took a sip.

"Oh man, your hand is shaking. Look we gotta get you some help," Howie said.

Ben slumped on his desk, laying his forehead on his folded arms and began to cry.

"Howie, I can't take it anymore. They all wanna kill me. I gotta save my family," Ben said between sniffles.

Howie stood up half way and looked around. It was early and there were no other brokers nearby. He ducked back down.

"Ben, ya can't have a breakdown here." Howie shook his shoulder. "C'mon, snap out of it. You can't do this here."

"All right, all right," he said, sitting back in the chair, wiping his eyes. "Why did this have to happen to me? I'm a good guy."

"Yeah, you are...I just wish you'd wait to panic. You don't know – Dracken may have been scared off by the will and Luke, well, he may be nothing."

"Maybe you're right. I'll just have to wait for Connie, that's all."

Ben's eyes now looked as though he had been in a prizefight. He sat at his desk with The Wall Street Journal held high, covering his face from all sides for half an hour. Howie reached over, pulling a corner of the paper away.

"You're good now. Now you're back to just looking like shit without the swelling."

Ben was able to crack a smile and for a moment felt euphoric. Maybe it would all work out and he'd have this nightmare behind him.

"You know, Ben, you never really told me much about Connie," Howie said, ruining Ben's moment of tranquility.

"Oh, yeah. She looks great. Brought back a lot of memories, Howie. Memories of growing up. Just wish we could've talked more about old times, but that never came up. Didn't have time."

"I was thinking about her last night. Really started to miss her," Howie said.

"You missed her? You missed a person? Wow, you realize that you felt an emotion there? You must be getting old."

"Very funny. No, seriously, what did she say when you told her all this. Did you have to push her into helping?"

"Actually, at first she gave the 'are you crazy routine,' but then – if I didn't know better, I would swear she sees it as an undercover thing. Almost excited about it...but she wouldn't show it."

"Maybe she's bored and looking for some excitement."

Ben's phone rang. Howie listened as Ben's conversation sounded upbeat. He stood up as Ben put down the phone.

"Hey, my truck's finally ready. Guy at the body shop says she looks like new. We gotta find a way of getting her today."

"Okay, we'll grab it on the way home." Howie popped open his briefcase and dropped his client book on his desk. "You ready to make some money here or what."

Ben answered half-heartedly. "Yeah let's get to it. I didn't have a chance to research anything but there's gotta be a stock with our name on it someplace."

Phones rang constantly as Howie and Ben placed orders for their clients. The busy morning gave Ben a much-needed break from his mind-consuming ordeal. One stretch afforded him forty-five minutes of murder-free thought.

"You check the e-mail lately?" Howie asked over the divider.

"Still nothing."

"Remember Ben, if you don't hear anything, it might be because there is nothing to hear. Stop thinking the worst."

"Howie, if I don't think the worst and let my guard down, I might get shot."

"Okay...I see your point. Just trying to be an optimist. By the way, we never spoke about – and I hate to bring it up but it is important – what are you going to do if Connie says that he knows?"

"God, I don't know."

"Well I know – you have to pack everyone up and head out west 'til it blows over."

Ben nodded. "Might be the only thing to do."

Lunchtime approached. Ben sat back in his chair with his hands folded in his lap. He rocked as he wondered when some news would come.

Please Connie, give me something.

Howie stood up. "Ready to head down? I'm starving."

"Yeah, let's go," Ben replied.

Howie was already at the back door when he turned to look for Ben, who was standing, looking at his monitor.

"Howie," Ben called out.

Howie could tell by the alarmed tone of Ben's voice that Connie had sent a message. He walked quickly back to Ben's desk, slowing his pace as he saw the panicked look on Ben's face.

"Bad news?" Howie sad quietly.

Without answering, Ben swiveled the monitor towards Howie.

I caught part of a conversation that Luke had. It was a guy but I don't know who he was. Can't tell anymore now. I need to see you right away. Can you meet me at 2:00 at the County Savings Bank on Northern Blvd? Just e-mail me yes or no. If no, we'll have to talk later on when to meet. -- C.

Howie finished reading. "Sorry for all the times I said everything would be okay. This ain't okay."

"No shit," Ben said unconsciously. "Now I'm in really deep shit. I'm more afraid of Luke than I am of Dracken."

Howie could hear Ben's voice cracking, and immediately grabbed his arm. "Let's go. We need to get some air," he said, fearing another breakdown like Ben had had earlier.

"Wait...don't worry, I'm all right. I feel better knowing than not knowing. At least now I can plan what to do next. Let me e-mail Connie back." He paused. "Howie, can you come with me later – to meet her, and when I go home to tell Claire?" Ben asked, his face looking like a child about to go to the dentist.

"E-mail her back that we'll be there," Howie said.

"Thanks man."

Ben typed in YES and hit the send button.

Ben knew from the conception of his plan that there would be kinks along the way – no plan is perfect. Never in his wildest nightmares did he expect to be hunted by two killers, two killers with entirely different temperaments. Dracken was a man with a lust for vengeance, but the possibility of dealing with him intelligently existed. Luke on the other hand was a different type of villain. He was ruthless, and any plan of attack would be thought out carefully but without the thought of future consequences. Ben now realized that he was in way over his head. He would need help to be released from the predicament he had created.

Chapter Eight

"What time is she supposed to be here?" Howie asked.

"Said two in the e-mail," Ben replied, shading his eyes. "I don't know what kind of car she's got, so keep your eyes open. I can't see cause of the sun."

Ben looked at his watch a countless number of times as they sat in Howie's car, waiting, sweating on the unusually hot, early fall day. Parking in the only spot that afforded them a line of sight to the incoming cars left them out in the open, away from the surrounding shaded areas.

"C'mon Connie, where are you?" Ben said.

"She'll get here. What's the rush? You already know what she's going to tell you." Howie turned the engine back on, flipping on the air conditioning. "Screw what the manual says, I'm leavin' the air on. Let it overheat."

"Okay, so we shoot out of here, get my truck and then you'll follow me to my house, right?" Ben asked.

"Told you I'd be there when you told Claire, didn't I?"

"Yeah, just making sure." Ben pointed to a cherry red, midsize car that had slowed coming into the lot. "That her?"

The car pulled up in front of them. Through the glare they could see Connie wave. Ben started to open the door but she motioned for him to wait. She drove around the lot, pulling up to the bank drive-up window.

"Move the car over there, out of the sun – and out of sight," Ben said.

Howie backed the car into a shady spot up against a fence, and cut the engine. Within minutes, Connie pulled in headfirst, her driver's door adjacent to Howie's. A quick smile of delight upon seeing Howie behind the wheel disappeared quickly as she scanned the parking lot from inside the car.

Ben opened his door and stepped out, keeping one hand on the door and the other on the roof. Without taking his eyes off the lot, he reached back, pulling the seat forward. Connie came from around the back of Howie's car and ducked into the back seat. By the time Ben followed her in, she was in an awkward embrace with Howie, who was leaning over the front seat.

"God, it's good to see you, Howie. Just wish it were under better circumstances." Tears rolled down her cheek.

"I know, Connie. Seeing you brings me back to younger times," Howie said.

"I'm guessing those aren't tears of joy," Ben said, now sitting next to her in the back.

She grabbed him, pulling him close. "Oh Ben, I'm so sorry."

He gently pushed her away to see her face. "What did you hear?" At the same time he pointed out the windshield. "Howie, keep a watch out on the lot, will you?"

"Well, they were trying to talk in code but it was easy to get the idea." Ben wiped a tear from her face with his finger. "The lawyer guy said to make sure it got done soon." She gave Ben a pitying look and dropped her face into her hands. "Ben, he's going to kill you," she blurted out between sobs.

"All right, calm down and tell me everything that you can remember," he said, taking out a small pad and pen from his inside jacket pocket. Connie gave him a puzzled look.

"You're going to take notes? How can you be so calm? Do you understand what this man is like?"

"Connie, after I got your e-mail, I kinda figured that he wanted to kill me. I've already been through the panic stage a couple times today already, right Howie," Ben said, meeting Howie's eyes in the rearview mirror.

"I thought he was going to have a breakdown right there in the office," Howie said.

"I decided on the way here that I have to stay strong to protect my family. Now I have to plan my next move."

"Your next move is to pack up the family and move to South Dakota - right now!" Howie said.

"Next move? Your only next move is to go to the police. I'll tell them what I heard if they don't believe you," Connie said.

"Look, I'll be okay. Just tell me everything you remember about the call."

Connie sank back into the leather seat, laying her head back and closing her eyes, trying to replay the conversation in her head.

"Well, the impression I got was that they know each other pretty well. I mean this definitely wasn't the first time they spoke."

Ben interrupted. "What makes you say that?"

"They were much too familiar with each other, not that they sounded friendly. It was more like they had dealings before."

"Okay, now did they mention anything like how, where or when?"

"No, it was a fairly short call and definitely not the first on the subject. I caught the call almost from the beginning because I answered the phone." She thought for a moment. "Oh, oh, wait," she yelled, causing Howie to jump. "I almost forgot - Luke is leaving tomorrow for some cabin. Not on the weekend like I thought."

"At least we know why he's going away. He needs to be somewhere else when it happens," Ben said.

Connie looked confused. "If he's going to kill you, how's he going to be in two places at one time?"

"Maybe Luke comes back for a couple hours from wherever he is, does it and shoots back to the cabin. He'd have to make sure that someone saw him wherever the cabin is so he'd have an alibi," Howie said.

Grabbing the back of Howie's seat, Connie pulled herself up to look at him as she spoke. "Yeah, but what if someone saw him around here around the time of the mur..." she caught herself in time.

"Maybe he uses a disguise and maybe he steals a car?" Howie said.

"Wait, he's got access to a whole bunch of different cars. I'll have to hurry back before he leaves; maybe I can see what he drives out in."

"Good idea. If you find out what car it is, e-mail me," Ben said.

"Okay, but wait, there's more. The last thing I remember hearing is the lawyer telling him to make sure everything got done. He emphasized everything – like there was more than just you, Ben."

"Simple, after he kills me, he's got to kill Dracken in order to get the bank account number and location," Ben said.

"That's one thing I don't get. After Dracken is dead, how does Luke get the number?" she asked.

"My other attorney will read or hear about Dracken's death and immediately send the info to Dan Perry, who will then give it to Luke. If Luke could find out who my other attorney is, he could put a gun to his head for the info. Then of course he would have to kill him, which would be easier because it would cut out one murder," Ben explained.

Connie ran her fingers through her hair. "Am I being stupid here? Why can't you just cancel the money side of this whole thing? If Luke knows there's no money, there's no killing, right?" she asked, looking back and forth at both men. "Right?"

"That's what we're going to do tonight. Tell Claire the whole mess and get it over with. Then hit the police station. I'll explain the whole 'will' thing, which I'm sure they'll have a field day with. Then I guess they'll find Luke and tell him that they know what's up. Since Dracken doesn't know who Luke is, he won't know that he's been told. He'll still think the will is on. Only problem is, if Dracken kills me, he gets away scot-free."

Howie turned to Ben. "Maybe we should get going. All this talk's got me nervous, sitting out here in the open and all. Plus we got shit to do – you wanted to get your truck, right?"

"Yeah, okay. Connie, someday I'll explain more in detail."

Ben slid out, holding the seat for her. A quick embrace, a quick look into each other's eyes, and she was gone. Howie and Ben sat in silence as her car disappeared around the bank. Both realized that they had left a good friend out of their lives for too long.

"Ben, we need to pack up Claire and the kids tonight in case they cant find Luke," Howie said.

Ben didn't respond.

Howie stopped his car across from the auto-body shop. Ben's truck sat parked along the side of the building. Only the rear was visible from their position. Ben got out and started across the street.

"You want me to come with you?" Howie asked.

"I think I can handle this," Ben said, without looking back.

He went straight across to the entrance without looking at the truck. As he came back out, he dangled the keys for Howie to see. His plan was to walk to the truck, hop in and drive home without checking the repairs or even looking at the vehicle, thus avoiding the flashbacks and the guilt. He pulled up on the door handle but stopped before the door opened – who was he kidding? There's not a man alive who has his car repaired who can just get in and go. He dropped his hand to his side and reluctantly walked forward, stopping before making the turn to the front grille. After a deep breath, he continued around, faced the new bumper and squatted down in front of it.

"I knew you wouldn't just get in and leave," Howie said, walking up behind him. "Ben, we really gotta get going."

"Looks a lot different from when I saw her last." Ben rubbed the bumper then pulled lightly on the grille. "It's all in one piece – and no more orange," he said sadly. He stood up, fighting the images of the girl entangled in the undercarriage.

"Ben..."

He raised his hand, stopping Howie from continuing. "I know, lets go."

Howie opened the door. "You gonna be okay?"

"This is a breeze compared to what's next," Ben said.

Placing his hand on Ben's shoulder, Howie held Ben still. "Ben, we're gonna get through this, all right?"

He nodded and hopped up into the truck. Howie walked back to his car, looking over his shoulder, hoping Ben would start the truck without hesitation.

To Ben's surprise, the deep sadness and the flashbacks that he had expected from sitting behind the wheel were absent. Was he becoming hardened? More likely the reason was the unenviable task that awaited him at home. Claire was about to find out how secretive he had been.

Pulling up to the house simultaneously, Ben parked in the driveway while Howie parked facing in the wrong direction in the street. Ben played nervously with his keys as he waited for Howie to come up the driveway.

"You ready to do this?" Howie asked, putting his arm around Ben.

"As ready as I'll ever be. This isn't gonna be easy," Ben replied.

"We'll get through it. As long as she knows you're going to the police and taking care of this." Howie held the gate open. Ben walked through and stopped on the first step to the house.

"Do you really think that's going to make her feel safe?" He fumbled finding the house key on his ring and slid it into the slot.

"Guess not."

Ben opened the front door and was relieved to see an empty living room. He listened for a second, keeping Howie from entering.

"What's the matter?" Howie asked.

"Nothing. I was hoping that the kids were taking a nap. This will go a lot smoother without them climbing all over us."

Claire, hearing voices, called from the bedroom. "Ben, is that you?"

"You were expecting someone else?" Howie called back.

Taken off guard by Howie's voice, she was speechless for a moment. "Howie?"

"Yeah Claire, it's both of us," Ben replied.

Claire ran into the living room and looked at the faces of both men. "What's wrong?"

"The kids asleep?" Ben asked.

"Yeah, they're out cold and the door's closed. What's going on?"

"Claire, I kinda got myself into some trouble."

"You did? What kind of trouble?" she asked with a sound of astonishment rather than urgency.

"Let's sit down. I'll tell you what I did." Ben led her backwards gently, and sat her on the couch.

She continually looked back and forth at both of them, waiting for either to give an explanation. Howie just stood with his face solemn. Ben opened his mouth to start his confession but was interrupted by the telephone. He ran to the kitchen to answer it, leaving Howie alone with a now panicky Claire.

"What kind of liquor do you keep in here?" Howie stepped to a small bar, set up in the corner of the room. Looking more like it was for show than for actual use, it held only three bottles of liquor.

"How about I make you a screwdriver, Claire?" he said, pulling out a bottle of vodka.

"Do I need a drink?" she asked.

Howie glanced in her direction. "I'll make yours a double...hey Ben, bring in the orange juice."

"Howie, I'm really getting scared. What's going on? Does this have to do with Dracken?"

"Please... let Ben explain the whole thing," he said as Ben returned.

Claire jumped up off the couch. "What's going on Ben, tell me," she insisted.

"Okay, okay, just sit and I'll tell you." He paused, handing a container of orange juice to Howie.

"There's no easy way to tell you this, but Victor Dracken threatened to kill me after the accident."

"What!" Claire screamed. Howie reached across the coffee table, handing her the drink. "Why didn't you tell me? I knew there was something wrong! I knew it!"

"I thought I could handle it without worrying you," Ben said.

"Handle it how? Did you go to the police? Ben, how could you not tell me this? I begged you to talk to me." Her eyes began to tear. "You lied to me."

Ben wasn't sure if she was more upset about Dracken or the idea that he hadn't confided in her.

"I went to the police but they couldn't do anything unless he actually did something to me. I could've gotten an order of protection, but they're useless if someone is going to have you killed." He pleaded for her to understand.

Claire took a sip out of her glass and grimaced at the strength of the drink. "You trying to kill me Howie?" She handed the glass back. "Could you put some more orange juice in here?"

"Sure Claire," he said, taking his already empty glass and hers back to the bar.

Claire stuttered, her brain working faster than her mouth. She smacked her hand across her eyes to calm herself enough to get one question out at a time. Ben sat, waiting for the barrage, but Howie spoke out from across the room before Claire could say a word.

"Ben, you better tell her the rest."

Ben shot Howie a dirty look. He was supposed to be there for support and remain as a quiet bystander, allowing Ben to explain slowly to keep Claire's panic level to a minimum.

"The rest? What else is there?" Claire asked, as she looked first at Ben and then at Howie. There was silence for a moment. "One of you better tell me what's going on." She grabbed Ben's arm, "Ben, tell me."

"All right...I set up my will so that if I died, a certain person would be notified and in turn would be paid by my estate to kill Victor Dracken."

Ben sat on the edge of the couch, and Howie stood still, waiting for her response. After a brief pause, she began to laugh. She reached out for Howie to hand her the now weakened drink.

Ben, knowing that Claire's laugh wasn't authentic, glanced at Howie who just shrugged his shoulders.

"I know I couldn't have heard that right. I thought you said you hired a hitman to kill Dracken." She raised the glass to her mouth and stared at Ben while drinking. From his pallor and guilty expression, she knew she had heard right. Lowering the glass, now half empty, she looked at Howie who quickly dropped his eyes to the floor.

"Howie, keep the drinks coming," she said.

"You sure Claire? That'll be two more drinks than you've had in a year," Howie quipped.

"You're making jokes now? Howie, how could you have let him do something so stupid? Or was it your idea... that makes more sense."

"No, no, it was my idea," Ben said.

Claire sat on the edge of the couch, elbows on knees, clutching the glass with both hands. Ben could see that her legs were trembling lightly, causing the glass to shake. She sniffled and wiped away a trickle of mascara that ran down her face.

"What do we do now? I mean are we safe here now?"

"Howie, run inside and grab the tissues, will you," Ben said.

"You gonna tell her..." Howie stopped short, causing Claire's head to snap toward Ben.

"You wanna let me do a solo here," Ben snapped.

Howie quickly left the room. Claire slammed her empty glass on the table. "I know it can't get any worse."

Howie gave Ben a wide berth upon returning, as he handed Claire the box of tissues.

"The person I had named in the will - who would kill Dracken if I died - kind of found out about it. Now I'm worried that he may try to kill me."

Claire sat silent. Ben reached his hand out for hers but she yanked it away. "Don't touch me."

"Claire...please, let me explain...Claire?" Ben watched the color run from her face and her eyes glaze over as she slumped toward the coffee table. He and Howie both dove towards her, Ben catching her first and laying her back on the couch. Howie grabbed her glass.

"What do we do? Should I call an ambulance?" Howie shouted.

Ben looked at him in amazement. "She fainted, you idiot. She's not dying. Haven't you ever seen a woman faint before?"

"Nah, I never stayed with one girl long enough to have her faint on me."

"Watch. I'll push her head between her legs and she'll pop right up," Ben said.

Ben knelt down, holding her head down for only a couple of seconds. She rubbed her eyes as she slowly regained consciousness. "What happened?"

"You fainted. You okay?" Ben asked.

Now realizing that it hadn't been a bad dream, Claire stood up. Still wobbly, she walked toward Howie, who reached out to steady her.

"Get away, just get away – both of you." Black mascara again streamed down her face and dripped off her chin. Black spots dotted her shirt as she ran for the kitchen. Ben followed close behind and watched as she opened her purse, throwing in a checkbook and a pen. Tears dripped onto the counter.

"Claire, what are you doing?"

"I'm taking the children and I'm leaving. They're not safe here." She tried to sidestep Ben to the children's room. "Move!"

"Claire, you can't leave. I'm going to the police in the morning. We are safe tonight." Claire looked hard at Ben's face, trying to read whether he believed his own words. "I think it would be more dangerous for you to take the children out in your condition. Come look." Claire stood with arms crossed, her defiance waning. She knew she couldn't leave – she had nowhere to go.

Ben led her to the bathroom. She gasped upon seeing herself in the mirror. Small globs of wet mascara clung to her lower lashes. Below her swollen eyes, the mascara had dried in spots and created black streams ending under her chin.

"God, I look scary," she said with a small laugh.

"Look, we'll be fine here tonight."

"I'm going to stay with you guys tonight – if that will make you feel better, Claire," Howie said.

Claire nodded, pushing past Ben and going into the children's room. She picked up Sarah out of her bed. "You're going to the police first thing in the morning, right?"

"Yes. I want to speak to the same detective that I spoke to before. He seemed like he really cared."

"Okay Ben, do what you think is right for us," she said.

Ben glanced at Howie, who stood at the living room entrance to the hallway. Both gave a sigh of relief that Claire had calmed. She bounced Sarah lightly in her arms as she waited for Ben to bring Michael out from the bedroom.

"Here's my sleepy boy. Say hi to Uncle Howie."

Howie bent over and kissed Michael on the head. He jingled his keys in front of the child's face. "All right, let me head out. I'll be back in an hour or so."

"Thanks Howie. See you in a bit."

Howie motioned for Ben to turn around. Seeing that Claire had begun to cry again, Ben handed Michael to Howie and rushed to her.

She held Sarah up so Ben could see her face. "Ben, this is our daughter," she said, her voice getting louder with every word. "These are our children for God's sake. I don't think we should stay here. Howie, what do you think?"

"I think you should pack up and leave for South Dakota...tonight."

Ben just looked at Howie in surprise. "How stupid are you?"

"Ben..." he cut her off before she could continue.

"Okay, okay, okay." Ben backed up, touching his fingertips to his temple. "We'll go."

"You know what?" Howie announced. "Pack it up. We're headin' to my place. I'm thinking this will actually work out well. I'll stay with Claire tomorrow while you're at the cop shop. I'll have Brenda forward all the calls to my place and I'll handle everything from there."

Ben looked back at Claire, who gave a quick nod of approval. "I'll back my truck into the garage so no one will see us packing up." Ben took a step toward the kitchen, stopped and took another toward the basement. "I don't know where to go first."

Howie had taken a seat on the couch and flipped the TV on. "Let me know if I can do anything."

"You're doing enough." Ben looked to see that Claire was out of earshot. "Tell the truth, I feel better this way. I wasn't a hundred percent on stayin' here."

"Absolutely."

Ben walked closer to Howie. "I told Claire that the police would help us. What do you think they're going to do?"

"I know exactly what they're going to do but no one's gonna be happy about it. Forget about that now. Just get packed. We got all night to talk about it."

Chapter Nine

Pulling into the parking lot of the police station gave Ben what he and now his family missed – a sense of security; a sense that almost everyone takes for granted – all except the hunted.

He stepped down from his truck, nodding to an officer just coming off duty. He remembered his last visit and the pitying looks he received from the officers who knew he was the man who had killed Victor Dracken's daughter.

Ben pulled open the door to a quiet station house, and approached the desk sergeant.

"I'd like to speak to Detective Casey."

"He's not in yet but I expect him." He glanced up at the clock. "Somewhere in the next half hour. Is he expecting you... wait, ain't you the guy that was here last week? The Dracken guy, right?"

"Yeah, that's me."

"I wondered what happened to you. I knew you wasn't dead though. That wouda made the front page."

Ben tried to understand the officer's lack of compassion.

"Look, I need help here. Can you contact Casey and find out when he's due in? This is an emergency."

"Okay, okay. Let me see if I can get him," he said, grabbing a folder and disappearing to the back of the station.

"Don't mind him," a female voice said. Ben hadn't seen her sitting to the side of the sergeant. "He's not Mr. Congeniality. I'll run back and see if I can locate the detective. Have a seat over there."

Ben sat on the same cold hard bench as last time, again imagining how the nights must differ from the now empty room. The stench of cigarettes and alcohol. Criminals and drunks cuffed to the bars along the wall. How lucky they were – only going to jail. They knew their fate; if only Ben knew his.

"Hey, Mr. Pearce," the female officer yelled. "I got hold of Casey. He'll be here in twenty minutes."

"Great. Thank you." Ben slumped back onto the bench in relief. He knew that Casey was the one he needed to tell his story to. He now had twenty more minutes to rehearse his lines, which had to be perfect in order to invoke the maximum amount of pity. Ben did feel that if there was a law against what he had done that Casey would look the other way and just let Ben void the rider – like it never existed.

Ben walked outside. Filling his lungs with the crisp air reminded him of the approaching fall, a refreshing thought, for he loved the change of seasons. His next breath filled his lungs with the smoke of a man who had come out and lit a cigarette behind him. Thinking that the man was an undercover officer, Ben returned inside, not wanting to converse about his situation or about Dracken.

Within ten minutes, Casey walked through the door. He carried a jacket over one arm and a cup of coffee in the other hand. Upon seeing Ben, he immediately stopped dead in his tracks. "They didn't tell me who was waiting for me."

Ben extended his hand. Casey switched the coffee to his left hand and grabbed Ben's. "I knew eventually I'd be seeing you again...Mr. Pearce, isn't it?"

"That's right, Ben Pearce. So you remember who I am?" he asked, not really sounding that surprised.

"Sure I remember. I'm just glad we're meeting here and you're still able to speak if you know what I mean," he said in a serious tone. "C'mon, follow me back."

The detective area was nothing like the lobby. Uniformed officers walked in and out through another doorway connecting to the main precinct offices. Phone conversations came from inside private cubicles, and the squawk of a portable police radio, mistakenly left on, carried over the walls.

"So, how you making out? Any more threats?" Casey asked while refilling his coffee at a small counter outside his cubicle.

"I really think I may have done something...illegal, which in turn has gotten me into some more problems."

Casey glanced back. "Coffee?"

"Please...cream if you got it."

He handed Ben a white Styrofoam cup and a container of cream. "Careful, it's real hot."

Ben emptied the cream into his cup and sipped slowly.

"Okay Mr. Pearce, you said you think you may have done something illegal? I'm afraid to hear this but I guess I've heard it all. You didn't shoot anybody, did you?" he asked smiling.

"No, but remember when I was here last, I told you that Dracken threatened to kill me? I couldn't sleep thinking about my family, so I went back to Dracken to see if I could reason with him."

Casey shook his head. "My guess is that didn't work."

"No, no it didn't. I think I may have made him angrier – if that's possible. He just told me again that he wanted to kill me." Ben sipped his coffee, getting ready to ease into his explanation of the will. "I went home and racked my brain for a solution." Ben placed his cup down and leaned forward, folding his hands on the desk. "To make a long story short, I came up with a plan to sort of adjust my will in such a way that would make him think twice about killing me."

Casey perked up, suddenly looking very interested. He uncapped a pen and pulled a pad closer. He hoped that this would be the escape from the mundane that every detective waits for. Escape from the everyday murders and robberies. Ben would not disappoint.

"What do you mean you adjusted your will?" he asked with intense curiosity.

Ben took a deep breath and in one fast sentence, summed up his plan. "I put a rider in the will that states if I die, a certain person would receive fifty thousand dollars to kill Dracken."

Ben waited eagerly for a response. Casey leaned back in his chair and rocked, contemplating what he had just heard.

"Is that illegal?" Ben asked, not able to wait any longer for Casey to say something.

"Well...I'm pretty sure that it's not legal but...wait; give me some more details here. Your will now has something that says if you're killed, a hitman then will get paid out of your estate for killing Dracken? Does your wife pay this money? How does he get it?"

"I set up an offshore account. If I die, my attorney notifies the hitman – if that's what you want to call him."

Casey jumped in. "What would you call him?" he said, scribbling notes without looking up. Ben hadn't thought of a better title for Luke, and was speechless for a moment. "Never mind. Go on."

"Okay, the hitman is notified that if he kills Dracken, he gets fifty grand. Once he does the deed, another attorney, who has the number of the offshore account, sends that info to attorney number one."

Staring at the ceiling, the detective again began rocking in his chair. He pointed his pen toward the ceiling, moving it around as if he were drawing a math problem in the air. He mumbled out loud. Ben was able to catch words like kill and dead, but that was all.

"Okay, I think I got the idea now." Opening a drawer, he took out a toothpick and bit down on it. "First question I have is, and please don't think I'm nuts, but am I being had? Is this a practical joke? I mean this kinda thing happens a lot here. The guys pull gags like this."

Ben's face remained somber. Casey could see that this was a real situation.

"I'm sorry for that, but I had to ask." He leaned forward, scratching his head. "Well, this is a first for me. Congratulations Mr. Pearce. You just blew my theory of having heard it all."

"Well, am I in trouble for setting this up?" Ben asked.

"Hold on a second. I need to get my partner in here for this."

"There's more..." Ben said.

"Hang on, hang on. I'll be right back."

Casey returned with his partner.

"This is detective Brent. He and I have worked together for many years."

Brent didn't look as much like a cop as Casey did. In his late forties, he appeared more like a banker.

"Nice to meet you Mr. Pearce," Brent said, shaking Ben's hand.

"Same here," Ben replied.

"Detective Casey has given me a quick synopsis of what transpired between you and Mr. Dracken. I'm not really clear on the part about the will. Why don't you give it to me again," he said as they all sat down.

"Look, I know this sounds crazy, but it was the only way that I could think of to stop this man. I put a rider in my will that says if I die, a man would be paid to kill Dracken."

Brent looked at Casey. "You weren't pullin' my leg."

Ben interrupted. "I didn't do this with the intent to have him killed. I just hoped to scare him enough that he would back off."

"Then why didn't you just tell him that you did it without actually setting up the will that way?" Brent asked.

Ben started getting nervous, thinking that these questions were going to lead up to him being put in cuffs.

"The reason I actually put the will into effect was..." Ben hung his head. The only reason could be the truth. "Well, I guess that I didn't really want him to get away with my death if he actually murdered me." Ben knew he wasn't making the case of an innocent victim. "I just got so enraged that the man would not listen to reason, and the fact that he was so callous. I made a decision that I have to live with. I know what I did was wrong and now I need your help."

"You want us to set up the order of protection like we spoke about last time you were here?" Casey asked.

Ben gave them a nervous look. "I'm afraid it gets a little more complicated - actually a lot more."

Casey pulled his pad closer again. "Okay, explain."

"Well, it seems my friend Howie ran into the guy - my hitman, on his way out of the Motor Vehicle building. I'm guessing that's when the second attorney, who has an office in that building, turned on me and tipped him off." He stopped and waited to see if the detectives understood.

"Your friend Howie talk to the hitman?"

"Yeah for a second. They knew each other from school too."

"Howie knows about the will?"

Ben nodded.

"Could he have mentioned anything about the will to him?"

"No. It was a quick hello goodbye thing."

"Okay, let's go back. What's the name of the attorney?" Casey asked.

"Dan Perry." Both detectives looked at each other oddly. "You know Perry?" Ben asked.

"Oh yeah, we know him. He's the sleaziest attorney around - love to put him away," Brent said.

"Now before we go on, who did you pick to kill Dracken, and how do you know he would actually go through with a murder?" asked Casey.

"The guy's name is Luke Stafford, and if you knew him, you'd know he'd have no problem killing someone."

The two detectives jerked with surprise. "Luke Stafford?" they said in unison. Casey rose and started pacing behind his desk while Brent just shook his head.

"You picked one of the most violent men we know. We would do anything to put him away too," Casey said, sitting on the edge of his desk. "You must know him well enough to know that he would commit a murder; how do you know him?" Casey asked curiously.

"I went to high school with him and heard over the years about his run-ins with the law."

Detective Brent had been sitting quietly while Casey and Ben conversed. He finally stood as Casey returned to his seat.

"Let me see if I can sum this all up. You kill Dracken's daughter. Dracken, one of the country's most notorious villains threatens to kill you. You go to Dan Perry, one of the areas sleaziest attorneys, and have him write a will to have Dracken killed by Luke Stafford, one of the area's scariest criminals. How am I doin so far?" he asked.

"That's right," Ben said sheepishly.

"Now... you think that Perry told Luke about the will..." Brent paused.

As they sat in silence, Casey's eyes opened wide. "No matter how you die, we're going to think it was Dracken. So Luke can whack you and collect... no wait. He has to kill Dracken first, then collect the money."

"And Perry takes a cut," Ben added.

Brent shook his head. "You're either the most unlucky bastard I've ever met or extremely stupid," he said as he chuckled.

"I think it's a little of both," Ben replied.

Casey sat, tapping the eraser end of a pencil on the desk. Ben could see he was in deep thought.

"Do you have a question?"

"Yeah, why can't you just go back to Perry and kill the rider? Let him know that you found out that he told Luke. By the way, how do know that Perry told Luke?"

"Perry is out of the country for three weeks and can't be contacted. I tried, but the office is closed; I mean there's nobody there. As for how I know he told Luke, I have a friend who works with him. I really don't want to bring this person into this whole mess, okay?" Ben started to get nervous. "Please, I don't want this person involved in any way. She's a good friend and has no part in this whole thing." He pleaded.

"We can't promise anything but we'll be careful. What's her name?" Casey asked.

"Connie Douglas...you know, there's really no reason to contact her..."

Brent interrupted. "We understand Ben; we'll only speak to her if we have to."

Ben started getting itchy in his seat and stood up. "Okay, look, I've explained everything. Now I need to know, can you help me and, more importantly, am I in trouble?"

"Ben, relax...sit, sit. What you did isn't illegal if no one knows about it," Casey said with a wink. "Of course we'll do everything in our power to see that you're safe."

"Did Connie hear Dan Perry tell Luke to kill you? I mean how does she know that he's after you?" questioned Brent.

"She listened in on a phone conversation. They kinda talked in code, but the gist of it was to take care of it. Oh...I almost forgot, Luke is taking some time off to go hunting by himself up in the woods somewhere. He's leaving tonight. Connie told me that he never goes alone, so I'm figuring that maybe he's going to try something this weekend. Maybe he never really goes away and tries to use it as an alibi."

"Yeah, that's a possibility," Casey said as looked over his notes. "Ben, why don't you give us a few minutes to discuss how we're going to handle this. Wait here; we'll just be in the office over there," he said, motioning toward a corner office with drawn vertical blinds.

"Okay, I'll be right here."

As the two detectives entered the office, he could see a name on the door and the person's title underneath, but he was too far away to read it. He thought for a moment of just sliding a little closer to get the letters into focus but decided that he would most likely find out soon enough whose office it was.

Ben sat for more than ten minutes; he could hear the muffled conversation from behind the closed door. He noticed that the fingers of one of the men inside had parted the blinds. A pair of eyes peered out at him. Another five minutes past and Ben was growing weary.

"C'mon guys, what's taking so long?" Just then the door opened and the detectives emerged.

"Okay Ben, we discussed this with our boss, and he agrees that we should take this as a serious threat. We want you to stay here while we pay a visit to Luke's work and have a talk with him."

Ben was silent for a moment. "If you tell him you know what's going on, he'll know that someone working with him turned him in. If he figures it's Connie, she'll be in danger." He had a look of anguish. "Isn't there any other way?"

"Don't worry, Ben, we've discussed that and we're going to make it look like Dan Perry gave it away. We don't really care what happens to him," Casey said, gathering his things. "The only way that Luke is going to give up is by realizing that we know what he's up to."

Brent, who had gone to grab his keys, returned. "Hey Ben, Casey said you've got a wife and what? Two kids? Where are they now?"

"They're at my friends. We moved them last night."

"Okay, good. Call them and tell them not to leave. Write down the address for me, and if they see a strange car outside in the next fifteen minutes, it's one of ours."

"Okay. Do you want the place where Luke works?"

"We've got that already," Casey said.

"I'm getting a bad feeling about this, guys. What are you going to say to him?" Ben asked.

"We're just going to tell him that we know that he's about to do something that will land him in jail forever. We're not going to mention your name. He'll get the idea. You see Ben, Luke is a very intelligent criminal. He'll plan everything down to the last detail, but if he knows that we're on to him, he won't continue on," Casey said.

"All we really have to tell him is that the money that he's expecting to collect is no longer there. That should do it...oh and by the way, close that offshore account as soon as you can. We'll forget that we ever heard about it. This way you haven't done anything illegal, okay?" Brent said with a big smile.

"We want you to stay here 'til we're back just to make sure nothing happens to you. You can wait in that office right there," Casey said, pointing towards a closed door. "There's a TV you can watch and there's a phone if you need to make calls."

Ben had taken two steps into the office when he heard Casey call from down the hall. "Oh and Ben, I probably don't have to tell you this, but don't call your friend at the junkyard."

"Right," Ben replied.

Claire sat upright on the couch in Howie's living room, her knees pulled in close to her chest. A small wastebasket half full with tissues sat next to her. She kept her puffy eyes hidden and muffled her sniffles from the children who lay on their stomachs, chins on elbows, watching a cartoon video.

Howie argued on the phone with a client, his voice echoing against the cathedral ceiling from his balcony office, which overlooked the living room.

"Everything okay?" she called up to him.

Howie leaned over the balcony. "Oh yeah, that's an everyday event with that guy. No big deal."

"Howie, what's taking him so long?"

Howie wound his way down the wrought iron spiral staircase into the kitchen, which was directly below the balcony. Coming up behind her on the couch, he placed his hands on her shoulders.

"It'll all work out. Nothing bad ever sticks to Ben."

"Hope you're right. I'm just so nervous. I jump every time the phone rings."

"He'll call."

"I keep saying to myself that we'll get through this. Then I get to thinking about what I have to look forward to after this – a move to South Dakota." She began to cry.

"Still haven't warmed up to the idea of being in the middle of nowhere, huh? Can't blame you for that, but that's between you and him. I could never do it," he said, walking back to the kitchen.

Claire looked surprised. "Thought you were on his side with this move."

Howie opened his mouth to answer just as the phone rang. They looked at each other for a second before Howie grabbed it.

"Hello?" He nodded to Claire that it was Ben.

Claire stood with her hands over her mouth, her body rigid, afraid to hear what Ben was telling him.

"Okay Howie, listen. First, you may see a car outside shortly. It's friendly. Don't mention it to Claire though. Our friends are going to see our other friend at his place to let him know that there is no ice cream."

Howie took the phone away from his ear and with a puzzled look stared at it for a moment. He covered the mouthpiece and turned to Claire.

"Ben's trying to talk in code in case the phone's tapped, but I think he's been watching too many episodes of M*A*S*H*."

"What's he saying?" she asked, reaching her hand out for the phone. Howie put his finger up for her to wait.

"So you think our friends are going to help you?" Howie asked.

"They're going to do whatever they can. We'll see," Ben replied.

Claire stamped her foot on the floor, again reaching for the phone.

"Okay, here talk to Claire before she lays an egg." Howie passed her the phone and whispered, "Don't say anything to Ben about what's going on, just listen."

"Okay, okay," she said, bringing the phone to her ear slowly. "Hi honey."

"Hi Claire. Everything's going to be fine. I'll see you later, okay. Kids okay?"

"Yeah, they're fine."

"Good, I'll call you later. I'm probably going to be here a while."

"Can't you talk for a minute?" She saw Howie shaking his head as he pulled the phone from her.

"Okay...bye," she said into the receiver which was already a foot from her mouth.

"Okay Ben, we'll talk to you later," Howie said, turning back to Claire. "I know you probably don't feel much better, but we don't know who's listening so we have to be quick."

She nodded her head and sat on the floor next to the children. Howie knew there was nothing more he could say to console her. Ascending the stairs, he stopped and watched her draw solace from gently caressing Michael's hair.

"I'll be upstairs if you need me."

Ben waited for over an hour watching TV and perusing police magazines, going over in his mind the scenarios that could follow once Luke found out that they were on to him. Although confident that the detectives would not expose Connie, the thought remained that Luke would connect her. The best-case scenario would be that she would lose her job. Ben didn't want to think about the worst case.

Filling his coffee cup outside the office, Ben's mind never left Luke. It didn't take him long to realize that there was another potential problem.

If Luke is spiteful enough, he could contact Dracken and tell him the will is off. I would never know if he did it and ... damn; I'm back to square one.

Ben sat behind the desk, deep in thought as the two detectives opened the door. He jumped to his feet, startled by their abrupt entry.

Brent threw his keys and radio on the table. "Well Ben, we have a problem. Seems Luke left a little early for his upstate cabin and nobody knows where it is. One of his coworkers did go with him once but they drove up at night. Unfortunately, he has no idea where it's at."

"We have to try to track down his other buddies and try other means in order to find him. We have our people checking if he owns the property. Maybe we can track him that way," Casey said.

"What happened with Connie?"

"We questioned her about his whereabouts just the same as his other coworkers. Didn't give anything away," Brent said.

"I'm glad to hear that, but now what do I do?" Ben asked.

"You're not going to like this, but the only way we can protect you and your family is to move all of you to a place where he can't find you," Casey said.

"You mean like a safe house?"

"Exactly," Casey replied.

"And my family?"

"They're going with you. They're at your friend's place you said, right?"

"Well yeah, but..."

Brent handed Ben the phone. "Call her; tell her to pack what's there and be ready to leave when we get there."

Ben, now alone again in the office, stared at the phone. Another possible scenario unaccounted for. Luke leaving early hadn't occurred to him. Ben's small slip left Claire open for a major letdown – the possibility of not being able to return home for days. He reluctantly reached for the phone but couldn't make the call, opting to tell Claire face to face instead.

Howie peered through the living room verticals and watched as a dark blue sedan carrying the two detectives along with Ben pulled into his driveway.

Ben waited in the back seat, sandwiched between the two baby safety seats from his truck. Casey and Brent scanned the area, sending two uniformed officers from an awaiting car around the back of the townhouse.

Claire watched from the window in disbelief as the officers came from the back, giving the all-clear signal to the detectives, who then whisked Ben quickly into the house.

Ben introduced the two detectives as he pushed past Howie looking for Claire. The consoling open-armed greeting that he had expected wasn't there. Claire sat on the living room floor holding the children who, upon seeing Ben, tried to break free. Claire seemed intent on keeping them from him but they wiggled free, running and wrapping their tiny arms around Ben's legs.

"What happened now?" Claire asked without taking her eyes off the floor.

"Why don't we go where we can talk."

Ben turned to Howie, who was being filled in on the situation by the detectives. Howie motioned for Ben to take Claire into the back bedroom.

"Okay you two. I want you to play with Uncle Howie for a

few minutes," Ben said, handing off the children. "Claire, let's go into the back."

She now sat with her back to him, her knees bent and her face buried under her arms. Ben reached down, pulling gently at her elbow.

"C'mon."

She jerked away and rose slowly, walking past the detectives without acknowledging their presence. Ben followed and closed the door.

"You guys want something to drink?" Howie asked.

"No, we're not going to be here long," Casey said, looking back towards the bedroom. "In fact, let's start packing their things. Should've been done already but he didn't want to tell her over the..."

Claire's raised voice stopped his sentence.

"Knew this would get ugly," Howie said as Ben's and Claire's voices grew louder.

Casey wandered the living room, picking up toys as Brent attempted to fold up the playpen. They stopped just for a moment as Ben opened the bedroom door.

"Claire, I am sorry but there is no other way. We have to go."

She didn't follow immediately. Ben leaned against the kitchen cabinets, his fist clenched.

"Ben, ya can't get mad at her," Howie said, still holding the children, who looked confused, in his arms.

"I'm not mad at her. This whole thing is Dracken's fault. You know Howie, after they find Luke, I might just kill Dracken myself. It might be the only way."

"We all clear?" Casey said into his radio as the two cars neared Ben's street.

"Yeah, you're good to go," the voice replied.

Brent turned to Ben in the back seat. "We have two more men at your house - plainclothes. They've checked the area."

Ben looked out the rear window at the car following. He could just make out Claire and the children in the back seat.

"Left here...half way down on the left. Right where that blue van is," Ben said, leaning between the front seats.

"That van is us. We figured it would be easier to haul your kid's stuff in it," Casey said.

"Good idea. Have them back the van into the garage. That way no one will see what's going on. Most of the neighbors are at work anyway."

Ben pushed the button on the automatic garage door opener, which he had taken from his truck. The van's reverse alarm beeped as it rolled backwards, disappearing into the garage. The two cars followed up the driveway next to each other, giving them more privacy from the neighbors than the open street would have.

"Do me a favor and get the uniformed guys into the house right away. I'll get the kids out of their seats," Ben said.

"Officer, take Mr. Pearce inside. We'll get the kids. Our job is to keep you out of sight. You shouldn't even be here, but we figured your wife...just go on in," Casey said.

With everyone inside, Brent pushed the button and closed the garage door. He opened the door to the house, slamming one of the officers in the back.

"Too many people in here," he said, making his way through the kitchen. Claire sat on the sofa trying to calm the children, who were now wailing in the midst of the confusion.

"You two guys wait in the garage and you two wait outside. Cover the back and front," Casey said from the couch, where he tried to help quiet the children.

Ben pulled their suitcases out of the closet. He dropped one to the floor in the children's room and threw the other across the hall. He spun around the room, not knowing where to start. Taking a deep breath, he leaned against the wall, which was covered in cartoon decals.

How lucky are my kids. Not even four years old and already heading for their first safehouse.

Feeling disgusted with himself, Ben went to the living room. The children's crying had calmed to a whimper. Claire had just put a tape into the VCR. Ben knelt down in front of them.

"I want you two to stay in here with these nice men and watch the TV, okay? Mommy and I will be inside."

They nodded their heads, already mesmerized by the dancing dinosaur.

Within half an hour, the van was packed and ready to carry them to their unknown destination. The children were strapped back into their seats. Claire climbed in-between. A fourth car pulled in front of the house, ready to escort them. Ben would travel in the van, which had no windows in the back.

He watched out the living room window as Claire and his babies pulled away. He gave a halfhearted wave, but she couldn't see him – and if she could, she probably wouldn't have waved back.

"Let me just take one more look around to see if we missed anything."

"We can always send someone back if you left something Ben," Brent said.

"I'll do it quick." He went from room to room. The house, once spotless and well kept, now resembled the scene of a looting. Clothes spilt over ransacked drawers. Children's toys scattered.

"What a nightmare," Ben said, leading the detectives towards the garage.

Ben sat on a small seat in the back of the van. Not more than twenty seconds into the ride, Ben had to ask the question that had been on his mind for hours.

"Okay, now tell me where we're going."

"Does it really matter? Better that you don't even know what town you're in," Casey said.

"I'm not concerned with the town. I'm concerned with what kind of a place it is. It's not like you see on TV – all seedy and grimy."

"No, no," Casey replied. "We do have places like that, but we use those for hiding drug informants and the like. You're going to be staying in a hotel that we use for cases like this. You'll be comfortable... well, as comfortable as you can be not being in your own home. Only problem is, the hotel is temporary. We're going to move you again if we cant find Luke by tomorrow."

"Oh no," Ben said loudly, angry that he hadn't been told before. "Where do we go then?"

"To an actual house. But a nice place," Brent said. "If you're lucky, we'll find him before then and you can go back home."

"Great, just great, can't wait to tell her that we're moving again. This just gets better and better."

"Sorry, but if you want to be safe..."

"Don't worry about – hey, I never asked: are you going to arrest him?"

"No, we really have nothing to arrest him for. He hasn't done anything wrong. Soon as we tell him we know what's up, he'll no longer be interested in committing that crime," Casey said.

Ben watched through the windshield, now spotted with light rain, trying to figure out where they were heading, but along the way he lost interest. Finding a new plan to fend off Dracken once again consumed him. His mind raced to come up with a new idea, but that kept leading him to remember how well his last plan had worked. Ben was now mentally exhausted, and he was rapidly approaching a breakdown, when a smile came to his face.

Uncle. I give up, Dracken. You win.

Even though the plan to move was already in place, Ben didn't want to give Dracken the satisfaction of thinking he caused him to flee but the decision was made. The instant they were back home, he would pack his family and head for the safety of the wide-open space of South Dakota. Nothing was worth the hell that he was enduring here.

A small speed bump jostled the van, snapping Ben back to earth. He wiped a single tear from his eye as the front entrance of the hotel appeared dead ahead. A large sign reading The Paramount Hotel adorned the front of the partially ivy-covered brick building.

"Looks like a decent place, but I gotta say I never heard of it before," Ben said.

"It's a converted office building, believe it or not. They even use it as a time share," Casey said.

"We're going to take you around the back entrance. I want you to duck down a bit – cover your face as we drive through the parking lot," Brent said.

Casey radioed to the other officers to be ready at the back door. They replied that all was safe and they were ready.

"Here Ben. Put these shades on and this cap. Just walk normally and don't take your eyes off the floor. Just look down," Brent said.

They walked him through the door and up the stairs to the third floor. Casey knocked; a plainclothes officer opened the door.

"You two know where to go," he said to the officers who had delivered Claire.

Ben walked to Claire, who was sitting on the bed rocking the children, trying to get them interested in the TV.

"Hi, how are they?" Ben asked.

"They want to run all over."

Ben knelt down in front of them. He stroked the children's faces and attempted the same with Claire but she pulled away. He leaned and looked past her at the detectives who stood side by side just inside the doorway.

"Maybe you could give us..."

"Oh yeah, of course," Casey said bumping into Brent as they both scrambled to exit. "We'll go down and start bringing your things up. There'll be an officer outside while we're gone."

Ben stood up and looked around for a subject to break the ice and get Claire talking.

"Nice place. I like the color of the room. You like this yellow don't you? It's a nice setup," he said, pointing toward the Corian counter, which separated the kitchenette from the bedroom. Ben moved the vertical blinds away from a set of sliding glass doors that led to a small balcony.

"Look we have a view of a golf course." He pulled the string to slide the blinds open.

"No, don't," Claire yelled. "They said to stay away from the windows and not to open anything.

"Right, I forgot."

"Let's get set up here. The bag is over there," she said.

Ben reached into the bag and pulled out a box with small plastic objects. He knelt down over an electric outlet. Claire set the children down on the bed. She lay a small blanket over them and walked to the sliding glass doors, taking the vertical blind cord in her hand.

A loud rap on the door gave them both a start. "It's Casey," the detective said, unlocking the door and pushing his way in carrying two suitcases. Brent followed with the playpen. Both had a puzzled look, seeing Ben on his knees and Claire by the doors.

"What are you doing?" Casey asked.

"I guess you don't have small children, do you?" Claire asked. "We're child-proofing the room. You know – covering the outlets, tying up the cords so they don't hang themselves."

"I see. Okay, we're going to leave you guys alone for a while so we can try and find Luke. A few rules to follow. Stay away from the windows. If you need anything, you ask the officer outside. Food, newspaper, whatever, you ask him, okay?" Brent said.

Ben and Claire nodded.

"Ben, only call your clients if it's important, and don't tell them where you are. I've already taken everything out of here that has the phone number on it so you can't give it out by accident," Casey said.

"Claire, call your neighbors and tell them you'll be away for a couple days. Tell them that you had a stalker and the police are trying to find him. Also that there may be unmarked cars around your house. Tell them as little as possible – just be brief," Brent said.

"Any questions?" Casey asked.

Ben and Claire both shook their heads even though they hadn't had enough time to digest all the information thrown at them.

"How do I contact you?" Ben asked.

"Here's my cell number, but only call if it's important," Casey said, handing him a card.

"Now remember, be ready to move tomorrow if we don't find him."

Claire spun towards the detective. "What do you mean move tomorrow?"

Both men looked at Ben.

"No I didn't have a chance to tell her."

Claire folded her arms and leered at Ben, who hung his head and backed away like a cowering dog.

"That's our cue. Ben we'll be back tonight to talk to you about a few things," Brent said.

"That's if she don't kill him," Casey muttered to Brent as they made their way to the door.

Chapter Ten

As evening approached, Ben grew impatient waiting for the detectives to return. He was sure that they would take him out to talk to him rather than talk in front of Claire, who was now only speaking when necessary. Being held in a room with two young children for hours was bad enough, but to have to endure a woman's scorn in such close quarters was nerve racking.

Finally, a knock came at the door. Ben rushed to it. "Who is it?"

"Casey."

Ben slid the chain off and swung the door open. Casey and Brent walked in.

"Nothing on Luke yet; he just disappeared," Brent said. "How was your day here?" he asked Claire.

"You ever been cooped up with two kids for a long period of time? The videos only go so far. Why can't I take them out for a while? No one's after me," she said angrily.

"Maybe we can get you out into the hallway for a while after. We can't have anyone see you who could associate you with Ben. The place we're taking you tomorrow has more room to move around, but you'll still be inside," Brent said.

"You made all your calls? Your neighbors and your family?" Casey asked.

"Yeah, I called everyone and told them we would be away for a couple days. My parents are a little upset cause I couldn't explain too much," Ben said.

"Okay... Ben, why don't you come with us," Casey said, then turning to Claire. "We're going to be just down the hall in a conference room. If you need anything, just ask the officer."

Claire glanced at her watch. An hour had past. The music from the cartoon videos echoed in her head as the same tape played for the tenth time. Having no more patience for reading, she searched through one of the bags and pulled out a portable stereo with headphones. After putting them on and adjusting the volume, she realized that she couldn't just stand there listening to music. She tried lying down but she got sleepy.

You know, they said if there was anything I wanted. Let's see how good a hotel this is.

Claire undid the chain on the door. The officer outside, who was dressed as hotel security, walked toward the door as she opened it.

"Hello Mrs. Pearce."

"Hi, listen, I'm about to lose it in here. I need something to relieve stress. Can I get the hotel to bring up a treadmill to walk on?"

The officer looked puzzled. "I don't know but I'll find out."

Within ten minutes, there came a knock on the door.

"Mrs. Pearce?"

She opened the door, allowing the officer to squeeze by her, wheeling in a fold-up treadmill.

"I really didn't think this was going to happen, but here it is."

Claire pulled down the tread section while the officer plugged it in.

"This is great. Thank you."

"If there's anything else just holler."

Claire poked her head out the door for a glimmer of freedom.

"Where are they?"

"Just down the hall there. Sorry I can't tell you how long they're going to be."

"Yeah, that's okay. At least I have something to do for a while."

Claire hopped on the treadmill and began walking.

Half an hour had past. Sweat poured from her body, soaking her jeans. Unfortunately, in their haste to pack, workout clothes hadn't been a priority. Looking at her watch, she realized that dinnertime was near and the children would be getting hungry. Bringing the machine to a halt, she toweled herself and walked to the kitchen area. She emptied the food bags that an officer had delivered earlier, rousing the curiosity of the children.

"You want to help Mommy make dinner?"

"Yeah," they both replied.

The sound of the television prevented them from hearing Ben come in.

"Claire?" he called.

"We're in here," she said, sending the children scampering around the counter into his arms.

"You're alone?"

"Yep."

Claire froze for an instant upon seeing Ben's face. Resembling a corpse, his eyes were set deep in their sockets, his skin pale white.

"Ben...have you been crying? What happened?" She began to panic. "What's going on, Ben?" she yelled.

"I'm okay. Everything's fine." He gestured toward the children whom he still held tight. "Why don't you two sit and watch the TV."

Ben took Claire's hand and led her to the other side of the bed.

"There were two FBI guys here. They wanted to know everything I could tell them about Dracken."

"Dracken? Shouldn't they be worrying more about Luke first?"

"They don't care about Luke. That's the detectives' problem. They've been trying to get Dracken for so long, they were hoping I could maybe give them something."

Claire shook her head slowly. "There's something you're not telling me. You look like you've seen a ghost."

"Well, I knew Dracken was dangerous, but they told me things that if I had known before, I never would have gone to his office."

"Things like what?"

"Doesn't matter." Ben stood up. "Claire, the second they find Luke, we're moving. I mean we're only taking what we need. Everything else can come later."

Claire's heart sank. She had always thought deep down that Ben, knowing her feelings on the move, would change his mind. Now she realized it was a necessity.

"Whatever you think is best," she said, walking back to the kitchen.

Claire pushed a can onto the electric opener and pulled the handle, turning it on. As she watched the spinning can, questions began to pop into her mind.

"Ben? What exactly did you tell the FBI about Dracken?"

"Not much. I really didn't have any info that could help them."

"It took that long for you to tell them that you don't know anything about him?" She watched from across the kitchen counter as he pulled a tee shirt over his head.

"Well they made me go over everything that he said and pretty much every step that I took in his office," Ben said quickly, not making eye contact with her. "You know there's a million dollar reward for information that puts Dracken away?"

"Yeah, and what's that got to do with you...ya know Ben, when you walked in here, you looked like hell. Now you just look guilty. You know I can tell when something's not right."

"Well, yeah, there is something. I guess I was putting it off as long as I could. They're moving us tonight." He cringed waiting for her response.

She stopped spooning sauce out of a can and placed it on the counter. "What time?" she asked with a deep sigh.

"Probably around ten."

"This morning if you told me that, I would've lost it. Now it gives me something to look forward to. Some fresh air."

"Don't get too excited. It's pouring out and it's not supposed to stop."

"Is it? Had that damn kids' tape on all day. I have no idea what's going on outside. I'm still looking forward to anything but here."

Claire took a moment while washing the dishes to watch as Ben sat in front of the children. He read to them from a red book with a white rabbit on the cover. To her surprise, the children were already nodding off, even though they hadn't used much energy during the day.

Without missing a line, Ben picked them up and placed them carefully into the playpen. As they curled up, both clutching a bear, Ben closed the book, but remained knelt over the mesh wall. He stood up and walked toward the bathroom, but Claire intercepted him.

"See? You're crying again," she said.

"I'm just upset for what I put everyone through, that's all."

Claire watched with a suspicious eye as he closed the door to the bathroom.

Ben sat with Claire on the bed, trying to come up with light conversation as they watched TV. She was restless and her mood was anything but happy.

Casey tapped on the door. "Ben, it's us."

Ben let the detectives in. Claire gave a quick wave. Brent motioned for her to come to the doorway, away from the children.

"Nothing on Luke yet, but he'll turn up - could be near your house or office," Brent whispered to Ben.

"You don't have to whisper," Claire said. "They have to get up anyway if we're going to leave."

"No not yet. This is how we're going to do this. Ben will come with me in the van. Two other cars will escort us. Once we're safely at the new place, we'll call for you and the kids. You'll also be in a van. Detective Brent will accompany you," Casey said.

Another officer pushed the door open slowly. Brent handed him Ben's suitcase and a duffel bag, which had never been opened.

"Okay, ready Ben?" Casey asked. "We'll wait in the hall for a few minutes."

Leaving the door slightly ajar, Ben turned to Claire, who wrapped her arms around his neck.

"I can't wait for this to be over. At this point, I'm even looking forward to South Dakota. At least I'll know we'll all be safe."

Ben didn't answer. He just pulled her in tighter, then slowly released.

"Let me say goodbye to the kids."

He bent over the padded rail of the playpen and stroked their hair. Pulling the blanket up that Michael had kicked off, he took one last look at them.

"They're angels when they're asleep," Claire said, hugging him again.

Casey, not wanting to interrupt an intimate moment, gave a fake cough from outside the door.

"Yeah, I'm comin'."

"Okay Hon, I'll see you in a little while," Ben said, kissing her on the forehead.

He walked past Casey, who in a low voice called to Claire. "Have them up in about a half hour or so."

She nodded.

"And remember, there's always someone right out here. You're never alone."

She smiled. "Thanks detective."

She sat on the bed, attempting to occupy her mind by watching TV. Flipping through the stations proved fruitless. There was nothing to keep her mind off the fear, and now some feelings of guilt. Had she been selfish by giving Ben grief over the move out west? After seeing what her husband was now going through, she promised herself that she would not complain again and would embrace the idea of a new life.

Reaching for tissues kept her updated on the time, since the clock sat next to the tissue box on the end table. Half an hour went slowly, but the time finally came to wake the children. Reaching into the playpen, she gave Michael a slight nudge, causing him to roll over.

Wait a minute - what am I doing?

She smacked herself on the forehead, realizing that if the detective were late, she would have to put up with two very cranky, half asleep children. Waking them would wait until he actually showed up at the door.

Forty-five minutes had past. Claire, now getting worried, jumped off the bed and walked to the door. She reached for the chain. A shiver ran down her spine as she opened it. Down the hall stood two officers. Upon seeing her one of them walked towards her.

"Yes Mrs. Pearce."

"It's been a while. Can you ask detective Brent to come down here?"

"I would but he got a call and ran out. Said he'd be back in a bit."

"Got a call? What kind of call? He's supposed to take us out of here now."

"I'm sorry. I just know what he told me. Soon as he's back, I'm sure he'll come get you," he said, guiding her back into the room.

Claire now felt very alone. Knowing that detective Brent was nearby had given her some comfort - a sense of security.

She switched off the lamp and sat at the edge of the bed. The glow from the television illuminated her shaking silhouette. She felt something was wrong. Wanting to talk to someone, she picked up the phone but didn't know whom to call. She realized that she had friends who were girls but no real girlfriends. Ben and the children were her whole life. At least there was Howie. She dialed his number.

"Hello," Howie said loudly.

"Hi Howie, it's Claire."

"Can't talk right now. I'll have to call you back," he said, sounding distressed.

"I don't know the number here."

"Claire, I gotta go. See you in a little bit."

She paused for a moment, then stood straight up. "What do you mean, you'll see me in a bit?"

"I meant call me back...in like an hour. I gotta go."

He hung up the phone, but not before Claire heard the voices of men in the background – one of them sounding familiar.

Claire lay under the covers, trembling and cold, the life having run out of her after the short conversation with Howie. She waited. Every car door that slammed outside caused another shot of adrenaline.

Then came the knock at the door.

She breathed rapidly through her mouth, her nose stuffed from crying. Sitting up, she sniffed in deeply, causing her to choke on the phlegm. She coughed all the way to the door, covering her mouth with a tissue as she slid back the chain. She opened the door a crack, praying that detective Brent would be there asking her if she was ready to go. As her tear-soaked eyes focused, her nightmare was coming true. Howie stood, his head hung. Brent and another man, both soaked to the bone, stood behind.

"Claire, there's been an accident," Howie said.

She stood frozen, attempting to speak, but her mouth had become instantly parched. Putting her hand on Howie's chest, she mouthed the words. "Is he...is he?"

He looked away and with a faint sniffle, nodded his head. She turned and took one step before falling to her knees. In an instant, her whole life passed before her, as if she herself had died. Flashes of their courtship, their wedding and the birth of the children played like a movie in her mind. Why did this have to happen to the perfect husband and father?

Howie knelt down next to her, trying to make sense of her sentences as she spoke incoherently between sobs. Placing one hand on her back and taking her by the elbow with the other, he coaxed her to stand. She jerked away. "Leave me alone!"

"C'mon Claire, you have to get up," he said more sternly, pulling on her arm.

As she gained composure, she stood, but still slightly hunched over. Howie led her toward the bed. "I'll get you some water," he said, making sure that she sat.

He ran water into the glass only to drop it into the sink as Claire's voice startled him. He turned to find her confronting Brent, who backed away. In two steps, Howie had her by the shoulders from behind.

"You were supposed to protect him," she screamed.

"Claire, it was a car accident," Brent tried to explain, as Claire became so uncontrollable that Howie had a hard time handling her.

"No Howie, he said everything was going to be all right. He said Ben would be safe. I want to see him." She tried to push past him.

Brent nodded to the other man who accompanied him. The gentleman opened a black bag and drew a syringe.

Their curiosity piqued, the two officers who stood guard outside walked toward the room as Claire's screams grew louder. The commotion inside intensified as Claire pleaded. The two officers looked at each other, the whites of their eyes shined as they opened wide with Claire's final shriek. Then silence as the doctor removed the needle from her arm.

"She'll come around in about an hour," the doctor said loudly over the now screaming children.

Howie picked them up and rocked them. "Shhh, shhh, shhh. You guys have to go back to sleep."

He trembled as he saw Ben in Michael's eyes, bringing tears to his own. "God, how do we tell them their father's never coming back?"

Sarah kept squirming, trying to see her mother. Howie placed them back in the playpen where they had no view of her. Michael yawned and lay down, Sarah followed. Brent joined Howie in leaning over the playpen, waiting for the children to fall asleep.

"Maybe you better call his parents now," Brent whispered.

"Yeah, I guess while she's out it'll be easier. Easier than what, I don't know."

Sliding Claire's limp body over, Howie noticed the small rivers of mascara that were already beginning to cake on her face. With a wet tissue, he carefully wiped her face clean. Sitting on the edge of the bed, he fingered through his wallet for Ben's parents' number and dialed the phone.

An hour later Claire began to toss and turn as she awoke from the injection. Her eyes opened but her sight blurred as she tried to focus on the figure sitting on the bed.

"Try to stay calm now, Claire," Howie said. "We're alone...except for the kids."

She tried to sit up but fell back. He knelt next to her, putting his hand on her back, helping her upright. "Take this." He handed her a glass of water. She sipped it while trying to focus on the television. She looked at Howie, handed the glass back, and began to cry.

"It really isn't a dream, is it?"

He stood up. "No, Claire, its not."

She fumbled for words, finally throwing her hands in the air and smacking them down on her thighs in frustration. "He's gone. He's really gone." As she cried, she grabbed a pillow and pulled it in tight to her chest, rolling on her side in a fetal position.

"What am I gonna do, Howie?" she mumbled into the pillow. "Can't believe he's really gone."

Howie needed to act fast to keep her calm. Brent and the doctor were near and if Claire were to go into another fit, they would have to sedate her again.

"You have to stay calm. Want me to bring the kids to the bed?"

"Okay...wait...no don't, don't. I don't think I can handle them asking where Daddy is."

She pulled the cover off her legs and swung them off the edge of the bed while reaching for the phone. "How do I tell his parents?"

"I already called. They'll be on the first plane here." He choked up. "Hardest thing I ever had to do. I told them that you were sedated and that you would call as soon as you could."

Claire sighed in relief, laying the phone in her lap. "I still have to call. What do I say? I don't think I can do more than cry when...when I hear his mother's voice." Tears streamed down her cheeks again.

"Why don't you wait 'til you talk to the detective? Maybe then you can give them some more details. I couldn't tell them much."

"Who'd you talk to?" she asked quietly.

"First to Wes, then Betty."

Claire picked up the receiver but held the button down until she could think of the right words. Dialing slowly, she psyched herself to remain composed, but knew that that was unlikely. As the phone rang, the suspense of who would answer grew along with the fear that maybe they had left the house already. Her hand shook as the phone rang for the fifth time.

"Hello?" the out-of-breath voice said.

Claire paused a moment. "Hi Dad."

"Hi sweetheart...are you all right?" Ben's father, Wes, asked. His deep voice and slow speaking gave Claire comfort. She now longed to be in his presence, for his manner was that of the true patriarchal figure.

"I got nervous that you had already left. I really needed to speak to someone out there," Claire said, holding back the tears.

"You hang in. We're runnin' around packin' and we'll be there soon as possible. Claire...what happened? Howie didn't say much but there was an accident." His voice cracked. "Wait a minute," he said, laying the phone down. She could hear him blowing his nose in the background.

Howie watched as Claire waited, her tears falling more frequently now in anticipation of speaking with Ben's mother. Feeling that maybe she wanted more privacy during the remainder of the call, Howie motioned that he would be outside. She nodded.

"Hi honey, I'm back. Sorry 'bout that."

"That's okay, Dad. I don't really have any details..." She stopped abruptly upon hearing Ben's mother, Betty, call to Wes.

"Who's on the phone?"

"It's Claire, pick up the phone."

"Cl...Claire? What happened?"

"Hi Mom," she said, bursting into tears. "There was an accident." Then no words were spoken for almost a minute as the three broke down. Howie stuck his head back in the door after hearing the continuous sobbing.

"You all right?" he asked.

She nodded to him and he stepped back out.

"Mom? Dad? You still there?"

"Yes honey, we're here," Betty said.

"I'm here but I best get on with the packin', sweetheart. I'll see you tomorrow. Talk to Mother for a bit," Wes said.

"Okay Dad, see you tomorrow."

"Claire, you must stay strong for the children. Howie will take care of you 'til they get there," Betty said.

"'Til they get here? Aren't you coming?" Claire asked.

"I want to dear, but we called the doc and he said I might not make it through the trip with my heart and all. The boys will come and bring my Ben home...and you too."

Claire now realized that her move to South Dakota was coming sooner than expected. There was no easing into what she felt would be a lonely life. Now, without her husband, it would be more a solitary existence. Suddenly, she sat up straight – a revelation. Without Ben she didn't have to move. An idea that crashed as fast as it had been born. Ben lived for the day that his children would breathe clean air and play on the ranch. How could she not carry out his plan – his dream? But it was his dream.

"Claire?"

"I'm here, Mom."

Howie poked his head through the door again. She waved him in.

"Mom, let me go. I'll call you soon as I find out more. Love you."

"Okay dear."

"Is his mom okay?" Howie asked.

Claire didn't answer. Feelings of guilt for finding an upside to her husband's death plagued her as visions of his body lying in a cold morgue swept through her mind. Convincing herself that living with his family in South Dakota was the best for all concerned would not be easy, but they were the only family she had. The closest thing in New York was Howie, who now squatted down in front of her.

"You okay?" He put his hand on her shoulder and shook her gently. "Hey, you all right?"

"Yeah, yeah, I'm okay."

Howie stood up. "You want anything?"

She looked up at him, her eyes so red and swollen that she could barely see him.

"Howie, where is he? I want to see him." She pulled a tissue from the box and dabbed the corner of her eye. "Will you come with me to see him?"

"I don't know, Claire. Might not be a good idea. Why don't I bring the detective back in. He said he wanted to talk to you as soon as you would let him." He sat down next to her. "Why don't you let me get him and he'll explain what happened."

She picked the glass of water off the end table and sipped while nodding. Howie went to the door and mumbled a few words to the officer outside. Within seconds, Brent came in, letting the door slam behind him. He mouthed the word "sorry." All eyes cast on the children, who stirred a bit but didn't wake.

Claire needed Howie's help steadying herself as she attempted to stand. Not wanting to face Brent, she wobbled to the sliding glass doors and moved the blinds. A sheet of wind swept rain hit the doors as the night still stormed.

"Claire, I'm very sorry for what happened," Brent said.

"Where is he? Take me to him," she said, her voice shaking.

"Claire, it was a car accident." Brent lowered his head. "There was a fire. It had nothing to do with Luke or Dracken. Casey lost control of the van going around a bend. He skidded and flipped it."

"What are you telling me..."

"Mommy," Michael called.

"Howie, help me get them to the bed," she said.

Howie placed Sarah on the bed followed by Claire with Michael. Retrieving their stuffed animals from the playpen, she sat down with them, kissing their sleepy faces.

Claire still hadn't made eye contact with Brent. "Detective, I want to see my husband."

Brent sat on the far corner of the bed. He opened his mouth but words eluded him. Claire finally glanced his way in reassurance that she felt no animosity. The look on his face was that of true concern, causing Claire feelings of guilt for her hostility towards him.

"I'm sorry for the way I acted. You showed us more compassion than most would have. Now, please can I see my husband?"

"Claire, there was a fire...he was burned pretty bad."

She let out a moan that caused Brent to shudder, he himself now finding it hard to hold back tears. Howie, who had been able to control his emotions thus far, let tears roll down his face. He walked towards the bathroom holding his stomach while his cheeks puffed out, as he pictured his friend screaming as he burned to death.

"Claire, I am truly sorry for your loss. I only knew your husband for a short time. His main concern was for you and the children. He was a good man."

"Please take me to the accident," she said.

"Do you really want to do that? It's a pretty ugly sight," he said, hoping she would change her mind.

"No...no, I really need to be where he died. I want to see it. I want to know what happened."

"Casey failed to negotiate a sharp bend in the road. The wet pavement caused them to skid off the road and flip."

"Oh my God, I forgot to ask. How's Detective Casey?"

"Oh wow, I forgot about him too," Howie said, returning from the inside.

"He made it out and was taken to the hospital. He's got some broken bones but nothing life threatening. Claire, he tried to get Ben out, but by the time they extinguished the flames, it was too late."

She nodded. "I'm glad he's okay. Maybe we could go see him," she said to Howie.

"Sure."

Claire picked up a suitcase and placed it near the door. Howie and Brent watched with a puzzled look as she moved everything they had brought towards the door. "Howie, do me a favor and fold the playpen."

"Claire? What are you doing?" Brent asked.

"I'm getting ready to leave. Should only take a few minutes. Then we can pack the car and you can take me to the scene. Then you can take me to see my husband."

"Claire, Luke doesn't know about Ben's death yet, and it isn't safe for you to be out," Brent said.

"You can't keep me here. I want to be in my own house."

"Claire, it's really not safe. I really think you should stay," Brent said more firmly.

She had started dressing Michael on the bed. She laid him down and walked within a foot of Brent. "My husband is dead. I have two small children who tomorrow morning are going to be asking for their father." Her voice wavered. "I have family coming to stay with me and a funeral to plan. And I was thinking that maybe I'd pull out some pictures of my husband and just stare at them." Her voice got louder. "If you won't take me home, I'll call a cab. I just want the comfort of my own home. Is that too much to ask?"

Brent backed away and nodded in agreement. "We'll still provide protection for you until he's found. I'll alert the other officers to ready the vehicles."

Howie came up behind Claire as Brent left the room. Placing his hand on her shoulder, he turned her and embraced her tightly. What little mascara remained on her eyes now marked his shirt.

"Don't worry, I won't let anything happen to you, and I'll take care of the kids like they were my own. I'm going to come stay with you. You can use the help."

"Thanks Howie, Ben couldn't have asked for a better friend."

Chapter Eleven

Escorted by a small caravan of marked and unmarked police cars, Brent crept along the wet roadways. The wiper blades intermittently swung across the windshield, the rain now reduced to a mist.

"This will be your last chance to change your mind," he said.

Howie sitting in the front passenger seat, turned back towards Claire, who sat between the children's car seats. She motioned her hand forward to continue. Having no windows in the back, she had no conception of how close to the scene they were until rays of blue and red light flashed across Howie's face, then filled the van as they drew closer. She pulled herself up and kneeled between the two front seats.

The van slowed at a stop sign. An officer holding a flare and wearing an orange vest walked to the window.

"When did you reopen the road?" Brent asked.

"About half hour ago. There's not too much traffic."

"Do me a favor. Close it down for a while again, divert the traffic away." Brent motioned to the back of the van. "We want to take a look."

"No problem," the officer replied, walking away and sending orders through his radio.

Brent turned right and pulled up behind a line of parked rescue vehicles. Two fire trucks, a small command center truck, and numerous policed cars remained.

Three hundred feet away, at the end of a sharp curve, stood the wreckage of the van – now upright. The twisted burned out shell sat in the midst of three maple trees, which formed a triangle around it. Light stanchions, set up by the fireman, focused their beams on the site, illuminating the burned tree trunks.

The three sat staring at the scene. Brent finally got out and came around to Claire's door, sliding it open. "You can still change your mind."

She shook her head. "No, I have to go there." She stepped out with a hesitant look as she glanced back at the children, who remained asleep. A female officer who had awaited their arrival, hopped up inside. "Don't worry about them, I've got five of my own," she said.

"Don't worry Claire, there won't be any cars going by and there'll be officers all around. Nothing will happen," Brent reassured.

Howie popped open an umbrella and held it over her as they walked on the sidewalk, passing the first fire truck. A loud fire call blasted over the PA system of the truck, jolting everyone. Claire felt her heart skip a beat and had to stop to catch her breath.

"You okay?" Howie asked.

She nodded and continued but then stopped short as a light breeze blew from the direction of the van. The burned rubber and plastic produced an acrid, eye-tearing smell. Claire breathed deeply into a handkerchief that Brent handed her. Howie covered his mouth with his jacket collar. They proceeded on. Firemen carried rolled hoses, their faces solemn as they passed Claire.

Amidst the colored strobe lights, white flashes became more prominent as they neared the scene. Brent's face grew a look of concern. "Uh-oh," he muttered.

"What's the problem?" Howie asked.

Brent stood on tiptoes, trying to see over the squad cars. "Stay here," he said as he cut between two vehicles. He ducked under the yellow police tape, which had been attached to the rescue vehicles along the street to form a barricade.

"What's wrong?" Claire asked turning to two officers who were bringing up the rear.

"Uh-oh," Howie now repeated, making a connection with the white flashes.

Brent returned and quickly turned Claire around, walking her to the command truck. "Step up inside. You too Howie. Glad we weren't spotted."

"Spotted? What..."

"Claire, there's a ton of reporters snapping pictures. They obviously found out that Ben was in that van," Brent said.

"How could they find that out so fast?" Howie asked.

"Oh it's amazing. It's like throwing bread in the air at the beach. One second there aren't any seagulls; next there's a thousand. Most likely an officer tipped them off. They trade info sometimes. Not always helpful in a situation like this, but other times they might break a case for us."

"So you think they know about Luke – I don't get it." Claire said.

"No, but they know about Ben killing Dracken's daughter. Speculation alone that Dracken had a hand in this will make the front page," Brent said.

"Do you think he did...have something to do with this?" Claire asked.

"Doubtful. I spoke to Casey and he said he just lost control. They'll inspect everything to make sure nothing was tampered with. Right now what we have to do is keep your picture out of the papers. I gotta warn you. They will be at the house in the morning. Right now they don't know that you're here." Brent jumped down off the truck and led an officer onto the grass, giving him instructions.

"Okay ready?" Brent asked Claire. "What we're gonna do is bring the van we just came in up on the grass. You're going to walk on the other side as we move toward the scene. It'll shelter you from the cameras. When you feel you've seen enough, we'll just put you back in the van and take you home."

Walking across the muddy field proved challenging. Claire's one hand held tight to Howie's arm, the other to a white towel covering her nose from the stench. She tried to dismiss the possibility that some of what they smelled might be burned flesh.

Now a hundred feet away, the severity of the accident came into focus. Large dents in the wet grass where the van had flipped led to the spot where the van now sat, its roof crushed in over the front seats. The driver's door still hung on one hinge, exposing the melted front seat and dashboard.

Claire hadn't noticed that as they drew closer to the wreck, the frequency of the camera flashes increased as curious reporters watched and questioned the officers who guarded the perimeter.

The van pulled along side the burned shell. Claire peered inside through the driver's door, but was unable to see through to where Ben had been seated. Brent stood in her way as she walked toward the back to see the other side. He had to speak loudly for her to hear over the portable generator powering the floodlights.

"Claire, I can't let you see the other side. Its been cut wide open by the firemen. That's where...he was taken out. I can't let you see it. It's not something you really want to remember," Brent said.

Amazingly, Claire kept her composure as she inspected the sight. It was as though she wasn't really looking at what was there – more like she was communicating with Ben at the spot of his final breath.

"C'mon Claire, let's head back to the house," Howie said. He had seen enough and didn't really see what Claire could get from being there. A sight such as this could only bring nightmares.

"Detective," an officer yelled.

Brent stepped out from behind. "Shit, it's a TV camera truck. How'd they get passed? They're going live. Let's get out of here."

Michael began to cry just as Brent slid open the door. The female officer hopped down.

"Thank you," Claire said.

"They were angels. My condolences."

Claire nodded and stepped inside, immediately going to Michael to calm him. Howie stood hunched over behind her to see if he could help.

"He's okay. Go sit," she said.

Howie stepped back out, sliding the door shut and climbing into the front seat. Brent, already in the driver seat, turned to Claire. "You ready?"

"I'm ready to see my husband."

Brent and Howie looked at each other.

"Are you sure? You saw there was a fire," Brent said.

"Just take me."

The van's tires sank inches into the muddy grass as it rolled toward the street. Reporters snapped photos from twenty feet away, held there by a line of officers, one of which Brent motioned to the van.

"Listen Jim, that camera truck and any car that these guys get into may have faulty lights. You wanna do me a favor and maybe inspect 'em all real slow like?"

"Sure, no problem. I think an inspection like that could take hours." They both laughed.

"Thanks Jimmy."

Brent pulled out followed by two squad cars.

"Detective, I understand that the reporters are there because they think that Dracken is involved, but is that big a deal to them?" Claire asked.

"Anything having to do with Dracken is a big deal, especially if it might have to do with a murder. Oh and by the way, I have a car at your house already and they tell me that there are a handful of reporters there too."

"How long are they going to harass us?" Claire asked.

"I'll be issuing a release to the press during the day, right after I get the report on the van. Soon as I tell them that Dracken had nothing to do with the accident, they'll leave."

Brent pulled into the morgue parking lot. "Claire, are you sure that you want to do this? I mean it might be better for just Howie to see him."

"I'm sure."

Howie looked up at the spotlights that were mounted on poles in the parking lot. A light mist still shone across them. He opened the back door and carried Michael out while Claire handed Sarah to one of the officers. Another officer held an umbrella over Claire as they followed Brent up the concrete ramp and through the double metal doors. Brent showed his badge at the desk.

"Call downstairs for Pearce," he told the officer. He turned to Claire. "What are we going to do with the kids?"

"Howie can stay with them."

"No, I'm going in with you."

She looked relieved to be accompanied by Howie but there was still the problem of the children. Unfortunately, the morgue didn't have a playroom.

"Well, if these two fine officers would volunteer to watch them..."

"No problem, sir," one of them replied.

Brent's hard-soled shoes slapped the tiled floor, echoing down the corridor. Howie, still carrying Michael, tried desperately to contain his shaking body. They turned a corner and headed down another hallway, stopping at the elevator.

"All right, we have to go down. We'll leave the kids here and the men can take them into one of the offices over there."

Claire looked a bit leery about sending the children off with strangers, but believing the officers had been trained to handle every situation, she relented. She kissed them both and watched as the officers took them inside an office.

"Now, we'll head down. You'll be able to view him from behind glass."

"I want to see...touch him," Claire said.

Howie was amazed – she wasn't even crying now. He on the other hand was already getting queasy and would much rather see his friend's body through glass if possible.

"Claire, these images you're going to see will stay with you for life. It's going to be very disturbing," Brent assured.

They stepped into the elevator.

"Yeah, Claire, maybe you want to rethink that?" Howie asked.

"Howie, if you don't want to come in, I won't hold it against you."

"No, if this is what you need to do, I'm there."

The doors opened. The air was cooling, exacerbated by their wet clothing. Claire shivered. They walked into a room, which had a glass viewing panel. A short Asian man wearing scrubs met them.

"This is Dr. Quan. He's one of the medical examiners," Brent said.

"I'm very sorry for your loss," he said, shaking Claire's hand.

"Thank you."

"They want to see the body up close," Brent said.

"Up close through the window you mean."

"No doctor, I want to touch my husband one last time."

She could see that he was about to attempt to talk her out of it but she cut him off.

"I know it's going to be bad, but it's something I have to do."

"Okay. If that's what you want."

The doctor opened a desk drawer and took out what looked like airsickness bags and masks. He handed them to Claire. "Are you going in too?" he asked, pointing towards Brent and Howie, who nodded. He handed them each a mask, and after looking at Howie once more, handed him a bag also.

"Please put the masks on," he said, pulling his own from around his neck. "Okay, come in."

Brent followed behind as Howie and Claire walked through a door and were now on the opposite side of the glass viewing panel. This room was colder than the outside room. A large stainless steel door equipped with a refrigerator-like handle stood before them. The doctor leaned his weight backwards while pulling the handle of the heavy door.

Howie put his arm around Claire and held her close. They could feel each other shaking. "You really want to do this?"

"No, but we have to," she said.

A rush of very cold air hit them as they watched the doctor push aside the hanging plastic flaps, which covered the entrance to the dark vault. The flaps lifted and slid along the top of the white sheet covering Ben's body as the doctor wheeled the gurney out. Brent, who had been through this a thousand times, quietly pulled two metal chairs behind them.

Ben's body now lay still covered before them. The doctor stood on the opposite side, holding the end of the sheet. "You can still change your mind."

"No...I need to see him."

The doctor removed the sheet enough to uncover Ben's head. Claire gasped at the sight of his colorless face. Over his left eye, a large wound, split wide enough to expose his cracked skull, was now crusted over with blood and surrounded with a massive bruise. A black handprint, obviously from a firefighter's attempt to free him, still remained smudged on Ben's neck. Both his lips were split and his right cheek had a smaller bruise. One small clump of hair on his right side, the size of a silver dollar, had been burned.

The sight was so frightful that Claire couldn't speak; even crying was impossible for her stunned body. Howie felt his legs weaken and his stomach turn as the odor of Ben's burned flesh filled the room.

Claire reached out and ran her hand through his hair, but pulled away quickly upon feeling how cold he was.

Howie stepped back and sat in a chair. He undid the mask and opened the air sickness bag and began to gag into it.

"I'm sorry Claire," he said, his voice muffled as he spoke into the bag.

She didn't respond – she just stared at her beloved husband. Brent took Howie's place standing next to her. "Maybe we should go?" he asked.

"No, not yet," she said in a calm voice.

Brent bent over to see into her eyes. She barely knew that he was there. The shock of seeing Ben's body placed her in a trance.

Howie, now feeling less nauseated, stood again. "Hey Doc, I thought he was burned. I smell it, but..."

"His body is very badly burned, but I don't think that's what he died of. I think it was the blow to the head."

Howie tapped Brent on the shoulder. He immediately moved over.

"Claire, it's time to go."

Howie waited, but she didn't move. She stood and stared, motionless. He pulled on her arm to try and lead her away. Finally she shook her head.

"What, oh, okay. Ben sweetheart, we have to go."

She took short deep breaths. The doctor stood only feet away with a rolling oxygen tank. The reality of the situation finally began to set in and her tears started to flow. As she became more cognizant, her moans grew louder. She laid her head on Ben's chest. The moans turned into screaming. Her voice echoed in the room.

"Ben...Ben. It's not fair!"

Her shrill outcries got so loud that the men started to panic. Howie pulled her away as the doctor fought to keep the sheet over the rest of Ben's body. Brent finally pried her hands free of the sheet. As they wrestled her a few feet away, she fainted.

"Wish that'd happened a few minutes ago," Brent said. "Let's get her a gurney and take her up. It'll be easier than bringing her to, here. Damn, look at the scratch she gave me."

Once upstairs in a warmer room with a blanket over her, Claire awoke, still on the gurney. Howie sat next to her.

"What happened?"

"Well, first you screamed so loud that you almost cracked that big glass panel. My ears still hurt. Then you fainted."

"God I'm cold. How long have I been out?"

"Not long. I brought your bags in so you can change into dry clothes."

"Where are the kids?"

"Right in the next room. They're fine. They're asleep."

She tried to sit up. Howie took her arm. "Still think it was a good idea that we came here?"

"Oh Howie, he's really dead." She started crying again.

She slid down off the gurney and sobbed into his chest.

"Look, let's get home so we can get some rest. We got a real lot to do tomorrow."

He handed her a tissue. She wiped her eyes and nose.
"Okay lets go. I can make it home in these clothes."

Claire's stomach churned as they turned onto her street. She leaned forward for a better view of the street. Neighbors stood in small groups, not knowing exactly what they were waiting for, but because of the presence of the police and reporters, they lingered.

"Don't these people sleep? I mean it's one thirty in the morning," Claire said.

"It's human nature to be nosy. You should see some of the stuff I see," Brent said.

"I'm sure it's not just being nosy. The neighbors loved Ben and they probably just want to give their condolences. Too bad they had to find out about it from the reporters," Howie said.

Pulling the van over a few houses away, Brent radioed to the other officers to keep the press away, then proceeded. Claire handed him the remote for the garage door from her purse.

"My God, I think every neighbor is out here. Look, Jerry even has Holly out. God, Ben loved that dog..."

Brent's voice startled her. "Okay, same routine as before. We back into the garage so no one gets near."

He swung the van across the street and stopped. He backed into the driveway as the other officers kept the media back. It wasn't at all what Claire expected. No one mobbed the van like in the movies. There were just a few flashes as the reporters called out questions, which - with the windows closed - she couldn't make out. The only word that was discernable was the name of Dracken.

"Claire, you know, your neighbors have probably been waiting out here for a while. It's a bit chilly - maybe you want to invite them in for a minute? I know it's late, but maybe for a minute?" Brent asked, backing into the garage.

As the garage door descended, Howie ducked under and walked-half way down the driveway. With the help of the officers, he separated the neighbors away from the reporters, and led them through the narrow passageway on the side of the house to the yard. Ten neighbors and one dog waited on the concrete patio while Howie went inside to see if Claire was ready to see them.

Brent stood in the living room holding a cell phone to his ear. He motioned toward the bedroom. "She's inside making sure the kids are asleep."

"Good, I'll bring everyone in."

Howie opened the back door. "Everyone, please keep as quiet as possible so the kids don't wake up." He led them through the office and up the stairs to the living room. "Let me see where she is."

Howie pushed open the children's door, but could only see them in the glow of the nightlight. He knocked gently on Claire's bedroom door.

"Come in," she said, coming out from the bathroom, wiping her nose with a tissue.

Howie took a step to the bed and picked up a photo album off of a pile of five that Claire had already laid out. He ran his hand over the cover.

"I haven't opened them yet. Figure I'd wait 'til later when I'm alone. Maybe you want to take the one with the two of you when you were young," she said.

Having looked through that album many times, he pushed through the pile and picked it up and nodded.

"Everyone's waiting in the living room, you know," he said.

Claire drew a deep breath. "I'm ready."

She walked down the hallway in front of Howie, and into the crowded living room. One by one they approached her, hugged her and cried with her. Paul and Gail, who knew Ben the best of all the neighbors, stood holding each other in the far corner, watching as each person broke down. Claire's eyes finally met theirs. She took two slow steps toward them then rushed forward, meeting Gail in a hug.

"I'm so sorry, Claire," Gail said, as they swayed in a hug that lasted more than a minute. The only sound in the room was an occasional sniffle until Holly became impatient and let out a small "woof."

Claire eased away from Gail and looked in the direction of the dog that sat, her tail sweeping the floor. Claire knelt down and put her arms out. Jerry bent down and unhooked the leash, sending the dog scampering into Claire's arms.

"Hi Holly. I hope you know how much Ben loved you." She looked up at her tear-filled neighbor. "Ben always said that when we moved, he was going to kidnap her, that he would miss her too much to leave her behind."

Claire's words became nothing more than loud sobs as she clutched the dog. Jerry bent over and put his hand on her back while Gail joined her on the floor. Howie backed away to let the others get closer and found himself part way in the kitchen.

"That is one of the most heart wrenching sights that I have ever seen," Brent, who was seated at the kitchen table, said. "She may need a sedative later. I have something that the doc gave me that you can give her to help her relax."

Howie bent over the sink and cupped his hands, splashing water into his face.

"Yeah, let me get her inside – better yet, I'll have Gail stay and take her inside while I let everyone out. I think it's time we said goodnight here," Howie said.

Howie touched each neighbor on the shoulder. One by one they backed away, creating an opening for him to help Claire off the floor.

"Gail, why don't you take her inside."

Claire stood up still holding the dog. Jerry gave Howie a look questioning whether maybe he should leave the dog to comfort her, but Howie moved in and passed the confused pup to her owner.

Before she turned to head down the hallway, Claire looked back at her sympathetic guests and gave a slow wave, then disappeared.

Howie stood waiting for someone to make a move toward the stairs, but instead the group began whispering and pointing at the wedding picture on the end table.

"People, it's been a long day," Howie said, walking towards the front door.

One by one they shook his hand and offered any help that he needed with Claire. Brent came up behind the group and excused himself as he pushed through to the door, putting his back against it. "Please don't stop to talk to the reporters. My men will escort everyone back to their houses," he said, opening the door.

"Listen Howie, I'm going to take off too. Wanna get some sleep before I start looking for Luke again tomorrow. There'll be men outside here all night. Call me in the morning first thing and get me the flight numbers of the family coming in. We'll pick them up. We have to protect them too." Brent pulled the door shut.

Howie's vision blurred from exhaustion. He rubbed his eyes as he walked to the bedroom to relieve Gail, who was still in with Claire. He gave a slight tap and pushed open the door.

Gail, who sat with her arm around Claire, looked up and gave Howie a frown as she motioned with her head down towards Claire's lap, where tears dripped onto the open wedding album.

"Claire, I'm gonna go. Try to get some sleep," Gail said. She walked past Howie and whispered, "Everyone's bringing food over tomorrow."

"Okay thanks," he said.

Claire remained seated at the edge of the bed, staring at the wedding pictures. For the first time, Howie didn't know what to say. He flipped open the album of photos of Ben and himself that he had left on the dresser but closed it again, deciding to grieve alone.

"The kids asleep?" he asked.

"Yeah," she said with a nod.

"Claire, I don't know what to do. Do you want to be alone? Do you want to talk? I mean you really should get some sleep."

"I'm okay." She stood up and wiped her eyes. "Let me fix the guest room for you."

"No, I got it. Just try and get some rest."

She pulled the shoulder of the shirt she was wearing to her nose. "I can still smell the smoke."

Howie wrapped his arms around her as she broke down once again.

"Howie, he burned. My God, he burned. The smell on my clothes could be the smell of his skin burning."

"No it's not. It's the rubber and plastic from the van," he said quickly. He held her tight as she squirmed to rip her shirt off. "Claire you gotta calm down. It's the smell from the van burning."

For a moment, he thought that she would really need to take the sedative that the detective had gotten from the doctor. He lightened up his grip and walked her backwards a couple of steps to the bed, sitting her down.

"Look, you have to try to get some sleep. The doctor gave the detective these pills to help you sleep. I'll leave them here if you want them."

"I won't need it." She paused. "I think I'm ready to be alone now."

"Okay, I'm right down the hall if you need anything. If the kids wake and I hear them, I'll go in."

"Okay Howie."

He stepped outside the room but didn't let go of the knob for a few seconds. He pushed the door back open and reached in, picking up the photo album off the dresser. Claire gave a small smile when their eyes met. He looked at the book as a priest would cherish a Bible, then tucked it under his arm and nodded. As he pulled the door closed, a low, steady squeak came from an unoiled hinge until the final snap of the latch as it clicked into place – then silence. She was alone.

Within seconds, she had her clothes in a pile at her feet and a long robe wrapped around her. Holding her breath, she scooped up the pile, running them into the bathroom and burying them deep in the hamper.

Coming back into the room, she sprayed air freshener wildly until she could no longer hold her breath. Gasping for air and feeling a bit faint, she held onto the dresser until the feeling passed. She sniffed the air for any remnants of the fire, but there were none.

The wedding album, still open on the bed, caught her eye. She sat beside it, running her fingers over Ben's picture. She pulled the book up onto her lap. Now in the silence and solitude,

Claire stared at Ben's image, realizing that it wasn't a dream and that he was never coming back.

Oh Ben, how do I raise the children alone? What do I tell them?

She pulled the album to her face, sliding her wet cheek along the plastic sleeves.

How could you let this happen? You were always so careful. Now you're never coming back.

In the still, quiet room, she grew conscious of her pounding heart. Every beat was louder than the last. She clutched her chest and then rolled onto her stomach, crawling to the nightstand. One click of the remote solved the problem of the unbearable silence. She flipped through the channels of the small portable TV that sat on the dresser.

She put the album aside for a moment to gather the pillows together and pile them behind her. Propping herself up against them, she now sat directly across from the big oval mirror mounted behind the dresser. She dragged the album back onto her lap. She tried to keep her attention on the photos, but her eyes were continuously drawn back to her own image in the mirror.

My God, I'm alone. I'm all alone. This is the way it's going to be... forever.

Now as she weakened with exhaustion, the simple task of lifting the album became a chore. She slid it off her lap and spread the pillows back along the headboard. While sliding under the comforter, she accidentally kicked the album off the bed. She sat up, her heart racing, startled by the noise of the book hitting the floor.

She fell back into the pillows. Feeling helpless and losing the will to live, a fleeting thought of suicide came and went as she envisioned the children as orphans.

The sound of a car door slamming, just loud enough to be heard over the TV, sat her up again. She rushed to the window, parting the blinds with fingers, expecting to see Ben walking outside. Maybe they were wrong. Maybe that wasn't Ben who lay cold and stiff on the gurney. She squinted and to her disappointment only saw the silhouette of a police officer smoking a cigarette against a car. She turned, taking two steps to the bed and falling face first into the covers.

She smiled as she watched Ben running, pulling a kite for the children. They giggled as they chased him in the afternoon sun. A gentle breeze blew her hair over her face; she flipped it back and walked after them.

Ben was standing over the kite, stamping on it as she reached him. Flames engulfed the tail. He tried in vane to extinguish them, but his pants caught fire. She reached out and grabbed his arm as the fire began to fully engulf him.

"Ben, Ben," she screamed, pulling on his arm with both hands.

"Claire, wake up."

She opened her eyes, still pulling on his arm – but it was Howie's arm she tugged at.

"Claire, wake up; you're having a bad dream. Wake up," Howie said.

"Ben?" she whispered as Howie slowly came into focus through the tears.

"No Claire, it's Howie. You were having a nightmare. I could hear you from down the hall. Hope the kids didn't hear you...you want some water?"

"I saw Ben on fire."

Howie nodded. "Let me get you some water."

"God, I could even smell it."

Howie came out of the bathroom and handed her a glass.

"It was so real. He was in such pain, Howie."

"Claire, we know he was dead before he burned."

"How do we know that?" she asked.

Finding it difficult to look at her, he turned away. Her face, in the short time since Ben's death, had aged a lifetime. She could see his pitied look, and she rolled onto her side, her back facing him.

"I'll be all right...I'm just having problems believing that he's really gone. I keep thinking that he'll come walking through the door and...and the children will run to..." She buried her face in a pillow and waved for him to leave.

"I'll peek in on the kids to see if they're okay. Try to get back to sleep."

He tiptoed across the hall, praying not to hear a sound from the children's room. After listening and hearing nothing, he returned to his room, quietly closing his door. He had taken one step towards the bed when he heard Claire's door open. He intercepted her in the hall.

"I can't go back to sleep in there. I'm going to just sit in the living room and watch TV until they wake up – which should be early." She closed her robe tight as she felt a chill.

"You want me to stay with you?"

"No, no, please just try to sleep Howie. I think after that dream it may be a long time before I can sleep normally. I'm surprised that I was able to even fall asleep at all."

"Okay, but I'm right here if you need me."

Howie stood staring at the guestroom walls. This room was unlike the rest of the house, which was bathed in warm colors. This room was cold and depressing. The walls were bare with a cheap off-white paint. The decision had never been made on what to do with it. Guests usually stayed in the downstairs apartment, which doubled as a play area.

A small bed, which hardly held Howie's large body, and a nightstand were the only furniture. He switched on the clock radio just loud enough to overcome the silence, then turned off the lamp. As before, he watched the red digital numbers change one by one.

If I can fall asleep right now, I can get three hours.

After tossing for ten minutes, he threw the covers off and sat up, cradling his head in his hands. He turned the light back on and reached under the bed, pulling out the photo album. He stared at the cover and took a deep breath. Until now, he had kept his feelings inside, trying to be strong for Claire, but he had to look through the book just once – just to remember the times he had spent with Ben.

With his eyes tightly closed and facing the ceiling, he opened the cover, slowly bringing his head down to see the first page. Not having looked at the album in many years, he opened his eyes wide with delight upon seeing himself and his best friend as teenagers. As he flipped through pages, his smile melted from his face, knowing that Ben was gone and this was all that he had left of him. He slumped over the album, wiping tears away as fast as they came.

How could I have let this happen? It my fau...

He sobbed, closing the album and sliding it under the bed.He fled the room for the liquor cabinet, walking quietly past Claire who was now out cold. Dragging a bottle of Scotch into the kitchen, he searched the cabinets for a shot glass but instead found a clear plastic cup. He filled it a quarter full and raised it up to eye level, judging it to be about three shots. He gulped it down and tried to decide what the perfect amount would be. It had to be just enough to knock him out but not too much to cause a hangover.

Six oughta do it.

He poured the second round and downed it, squinting and shaking his head from the harsh taste.

Once lying back on the bed, he folded his hands behind his head on the pillow. He reached and turned out the light. A small ray of moonlight breaking through the clouds cast a ghostly image on the wall and he quickly turned the lamp back on.

He rolled onto his side and again faced the clock, waiting for the alcohol to put him out. Within ten minutes he began to feel sleepy, but instead of achieving the desired effect, he was put more into a daydream where he relived many of the good times with Ben. He smiled and cried at the same time, cherishing the memories until finally he passed out.

Howie was snoring loudly when the cordless phone that he had left on the night table rang. He sat straight up, not knowing for a second what the sound was, then felt his way around the top of the table for the phone.

"Hello," he said in a groggy voice.

"Howie, that you?"

Howie stood up, his mouth and eyes wide open; a shiver ran down his spine. "Ben?" he asked in astonishment.

"No, no. Howie, Howie listen to me. It's Wayne, Ben's brother."

"Oh jeez. God you sound just like him. My heart's racing. Where are you?"

"We're in Chicago just getting ready to board again. We'll be there in a few hours."

Howie switched on the lamp and pulled open the small drawer in the table.

"Okay, give me a sec to find a pen to write down the flight info."

"No, don't worry, we'll get a cab. Don't want you to leave Claire. How is she?"

"She's kinda in denial but I guess that's normal. I'm kinda glad she didn't hear the phone with your voice on the other end."

"Okay, listen, we gotta run. See you in a few hours."

"Okay." Howie laid the phone back on the table and fell backwards on the bed, his heart still pounding.

It's gonna be a long couple days.

Howie lay with one leg hanging off the bed when the doorbell rang. He rolled to his side and with his eyes half open looked at the clock.

Six thirty.

The doorbell rang a second time. Howie sat up rubbing his temples, hoping to alleviate a slight headache.

Well, here we go.

Just as he made it into the hallway towards the front door, the phone rang, spinning him around back towards the bedroom. He took one step for the phone when the doorbell rang once again and spun him back around. Confused and still half-asleep, he ran back to the room and answered the phone as he walked quickly to the front door.

"Hello."

"Yeah Howie, its Wayne. We're here and should be there in less than an hour."

"I thought this was you at the door – hold on."

Howie opened the door. Brent stood on the stoop with his back to the door, newspapers in hand.

"Thought you weren't going to wake up. I just stopped in to make sure everything was okay," Brent said.

"Yeah Wayne, the detective is back, so I'll see you in a bit."

Howie held the door open. "That was Ben's brother. They'll be here in a little while. They didn't want you guys to pick them up. They're takin a cab."

"That's fine. Glad they got here so fast – she's gonna need the support...she up yet?"

"No, let me go wake her."

"Guess you haven't seen any papers yet?" Brent handed him a copy of the newspaper. A small two inch square picture of the accident scene appeared in the upper corner with the headline "Dracken's revenge?"

"They must've just made the deadline getting the story in. Surprised it didn't make the full cover but it's big enough for Luke to see...this way he won't be around here. It's making all the TV news too." Brent followed Howie into the kitchen where Howie leaned over the paper on the table, scanning the full story.

"Nothing in there that we don't know, just lots of conjecture. I'm going to make a statement to the press on the van – it checked out okay. No foul play; he just skidded out on the wet surface." Brent said.

"That's some good news at least. Now these vultures will leave us alone, and like you said the story will keep Luke away from here."

Brent had the coffee maker pulled out onto the center of the counter and was opening cabinets. "Where's she keep the coffee? I think we're going to need a continuous supply – wait, I found it."

"Well, let me go in and see what's up with her. I would think she's awake with the doorbells and phones and us talking in here. She went back into the bedroom though. Last I saw her, she was on the couch here."

Howie walked down the hall, first pushing the children's door open a crack, then wider as he saw Sarah's crib empty. As he leaned into their room, a faint giggle came from Claire's bedroom. He tapped on the door and opened it.

On the bed sat the two children amidst hundreds of photos of their father. Claire sat with her back against the headboard, an album on her lap.

"How you feelin?" Howie asked

Claire just nodded.

"How long have you had them in here?"

"Most of the night - well most of whatever you want to call it - couple hours."

"The detective is here - it's in the paper already."

"I saw it on the news already." Her voice cracked and she cleared her throat. "It was one of the first stories."

"Did you sleep?" She looked at him with her swollen, bloodshot eyes and he quickly changed the subject. "Spoke to Ben's brother. They'll be here in less than an hour." Howie walked in and sat next to Michael, who held up a picture for Howie.

"Daddy."

Howie didn't know what to say; he just looked at Claire.

"I've been trying to hint to them that he's not coming back." She had to stop. She closed the album and moved to the edge of the bed, picking up Sarah. "How do you get them to understand at this age that he's... never...coming...back?" Her words tailed off into quick breathing.

"I don't know," Howie said, walking around to the side where she sat.

"Can you watch the kids while I get ready?"

"Sure, you want me to feed them?" he asked.

"I don't think you're ready to try that. Call Gail. She'll come over and do it."

"Okay."

"You know, I don't feel like taking a shower - I don't feel like doing anything right now. I just want to lay in bed with the kids."

Howie put his finger over his mouth to shush her. "You hear the bell?" He walked to the door and could hear Brent talking to someone.

"It's Gail. Great, let me take the kids out to her. You get ready - they'll be here soon."

"I'm looking forward to seeing them, but at the same time I'm dreading it. Wayne looks like Ben and I'm afraid...I'm afraid the kids might mistake him. By the way, who else is with Wayne?"

Howie gave a confused look. "You know, I didn't think to ask."

"Hey Howie," Brent yelled from down the hall. "Everything okay? You know Gail is here."

"Be right there," he called back. "All right, let me take them in."

Claire stood with her arms crossed, her hands inside the sleeves of her oversized sweatshirt. "Thanks Howie – for being here."

He stood in front of her. "I made a promise to Ben that if anything happened to him that I would see to it that you were taken care of."

She nodded and whispered, "Thank you," as she hugged him and began crying again.

"C'mon now. We got a long day ahead and you gotta get ready."

He gently eased her away and watched her close the door to the bathroom. With a child in each arm, he came into the living room. A strong smell of coffee already filled the air.

"There they are – my two buddies," Gail said.

Howie bent down, letting them go. They ran to Gail's open arms where she hugged them. She looked up at Howie. "How is she?"

"I don't really know how to answer that. I'm sure that I'll be asked that question a lot, but what do I say? She's going to be a wreck for a long time. What other way could she be?"

"Yeah, you're right but I guess its kind of a standard question in this situation. How about them?" she asked, looking down at the children.

"Hopefully, for their sake now, they won't miss him for too long...but I don't know the mind of a child."

"Howie, you want coffee?" Brent asked.

Howie walked into the kitchen and pulled out a large mug, filling it to the brim. Not able to wait for the caffeine fix, he sipped immediately, burning his lip.

"Listen Howie, I'm gonna get going. Still gotta find Luke. With all the publicity, I'm sure you're safe, but I'm going to leave a man outside and have another accompany her wherever she goes. You want me to talk to her?"

"No, I'll tell her."

Gail brought the children into the kitchen.

"Maybe you guys could go inside? I have to feed them. I don't know if they'll even eat this early and they'll never eat with you distracting them."

"That's okay, I was just leaving," Brent said.

The phone rang as Howie shook the officer's hand. "Call us if there's anything on Luke," he said turning to find the phone.

"Hello...yeah, hi Gus. Yeah, I'm sorry to say it is true, Ben's dead. I don't have time to go into details but do me a favor and tell the guys at the office that I'll be in touch with the arrangements. Oh and tell the boss I don't know how long I'll be out for, okay?"

Howie walked back into the kitchen for his coffee. "That was one of the guys from work. Saw it on TV."

Gail nodded while spooning puréed fruit from a jar into Michael's mouth.

"Gail, do me a favor. Go see if she's okay in there."

"You wanna take over the feeding?"

"I'll give it a shot."

Gail got up. Howie was about to sit when the phone rang again and a horn blew out front.

"You get the phone and I'll see what's up outside."

Howie peeked through the blinds. A taxi driver was unloading luggage from the trunk of the yellow cab.

"They're here. Shit that was fast."

He opened the door, knowing that he was about to face a difficult task. Wayne and Wes, having made it past the two remaining reporters with the help of the police, walked up the driveway. Each carried a suitcase and both wore cowboy hats and boots.

Howie set the storm door to stay open as Wayne came up the stairs, dropping his suitcase at the top. He and Howie embraced, rocking back and forth, both trying to find words to comfort the other, but neither could speak. Wayne backed up, keeping his hands on Howie's shoulders. He grabbed his bag and moved inside. He turned and watched his father remove his hat and put Howie in a bear hug.

"Howie, as far as we're concerned, you are Ben's brother. He always told us how you took care of him better than a friend ever could. For this we are forever grateful."

Howie again speechless, caught off guard by the profound words, dropped his head as Wes wiped his tears with a red bandana. Wayne still had his back to Gail, who now got her first glimpse of Wes. Rough and rugged, graying brown hair and mustache with tough weathered skin and a denim jacket – a true cowboy.

"Howdy," he said, his deep voice resonating through the house.

"Wayne, Wes, this is Gail. She lives next door. Gail, this is Ben's father and brother," Howie said.

She stepped on tiptoes and kissed Wes on the cheek. "I'm very sorry for your loss." She turned to Wayne and froze. Though stockier and having a mustache, his resemblance to Ben, especially in his eyes, was eerie.

"Pleasure to meet you," Wayne said, taking off his hat and extending his hand. Gail covered her mouth with one hand and took his with the other. Up close, it was like speaking to Ben.

"I know I look and sound like him. Hope it doesn't frighten you." Gail shook her head. "Don't forget Gail, Claire's seen me before. She knows what to expect."

"Yeah, but what about the children?" She asked.

They all looked at each other in silence.

"We'll know in a second," Howie said. "Gail, why don't you see if she's ready."

Gail walked away, never taking her eyes off Wayne.

The children leaned and twisted in their safety seats, attempting to see into the living room. Howie lifted Sarah out first, blocking her from going inside until Michael was out.

"You ready Wayne?" Howie asked, kneeling down in front of the two curious children.

"Yup"

"Okay now kids, listen to me." Howie looked into their eyes, making sure they were paying attention to him. "Your Uncle Wayne is here. He looks like Daddy but he's not, okay?"

Howie backed out of the room still on his knees, repeating, "That's Uncle Wayne" until the children finally caught a glimpse.

"Daddy?" Sarah said loudly.

"No, no honey, that's Uncle Wayne."

Relief fell over the three men as Sarah and Michael were swept up in Wayne's arms, yelling "Uncle Wayne, Uncle Wayne." Even though they hadn't seen him in a year, Ben had told them many a bedtime story about Uncle Wayne and Grandpa.

"Sarah? Do you know who that is?" Wayne asked, pointing to Wes. She blushed and hid her face.

"That's Grampa. You remember him don't you?"

Sarah kept her head buried, but Michael perked up. "Grampa?"

Wes reached over and rubbed the boy's head. "I'm your Grampa." He looked toward Howie. "They don't see us enough to know what grandparents are all about. I was looking forward to having ...having my boy and his family back home. Now I'm just going to have his family – I hope."

Gail walked out from the hallway; Claire followed. She stopped, and the house fell silent. Gail took the children from Wayne's arms and rushed them into the kitchen.

"Oh Dad...I can't believe he's gone," Claire sobbed as she ran to his outstretched arms.

Wayne came from behind her and rubbed her shoulder. She reached one arm around him and pulled him in until all three of their heads were touching. The sobbing grew louder to the point of frightening the children. Gail tried to calm them but in seconds the children were bellowing louder than the adults were.

Howie turned from the three as they stood huddled in the middle of the living room, not wanting to watch but still able to hear. The agonizing moans echoed in his head, and for the first time in his life he felt faint. He fell back onto the couch, immediately putting his head between his legs and forcing blood to his brain. Within seconds, he was coherent again, but now felt nauseated. Gail watched Howie lose color in his face and struggle to get up but was helpless having her hands full of children.

"Wayne," Howie called, bringing both men over to help. "Just get me up and toward the bathroom. I don't feel so hot."

Kneeling on the floor leaning over the bowl, he heaved three times, producing only a strong taste of alcohol but no vomit. Feeling weak, he stood and looked in the mirror, splashing water into his face. He squeezed toothpaste onto his finger and rubbed it in his mouth, then rinsed. He took a deep breath and walked out.

Claire sat on the couch, rubbing her eyes with a tissue. Wes talked on the phone near the front door.

"You okay?" Claire asked.

"Yeah, I'm okay. I feel kinda stupid." He ducked into the kitchen and filled a glass with water.

The children had stopped crying. Gail wiped their eyes and dried Sarah's hair, which had stuck to her face from the flowing tears. Gail looked at Howie, but figured he didn't need to talk about what had happened.

Howie knew the stream of well wishers would run all day, but didn't realize that they would start so early. The doorbell rang. He first looked through the window and recognized one of Ben's neighbors. He opened the door and she handed him a bag filled with plastic containers.

"There's eggs and bagels there. We're all going to make sure there's plenty of food," the neighbor said. "If you need anything, Claire has all our numbers. Please call us."

"Thank you very much," Howie said. She waved and walked down the driveway.

Howie laid the food on the dining room table. Within seconds the house was filled with the smell of eggs and sausage.

"Anyone feel like eating?" he asked, but there were no takers. "Better put this in the fridge then...Do bagels go in the fridge?"

"Howie, leave it. I'll do it," Gail said.

Wes had handed the phone to Claire, who began to cry before saying any words. Howie came up behind, tapping Wes and motioning to the dining room table. "I'll sit with her. Go ahead, eat."

"Yeah okay. Oh, that's my wife on the phone."

"I was meaning to ask why she didn't come."

"Doc didn't want her to travel. Her heart's not so great and he's afraid the strain could kill her. She's got my daughter and other people to take care of her back home. Anyway, we'll have a service out there."

"That's what I figured," Howie said.

Claire's crying grew louder. Howie sat to comfort her, but instead she stood up and handed him the phone. "Gotta go to the bathroom. Talk to Mom."

He covered the receiver. "How is she?"

"Just talk to her."

"Hi Betty."

"Hi Howie, how you making out?"

"I'm okay. Claire's not doin' so well. Soon as we're off here, I'm going to try to get her to eat."

"Okay dear. Go take care of her and we'll talk to you this afternoon."

"Okay Betty, I'll talk to you later."

Wes and Wayne had waited for a moment alone with Howie.

"Howie, we need you to explain what happened here. We got bits and pieces last night on the phone but still don't understand what Ben was involved with," Wes said.

"Yeah, why were they under police protection? We're guessing the father of the girl that he hit was involved but who was the other guy that Claire talked about?" Wayne asked.

Claire walked into the kitchen and picked up Sarah, bringing her into the living room. Gail carried Michael in and set him down. He immediately ran to Wes who propped him up on his knee. Sarah squirmed in Claire's arms, wanting to join her brother in play.

"They were just asking what the whole story was," Howie said to Claire.

"Gail, could you take them downstairs to play for a while. We're gonna need some time to talk," Claire said.

"Sure, I'll take them to the playroom and maybe for a quick walk outside."

"No! Not outside! Not yet. Not till they catch him. Just downstairs," Claire said, sounding petrified.

Gail looked shocked at Claire's outburst, not knowing about Luke. "Not 'til they catch who?"

"Can I explain it later, Gail?" Claire asked.

"Oh, yeah, sure." She coaxed the children away from Wes and Wayne and steered them down the stairs.

Howie spent the next hour explaining every detail of Ben's plan and how it backfired. Claire sat silent, having to relive the ordeal over again. Wayne and Wes peppered Howie with questions until they understood how the whole scenario unfolded.

"Seems to me that his plan would've worked if it weren't for the lawyer tellin this guy Luke," Wes said. "I mean from the way you explained it, there was no other way out. What'd you say that lawyer fella's name was?" Wes motioned to Wayne to write the name down on a pad on the table.

"Whoa there, Wes. This ain't the Wild West here. You can't take the matter into your own hands. The police will talk to him once he's back," Howie said.

"Seems the police couldn't help him when he needed it..."

"Dad, look, now ain't the time to look for revenge. Let's take care of the funeral, all right?" Wayne said.

Claire sat with her hand covering her mouth and her eyes open wide. She had looked forward to having Wes and Wayne around but all the while never gave thought to the possibility of them looking for revenge.

"Now don't you worry Claire, we're not going to cause any problems. Let's just take care of matters," Wes said, but not sounding convincing.

"Please promise me that you won't do anything foolish Dad. Aren't we going through enough already?" she asked.

"Okay Claire, I promise."

She looked him in the eye and felt he was telling the truth. "Okay, let me go down and talk to Gail for a minute. Why don't you get unpacked and showered?"

Wes sat up straight and raised his head high to watch Claire go down the stairs.

"Okay she's gone. Now Howie, where would I find this Dracken fella?"

"Dad," Wayne snapped. "We're here for only two reasons. One to take care of Claire and the kids and two to get Ben back home. That's it."

"Wes, seriously, this isn't like what you're used to. You go and talk to this guy and he'll have you killed."

Wes picked up a mug of coffee, took a long sip and placed it back on the table. Howie and Wayne waited for a reply to their comments. Wes stretched his arms open and clapped his hands together.

"I just want to talk to the man is all."

Chapter Twelve

Shortly after noon, Wes, accompanied by Claire, drove her car, followed by an unmarked police car into the funeral home parking lot. Wayne was left behind as a precaution. His close resemblance to Ben could easily result in a double funeral if Luke hadn't seen the news of Ben's demise.

"Now we're not goin' to let this guy sell us anything we don't need. They know they got you feelin' sad and all," Wes said.

"Dad, I discussed this with Ben and I know what we want."

Wes stepped out and walked around to Claire's side. The two officers walked up behind, scanning the area for signs of reporters or Luke.

Claire stepped out and squinted in the direction of the backyard of the church rectory, which bordered the parking lot of the funeral home. She waved to a priest who sat reading a newspaper in the cool air.

A shiver went down her spine as Wes held the building door open. Inside, drab colored walls and dark carpet lined two sets of stairs. She looked up then down, unsure which way to go. A man carrying a heart-shaped bouquet started up from downstairs. She breathed in deeply, taking in the beautiful scent of the roses in the arrangement.

"Need help?" he asked.

"We're looking for the office," Claire replied.

"Up the stairs and to the left."

They nodded their thanks and began up the flight. Claire held tight to the wrought iron rails, pulling herself up. At the top, a large chandelier hung, shimmering in its light. Claire stopped to look at it sway ever so slightly in the breeze of an air conditioning duct. Anything to put off having to go and see the box in which Ben would spend eternity.

"Claire, we have to do this. It ain't gonna be easy for either of us, but let's get it done."

"I know...I know... ever wonder why the air in these places is so...so... I can't explain it."

Wes led her to the receptionist's desk. "Feels like death." He said.

"We'd like to see the director about a funeral," Claire said.

"Certainly, your name please?"

"Pearce, Claire Pearce."

"Oh Mr. Shane is expecting you," the girl said, picking up the phone. "The Pearce's are here."

Claire and Wes looked at each other. "We didn't call before we came," Claire said to the girl after she hung the phone up.

"Mr. Shane will be right out to explain."

The office door opened. A distinguished looking gentleman greeted them. He reached his hand out. "I'm Mr. Shane. I'm very sorry for your loss. Please come in."

He offered them two chairs at a large oval cherrywood desk – more like a table than desk. It had drawers but it was set up to allow the director as well as his customers to pull their chairs under on both sides, making it more comfortable and easier to pass brochures.

"Your secretary said you were expecting us. We didn't call here," Wes said.

"I actually tried to call you, but you had already left. I heard the news just a little while ago. You see your husband came to see me. He told no one, nor did I." He opened a drawer and took out a large manila envelope and sliced it open. "Your husband made his own plans for his funeral in case there was an accident."

Wes looked slightly surprised, but Claire had no reaction. She had become accustomed to his cautious planning and this was just typical. She reached across and took the list of what Ben had asked for along with a brochure picturing a modest casket. She handed Wes the brochure while going over the list.

"If you'd like to see the actual coffin, we have a room with models."

"That won't be necessary. The picture is good enough," Claire said.

The director took out a pair of glasses from an inside pocket. "I see from my notes here that the final interment is to be in South Dakota. What we'll do is, immediately after the funeral deliver his body to the airport and have it sent to the destination that he indicated. Is that what you want?"

Claire looked at Wes and nodded. "That's what we want. We'll do it just like he asked."

"What's this all gonna cost?" Wes asked.

"Dad...doesn't matter. It's what he picked and we'll go with it."

Wes starting to choke up. "My boy... in this box." He threw the picture of the casket on the desk and stood up. "I'm sorry." He pulled a handkerchief from his pocket and walked to the window.

Hearing Wes cry started Claire sniffling. The funeral director pushed a box of tissues in a silver holder toward her. As she reached for the box, she could see that there was actually a path worn on the desk from his pushing the tissues to so many others before.

"Dad, you all right?"

Wes walked back over and nodded as he sat down.

"Okay," Claire said, "do everything the way Ben wanted it. I want a special bouquet from me and the kids."

She broke down in tears. Wes pulled her close, setting her head down on his shoulder.

"I'm okay." She wiped her eyes. "I know there's an arrangement that the wife usually gets."

"Usually a spray for the top of the coffin," Mr. Shane said.

"Okay, that and a heart-shaped bouquet of red roses from the children. Oh, and before I forget..." She reached into her handbag and pulled out an envelope. "Here are some pictures. I know sometimes you do a collage thing. I think I'd like that."

"Certainly, Mrs. Pearce."

"Can I call you later?" Wes asked. "I'd like to call my wife and ask what she'd like. Can't believe I forgot to ask before and I didn't think to ask Wayne either. Yeah, we'll call you later with the rest, okay?"

"That's fine. So we'll have a one-day wake with two viewings. One between two and four and the other in the evening, seven to nine. I'll set the funeral up with the church and have the exact time for you later. Here's a brochure with floral arrangements to choose from. Do you have any other questions?"

Claire looked at Wes, who shrugged his shoulders. "Not right now, but I'm sure I'll think of some later," she said.

"Very good then. I just have some papers for you to sign."

A block away from the house, Claire said a prayer, hoping that the reporters had given up their relentless vigil. She closed her eyes as they approached; Wes broke the good news.

"They're gone."

"Thank God," she said as they pulled into the driveway.

"Don't get out yet. Let the officers tell us when."

The two officers pulled in behind and hopped out, checking the area. Howie came down the steps to greet them. Wayne waited inside, still under orders not to even peek out a window.

One of the officers called to them that all was clear.

"Howie, did Ben mention anything about his going to the funeral home and making arrangements?" Claire asked.

"Didn't say anything to me. Why, did he?"

"Yep, he had it all set up," Wes said as they walked up the stairs.

"Thought you were back kinda fast - how did it go?"

"As good as planning a funeral could I guess. There wasn't much to do. He had it all done," Claire said. She stopped short in the living room and pointed to three fruit baskets. "Where'd these come from?"

"The doorbell and the phone have been ringing ever since you left. I left the cards on them and here's a list of the people who called – the most important being Ben's lawyer. He had a messenger drop off this envelope."

Claire fell back onto the couch staring at the large manila envelope with her name written in Ben's hand.

"Claire, what is it?" Wes asked.

She didn't answer.

"Claire?"

"Oh I'm sorry. Ben told me that he had left a letter for me to open if he died. Guess this is it." She stood up. "Where are the kids?"

Howie was about to answer when they heard Wayne talking to the children from downstairs. He led Michael by the hand and held Sarah in his arms coming up the stairs. "See, I told you Mommy's here."

Claire noticed Howie had an unsettled look. "What's wrong now?" she asked.

"I spoke to the detective a little while ago," Howie said.

Wes looked at Wayne and Howie in anticipation as he sat Claire back down on the couch.

"Nothing on Luke yet, but he got the medical examiner report back already," Howie said.

Wes wrapped his arm tightly around Claire's shoulder. Their bodies tensed.

"Cause of death was a broken neck. The fire was afterward. There was no pain – no suffering."

The only sound in the room was the ticking of the grandfather clock. Wayne held the children still on the other end of the couch, waiting for Claire to break the silence. Her lip quivered as she pictured how the accident must have taken her husband's life – the van flipping violently, coming to an abrupt stop, snapping his neck with a loud crack. She gasped loudly, covering her mouth.

"You okay sweetheart?" Wes asked.

"Huh, oh yeah." She looked at Howie. "Are they sure...that it was quick?"

"Positive...he died...instantly."

She stood up and waved the children towards her. "I guess that's good news – if you could call it that." She held back her tears. "I'm going to lie down for awhile. I'll take them with me."

"Oh, I almost forgot," Howie said. "Gail picked this up for you. Said it would be helpful." He handed her a large thin book. She read the title and tucked it under her arm along with the Manila envelope containing Ben's letter. As she reached for the bedroom door, Howie called to her from the living room.

"Oh Claire, I forgot to mention that Detective Casey is doing well."

"Oh my God, I forgot all about him. We should send something to the hospital."

"Go ahead and rest. I'll take care of it. I'll send him one of these fruit baskets."

"Howie, don't you dare."

"I won't, I won't."

Claire sat the children on the bed and walked into the bathroom, returning quickly to turn on the TV to a children's' channel. After a small fuss, she took the remote from Michael to prevent him from surfing the channels and accidentally seeing his father in the news.

She stared into the bathroom mirror, psyching herself up for the first real attempt to explain to the children that their father wasn't coming home. She splashed some water into her face and slowly wiped it dry.

C'mon Claire, you can't stall forever. You have to do this now. God please give me strength.

Michael unexpectedly helped break the ice. "Mommy, when's daddy coming home?"

"That's something I wanted to talk to you both about." She picked the book up off the dresser and opened the cover as she walked around the bed. This was indeed a special book – a book to help children understand and cope with losing a parent. The pictures were bright and cheerful, yet without even reading the words, Claire could see that it easily relayed its message.

Both children had crawled to her, their curiosity piqued by the book. Claire had become entranced as she skimmed through the pages, not even noticing that the children had crawled up behind her in an attempt to get a glimpse.

"Daddy?" Sarah asked, pointing at a cartoon picture of a man with blonde hair and wings.

Claire snapped the book shut, and after a moment of thought she laid the book down. "Yes Sarah, that's Daddy." They looked at her in confusion. She reached back for the book but decided to explain in her own words until she had a chance to read the book herself first.

"Daddy is an angel now. He's in Heaven."

"When will he come back?" Michael asked.

Four big blue eyes stared up at her, waiting patiently for an explanation. Claire hoped that Sarah was just imitating her brother and not fully understanding what was happening.

"Daddy can't come back." She waited for their response. Sarah, too tired to comprehend, almost fell over on her side. Without getting off the bed, Claire lifted Sarah and laid her down with her head on a pillow, covering her with the sheet.

Michael still stared, now with a million questions filling his head. "He's never coming back?"

"No Michael, never."

"But why?"

"He was in a bad car accident."

"Our car?"

Not wanting to go out on other tangents, she decided against mentioning the police. "Michael, do you understand that Daddy isn't coming back?"

He pouted and started to cry. "But I wanna see him."

"I know, I know honey," she said, hugging him while trying to muffle his moans from Sarah. Hoping that he was as tired as his sister was, she rocked him and stroked his head, praying that he would fall asleep. She needed the opportunity to read the book on a parent's death. So far she was not confident in her own ability to explain in a manner that would not cause them unwanted stress. Thankfully, only minutes were needed until he was nodding off.

Michael's head had barely hit the pillow before Claire forced Ben's envelope open with her finger, giving herself a paper cut in her haste. She put the finger in her mouth while dumping the envelope's contents on the bed. Five sealed white envelopes and one sheet of folded paper fell out. She opened the folded page and quickly read the short message telling her to give the children their envelopes when they were old enough to understand.

She flipped through each envelope. The first had Sarah's name, then Michael. The third had her name on it. She dropped the others on the bed, quickly glancing to see that of the other two, one was for his family, and the other read: "Investments and Insurance."

She slid her finger under the sealed flap – this time taking care not to cut herself. Tapping the envelope upside down on her knee forced the two pages to fall out. She unfolded them, and to her surprise, they were hand written. Tears immediately dripped onto the top page. She quickly grabbed a tissue out of the box, which she had already placed at her side, and dabbed the drops, smearing the ink slightly but not totally obliterating any of the words.

Claire grew excited, her heart pounded. Seeing Ben's handwriting almost made her feel that he was still with her, and although heartbroken, she became almost joyful for the moment in anticipation of Ben's final message. She looked back at the children who were fast asleep at the head of the bed. In a way she wished that they were older, so she could cuddle with them and read the letter aloud, but at the same time she was thankful that they had a lesser chance of emotional scarring at their age.

Claire moved to the center of the bed and sat Indian style, steadying her elbows on her knees to keep her hands from trembling. She began to read.

Dear Claire,

This letter holds my last wishes and my final goodbye. I can only blame myself for the mistake that I made that brought us to this fateful situation. I know that telling you not to cry for me won't stop the tears, but please think of where I am now, watching you and the children from above. I am only gone in body; but as the church has taught us, I am not dead. I will live on until we meet once again, and that alone should make you strong, which you must be for the children.

Our lives together were as close to perfect happiness as is possible on Earth. You are and always will be the finest wife and mother that the world has ever seen. I know that you will raise our children with the virtues and kindness that we both possess. Teach them what I would have; that honesty and integrity are the only tools that a person needs to create a path to success. Tell them that I did my best in the little time that I had to raise them and that I will always be watching over them. I am enclosing a letter for each of them also to be opened when you feel that they are old enough to understand and appreciate it.

Please promise me now that you will still continue with our plan to raise our babies in South Dakota. My family will be a great help to you, and my parents as you know will treat you as their own daughter. Howie will help you with the move West and you are to put your full faith in his ability to handle the investments. I will instruct him on what I want done, and there is a list accompanying this letter showing you where all the accounts are along with the insurance policy.

As for my funeral, I have taken care of most everything. If you haven't been to the funeral home yet, you may be surprised to know that I have been. More important than an expensive casket are the memories that will join me. I would like of course pictures of you, the children and my family inside along with the one other item that I hold sacred, my wedding band, which I will wear for eternity. This doesn't mean that you have to wear yours forever. If you, sometime in the future, meet another, I will not hold it against you to remarry. I don't want to see you alone in life, and the children deserve the benefits of two parents.

I would also like you to put the mementos from our vacations in with me. I have separated a group of them on my shelf above my desk, and they are the ones that remind me of the best times of my life; the times we had away together.

I have also enclosed a letter for my family. Tell my dad that I want him to read it to everyone in the great room at their house. You and the children have been my life, and I pray to God that this letter never gets opened but in the event that it does, you will know that I will always love you, and with you and the children I had the perfect life.

Love always,
Ben

Two tissues, soaked in tears, sat next to her as she sat holding a page in each hand, looking back and forth at them. The letter was not at all what she had expected. It was too serious – there was no joking. Even though this was to be Ben's final communication, he would have added some levity. Claire almost began to question the authenticity of the letter, but speculated the reason for the straightforward writing was fear. Fear and maybe lack of sleep caused by one man – Victor Dracken. She dabbed another tissue under her eyes, but to her surprise they had dried. The sorrow that she had felt for a moment had turned to anger.

What he must've gone through in his head. Constantly fearing for his life and never once showing it.

She started reading the letter again, stopping to rub her finger on an indentation where Ben had crossed a word out.

God, if I could kill Dracken and get away with it, I would.

Leaves and papers swirled as stiff winds fueled a small tornado in front of Victor Dracken's office building. Brent's tie blew over his shoulder as he held the door for Casey's temporary replacement, Detective Gant. A young aggressive officer, Gant stood tall with slicked-back black hair, and unlike Brent, he was dressed to perfection.

"Can't believe we have to protect this guy," Gant said.

"We took an oath, remember?" Brent said with a smirk.

"We took an oath to protect the law abiding citizens, not garbage like Dracken."

"My heart's not in this either. Let's just get it over with," Brent replied as they entered the elevator.

"You ever meet him before?" Gant asked.

"Dracken, yeah couple times. Meanest prick you ever wanted to meet. You'll see – he just loves cops."

Brent pulled open the glass door to Dracken's suite. Both detectives flipped open their badges at the receptionist.

"We'd like to speak to Mr. Dracken," Brent said.

"Just a minute, I'll see if he's in," she said, getting up and disappearing around the bend to the corridor.

"What's the matter? Phone don't work?" Gant said loudly.

The other receptionist turned away and continued to flip through a magazine, unfazed by the officer's outburst. Gant looked at Brent and pointed at the girl. "Believe this?"

"No big deal to her, we're here all the time," Brent said, leaning his elbow atop the reception partition.

"This way gentlemen," the girl said, standing at the entrance to the hallway.

The two men followed. Gant waved his hand occasionally in front of his face, getting an intermittent whiff of cigar smoke.

"Go right in," she said upon reaching the office.

Brent opened the door and stepped in with Gant right behind. Dracken pushed and twisted a cigar into an ashtray. Gant choked for a second, but was more overcome with the beauty of the office.

"Detectives, how are you? So nice of you to stop in. It's only been a week or so since some of your colleagues were here." He walked out from behind his desk, offering his hand, but both men, after the patronizing comments, snubbed his offer.

Dracken brought his hands together with a clap. "Can I get you gentlemen a drink?" he asked, walking to the bar.

"This is not a social call, I assure you." Brent said.

"Mr. Dracken, I'm sure you know why we're here," Gant said.

"Oh yes," he said, dropping an olive into a martini glass. "I recall hearing something about the gentleman who killed my daughter being killed in an accident." Dracken's face turned to

stone. "I was home with my wife and... and with my only child."
He walked back behind his desk. "Please have a seat," he said,
motioning to the two chairs in front of the desk.

"No thanks, we're not going to be here that long," Brent
said. "And we don't think you had anything to do with Mr.
Pearce's death."

Dracken stretched his arms wide. "Then why are you here?"

"We understand that Mr. Pearce paid you a visit and
explained the little extra amendment to his will."

"You're not taking that seriously are you?" Dracken asked
looking surprised. "I really thought that was just desperation."

Gant put both hands on the desk and leaned toward
Dracken. "Desperation for what? Did you threaten him?"

Dracken, not fazed by Gant's get-in-the-face approach, stood
up and faced the window.   "Mr. Pearce had some
delusions that I wanted him harmed for what he did to my
daughter." He turned back to them. "I assured him that I wished
no harm to him and that I understood that it was an accident."

"I'm sure you did," Gant said. Brent immediately cut in.
"Mr. Dracken, the reason we're here is that the will is no joke
and you may be in danger."

Gant laughed. "And we can assure you that we wish no
harm to come to you."

"Trust us Mr. Dracken, we don't want to be here but we
have to; it's our job. You might want to keep your eyes open for
a wild man named Luke. Right now, all he knows is that if he
kills you, he gets fifty grand."

"This Luke, does he know who I am? And why can't you
tell him that you're on to him?" Dracken questioned in a
nonchalant manner.

"I'm sure he does know who you are and I'm sure he doesn't
care," Brent replied. "As for your other question, we can't find
him...he's disappeared. All he knows is that Ben Pearce is dead
– at least we're assuming he knows. Now he wants you."

"I see. Why not put his picture on TV? Let him know
people will be looking out for him?"

"Well the main reason we're not doing that is we don't want other people getting the same idea about the will. You know, copy cats," Brent said.

Dracken, unconvinced by the officer's explanation, sat down slowly in his seat. "Then why mention the will at all?"

Gant propped himself up on the glass desk, facing away from Dracken. "Say we put out to the press that we need to find Luke but can't tell them why. How long do you think it will take them to find out." He hopped back off the desk. "We're doing you a favor at the same time. If all the people that you pissed off in your life were to hear about this, how long before you're duckin' bullets and they're blaming Luke. Oh wait – I forgot – you don't have any enemies, nice guy like you."

For the first time Dracken had a slight look of concern. "Not that I don't trust your detecting skills, but why don't you give me some information on this Luke," Dracken said as he took out a black Mont Blanc pen from his desk drawer.

"Unfortunately, we can't give you that info. See, the same laws that say we have to look out for your life also protect him," Brent said. "We'll leave a car outside here and at your house for your protection."

"No need," Dracken said smugly. "I have people to take care of me; one phone call and my home and office will be surrounded with my men." He leaned back in his chair, holding a gold lighter under a cigar. He puffed until the smoke became thick around his face. "Good day gentlemen...oh, let's hope for his sake that you find him before I do."

"You ready to go?" Brent asked.

"Yep, we're done here," Gant replied.

Claire entered the living room with the two half-asleep children right behind. "C'mon, time to get the sleepies out."

Wes jumped up off the couch, looking half-asleep himself.

"Did you sleep?" Claire asked.

"I nodded off a couple times but the damn phone rang on forever." He handed her a pad. "Here's the people who called."

Claire skimmed over the names, and then glanced at Wayne who was asleep with his cowboy hat over his face. "He slept through the phones?"

Just as she finished her sentence, a yawn came from under the hat as Wayne reached up and removed it.

"Nah, he's been up and down past couple hours," Wes said.

The children climbed onto the couch, pulling on Wes's shirt to get him to sit back down. Within an instant they were on his lap, their heads against his chest, looking for more sleep.

"Don't let them go down again – they'll never sleep tonight."

Wayne walked to Claire and put his arm around her. "You doin' okay...how'd you sleep?"

"Every time I dozed, I'd have a dream about him. I'd be pulling him out of the wreck and my hands would fly in the air and wake me. I had to sleep at the other end of the bed 'cause I was afraid of hitting the kids."

"That'll all pass in time. I know it won't be easy, but maybe you don't want the kids in the bed too often. You don't want them to get used to it."

"I know Wayne," she replied. "Dad, don't let 'em sleep. Bounce them around."

"Oh yeah, there were some more deliveries and more neighbors brought food. Howie disconnected the bell so it wouldn't wake you. There's a ton of food over there. Why don't you grab something to eat?" Wes said.

"You know what? Why don't I take them outside to play?" Wayne said. "Who wants to go on the swings?" he yelled.

The children jumped up and scampered down the stairs toward the back door.

"Claire? Did you eat anything today at all?" Wes asked.

"No, not hungry," she replied, shaking her head.

"You have to eat or you'll wind up fainting. At least have some milk or juice."

"I will Dad."

Nearly tripping over a wrapped fruit basket, she pulled the stapled envelope from the cellophane and took the card out.

"Don't know who this is - maybe from his office. Hey by the way, where's Howie?"

"He took off to get some stuff from home and said he wanted to stop at the office in the evening so there wouldn't be anyone to question him yet."

Claire moved newspapers and fruit baskets into a corner. "What a mess."

"Claire, why don't you just relax? We'll take care of all that."

"Dad, what am I supposed to do...just sit around? If I clean it'll occupy my mind a little." She made her way into the dining room where bagels and cakes covered the table. "Did you guys even check to see if any of this stuff needed to go in the fridge?"

"I don't know. Howie was taking care of that." Wes walked around the table, looking in bags and plastic containers. "This should maybe go in." He slid a small tray of carrot sticks and celery out of a bag.

"Yeah, put it in."

Keeping a stalk of celery in his hand, he put the tray back into the bag and laid it down. He bent the celery into a bow until it snapped with a loud pop. Claire shrieked, dropping a cake box on the floor and covering her ears like a child hearing a thunder clap. Wes rushed around to where she stood.

"What's the matter? What's the matter?" he yelled, coming up from behind, turning her around to face him.

"The crack...that noise."

"The celery?"

She nodded, crying and looking embarrassed. "I know this'll s...sound stupid but...the cracking noise reminded me of the accident."

Wes tried to understand but shook his head. "I don't..."

"Howie said that he snapped his neck."

"Oh, now I get it. I'm sorry sweetheart."

"That's okay Dad, I'll be okay." She bent down to retrieve the box and wipe up a few crumbs that had fallen out.

The front door pushed open, startling her again. She spun on one knee to see over the table but Howie's voice got to her before she saw him.

"What's going on? What's she doing down there?"

"She dropped a cake," Wes replied.

"No big deal," she said.

"Need help?" Gail asked.

Claire popped her head up again, happy to hear Gail's voice. They knelt facing each other.

"I met Howie half way up the driveway," Gail said.

"Listen, can you and me go out into the yard later or something? I've been with the men all day. I need to be alone to talk to you." Claire said.

"Sure, let me know when you're ready."

"Yeah I just gotta make a bunch of phone calls, discuss the plans for going out west and pack. I don't know when I'm going to have time for anything." She dropped the cake back to the floor and held her face in her hands. Gail rubbed her back.

"Why don't we go to my house for a little while. There's no distractions – we could talk."

"They don't want me to leave – oh yeah that reminds me." She stood up. "Hey Howie, anything from the police on Luke?"

Howie called back from the guestroom. "I spoke to Brent but nothing yet. Still can't find him."

"They'll never let me go over alone." Claire perked up. "How about the garage? Ben's truck is in the driveway and there's a couple of chairs." She sprang up. "Let's go."

"I was wondering when you gals were going to come out from there. What was all the whispering about?" Wes asked.

"We weren't whispering, Dad. Just trying to figure a place where Gail and I could talk. We're going to the garage." She took a step down the stairs but backed up quickly, bumping into Gail. "Sorry, I forgot something."

Opening the refrigerator, she rummaged past all the bags of food, pushing her way to the back, taking out an already opened bottle of red wine. Gail, who had picked up on the plan, already had two glasses in her hand by the time Claire had the bottle clear of the shelf.

Howie was now back in the living room after unpacking two suits and hanging them on the inside doorknobs in an attempt to make the room look a little less lifeless. The small television that he brought up from Ben's office sat atop a milk crate that he had found in the garage. Now came the problem of splicing in the cable line without anyone tripping over it.

"Where are you girls off to? And with a bottle of wine no less." Howie asked.

"Off to the garage for some girl talk. I've been around you guys so much, I need a break."

"Have you eaten at all?"

"She hasn't eaten a thing," Wes said.

"Claire...c'mon, you gotta eat."

"All right, all right," she said.

"Tell you what, go ahead down and I'll bring some stuff," Howie said.

As soon as the women were out of sight, Wes motioned for Howie to come closer. "See if you can explain to her that she don't have time for this stuff. She needs to get packed and tell us what needs to be done around here. I'm not doing anybody any good sittin' here watchin' the tube."

"I agree. I'll say something when I go down."

Howie tapped on the door and opened it. The garage felt a bit damp. He struggled to understand how sitting on metal fold-up chairs on a cold concrete floor while drinking wine would make Claire feel better. He picked up a small folding table and opened it, placed the tray of assorted foods upon it and sat it between them.

Being more preoccupied with setting up the food, Howie hadn't really looked at either of them. Squatting next to Gail, he saw that the white light of the fluorescent bulb showed the deep emotion on their faces. He had seen Claire from the moment that she found out about Ben's death – he watched her cry uncontrollably – he saw all the pain, all the agony. But now her face was different – as though she was able to communicate her feelings in a way that a man wouldn't comprehend. Now he realized that the surroundings weren't important, it was the female companionship. Without saying a word he left them to be alone.

* * * * * *

By nine o'clock that evening, Claire had most of the children's clothes packed for the trip to South Dakota. With them now sound asleep, she dragged a suitcase into her room from the hallway. Lack of sleep and nourishment had diminished her strength to the point that she fell to one knee while trying to lift the relatively light bag onto the bed. Howie heard the thud from down the hall, and thinking that she had merely dropped something, came into the room where he found her with her face in her hands, sitting on the floor, leaning against the bed.

"What happened?" he asked.

"I'm okay, I'm okay. Just a little weak."

He sat on the bed above her, pushing the suitcase to the side. "What's the story with the kids tonight? You gonna try it alone in here?"

She nodded her head in a quick jagged up and down motion while running her hands across her eyes and down her cheeks to her neck and finally dropping them to her lap.

"Howie, be honest, how do I look?"

"Your husband was just killed. You look like hell - how else you supposed to look?"

She cracked a smile. "You didn't have to be that honest." She pulled herself off the floor and with Howie pulling up on one arm, she sat up on the bed.

"I see you did some packing."

"Kids stuff so far. I think I'll wait for tomorrow to do any more. How 'bout you, you pack at all?"

"Did some. I'll run home again tomorrow between the viewings," he said

"You know you don't have to stay here. I'll be fine with the guys here."

Howie gave her a sheepish look. "Tell you the truth, I really don't want to be alone either. When I went home before, I felt like... like, well every noise I heard made me turn and look. Felt like I was being watched. Kinda eerie."

"I know the feeling. Even though I know he's gone, I still think he's going to walk through the door. Or when I hear a car door, I automatically think it's him."

A picture of Ben and the children on the dresser caught Howie's eye. "You know, I'm really going to miss you and the kids...you know, when you move out there for good. I am assuming that's what you plan."

"Yeah I'm pretty sure," she said sadly, then perked up. "But you can always come out there and we'll come here."

"Yeah, but you know how it is. For a while you stay in touch, then you talk less and less 'til you're almost strangers."

Claire knew that he was right but he looked so dejected that she thought quickly. "You and Ben were like brothers. He would never want us to lose contact – that'll keep us together. I promise."

Howie's frown slowly turned to a smile. "I'll buy that."

"And who else can tell the kids stories about their father as he grew up?"

Howie stood and picked up the picture off the dresser. "Yeah, you're right," he said. "Well, maybe we better try to get some sleep – if possible. You gonna come out and say goodnight?"

"Yeah, I'll be right out."

Howie had already left the room when Claire spotted the suitcase still on the floor.

That dummy forgot to put the bag on the bed for me.

She opened her mouth to call him back but decided that she had had enough for one day and walked down the hall to the living room.

Wes sprang to his feet upon seeing her. "Need help with anything?"

"No Dad, I'm just coming out to say goodnight. Actually, I'm a little hungry."

Wayne ran to the refrigerator and pulled out platters of food, startling Claire with his quick movements. She looked at Wes in confusion.

"We were just talking about your not eating. He just figured before you changed your mind..." Wes said.

"What do you want Claire? We got everything," Wayne asked.

She glanced over. "Just let me take that small tray of sandwiches and a glass of milk in with me."

With the brighter lighting in the living room, Claire could see Howie's face more clearly now. Appearing drained and pale, he scratched his head.

"You're finally going to eat something?" he asked as Wayne handed her the tray. "Not a bad idea. Maybe I'll grab something before bed."

Claire put the tray on the end table and, on tiptoes, kissed Wes on the cheek. "Goodnight Dad"

She turned and hugged Howie, then Wayne. "See you in the morning."

"If you need me, just wake me if I'm lucky enough to sleep – without booze to put me out," Howie said.

Claire had disappeared around the corner.

"She forgot her milk," Wes said, taking the glass off the kitchen counter and walking it down the hall. "You forgot your milk." He reached his arm in and put the glass on the dresser, then closed the door.

"Hey Dad?" she called.

He opened the door wide and walked right to her, knowing from the tone of her voice what she needed. She wrapped her arms around him as far as she could reach and they together had one last cry.

Sitting on the bed, she picked at the sandwich, tasted a pickle and finished the glass of milk. She watched TV to occupy her mind, but haunting her was the fear of dreaming and the thoughts of the impending wake and funeral. Her body was now stressed to the limit and with her heart pounding so hard there was no chance of sleep. Sleeping pills were the only solution.

Keeping the arrows lined up on the bottle and its top proved difficult as she attempted to remove the tablets. In frustration, she slammed the bottle into the bathroom sink, hoping the impact would break it open. Instead the bottle used the sink like a ski jump and soared through the air, landing behind the toilet.

Seeing this as a sign, she surrendered the idea and sought alternatives – but what? As she stared into the mirror searching for an answer, she found herself humming to the music of a television commercial – a lullaby that soothed and calmed. She laughed at the irony when she saw it was an advertisement for a sleep aid, but it gave her an idea. She remembered that Ben had once told her that when he got up at night with the children, singing to them put him to sleep faster than it did them.

It's worth a try...but I have to take one of them out to sing to. She nodded her head. *Yep, Michael's the one. He'll fall right back if he even wakes at all. God, if anyone found out about this, they'd think I was nuts—singing a lullaby to Michael to put me to sleep.*

She peered down the hallway, then slipped across into the children's room. Leaning with her back against the wall just inside the door, she held her breath and looked up at the decals of planets and stars that glowed in the dark. Once satisfied that she hadn't been detected, she took a few short steps and stopped, waiting for her eyes to become more accustomed to the dark. She continued to Michael's crib. A small nightlight plugged into an outlet guided her way.

Michael had already kicked his blanket off down to his knees, making the job of lifting him out in the dark that much easier. She reached in and stopped – what if she frightened him while singing? A crying child would surely bring Howie running. After a deep breath, she carefully slid her hands under his body and lifted him, still not sure exactly what she was doing.

I'll just do what he did and hope it works – although I don't see how.

She closed her eyes and pictured Ben holding the child in the dark. Slowly she began to sway while rocking the baby as Ben did, humming his favorite song for the children – Danny Boy. Ben's voice filled her head as she sang along with him, half singing, half whispering.

Minutes past as she waltzed the room, entranced, holding the still sleeping child. Deeper and deeper she slipped as Ben danced with her, holding her, Michael in between them. A wide smile spread across her face and tears streamed – it was all so real.

The blissful dream suddenly came to an end as Claire backed into the children's dresser, causing a small mirror to fall face down on the wood. She gasped as her eyes snapped open as if a firecracker had gone off behind her. Few seconds were needed for her to realize that it wasn't real and Ben was again taken away from her - disappearing in front of her watery eyes. A chill shot through her body and her heartbeat accelerated as she squeezed Michael tightly, causing him to cough. She eased her grip and laid him back into the crib, praying that he wouldn't wake.

"Claire?" she heard Howie whispering in the hallway.

She rushed to the door and put her finger over her mouth to quiet him until the door was closed.

"I heard something - everything okay?"

"Yeah, come in here," she said, dragging him into her bedroom. "Ben was just with me." Grabbing him by the shirt, she pulled him back and forth. "Do you believe in the after life?"

"Wait, now calm down." He took her by the arms. "You're trembling."

"No...I mean do you really believe...that they can contact us and stuff."

"Yeah I guess, why? You going to tell me that Ben contacted you?"

"Not real contact. I mean he didn't say hello but..." she paused, "he was there when I was singing to the baby."

"I can believe that. I'm sure he'll be with you for the rest of your lives," he said, putting his arms around her.

Claire didn't try to explain further, knowing there was no real way to express what she had felt. At least she was more at ease. Sliding under the covers was a little less frightening, but unfortunately she was more wide-awake than ever. She lay down and covered herself. Her body felt heavy, giving her the feeling of sinking into the mattress. The mind raced but the body begged for sleep, and in minutes it came... as the last tears of the day trickled from the sides of her eyes across both temples.

* * * * * *

Claire woke abruptly to the sound of a spoon dropping in the kitchen. She peeked through crusted eyes.

7:00. Wow I slept through.

She sat up. To her amazement, the bed was a wreck. The covers were twisted and kicked to the foot of the bed. The pillows were on the floor and even the mattress cover was off at the corners. She saw herself in the dresser mirror and tried to run her fingers through her hair, but the top was knotted and the back soaked with sweat. Frightened by the disturbing appearance of the bed, she tried to call out for Howie but her first attempt only yielded a low hoarse cry. After clearing her throat and moving her tongue around in her mouth, she was able to get his name out.

Within seconds, Howie swung the door open; Wayne and Wes stumbled in behind him. Claire sat with her back against the headboard, her arms over her knees. "What happened here?" she asked.

"I looked in on you a couple times. You were tossin' pretty good," Howie said.

"I slept, but I feel like I did manual labor all night. I'm still exhausted."

Wayne picked up one of the pillows and handed it to her. She laid it on top of her knees and leaned into it. Wes left the room, seeing that there was no emergency, then yelled, "Oh no," from the kitchen. Howie looked at Wayne, and then together they ran back out with Claire on their heels.

"No big deal, no big deal. Sorry I yelled," Wes said.

Oatmeal covered the floor and cabinets. Even Sarah wore some, as Michael was obviously dissatisfied with his breakfast. They all stood and stared. Michael looked up with sad eyes, waiting for his reprimand. Howie looked at Claire and started a chain reaction of laughter.

With oatmeal dripping off her nose, Sarah giggled while Claire wiped her clean.

The three men fell silent and backed up into the living room as they heard someone attempting to open the front door.

Claire glanced over her shoulder. "That's Gail. I gave her a key. Said she'd come early and I didn't know who would still be sleeping. Help with the door, it's tricky."

Wes reached for the knob, but Gail had already unlocked it. She put her hand on her chest in surprise, not expecting Wes to be standing right in front of her as she walked in.

"Everybody's up?"

Claire came in from the kitchen. "Thanks for coming so early. I've got a lot to do. Lots of calls to make."

Gail stopped short when she saw Claire, her eyes immediately drawn to Claire's hair.

"I look that bad don't I?"

Gail tried the best she could to look believable, but she wasn't a good liar. "You look a little tired, that's all. C'mon, let's go inside. Show me what you're going to wear today."

"Okay listen, I'm gonna run home and pack the rest of my stuff and run some errands. Be back around noonish," Howie said.

"Okay buddy, we'll see you later," Wayne said, wrapping him in a hug.

Howie gave Wes a nonchalant salute and walked out the door.

Only two cars occupied spots at the funeral home as Wes pulled Claire's car into the lot. Claire sat in the passenger seat, already clinging to a tissue. Howie pulled in along side in his car with Wayne and what was now becoming fairly natural to them: an unmarked police car brought up the rear.

Claire stepped out, clutching a small black handbag. She shuffled her feet on the pavement in an attempt to scuff the bottom of her new low-heeled shoes – also black, matching her dress. A small diamond pin, a gift from Ben, showed brightly against the dark background of her collar. The only other jewelry she wore was her wedding band and engagement ring – both wrapped in the back with Scotch tape to take up the space from the weight that she had already lost.

"God, I don't know if I can do this...take my arm. I'm feeling a little shaky," she said to Howie.

Wayne held the door, but Claire paused. "Okay, I'm ready."

As they entered, Claire noticed that the sweet smell of flowers present the day before was gone. Now the smell reminded her of her grandmother lying in a casket at her wake when Claire was just a child. Wayne led the way up the stairs where they were met by the funeral director.

"This way please."

Wes and Howie flanked Claire as she held each by the arm. As they approached the room where Ben lay, Claire held both men back, afraid to go any farther.

"Take your time. We can wait here 'til you're ready to go in," Wes said.

The truth was that no one was in a rush to enter, not knowing how they would react to seeing the coffin. The funeral director, not realizing that they hadn't followed him in, returned to the hall.

"This may take a few minutes," Wayne said.

Without any further words, the director knew they wanted to be alone. He gave a slight bow and backed away. "Again, my deepest sympathies. If there is anything you need, please find me."

"Thank you," Claire replied.

Breaking free from the three men, Claire made the first attempt to peek inside. She took one short step then another – she was in. Howie took one step towards entering but Wes put his arm out. "Give her a second alone."

Claire looked back and gave a look of thanks for the time alone, then turned and took another step. The smell of flowers again filled the air. Bouquet after bouquet of flowers of every kind and size lined both sides of the room. She covered her mouth in astonishment at the outpouring of sympathy from Ben's friends and family.

She stood in the middle aisle between two sections of chairs facing the coffin; her eyes focused on the floor. The three men had now taken one step into the room. They watched as Claire raised her head slowly to see the casket for the first time. She showed no outward emotion as she took steps like that of a march towards Ben. Finally face to face with her worst nightmare, she reached out and placed her hand on the beautiful cherrywood coffin and knelt down. She sobbed quietly as she stared at the picture of Ben that sat atop the coffin. She admired the beautiful red rose spray, highlighted with two white orchids – one for each child. She turned and motioned for the others to join her.

Wes's concern was so great for Claire that as he approached her, he almost forgot that Ben lay only yards away. Howie and Wayne followed him, almost colliding as he stopped short upon seeing the wedding photo.

Claire held her hand out for Wes to join her. He knelt down next to her where they embraced and cried. Howie and Wayne both broke into tears while watching the emotional outburst. Wayne immediately sat down with his head in his hands. Howie put his hand on his shoulder and squeezed.

Claire reached out, taking the wedding picture off the casket and stared. A single tear fell and slid down the edge of the frame.

"He's at peace," Wes whispered.

She nodded and together they stepped aside, allowing Wayne and Howie to take their turn saying goodbye.

A black metal stand held a collage of pictures of Ben from when he was a boy until only a month before his death – the last picture taken of him holding the children at the beach. Claire ran her finger over the photo.

"God, I remember that day. It was so hot, but we had the greatest time...the kids in the water...eating ice cream..." Out of the corner of her eye, a bright red arrangement caught her attention. She took Wes's arm and walked him in front of it. White roses outlined the red center of the heart shaped arrangement. Wes lifted the gold ribbon that hung from the bottom and read the inscription aloud. "We miss you Daddy. Love Michael and Sarah." Claire started to cry again. Wes pulled her close. For a moment the sadness of his son's death was replaced with anger as the face of Victor Dracken flashed in his mind.

Claire continued down the line of bouquets, reading the cards, but her eyes were continuously drawn back to the casket. She watched as Wayne and Howie looked at the pictures on the board. She looked across at the opposite wall also lined with flowers and realized that there was no escape from the memory of Ben here. At least at home there were distractions, giving rest to the sadness on occasion. She shuddered, thinking about all the people who would soon fill the room crying. Feeling a bit nauseated, she sat immediately. Wes, who had walked up front noticed and rushed back to her.

"Wayne," he whispered loudly.

"What's up?" he asked rushing back.

"Get her some water outside."

"Sure, and Dad, you don't have to whisper."

"Just get it."

Howie came down the center aisle, then cut over to sit next to Claire, but before he made it to her, Connie and her husband walked in tentatively. Howie held his finger in the air indicating to them to wait for a moment.

"You okay?" he asked Claire.

"Yeah I'm all right."

"Maybe you should get up to the front. People are starting to show up."

Claire turned to the back and squinted through watery eyes. "Who is that? Oh it's Connie."

She walked across the row and met Connie in the center aisle.

"God Claire, I'm so sorry. If there's anything we can do..."

Connie's husband shook hands with Howie, who had come up behind Claire.

"Oh I'm sorry," Connie said. "Claire, you remember my husband Jim."

"Nice to see you again," she said.

"Very sorry for your loss. I've heard a lot about Ben," he said.

"Thank you," Claire replied, looking past them as more people walked through the door.

"Connie, why don't we talk more later; I'd like to hear any stories you have about Ben. Right now I think I'll go up front and sit. I'm about to meet a thousand of Ben's coworkers that I never met before." She stepped aside, giving the full view of the casket to Connie, who took her husband's hand and walked forward.

"Okay Claire, how about we do it like this? Wayne and Wes sit on both sides of you up front. I'll bring the people to meet you and I can introduce them that way," Howie said.

"Yeah okay."

Howie walked to the back while Wes and Wayne both hobbled as they escorted Claire to the front row. She sipped water from a styrofoam cup.

"What's the matter dad? You okay?" she asked.

"Its these damn shoes. We're used to the boots and how in the hell men go all day with ties on I'll never know."

"I thought it was me," Wayne said, tugging on his collar.

"Oh Wayne, before I forget and it gets crazy here, do me a favor and call the house. See if Gail is having any problems with the kids. By the way, are you ready?"

Wayne gave a puzzled look. "Ready for what?"

"You're going to freak a lot of people out here today. You know – looking so much like Ben and all."

"Yeah, I thought of that. Maybe we should've put out a warning sign on the doors as people walk in."

Claire turned around in the seat and watched Wayne walk down the aisle just as Howie was bringing the first couple to pay their respects. Initially, there was generally a break of a few minutes between mourners, but after the first half-hour there was a steady stream.

"I never been hugged and kissed by so many strangers in my life. Never knew Ben had so many friends either."

She fanned herself with a piece of paper as the temperature of the room soared with unexpected crowd. Wayne continuously brought refills of water.

"Please everyone, may I have your attention," the funeral director said in a loud, authoritative voice. "If you will all please take your seats. Father Burns is here to say a few words."

"This the priest you were telling me about?" Wes asked.

"No, he wasn't available for the wake, but he'll be saying the mass tomorrow," she replied.

The elderly priest began his prayer, but Claire was already in another place. For the first time in over an hour she had an unobstructed view of the casket, and her eyes were drawn to the wedding photo. She closed her eyes, letting her life with Ben play through her mind like a movie.

"You all right?" Wes whispered into her ear just as the priest asked everyone to rise for "The Lords Prayer."

She mumbled the words along with the mourners, but could only think of how badly she wanted this day to end. The priest joined her after the prayer in an attempt to console her.

"I know that no words that I can give will make you feel better, my dear. But if you have faith and truly believe in the words of the Lord, you must believe that Ben is in a better place – and one day you will join him for eternity." He kissed her on the forehead and blessed her. "If you need anything, the rectory door is always open."

"Thank you, Father."

The level of noise increased as the priest passed through the room. Claire sat back in her seat and waited for the next person to hug her or kiss her. She knew they all meant well but a person only wants to get pawed so much in one day.

"Hello Claire," said a familiar voice.

"Detective Brent," she said, standing and taking his hand. "Thank you for coming."

"Again Claire, my deepest sympathies."

She leaned and whispered in his ear. "Anything on Luke?"

"Sorry to say not yet. He's just vanished."

"Hi Detective," Howie said, coming up from behind. He laid his hand lightly on Brent's back.

"Hey Howie, how you feelin'?"

"You know – with all the commotion here it's okay but it's when you're alone and have time to think."

"Yeah, I can imagine – well listen, I just wanted to stop for a minute. I've gotta get back. I'll see you before you leave for South Dakota."

"Wait – how's Detective Casey?" Claire asked

"Oh...yeah, he's doin fine. He'll be okay."

Just for a second, Claire didn't trust the look in Brent's eye and opened her mouth to quiz him further, but Wayne talked into her ear, turning her away from the detective.

"Kids are fine by the way," Wayne said.

She turned back, but Brent was gone.

Howie knelt on one knee. "What's the matter? You looked puzzled."

"Howie...did you..." she looked toward the back of the room. "Ah, never mind."

With fifteen minutes left in the viewing, the room thinned. One by one the mourners approached Claire with their condolences until finally the four were once again alone. They sat silent, staring at the coffin until Wes finally stood.

"We should get going. We're back here in a few hours," he said.

"Let me just say goodbye," Claire said.

She handed her purse to Howie and approached the casket. Instead of kneeling, she stepped to the side of the kneeler and rested her head on the coffin.

"I miss you Sweetheart. I hate...I hate to leave you here alone. You should be coming home with us." She sobbed loudly.

Wayne put his arm around her to lead her away.

"Saddest thing I ever seen," Wes said to Howie. They turned and walked down the aisle.

Nine thirty that evening, Gail waited at the front door as the two cars pulled into the driveway. With a light chill in the air, she crossed her arms and walked down the stairs to greet them. Even in the dim light of the exterior bulb, she could see the wear on their faces.

"Just wanted to come out and warn you the kids are still up. Paul's inside – they just wouldn't sleep."

"That's okay, I need to see them," Claire said.

The two children slid off the couch upon hearing the voices outside, and ran to the door where they yelled for their mother. She wrapped them in her arms and attempted to pick them up but instead almost fell over. Wes took Michael from her. She stood with Sarah and kissed her, then reached over and kissed Michael. For a brief moment, Claire was allowed to be happy and was able to forget what she had gone through during the day.

"Oh, hi Paul," she said.

"Hi Claire. They just wouldn't sleep. Every time we put them inside, they cried. They kept asking for..."

Claire finished the sentence for him by mouthing the word, "Daddy."

Paul nodded his head.

"So how did it go?" Gail asked.

"Faster than this afternoon." Claire picked up a piece of paper on the kitchen table with phone messages. "All the neighbors were there tonight. I had people that I knew to talk to and my boss showed up with his wife. Hey Howie, could you make me a drink?"

"You read my mind," Wes said and headed for the bar.

"So Gail, you have no problem sitting again tomorrow?"

"No, but I do feel bad that I can't be there and at least say a prayer."

"Don't feel bad; you're doing us the biggest favor that we could ever ask. While the kids are with you, I don't worry."

Wes handed Claire a glass. "You want one too Gail?"

"No, thanks. We're just going to head home."

Before Gail and Paul had pulled the front door closed, all four had a glass in their hand and sat heavily on the couch. Wes and Wayne propped their stocking feet up on the coffee table, having taken off the uncomfortable shoes before completing one step into the house.

"Wes, could you give me a hand getting them to bed? I have to do some more packing anyway, so I'll say goodnight," Claire said.

Howie waited until he and Wayne were alone. "So how's the old man hanging in?"

"Howie, I'm really worried about him. You know things are done different out West. We need to handle a lot of our own problems. He don't say much about it, but I know he wants a piece of that Dracken guy."

Howie shook his head. "You better talk to him because if he tangles with Dracken, we'll be having another funeral. Dracken is a bad dude. He don't fuck around."

Wes's footsteps could be heard coming down the hall, silencing them.

"You all packed Howie?" Wes asked.

"I got a little more to do. Do it tomorrow late." He stood up and stretched. "I'm pretty beat myself – what time we leaving here in the morning?"

"Well it starts at ten, so I guess we leave at what, nine fifteen?" Wes said.

"Good, see ya in the morning."

Wind-driven rain pelted the windshield of Claire's BMW as Wes parked facing the church. Howie and Wayne watched out the back window, waiting for their unmarked shadow to pull in behind.

They sat in silence, watching the large maple trees surrounding the church bend in the wind. People ran past the car, crossing the street and up the three levels of stairs to the white columns that marked the entrance.

Claire sat with her index finger in her mouth, biting down on her nail. The men waited for her to give the signal that she was ready to go.

"You know, if I saw a light at the end it would be easier," she said. "We have to do this, then everyone is coming back to the house. Then we have to do it all over again on Tuesday."

"I know sweetheart, but we really have to go in," Wes said.

Without warning, she opened the door and stuck her umbrella out, pushing the button and springing it open. The men quickly followed, slamming the doors and making a mad dash for the church. Once on the top landing and sheltered from the weather, Claire turned back. Cars packed the lot and more were waiting in a line.

"Are all these cars for Ben?" She backed up, finally turning and going through the door, which Howie held open.

"You ready?" Wes asked.

She nodded and he opened the door from the vestibule into the church. The silence of the mourners was broken with whispers and shuffling of bodies that spread like fire as they turned to see Claire. Slowly they all stood. Claire walked down the center aisle not looking up once.

Wes and Wayne, though preoccupied with the thought of Ben, still couldn't help but admire the splendid interior of the church. They were used to small-town houses of worship, and the three-story ceiling with massive hanging chandeliers, drew their eyes upward and then back down the walls. The colorful stained glass windows depicting the life of Jesus Christ held them in awe.

Claire raised her head as she neared the first few pews. Ben's coffin sat between her and the altar atop a wheeled cart skirted with a white satin shroud. The wooden box with its brass adornments shined in the bright lights. Even in its beauty, Claire knew that all eyes were focused on her and not the coffin.

Reaching the front pew, Claire stepped aside, allowing the three men to slide in, leaving her the aisle seat, only ten feet from Ben. As she stepped in and sat, so did the entire group of mourners.

The temperature inside was cool and Claire, still damp from the sideways rain, was chilled. Wes, almost feeling her shiver next to him, removed his jacket and coaxed her to lean forward, wrapping it around her. She gave a smile of gratitude, then jumped with a start as the organist began to play.

The priest and two altar boys walked onto the altar, genuflecting in the middle and returning to their positions. Everyone rose as the mass began.

"That the guy?" Wes whispered into Claire's ear.

"Yeah, that's Father Shehan."

The priest began to speak, and immediately Claire could feel the confusion from the crowd. Father Shehan spoke with a thunderous voice, but his heavy Irish brogue made his words indiscernible. Claire disguised her laughter with a cough, remembering the first mass said by the Father that they had attended. She and Ben almost had to leave the Mass, laughing under their breath trying to understand what the man was saying.

But over the years, he became their favorite priest and they always attended his services.

She turned her eyes away from the priest and onto the coffin and began daydreaming about her life with Ben. She no longer heard the words of the priest; she just stood and sat like a robot, following the lead of the mourners.

Half way through the mass, she glanced at her watch and then over to a side entrance. She continued this until finally it caught the attention of Wes.

"What's the matter? Why do you keep looking over there?"

"You'll see."

With only a short time left in the mass, Wes caught sight of the door closing but didn't see who had opened it. His interest piqued, he stared until it finally reopened. Paul and Gail walked in carrying Michael and Sarah. Detective Brent walked in behind, sliding in next to them on the opposite end of the front pew. Howie leaned forward to see Claire, raising his shoulders up in question. She leaned over Wes's lap so Howie and Wayne could both hear.

"I just wanted them to be with their father in our church one last time."

They sat back confounded as to how Claire arranged this without any of them knowing.

The mass came to a close. Three pallbearers walked up each side of the church and stood waiting for the priest's final blessing over the coffin. He sprinkled it one last time with holy water and nodded to the men. Claire motioned to Paul and Gail, who slid down and handed the children to Wes and Wayne. Howie waited in the pew as Claire stepped out following the rolling casket. Wes and Wayne walked side by side carrying the children behind Claire. She again looked straight ahead, not wanting any eye contact, fearing it would lead to tears, which she had been able to control for most of the Mass.

As the casket moved through the vestibule, Father Shehan stepped aside.

"Claire my dear, my deepest condolences." He made the sign of the cross over her. "If you need someone to talk to, please come see me."

"Thank you Father. It means a lot that you said the mass."

Mourners gathered behind, umbrellas opened, watching the pallbearers carefully step the coffin down the stairs to the waiting hearse. Facing each other, they sidestepped the casket into the opened door, two at a time stepping away as it disappeared inside.

A line of people formed, waiting to console Claire. This was the part she dreaded most. Everyone who had hugged and kissed her at the wake the day before was about to do it all over again.

The funeral director appeared from nowhere and tapped Wes on the shoulder.

"Everything is set. The body will leave on a flight today and be delivered to the funeral home that you specified."

"Very good. I thank you."

With the majority of the mourners still on the front steps, the church bells rang from its spire playing Ave Maria. Quiet fell over the crowd as they watched the hearse pull away from the church, carrying Ben on the next leg to his final resting-place.

Chapter Thirteen

By three thirty the following day, the four adults and two children had already made a connecting flight in Chicago on their way to Rapid City, South Dakota. They sat six across - Howie and Claire on the aisles, the children next to her.

Wes sat nervously, worried about the health of his wife. Would the stress of the death of her son take her life as well? Playing country music through the airplane headphones helped calm him, but the thought of another funeral mass, and this time a burial, made him restless.

The children watched a kiddy show on a DVD given to Claire by the stewardess.

"This is the greatest idea I've ever seen," Claire said, looking at Howie and pointing to the TV monitors on the seat backs.

Not getting a response, she waved her hand in front of his face as he leaned slightly to his left, allowing him to stare straight down the aisle. Snapping out of his daydream, he shook his head and rubbed his eyes.

"Sorry, did you say something?"

"You okay?"

He took a minute to answer. "You know, I really miss him. I'm so used to having someone to call and talk to about - you know, stupid stuff – stuff you can only talk to someone about that you know forever."

"Yeah, what did you guys talk about? Whenever Ben was on the phone with you, he never stopped laughing."

Howie smiled. "Just guy stuff."

The seatbelt alert rang as they began their final descent. The plane banked hard to the right allowing Howie to see past Wes and Wayne and all the way to the ground. Colored squares blanketed the countryside, each shade a different crop. He wondered how anyone could live in a place so wide open that it takes an hour to get to a gas station.

"Howie, switch seats," Wayne said. "You can get a better look."

Howie sat and pressed his nose against the glass to see down.

"Get a better look at what? There's nothing there. There was nothing here when I came out with Ben when we were thirteen. Don't remember much of that though."

With the plane approaching the airport, Rapid City showed itself, surprising Howie on its size. There were no buildings taller than what looked like ten stories, but there was life – and definitely more metal and concrete than cattle.

"We're about an hour and a half outside the city," Wes said.

The plane's wheels chirped as they made contact with the runway. The engines reversed and the aircraft came to a slow crawl before turning towards the terminal.

Claire, already crying, turned to Wes, who now sat in the opposite aisle seat. She choked to get words out. "Dad... I'm so nervous. I don't know how I'm going to react when I see Mom."

He reached across and took her hand. "You'll be just fine...just fine. How 'bout I take Sarah, and Howie takes Michael," Wes said. "You'll need your arms free, and Wayne's never been away for from his family for more than a workday, so let's stay out of his way."

Wayne led the way through the half-empty plane, carrying two small suitcases. Claire followed right behind. Once into the arrival area, Wayne walked ahead quickly, his head darting back and forth looking for his wife and mother. Claire was more apprehensive, walking slowly, then stopping short when she heard Wayne's wife call out his name. Wes and Howie caught up to her and waited. They watched Wayne hug his wife off the ground.

"Where's Mother?" Wes asked in slightly alarmed voice.

"She's okay Dad," Jill said as she walked to Claire. They stood face to face for a second then grabbed each other tightly. Their moans and sobs echoed through the small arrival area. Travelers stopped upon hearing the wails, looking up at the ceiling trying to locate the source.

Wayne put his arms around both of them. "C'mon gals, let's get home."

Wes stood right next to Jill, waiting for an answer. "Everything okay?"

Jill wiped the tears and stepped up to Wes, kissing him on the cheek. "Mom's leg was a little swollen, so we figured it'd be best that she wait. Was like tyin' down a lion to keep her from comin' though," she said, taking Sarah from him. "Hi Sarah honey. You're such a big girl now."

"Hey Howie. This is my wife Jill," Wayne said.

"Hi Howie, I've heard all about you. Ooh, you are a lady killer." She handed Sarah back to Wes and took Michael from Howie. "You remember me? I'm your Aunt Jill."

"Hey Jill, let's skip all this 'til we get home. We're a little beat," Wayne said.

Claire sidestepped over to Wes. "Dad, there's a guy over there who's watching us and makin' me nervous."

"No, no that's Jeff Eagle. He's one of my ranch hands. Came to help out." Wes waved him over. "Jeff, this is Claire – my boy's wife."

Jeff removed his hat, showing his jet-black hair, which was tied in a ponytail. "I'm very sorry for your loss."

"Thank you," she replied.

"Okay everyone, start headin' over for the bags and let's get outta here," Wes said.

Jeff and Wayne pulled two black Chevy Suburbans to the pick-up area just as the rest wheeled out two carts of luggage.

A stiff wind blew from the west, giving a slight hint of the upcoming winter. The men held tight to their hats as they loaded the bags while Claire and Jill strapped the children into their seats. Jeff climbed into the driver's seat of the first truck.

"Everyone ready?" Wes yelled. "Howie, you're with us."

Howie looked a little surprised, assuming he was traveling with Claire. He opened the back passenger door and sat.

"Howie, I didn't really introduce you to Jeff. He works for me."

Howie reached up and shook his hand.

"We're going to make a stop along the way about an hour down the road. A place where Ben used to go a lot. It was real important to him and I think you should see it."

Howie thought for a moment and then his eyes lit up. "I know where you mean. Ben used to talk about that spot all the time. He showed me pictures, but after a while I got sick of hearin about it."

"Yeah, well I just want you to maybe feel what he felt there. Claire's been there, so we'll just stop quick and meet up with them at the house after."

The suburban cruised down the interstate at eighty, passing eighteen-wheelers every few minutes. Howie stared through the window expecting to see green fields and corn, but instead the farmland was more a dry, hay colored grass close to the ground.

"God, we are in the middle of nowhere. There's nothing but flat land and fat cows... and more cows." They drove past a roadside truck stop with twenty semis parked in a row. "And why are all those trucks parked like that?"

"A lot of the truckers like to drive at night when there's less traffic."

Looking out the back window, Howie could see miles of the road that they had just covered. "Less traffic than what? There's like four cars and a few trucks for miles and the exits are like ten miles apart."

Wes and Jeff just laughed at the city boy who would soon understand the beauty and spiritualism that was South Dakota. Howie continued watching out the window, waiting for something of interest to keep him from dozing.

"Okay, I give up. What are the windmills for?"

"They pump water up for the cows. Makes small watering holes."

With that mystery solved, he sat back, but perked up upon seeing for the third time a billboard – not huge like in New York but about ten feet high, with the words "Wall Drug." He became more curious as they passed more and more – "Free ice water at Wall Drug" – "Native American art at Wall Drug" – "T-rex at Wall Drug".

"Okay, I give up again. What's Wall Drug?"

"Wall Drug is one of the biggest tourist attractions in the state. Started back in the nineteen thirties. Got every kind of South Dakota souvenir ever made."

"Great, a drug store is one the biggest attractions. Probably the only drug store in the state," Howie muttered under his breath.

Jeff slowed the truck and headed off the interstate, down a two-lane road with more billboards advising that they had just missed Wall Drug. They approached a booth where a park ranger checked Wes's pass. Howie's now sat up straight, reading out loud, "Welcome to Badlands National Park." What was so great about this park that Ben couldn't get enough?

The truck continued on, finally turning right onto a dirt road for a half-mile. The dust that the truck had kicked up was blown by the wind, overtaking them and making it almost impossible to see ahead.

"This is it," Wes said as the truck came to a stop.

Howie was still unable to see through the dust.

"Hop out. We'll wait here. This is something that every man should see by himself for the first time."

Howie stepped down and waited for a few seconds for the dust to settle. Walking in front of the truck and across the dirt road, Howie stopped short. His mouth hung open as he took a few more steps. He took a deep breath of the cool crisp air and continued to walk into an area that was rocky and vegetated with small grassy plants.

"Watch where you're walking," Jeff yelled.

"What am I watching for?"

"Snakes...scorpions."

Howie jumped straight up in the air, then quickly tip toed back to the flat dirt. He bent down and wiped the dust he had kicked up onto his new white sneakers.

"We have to get that boy some boots. He looks retarded," Wes said to Jeff.

Howie walked out to the edge of the cliff which didn't drop straight down but sloped out, blending from a rock face to a mixed grass prairie about two thousand feet below. A half mile in the distance, mountainous formations carved from years of erosion spiked up, resembling a lunar landscape. Horizontal bands of color, reddish to white to gray, stretched as far as the eye could see. He looked back at the truck and then overhead upon hearing the screech of a red tailed hawk. He followed the bird until it disappeared into the sharp spires of the badlands.

It was so quiet, so peaceful, like nothing he had ever experienced.

"Hey there's buffalo down there," he whispered.

"Why you whispering?" Wes called.

"I don't know. It's so quiet that...I don't know."

"All right c'mon. You can come back again."

Howie took a few steps backwards toward the truck, almost unable to turn away, but finally sat back inside.

Wes turned to see Howie's face. "Well? Was Ben right?"

Howie, too stubborn to concede that South Dakota wasn't the vast wasteland that he pictured, didn't answer. Wes reached back and slapped him on the knee.

"It's good havin' you here Howie. You're the...you're the closest thing to Ben – I mean besides Claire and the kids, that I have. You can tell me what he felt. What he was like – I mean he was my boy and all, but when you live so far away, it's real hard to stay real close. You know?"

"Yeah I know, Wes."

The sun was just beginning to set as the Suburban exited the highway onto a narrow two-lane road – both sides lined with three-foot wire fences. The smooth ride of asphalt lasted only minutes as the truck slowed, approaching the entranceway to the ranch. Two massive wooden columns almost twenty feet tall held a log cross member. Engraved with a carving of a full ranch, horses and wagons, it spanned the entire drive, holding beneath it a hanging sign reading, "Lone Prairie Ranch."

"I can't believe that in a matter of minutes of being off the highway, we're on a dirt road," Howie said, leaning up between the front seats. "I don't even see a house - just lots a cows. Hey, you got inside plumbing here, right?"

"Yeah, we had the pipes put in just last month." Wes started to laugh, but the smile left his face as the house came into the distant view. "We'll be there in a few minutes."

Howie could see the outline of buildings, encircled by trees like an oasis in the desert. He wondered why the house and barn were surrounded, but before he could ask, Wes started to explain as if he had read Howie's mind.

"See Howie, the whole compound is surrounded to block the wind and snow - mostly cedar and ash trees."

The truck climbed a small hill, nearing the house, allowing Howie to see the mile long trail of dust that they had kicked up behind them, now hover over the dirt road like a fog.

A slight bump signaled an asphalt road again as they drove through the wooden railed gate and over a large metal grate. Wes turned back to Howie again "the grate keeps the cows away from the house."

Large pines in the center of a circular drive still blocked his view of the house but not the two barns, one white, one red, directly behind it. Howie's jaw dropped in amazement as they came around the final bend, putting the house in full view. Ben had mentioned that the house his parents were building only three years before was on a grand scale, but Howie never expected this.

"Wes, this is incredible."

"Thanks, we put a lot of hard work into it."

Rising three stories at the center peak, the magnificent log house looked more suited for a Colorado ski chalet. A tremendous triangle window above the front doors followed the lines of the frame to the crest, allowing a view of the center hall chandelier. A staircase of halved logs led to a porch that spanned the entire width of the house. Forest green trim around the windows beautifully highlighted the stained log façade.

Along with the Suburban in which Claire had ridden, there were four pickup trucks and a Lincoln Continental parked in the small lot directly in front of the house. Howie stepped out, his eyes immediately drawn to the three stone chimneys atop the house. Smoke poured from the largest in the center. He took a deep breath. The smell of the burning pine permeated the crisp and now cold air, which had dropped twenty degrees since they had left the airport.

Howie and Wes stood in silence as they looked up towards the front door – neither wanting to be the first to go in, neither wanting to be the first to cry. Howie turned back towards the truck.

"Maybe we better grab the stuff."

"No, leave it. Jeff will bring it in."

The front outside lights on the house switched on in the now twilight. Ben's mother opened the front door and stood directly under a recessed light in the overhang, illuminating her silvery gray hair. Her appearance was not that of the typical matriarchal figure. She stood only five foot two and very overweight with a face that seemed much too kind to take charge. She came off more like the proverbial grandmother in a holiday movie – but her looks were deceiving.

"You two going to stand out there all night?" The resonance of her voice made Howie crack a small smile – she was undoubtedly in charge.

Jill came out behind her, crossing her arms in the cold. The two men climbed the stairs, steam coming from their mouths.

"It's good to see you Howie," she said, her tone changing from the dominant family figure to the grieving mother. He bent down and wrapped his arms around her.

"It's good to see you too, Betty."

Wes stretched out his arms and herded them all inside to the main foyer. Howie, Betty, Wayne and Ben's sister Jessica huddled and cried, while next to them Wes and Jill held each other. Other members of the family stood nearby, feeling helpless. Howie felt a tug at his pant leg. He backed away, wiping his eyes to see.

"Hi Uncle Howie," Sarah said.

"Oh hi sweetheart." He bent down to pick her up just as Michael came running in and between the grown up legs like an obstacle course to get to Howie. All eyes focused on the children as Howie held them tight.

"Have you two been good?"

Sarah reached out and touched a tear on Howie's cheek and rubbed it between her fingers.

"For Daddy?"

"I told them that the tears were for their daddy," Claire said, coming down from upstairs.

"Howie, put them kids down for a minute and let me introduce you to everyone."

"Okay, you two go inside and I'll be there in a few minutes."

Wes walked Howie down the line. "This is my brother Justin and his wife Tammy...Betty's sister Margaret...and this is Tom and Judy, my brother's kids."

"Hey Dad," Wayne yelled.

Betty was taking deep breaths. Wayne was already helping her through the tight gathering into the great room. Wes took her other arm.

"Get her to the couch – get the tank."

Everyone huddled around the couch. Jessica wheeled a green oxygen tank up and quickly placed the mask over Betty's face.

"I'm fine, I'm fine," she said in a muffled voice. Within minutes she had the mask off and was attempting to get up to help with the cooking.

"Just stay there," Claire yelled from the kitchen. "We got it under control."

"Just stay here Mother – they can cook," Wes said, massaging her shoulders from behind the couch.

"Make sure you don't burn those steaks," she yelled back.

Howie sat back in a soft rocker, off to the side of fire. Wayne sat opposite him and leaned back, sipping a beer. Wes came around from the back of the couch, not taking his hand off Betty's shoulder, not giving her a chance to get up. Howie laughed as they both looked lost on the custom-made tan leather couch – a twenty-foot semi-circular piece. Tom and Justin sat on a smaller couch further away from the heat of fireplace.

Howie sniffed the air as the scent of burning pine occasionally slipped past the overwhelming smell of the steaks cooking in the kitchen. He watched as the rest of the women hurried back and forth to the dining room, setting up for dinner.

"So Howie, what do you think of the place?" Wes asked.

"Very impressive. Not what I expected – especially outside. Kinda expected a place to tie the horses up and in here... well, there's no animal heads on the wall."

"Well, we tie the horses in the back, and there ain't much big game around here for trophy heads."

Howie gazed up to the top of the three-story ceiling, past the massive log beams that traversed the room to the pitched wooden ceiling. Everything was wood; the walls were wood, the floor was wood. The arms on the couches and chairs were a beautiful stained oak that matched the stain of the log staircase that went up from the foyer to the balcony overlooking the room and leading to the north wing of the house.

Howie jumped to his feet when the tree trunk sized log in the fireplace broke in two with a loud poomf. A blast of heat shot through the room as the flames and a shower of sparks were sucked up the chimney. As fast as it had flared, it calmed and Howie was able to walk up to the massive fireplace, slapping the solid stone.

Betty's sister came up behind him with a tray. "Here you go Howie, you wanted beer right?"

"Yeah, thanks."

"Howie, move the chair away a little, you're too close," Betty said.

He dragged the chair to the side more, facing it towards the kitchen, which was separated only by an oak and marble island. Country music played lightly as the five women readied the food and carried trays to the dining room.

Claire bent down, taking a dish from the oven, setting it on the counter. She stirred whatever it was with a fork – Howie couldn't see well from his vantage point. She lifted the fork to her mouth and tasted what he thought looked like squash. Jessica came up behind her and they looked into the glass dish. Jessica made a comment and laughed. Claire said something back and smiled. She took a sip of a drink.

"Too bad she can't be kept busy like this all the time," Howie said to Betty. He pushed his chin forward, pointing it toward the kitchen so that she would look. "She's actually eating something and smiling."

Claire looked up and stopped chewing as she noticed all eyes on her.

"What?"

"Nothing, dear," Betty said, standing with the help of Wes. "Let's head in."

As Howie stood up, he looked around quickly. "Hey, Claire, where are the kids?"

"They're in the south side playroom with Jill," Betty answered.

"Wow, I didn't even notice they were missing."

He walked past the back door and into the dining area, which was not divided from the great room. The beams that ran overhead were closely spaced, giving the illusion of a ceiling, making it warmer and homier as compared to the great room's wide open space. Glass made up the back wall from bottom to top.

Pressing his face against the cold glass, he shaded his eyes with his hand, but the glare from the bright lights of the wrought iron chandelier prevented him from looking through. He turned to the table. Lashed together with metal straps and wooden pegs, its immense size brought to mind the immediate question of how it was fit through the doors.

"This is some table, Wes. How old is this thing?"

"It's from the eighteen hundreds – used in an old meeting house. Bought it at an auction and cleaned it up."

"Howie, you sit right there across from me and next to Claire. I want to look at you both while I'm talking," Betty said.

Claire had just finished seating the children in their

highchairs. She stood up straight upon Betty's instruction to Howie and looked at him, shrugging her shoulders as he approached.

"I don't know," he mumbled to her. "But I'm sure we're gonna find out."

The sound of chairs being dragged under the table stopped. Wes glanced at his wife.

"Mother, I think you should say it."

"Everybody bow your heads. Lord, it is difficult to give thanks as we are all brought together on this saddest of occasions. We do thank you for the food we are about to receive and pray that our son is in your hands, amen."

"Amen," they answered together.

Claire stood up and took two plates that she had made up for the children, and set them down in front of them. Jill did the same for her kids, who Wayne had seated.

Slowly hands reached out across the table, picking up trays and passing them. The country music played just loud enough in the background to prevent dead silence.

Howie kept his head down while he ate, fearing eye contact and the start of a conversation. He knew that he and not Claire was the focal point because of Ben's secret life on the run from Dracken. He was the only one left to fill in the blanks about what transpired; he was their only link to Ben outside of his family life. He could feel the tension in the air as each one there yearned to ask a question, but none wanted to be the first.

Without turning his head, he strained to see Claire's face and her plate. She ate slowly, pushing the food around the plate with her fork. Now that there wasn't as much activity, she had time to think, and he could see that she wasn't really in the room. A conversation about the weather or the kids would surely bring her back and keep her eating, but on the other hand, anything leading to talk of Ben would stop her. He leaned back in the chair to get a better look at her plate. She turned her head quickly and leaned towards him.

"Don't you think I see you watching me?" she said loudly, but lowered her voice in mid-sentence to avoid upsetting the children. "I know you're worried about my eating, but you have to stop protecting me. I have to learn to take care of myself now." She looked around the table. No one even chewed. "You haven't mentioned Ben once here at the table. You all need to talk about him and ask questions, you need to reminisce - you can't keep it inside." Her voice dropped low. "We lost one of the kindest, most loving men in the world."

"We just figured when you wanted to talk, you would," Wes said.

"So let's talk, Dad," she replied.

Betty wiped the edges of her mouth with her napkin. "Okay dear, I guess you're ready. There's something I've been waiting to tell you Claire... and Howie. I wasn't sure if I should tell you alone, but then I decided that we are a close family and you've opened the door, so here goes. You never asked where Ben was to be buried." She waited for Claire to think for a moment.

"I assumed in the local cemetery - near your church...no?"

Betty shook her head with a look of guilt. Howie's fork hit the plate as he sat back, not having any idea what she was leading up to.

"Ben and I had talked a little more frequently recently. He probably didn't mention it to you - didn't want you to worry, but it did concern me. He talked a lot about how much he missed it out here and I just took it as homesickness. Whenever you leave the West, you always need to come back." She wiped a tear from the corner of her eye with a napkin. "Anyway, Ben, knowing that he was in trouble, worked some things into our conversations without me suspecting too much. I have to say that he really played me."

"Mom, what are you talking about?" Claire sounded a bit annoyed that Betty wasn't coming to the point.

"Ben told me that he wanted to be buried here on the ranch."

Claire's mouth dropped open. "Where, in the back yard here?"

"No, no, dear. There's a hill...with a weeping willow tree. It was one of his favorite places from when he was a boy."

"I know the place," Claire said. "Ben used to talk about it and he had pictures...oh my God - I remember seeing the picture out on his desk recently."

"Where is this place?" Howie asked.

" 'Bout three quarters of a mile out that way," Wes said, pointing towards the back of the house. "You can see the top of the tree from upstairs."

"You knew about this, Dad?" Claire asked.

"She told me over the phone in New York."

"Claire, it's a beautiful place – very peaceful, quiet. Horses and cattle drink there at the stream," Betty said, beginning to yawn. "Forgive me, the doctor has me on a light sedative and into the evening I get very tired."

"Well, if that's what Ben wanted." She looked at Howie. "He mention this to you?"

"Nope but it don't surprise me. He loved it here."

"Listen, the service is at ten tomorrow. We can all get up early and take a quick trip to the spot," Wes said. "Okay with you Claire?"

She nodded and then froze upon the realization that the time was nearing where she and her two young children would be standing at Ben's open grave. She took a couple of deep breaths in panic but then quickly calmed at the thought of being near him again.

"You know – if nobody minds, I think I'll take the kids up for a bath and spend some time alone with them. I'll see you all in the morning."

"Oh Claire, I was hoping to talk by the fire later," Betty said.

"I know Mom, but I need a little time alone with them. I'll be here all week. Besides, I'm sure you all want to know exactly what happened. Howie knows best, and I really don't want to hear it all again."

The men all stood as Claire picked up Sarah. Howie wiped his mouth with his napkin and picked up Michael.

"You know where your stuff is, right?" Wes asked.

"Yeah Dad, Jill showed me before."

* * * * * *

A rooster crowed loudly, startling Claire out of her sleep. She gasped and looked around the room, not knowing for a moment where she was. She had slept for a good portion of the night, although it wasn't a deep refreshing slumber. It was more like the kind of sleep where a dream is repeated and becomes a chore, not allowing for rest. She sat up to see if the children were moving, but they were still out cold.

How do they sleep through that racket?

The room was chilly. She could feel the heat coming up and pulled the comforter tightly around herself. That would be another thing she would miss – Ben's warm body throwing off heat like a fireplace on the cold nights.

A knock on the door startled her again. "Yeah?" she said sleepily.

"It's Howie; you awake?"

"Who could sleep with those damn roosters squawking out there?"

"I know, they got me up too. Can you be ready to go soon? They're already downstairs eating and Betty wants to show us this hill with the tree."

"Okay, give me a few minutes...and what time is it that they're up and eating?"

"It's six thirty. Jill said to leave the kids and she'd be right up to take care of them so you could go. Betty wanted to go now so we don't have to rush around when we get back."

"Okay, I'm coming," she said, swinging her feet to the floor.

The children, now both awake, looked at her with sleepy eyes.

"You two stay here with Aunt Jill and I'll be back in a bit." She kissed them both and quickly got dressed.

She stepped down the stairs. Still a bit sleepy, she could hear utensils hitting the plates in the dining room. She stopped to listen, but there wasn't much conversation. Claire could hear Jill's voice in the kitchen so she continued down the stairs, meeting her at the bottom where they hugged.

"How'd you sleep?"

"Not real good but enough."

"Go on and eat real fast. I'll keep the kids up there 'til you're gone, then I'll feed em."

"Thanks Jill."

The room was still when Claire walked in. The men all stood while she pulled out a chair and sat.

"How did you sleep dear?" Betty asked.

"Okay, Mom." She reached for the coffeepot and poured. "Let me just have a quick cup to help me wake up."

"Why don't you eat something?" Howie asked, then regretted it as Claire's cold stare shriveled him into the chair.

"Wes, Howie, finish up so we can leave," Betty ordered, which translated into drop everything and we'll heat it up again when we get back. "Just the four of us going. No need to drag the others; they've seen it."

Jessica handed Claire a travel mug to pour her coffee into for the ride.

"Hey Claire, how'd you like the roosters this morning?" Wayne snickered.

"Very funny."

"Don't worry dear, once you're living here for a month or so, you won't even hear them," Betty said.

Howie was still eating off his plate as he walked to the kitchen. Stopping short on Betty's comment, he spun back to see the guilty look on Claire's face.

"You're definitely coming out here for good?" Howie asked.

"It's what Ben wanted," Claire replied.

Howie erred in judgement and questioned further. "But what do you want?"

Betty shot daggers with her eyes, then turned and carried a plate to the kitchen.

"What I say?" Howie asked, almost whispering.

Wes stood up and unhooked his keys from his belt. "Boy, are you just playin' dumb or do you have a death wish?" He shook his head. "My wife gets a hold of you alone later and you're gonna be the sorriest son of a bitch ever."

Howie swallowed hard and slid his plate across the counter to where Betty stood on the other side. He avoided eye contact and went looking for his jacket.

"Okay let's go...Claire, c'mon," Betty called.

Once outside, still clutching her coffee, Claire wrapped her arms around herself and shivered. Howie walked up next to her. "Guess I shouldn't have said anything."

Claire turned around looking for Betty, who was helped down the stairs, which were slippery from a light dew.

"Probably not. Let's talk about it later, all right?"

"Right."

Two chickens ran in their path.

"Hey Wes, is that the one that woke us up this morning?" Howie yelled back as he and Claire waited at the truck.

"Those are hens ya dope," Wes said with disgust as he approached. "Get in the truck, ya turnip."

Claire started to giggle and by the time she was seated next to Howie in the back seat, she was doing all she could to keep from bursting out laughing. She faced out the window so as not to look at Howie, his face like a two-year-old who just got yelled at.

Wes turned to the back. "Didn't they ever teach the difference between roosters and hens in them fancy schools of yours?"

"I musta been out that day."

Claire couldn't hold it in anymore. She burst out laughing and couldn't stop. Wes, who had just started to pull away from the house, brought the truck to an abrupt stop. He looked at Betty and they both looked to the back.

Claire raised her hand, still having trouble containing herself. She wiped tears from the corners of her eyes. "I don't know...I just found it funny. Maybe it's my body's way of coping with what I'm about to see."

Wes drove along the narrow dirt road, which meandered through and over rolling hills. Small groups of cows and sheep grazed along side.

Howie shook his head. "I need more concrete around me...I mean there's nothing here."

"Just wait," Wes said. "We're not even close yet. Where we're going is way out in no-mans-land, and the road starts gettin a little bumpy right about now."

He steered the truck sharp to the right and headed up a steep hill. The truck bounced as it drove through a muddy puddle; Claire held tight to her coffee. She looked at Howie as they jostled in their seats. The only picture in her mind now was Ben's casket bouncing around in the back of pickup truck.

Wes brought the truck to a stop at the summit. "This is one of the highest points on our land, beautiful ain't it?" Wes asked proudly. Claire and Howie stared out the window. They could see for miles, mostly grassland with an occasional tree.

"Drive on dear, we're not here to sightsee," Betty said.

After riding for another ten minutes, Howie envied Claire for having an empty stomach, wishing that he hadn't powered down everything on his plate when Betty put the rush on.

In the near distance, a large weeping willow tree appeared. Claire sat straight up, looking out different windows, trying for a better view.

"There it is," Betty said, pointing. "Stop here and let them walk up to it."

As Claire stepped from the truck, her heart pounded. Two hundred feet up a small hill was Ben's final resting-place.

"Howie, walk her over. Once you're there, I'll drive Betty up." He cut the engine.

They took a few steps and stopped. The tree, whose leaves were shriveled and dry but still clinging, stood directly in line with the rising sun. Ever-changing shadow patterns danced before them as the wind swayed the long hanging branches.

Howie waited for Claire to gain the nerve to approach. She took a few more tentative steps and then walked a bit faster. He stepped quickly to catch up. An eerie calm had come over her. She no longer feared the spot but felt warmed by its tranquility.

"Look how it's shaped like a courtyard," she said, pointing to the six large rocks that formed a semicircle fifty feet wide. The tree was centered but near the edge of the back side of the hill, which dropped away.

Branches swayed in the slight breeze. Dried leaves fell to the ground, rustling and blowing in small waves. Howie stepped out of the shadows, allowing the welcome rays of the sun to warm his face.

Now under the tree, Claire looked back at the truck and waved them over. Wes pulled it around near enough, with Betty's side facing them so she wouldn't have to get out.

"It's a beautiful spot, Mom," she yelled.

"I told you."

Leaves and prairie grass crunched under her feet as she approached the far side, which was steeply sloped into a small stream that lay two hundred feet below. Looking out into the distance, she saw hundreds of white puffy clouds, the bottoms flat and dark, filling the sky to the horizon. Howie and Wes leaned against the truck, watching her as she stared out over the small valley.

"Hey Wes, the service is in a little while – when's the hole gonna be dug?"

"When we head to the church, they'll come in with a backhoe and dig it. By the time we get back here, the coffin will already be in place."

Betty sniffled from inside the truck. "What do you think Howie?"

He spun around. "Couldn't ask for a more peaceful..." he stopped short noticing that Claire had dropped to one knee in tears. He took a step in her direction but Betty barked an order.

"Leave her – just let her alone for a minute. Let her get it out of her system."

Both men watched and waited for Betty to give permission to retrieve Claire. Howie was noticeably agitated, and finally Betty nodded. He moved swiftly toward Claire, bending down and taking her by the elbow, lifting her. As she cried into his chest, Wes joined them and noticed tears running down Howie's face as well.

"C'mon sweetheart, lets get you back to the house. We have a long day ahead."

"Okay Dad," she said, and together they walked toward the SUV.

What was a light breeze was now turning into a stronger wind. The sound of a diesel engine off in the distance grew louder and waned with every wave of calm and gust.

"What's that?"

"Damn, talk about bad timing." Wes sighed. "That's the backhoe. Let's go."

Within an hour, Claire found herself dressed in black and again in the back seat of the truck. They drove in a small caravan, which included the second black truck, a four-door pickup, a Jeep, and a Cadillac, winding their way back to the main road. She took her sunglasses from her purse to help block the sun, which shined brightly through her window. Having only been in South Dakota for less than a day, she was already unhappy as they drove for miles, seeing nothing and more nothing, she contemplated going back on her promise to Ben.

"How far's this town, Wes?" Howie asked.

" 'Bout six, seven miles. A stone's throw for out here."

"And there's two thousand people living there?"

"Well not right there. When we say there's two thousand in the town, it includes all the surrounding farms and ranches. Town may only have a thousand right near."

Howie nudged Claire lightly and whispered. "You okay?"

She just nodded and looked away. He couldn't tell if she'd been crying – her sunglasses were big and round and covered her eyes.

"There it is," Howie jumped a bit as he announced it. "It's amazing. There's nothing for miles and miles but grass and cows, then poof, there's a town out of no where."

Wes slowed the truck, heeding the warnings of the lowered speed signs. The two-lane, seventy-mile-an hour road magically turned into downtown Main Street – almost typical of a modern TV western. Small shops lined both sides – everything from a tack and feed shop to a general store. Cars parked head first, but only on one side of the street. Wes stopped the truck for car backing out of a spot. Howie bent low in his seat to read a banner hanging across the road announcing a dance for that Saturday night. He marveled at the simplicity of the quaint town as he watched a man climb off his horse and tie it up in front of a store.

"Believe this?" he said to Claire.

She mumbled a response; Howie didn't ask her to repeat it.

The small procession continued for two blocks, turning left between the pharmacy and the tiny movie theatre and down a very wide, gently sloping road, which lacked sidewalks. People walked along the grass in front of small houses set back on their property on the way down the hill to the church.

Orange cones blocked off the remaining three parking spots on the street directly in front of the church. Wes waited as a man removed them and pulled in; the other two vehicles came in right behind. The remaining black SUV double-parked along side.

The church, painted all white with thirty-foot columns and flanked by tall pines, resembled the picture that one might find on an old western Christmas card. The two round stained glass windows over the front doors stood out, catching the eye with their pictures of Jesus and Mary in beautiful blues and reds.

Recognizing Wes's truck coming down the hill, mourners hesitated to enter the church, instead gathering outside the front doors. Men removed black cowboy hats in respect as Howie stepped out and opened the door for Betty. Wes, on the opposite side, helped Claire out.

"Oh my," Betty said, as the crowd took small steps toward them.

Wes walked into Claire who had stopped short, overwhelmed by the number of people. At the same time, the priest came from the back of the crowd. "Listen people, you will have more than enough time to console them afterward. Please come inside," he said sternly, putting his arm around individuals and turning them toward the front doors.

As the entryway cleared, Jeff Eagle walked past the family to hold open one of the doors. Wes and Betty walked in first, followed by Howie with his arm around Claire. With Jill at home watching the children, Wayne escorted Jessica, followed by Wes's brother and his wife who split off to the side aisle and slipped into one of the front pews.

The church interior had a slight musty odor and looked much older than did the outside. A slightly worn blue carpet lined the center aisle. Frayed edges bordered the wooden floor on the entrance to each pew, which were in dire need of staining. The ceiling had watermarks and shoddy patchwork where obvious non-professionals had attempted repair.

Claire felt very uncomfortable and she stared at the tattered carpet as Howie led her behind Wes and Betty. This wasn't her church and the hundreds of pairs of eyes weren't those of people she knew. Many didn't even know Ben but attended out of respect for the family.

Half way down the aisle, Claire couldn't help but look past Wes and Betty to the coffin, resting before the altar. The wide rimmed sunglasses couldn't hide her weak eyes as tears flowed down her cheek.

Allowing Wayne and Jessica to enter first, Wes and Betty slid into the front pew, letting Claire take the end seat closest to the coffin. Raising her head slowly and to her own surprise, she was not frightened by the presence of the wooden box. She wiped the tears from under her glasses. She felt different – she felt at peace knowing that Ben was close by and had she been alone, she thought, she would have actually liked to talk to him while laying her head atop the coffin.

"Are you smiling?" Howie whispered.

She covered her mouth. "God, I kinda zoned out I guess." She leaned closer to him. "It's weird but I feel better with him near and it's like he's talking to me."

"Okay," he said, then leaned toward Betty. "Why is this church in such bad shape?"

Betty opened her mouth to answer, but the choir of nine women who began to sing in the balcony muffled her words. The thought was quickly forgotten as the entire group turned to see the female chorus, but most eyes didn't look up. The entire back of the church was standing room only but mourners continued to squeeze in.

"Gosh, the whole town's here," Betty said.

"Wouldn't expect nothin' less in this town. They're good people...just like Ben," Wes said quietly.

The priest now stood behind the altar waiting for the choir to finish.

"Let us pray," he said, bringing the congregation to their feet.

As in the Mass in New York, Claire sat and rose with the others by reflex alone. Even with her new-found feelings of comfort, she knew there was still the ceremony under the weeping willow tree with Ben's coffin supported above his grave. How would she seek comfort when she could no longer reach out and touch any physical remnants of her husband?

Howie lightly nudged her. "Wes is going to give the eulogy."

She stepped out with Howie, allowing Wes to get through.

"I didn't know he was going up there," she said.

"I didn't either 'til Betty just told me."

"They don't expect me to say anything, do they?" she asked, her heart quickening.

"No."

Walking past the coffin, Wes placed his hand on it for a moment and then continued up the one step onto the altar. His legs looked heavy as he crossed to the pulpit and climbed the two small steps.

He cleared his throat. "Thank you..." were the only words he got out before realizing that he didn't have to yell. His deep voice, as loud as thunder, echoed from the high ceiling, startling the crowd.

"I'm sorry about that. I've never used one of these before," he said in a much quieter voice while tapping the microphone. "Thank you all for coming here today. I wish we could all be meeting under better circumstances." His voice trembled. "Many of you remember Ben as a boy. Many of you never knew Ben. That's because I sent him to New York so that he could get a better education – at least that's what I thought would happen. And it did, but turns out the boys that stayed here did just as well. Shows what I know."

"Don't you blame yourself for this Wesley," Betty called out.

"Please Mother, I'm doin' a solo here."

The crowd let out a faint laugh. Wes cracked a small smile even though he hadn't intended to be funny. Betty, agitated by Wes's joke, pulled Wayne by the sleeve and talked into his ear.

He continued. "Ben was a great son. Kind, respectful...loved his family. The way most of our children out here turn out." He took a handkerchief from his jacket pocket. "Why anyone would want to hurt him...unfortunately things are handled differently in New York. Well most of you know what happened."

With his mouth now dry like sawdust, Wes had trouble finishing sentences. Feeling a hand on his back, he turned to see the priest pointing under the pulpit shelf. Wes stepped backwards down one step and took a glass of water from underneath. With a look of surprise and gratitude, he sipped the water.

"I guess I'm not the first person to stand up feelin' like his tongue was three sizes bigger than normal. They had this waiting for me." He lifted the glass.

His words came slowly now as he reflected on Ben's life.

"Ben left a wife, Claire, and two small children who were his life. He was only months away from moving the family back out here. Now we hope they still come to stay here – a safer and gentler place where a man's word is his bond and family means something...and human life means something."

Wes stood silent for a moment, almost looking drunk. The stress of the past days was now evident on his hardened face, and the words that he had rehearsed over in his mind were lost looking down upon the coffin.

"He was such a good boy. Why would anyone..." he fought to hold back tears and at first was successful, but Claire began to sob, causing a chain reaction. Tears rolled down his cheeks. He stepped down one step, then leaned back up and hoarsely said, "I'm sorry," then stepped down, walking off the altar and past the coffin without looking at it.

Claire stood waiting for him. She reached out her arms. The crowd watched as the two swayed crying in the center aisle. Not a cowboy among the mourners was immune to the touching seen and many cried like babies, some for the first time in their lives.

Claire's body went limp. Wes lifted her gently, placing her back in the seat. The priest came down off the altar.

"Is she all right?" he asked.

"I'm okay. Just a little weak that's all."

The priest quickly started the service again, hoping to direct the attention of the mourners away from the family. He kept watch from the corner of his eye, making sure that Claire was all right, as he continued, nearing the end of the Mass.

Coming off the altar carrying incense, he motioned to the front pew. They all stepped out. The three men took their place on one side of the casket while three of Ben's cousins lined up on the opposite side. The women followed behind as the coffin was wheeled down the aisle behind the priest and two altar boys.

Betty stopped twice along the way to hug friends in the aisle seats. Claire just looked back as she and Jessica kept walking arm in arm, both covering their noses from the intense smell of the incense.

In the vestibule, the six men lifted the coffin to their shoulders and carefully carried it out the main doors and down the two small steps to ground level.

The tires of the black Suburban were backed up against the curb in a space left between Wes's truck and the car in front of it. With its tailgate opened facing them and back end of the vehicle overhanging the sidewalk, the pallbearers lowered Ben's body and slid it inside.

"Okay Jeff, take my boy home for good." Wes pulled the tailgate down and pushed it shut.

Claire watched as again Ben was leaving her. She wanted to follow immediately but the crowd enveloped the family and people she had never before met, hugged her. Howie came from the truck and worked his way through the crush of people, finding Claire almost cowering next to Betty.

It took almost half an hour for the crowd to dwindle, leaving only the close family and the priest.

"Well let's head out," Wes said, pushing down on the top of his hat. "Anybody ridin' in a car might wanna catch a lift with a truck. It's bumpy," he yelled to get their attention.

Wes led the line of twelve assorted four-wheel drive vehicles up the hill. Turning onto Main Street, he watched in his mirror, making sure all the trucks made the turn together. The procession with their lights on headed back to the ranch. By now Ben's coffin would be resting over his grave.

Howie watched while Claire nervously played with something in her hand.

"What's that?"

"Ben's Mass card."

"Where'd you get that - I didn't see them."

Betty turned to the back. "They were in the vestibule. You couldn't have seen them while you were carrying the coffin."

Claire handed it to him. "Saint Francis of Assisi, the patron saint of animals."

"That's what he would've wanted." He flipped the card over and quickly read the prayer. "I'll keep this one," he said, sliding it into his inside jacket pocket.

"Claire, I'm not feeling so good and I don't think I can stand to see the coffin again so I think I'll stop at the house and watch the children and let Jill go with all of you - that's if you don't mind, dear." Betty said. "Or maybe you want to bring the kids?"

"No, I don't want them to see that. It's not something I want them to remember. I'd like to bring them back later though, once he's buried. Maybe someone could bring me."

"I'll come back with you later," Howie said.

After a quick stop at the house, the procession continued on along the bumpy road, parking at the gravesite. Wes shut the engine and, like the others, looked straight ahead. He then put his hand on Jill's knee.

"Ready?" he then glanced up to the rear view mirror. "Claire, you ready?"

She looked down at the floor, then raised her head. The priest already stood behind Ben's shiny casket, which rested on two metal poles stretching across the open grave. A mound of dirt four feet high had been piled away from the grave to allow room for the mourners.

One of Ben's cousins stood between the trucks and the grave, holding red roses. As the mourners passed she gave each a single flower.

Claire opened her door and stepped down. Off in the distance, she could see two men leaning against the backhoe, waiting to finish their job. Howie hurried around to meet her almost bumping into Wayne who had come to escort his wife.

Howie and Claire were the last to join the others, and just as at the church, Claire only heard the first few words that the priest said.

"We are gathered here today..."

She would have liked to have reached out and touched the casket, or better yet, laid her upper body across it but if she got too close, the possibility of sliding into the hole under the casket was too great. Her nightmares would come easily enough and she wasn't going to help them along. But she just needed to be closer to Ben somehow. Suddenly a strong urge to hold the children came across her. Her face lit up through the tears just for a moment as she felt this yearning as Ben's way of bringing himself close.

With the end of the service near, Claire's thoughts actually left Ben and returned to a recurring internal struggle - living the rest of her life in South Dakota - bringing the tears down her cheeks faster than before.

The priest ended the service by blessing the grave, and with a low "amen," the family one by one walked past the head of the coffin, each laying their red rose on top.

Claire found herself alone as the others walked back to their trucks. She laid her rose. "Goodbye Sweetheart, we'll miss you. I'll bring the children back later and try again to get them to understand."

The drive back was quiet. Claire wasn't looking forward to being back at the house where it would be filled with people. Howie had the same feelings. He would be the one at center stage for questions of exactly what transpired in New York.

"I'm not really up to seeing people when we get back," she said.

"I'm not either," Wes said. "But no one's gonna expect you to be sociable."

"You know what - I'm not going in when we get back. I think I'll just go for a walk or something. When the sun's out from the clouds, it's not that bad. Howie, you go in and get the kids and bring them to me, okay?"

"Good by me, but where you gonna be?"

She thought for a moment. "Drop me behind the barn. I'll wait there but just don't leave me there too long, Howie."

"Know what, call Betty right now and tell her to have the kids ready to go."

Nearing the house, Wes stopped the truck. Claire walked down a small slope to the barn where she found a wooden chair. She dragged it from the shadow of the building and sat. She strained to hear the sounds of laughter, and soon Howie's voice and giggling children grew closer.

"Right around there. That's where she is," she heard him say and the two came into sight yelling "Mommy, Mommy."

"Listen, Wes said to go in the barn. It'd be warmer in there."

The front doors to the barn were in full view of the house, but Claire, now distracted by the children, didn't think about or care at this point who saw them go in. Howie looked up to the top of the ten-foot doors and lifted the wooden latch that held them shut.

He leaned back, swinging the right side door open with a loud squeak. With the children growing excited behind him, knowing from their books that farm animals lived in barns, he peeked in.

"Should we really be going in here? I mean we're from New York, what do we know from barns?" he asked.

"It's a farm Howie. I don't think that farm animals hurt people. Besides I don't think Wes would let us go in if there were danger."

"Oh yeah."

"Coward," she mumbled.

Once inside, Howie formed bales of hay to make a couch, but before they could sit, the children dragged them toward the back stalls. After petting a cow, some sheep and a pony, the two children found great pleasure in chasing a chicken, giving Howie and Claire a chance to sit.

"I think every house with kids should have a chicken. Keep 'em busy for hours – they'll never catch him. Guarantee they tire out before he does...or is this one a she?" Howie asked.

"I'll have to show you one of the kids' books so you can learn the difference."

Howie put a piece of hay in his mouth, letting the end hang out.

"Why are you eating hay?" she asked, looking puzzled.

"I'm not eating it. I'm just doing what they do in the westerns. The guys always have a piece of hay stickin' out of their mouths. I figured maybe it tastes good or something." He shrugged his shoulders.

"Well does it?"

"Does it what?"

"Does it taste good?"

"Oh," he laughed. "No not really. Doesn't have much of any taste actually. I don't know what the cows see in it."

The childrens' giggling as they explored the barn was the only sound keeping Howie and Claire out of an awkward silence, both uncomfortable about what they needed to talk about.

"Everything went smoothly today just like the service in New York did," Howie said.

"Yeah, I guess."

"Now I'm flyin' back tomorrow and you'll be back when?" he asked.

She looked down at the floor as she spoke, pushing hay around with her foot. "I think the flight is Friday. I don't know who's coming with me yet. Probably Wayne, maybe Wes or Jessica... They're going to help me pack up the house." She flashed her eyes up at him and saw his disappointment.

"All right, let's talk about this." He swung his knee up on the bale and faced her. "Do you really want to move out here? Or is it what everyone else wants?"

"It's what Ben wanted."

"I understand that, but do you believe the children will do better here? You heard what Wes said in his eulogy. That the boys that stayed here did just as well as Ben did."

"You heard that too, huh?"

"Yeah, and once you're gone everything having to do with Ben is gone. It'll be like he was never there." He hung his head.

"But Howie...I have no family there and I can't take care of that house alone. I've weighed all the pros and cons, and even though I'll die a thousand deaths out here, what other choice do I have?"

He perked up. "I could help you."

"Howie, that's sweet, but some day you'll have a family of your own and for now you've got enough with work and your little girlfriends."

"Well it's your life. I guess we could visit, but I really think you should consider what you're doing. I know it's what Ben wanted and all."

Michael yelled out, "Mommy, a mouse."

Claire pulled her legs up to her chest. "I think it's time to go," she said nervously.

"Yeah I guess you ought to go in and see everyone. I know you're not up to it, but it's gotta be done. Then I'll take you back to the grave."

It was only a short walk to the house. Howie, carrying Michael, kicked a basketball-sized tumbleweed along the ground, which was packed hard and imprinted with hoof marks. Claire lagged a bit behind, not in any rush to go in.

"Howie listen, don't leave my side. I don't want to caught up in conversations that I can't get away from."

"Deal! But only if you help me from being alone with Betty. She'd like nothing better than to beat me to death for asking you if you really wanted to stay out here."

Once inside, Betty greeted Claire with a hug and took Michael from Howie. She walked him and Sarah to the center of the great room, which was filled with people.

"These are my other grandchildren," she announced. "Spittin' image of Ben, the boy is. They're coming out here to live with us." She turned to look at Howie, but he had already slipped off to the kitchen with Claire.

"You know Claire, you have to go out there and say hello – even if its only for a second," Jessica said to her.

"All right, Howie lets go."

Betty could see them making their way through the small gathering in the kitchen.

"This is my daughter-in-law, Claire."

She gave a small wave, leaning against the outside of the kitchen counter, which divided the rooms. Betty coaxed her over. Reluctantly, she joined her.

"Look Mom, I really want to take the kids back to the grave while it's still warm out," she whispered.

"Nonsense dear, there's plenty of time for that."

"No, Mom...I'm not doing this now," she said more firmly. "I'm sorry everyone, but I'm not up to talking right now."

She walked toward the stairs, passing Howie. "I want to change my shoes. Be ready to take me in five minutes."

Betty looked embarrassed. "Can I get anybody anything?" she asked to break the silence.

Wes stood up. "Hey Jessica, turn that music up a little will ya?"

Howie stood by the front door, jingling the keys on the many key rings that hung from brass hooks. As he unhooked a set of keys, he stood up straight, realizing that he wasn't alone. He could feel an angry presence. He turned slowly. Betty stood in front of him. She reached out and with an open palm, smacked him on the forehead.

"What kind of ideas are you putting in that girl's head? Did you see how she acted?" She started to shake her finger in Howie's face as Claire came down the stairs. Claire took Betty's arm and gently guided her away from Howie.

"Mom, look, I'm sorry but I have to go there...now."

Betty sighed. "I understand – Howie, I'm sorry." She walked away.

"Thanks for saving my life. I thought she was going pop me again."

"Again? She hit you?"

"Just a little love tap. C'mon, let's go. Get whatever stuff you want to bring."

"You gonna be all right out here alone with the kids?" Howie asked, pulling up to the gravesite.

"Howie, there's no wild animals out here. It's not Africa. Besides I've got the radio. I'll call you if there's any problems." She opened a small collapsible cooler and peeked inside. "I've got some munchies for them and water and I brought a small case with toys to keep them busy."

"How long you plan on stayin' out here? I mean it's not summer."

"We'll be fine."

"Okay, c'mon I'll walk you over."

With great apprehension, she walked towards the grave, leading both children by the hand. Howie followed, carrying three folding chairs.

The metal supports were gone and the previously open grave was now a carefully shaped mound of dirt, three inches above the surrounding area. The newly packed soil, darker than the surrounding earth, was still moist from the depths.

At the head of the grave was a log, two feet long and standing on end. The top was cut at an angle facing the mound, and mounted there was a bronze cross bearing the likeness of Jesus – a temporary marker until the permanent head stone was cut.

"Remember what I told you about Daddy?"

The children both shook their heads, confused about what this had to do with their father. Claire had a look of frustration. Explaining to young children the concept of death and that their father was buried would be trying.

"You sure you're going to be okay out here alone?"

Not feeling as secure as she did in the truck, she looked out in all directions.

"Yeah...I guess so."

"You don't sound as sure as you did before. You want me to stay?"

"No, I'd rather be alone with them. Less distraction that way."

"Okay, call me when you want me back."

The children waved as he drove off.

"Okay...Michael, you come on this side and Sarah, you come over here," she said, positioning them on either side of her. She knelt down beside the grave and leaned back on her heels. "Now we talked about Daddy being in heaven, right?"

"Yeah," Michael said.

Sarah nodded her head in a big motion. Michael bent down and took a handful of the loose dirt and threw it across the grave.

"No, no, Honey." She pulled him back so he couldn't reach the mound.

How do I tell them that their father is buried under here? What if it scares them? It can wait.

"You know what? I brought some potato chips and some things for you to play with." She stood up and brushed her knees. "Here, sit in these chairs or better yet..." She opened a red blanket. Play on this. Michael, I brought some trucks for you, and Sarah, your dolls are in the case."

Claire took a chair to the other side of the grave where she could talk to Ben and still see the children. She reached down and took a handful of the dirt, letting it fall through her fingers.

"Well Honey, this is it. This is where you wanted to be." She spoke quietly. "I guess I'll be able to visit you every day once I move out here." She looked around almost as if waiting for a voice to tell her that it was okay to stay in New York.

She stood up, reaching into her back pocket and taking out three photos. One was their wedding picture and the others were one of Ben in a suit, and the other of him playing with the children on their living room floor on Christmas.

"Ben, you were right. This place is peaceful." She felt a chill run down her spine, feeling that Ben's spirit had gone through her. She gasped. "You really are here...watching us." She took great comfort in the feeling.

"Mommy, I'm cold," Sarah said.

"Aw Honey, we've only been here a few minutes." She sighed. "Okay, I'll call Uncle Howie in a bit and we'll go soon as he comes back. You wanna come over and sit on my lap to get warm."

"No."

"Okay, Howie, give us ten minutes and come get us – they're cold," she called into the radio.

While waiting, Claire took out a small camera. Wanting pictures for the people in New York, she shot a whole roll from different angles. Getting the tree and the grave together proved difficult, as she had to continuously back up to fit them both in the frame.

"I'll be back tomorrow, Ben. We'll talk some more."

She leaned back and watched the gentle motion of the weeping willow tree, crying quietly. Her sorrow was for Ben, but as she looked out into the empty distance, the tears were also for herself.

Chapter Fourteen

Simultaneously in New York, another event was unfolding. Ben was about to reach out from the grave and strike a blow of revenge.

The ruins of an eighteen-hundreds building fashioned after a medieval castle sat hidden high on the slope of the tree-covered hill overlooking Victor Dracken's office building. Dark stone walls had crumbled into mounds; the lighter colored mortar that had once held them in place was now brittle and would turn to dust with just slight pressure.

Surrounded by tall maples, the building was camouflaged from the parking lots and buildings below. Through a window in the still-standing turret, the parking lot of Dracken's building was visible, although it was three quarters of a mile away. Standing almost three stories tall, the vine-covered tower, obviously once used as a lookout post, fared better than the adjoining building. Constructed of two foot square flat stones with smaller baseball sized stones in between, it had been added later, and a better mortar had been used.

Some of the smaller stones from the broken walls were fashioned into a circle and were scorched black. Ashes and burned wood pieces from a campfire still remained.

The ground was moist, the thick canopy above keeping out the drying rays of the sun. Wet leaves mixed in with broken glass and crushed beer cans, which littered the area.

In the doorway, remnants of the wooden jambs clung loosely to the stone. The door, long gone, left only its rusted metal hinges with pieces of rotted wood still clinging.

Inside was a single round room, twelve feet across. Once white-walls were now marred with graffiti and dirt from decades of exposure to the elements. A staircase, made of the same stone as the exterior, hugged the wall, half way around.

The ceiling was blistered and cracked from the invading rainwater. Huge gaping holes exposed the massive timbers used to construct the floor above. A drop fell every three seconds into a puddle, echoing throughout the structure.

A strong mildew odor came from a mattress, partially propped up against the wall. Torn open and exposing its coils, it was the only thing in the room.

The stairway leading upward was still solid. Splintered wood sticking out of mortar filled holes in the stone were all that was left of the rails.

Broken bottles and wet newspapers covered the floor on the next level. Here the smell of mildew was replaced by the odor of beer, which had permeated the wooden floor.

A wooden ladder rose to a square hole in the ceiling – the entrance to the third tier. A metal chair that sat next to the ladder was probably used to bypass the broken rungs, which were snapped in the middle.

Only a semblance of a roof still remained over the turret's final level. Old beams and roofing material hung precariously overhead. Plywood strips that appeared to be only years old were cut narrowly enough to fit through a small entrance hole and placed over the existing rotted floor. A blue tarpaulin covered an area directly under the only window in the room.

A long black nylon duffel bag with many zippered and Velcro pouches sat to the left of the window. A hand unzipped a pouch and removed a large set of binoculars, raising them to a pair of deep blue eyes. Luke sat at his perch waiting for his prey to appear. Nesting pigeons cooed quietly as they watched the intruder unpack his bag, piece by piece.

Luke's long blond hair and ponytail were now shaved, as well was the rest of his body. His acne-scarred face was the only visible skin. With the increased technology of forensics, he knew not to leave a trace – no hair, no blood, no saliva. A police trained dog could pick up almost any scent, so even his waste would have to leave with him in containers.

His black military boots were wrapped in heavy plastic bags to prevent footprints and were two sizes too large in case they did sink into the soft dirt outside. Camouflage pants were tucked into his socks, and tight elastic gloves covered his hands. The woolen cap that just covered his ears could be pulled down to a full ski mask in an instant if he was confronted.

Having been to the building briefly the day before, he had spent most of the night rehearsing his plan, as he lay hidden in the forest. The evidence of teenagers using the turret as a hangout had kept him at a distance but now he would have to chance being caught.

The powerful binoculars brought Dracken's building within inches, but his line of sight was obstructed by two branches, both over twenty feet high. He was prepared. Using a telephone lineman's belt and climbing gaffs, he shimmied up the first tree. With a small, battery operated reciprocating saw; he easily cut through the branch, watching it plunge to the ground. Within ten minutes, the branch on the next tree fell just as easily.

With his binoculars back in hand, he peered through the eyepieces, turning the adjusting wheel slightly to focus. A slight smile showed his yellowing teeth. He now had a clear line of sight.

He kneeled over the duffel bag and pulled the zipper down the length of the bag. He carefully lifted out a fifty-caliber semiautomatic sniper rifle and laid it on the ground. Taking a padded case out next, he unzipped it and removed a scope. He peeled off his gloves revealing a second pair of surgical gloves. Under them, his palms and fingertips were covered with clear silicone rubber to avoid leaving any prints. Nothing was left to chance.

Sweat build-up between the thin rubber gloves and his skin allowed two tattoos, one on each hand, to show brightly. A blue skull and cross-bones on the left, and on the right, the letters RIP in red.

Placing the scope onto the rifle, he screwed down the locking knob, joining them securely. He raised the scope to his eye and panned the area. The lane between the trees afforded him a view from the main doors of Dracken's building to half way across the adjacent parking lot. He zeroed in on a white stretch limo parked against the sidewalk next to the building. The license plate read Dracken II, Dracken's vanity giving away his presence.

Luke was not unfamiliar with Dracken's cars or his routine. From the moment he had learned of the will, he had on occasion staked out the building – before the manhunt for him had begun. He still had no idea that the police were searching for him.

Luke broke the gun down and placed it back into the duffel bag. He took out a set of range finding binoculars, much smaller than the first pair, and flipped on the switch. As he panned the target area, digital numbers increased and decreased rapidly inside the lenses. Focusing on the limo, he pushed a button, locking in the number. It read .72.

Three quarters of a mile.

Luke was no genius – he knew only two things, cars and anything to do with hunting. He knew that the sound of a gunshot would take between five to six seconds to reach someone three quarters of a mile away, depending on wind speed. With that he concluded that he could get off three to four shots before Dracken even knew he was a target. And at that distance, making the first shot would be difficult. He would probably need all four.

He lifted his sleeve to see his watch.

Noon

He packed his equipment. He would return at four o'clock and wait for Dracken. If the shot couldn't be made today, he would return the next day. The longer the hunt lasted, the more of a rush he got.

* * * * * *

For the first time in his life, Victor Dracken was afraid. A stealthy enemy that neither the police nor his men could locate kept him out of sight.

"I can't believe the cops can't find this guy," he said to Willie. "I can't believe my guys can't find this guy. That's what makes me nervous."

He paced the floor in front of his desk.

"I never seen you scared before boss," Willie said. Dracken glared at him. "I didn't mean nothin by it boss, just that I figured no one scared you."

"This is different Willie." He filled a glass a quarter full with scotch. "This guy has just disappeared off the face of the earth. I have to watch everything I do, everywhere I go. I went to my daughter's grave yesterday and had to worry that this guy would jump out from behind a headstone even though I had eight men with me," he said, almost in a rage. "This guy isn't like everyone else, he's not afraid of me. I've done some checking," he sat back in his chair and swished the scotch around the glass. "This guy is crazy, makes me look like a saint."

"Why don't just go away for a couple days? They'll find him eventually," Willie said.

"I can't do that you idiot," he downed the scotch and stood up. "You want the cops to think I'm scared of this guy?"

Ironically, from his top floor office and from almost the same elevation, Dracken stared across to the tree-covered hill where Luke sat in wait.

"It's almost four-thirty. Another day gone and these fucking cops haven't caught this guy."

"Hey boss, tell me again why they can't put this guy's face on TV. You know, like that Most Wanted show – I love watchin' that."

Dracken gave him a slow dirty look and then explained. "They don't want every idiot to try this will thing. Reporters would want to know what he's wanted for and they think the will story will leak out."

Dracken sat back in his chair and rekindled a cigar that had sat in an ashtray.

"Maybe they don't wanna find him. You know these cops got it in for you."

"I thought of that but...you know...fuck them. Let's pay the TV station a visit and offer a reward for this guy. Fuck the cops." He paced the room again. "Yes, yes, let's do that. Call downstairs and have them sweep the lot with the cameras. Let them know I'm coming down in ten minutes."

Willie grabbed a radio and alerted Dracken's men outside to be prepared. Dracken went into the bathroom.

Coming back out, he buckled his belt. "Any problems?"

"It's clean out there, Boss."

"Good, let's go."

Luke kneeled back at his perch and rested his elbow on a piece of foam rubber, which was laid on the rock sill of the window. He brought the rifle scope to his eye and waited. Expecting Dracken to exit the front of the building, he pointed the gun at the front doors then panned to the car. He jerked his head back when he saw three men standing next to the limo. While laying the gun down quickly, he grabbed the binoculars with the other hand for a wider field of vision.

Three?

He watched as the men in suits looked around nervously, but quickly shrugged it off and brought the gun sight back up to his eye. He planted his elbow firmly into the foam and waited, scanning back and forth.

Most men's hearts would now be racing, but Luke was not like most. He thrived on the hunt – his heart actually slowed. A rapid pulse now could throw off the shot.

While he was putting each of the bodyguards in his cross-hairs for practice, Dracken emerged from a side door, leaving Luke with less time to set up the shot.

Shit.

From the side door, Dracken only had thirty feet to walk to the car, as opposed to over two hundred from the front. The other difference was that Dracken was now walking towards Luke instead of crossing past him. A bullet straight to the

forehead rather than the temple excited Luke; he would be able
to see the hole as Dracken fell. Luke pulled away from the sight
for an instant to rub his eye, which teared from the strain.

With Dracken back in the cross-hairs, he followed him
towards the car, waiting for the perfect moment. The best case
scenario was that Dracken would stand still outside the car for
just one second.

Because of the great distance the bullet would travel, Luke
would have to compensate for a light breeze. Gravity would
play an even bigger role in the shot, pulling the bullet down
over the long trajectory. He would have to aim above his target.
Complicating the shot further was the angle downhill.

Dracken reached for the handle of the limo's rear door.
Willie stood directly behind. Luke braced himself and drew in
a deep breath, holding it. He squeezed the trigger until the gun
fired. The first shot took out the headlight of a car parked behind
the limo.

Too high!

Compensating quickly, he squeezed the trigger and fired
off two more rounds, the first hitting Dracken over the left eye
and the next grazing Willie's shoulder. Dracken was knocked
back into his bodyguard's chest. Willie kept his balance while
falling backwards, but he was unable to catch Dracken, who
slid down, the front of his body leaving a smeared bloody trail
from Willie's shoulder to his thigh.

A small entrance wound through Dracken's left eyebrow
was not bleeding, but the exiting bullet had blasted a huge hole
in the back of his skull, sending shards of bone onto the
pavement.

Luke continued to watch as chaos erupted in the parking
lot. Bodyguards with guns drawn pointed them wildly in the air
looking for the shooter. An unmarked police car screeched to
a halt near the limo. Pedestrians close enough to see the blood
ran for cover. Those more than fifty feet away just froze, the
gun shots to them sounding only like faint pops.

The two officers, after calling for backup, ducked low
running toward Dracken, who lay flat on his back near the rear
of the car. The first officer lifted Dracken, sitting him upright to

drag him aside. But as Dracken's head fell forward, the officer found himself staring directly into the massive hole in the back of his head. A three-inch wide piece of scalp hung off to the side still clinging to the head, but the bone was missing. Startled, the officer jumped back, allowing Dracken's head to smack the pavement in a splash of blood. The officer retreated for cover behind the limo.

Willie sat on the curb holding his shoulder wound, which bled heavily, but wasn't serious. His face was splattered with Dracken's blood, and gray matter covered his jacket.

"He's dead, ain't he?" he asked the officer.

"Very dead, sorry."

Luke continued to watch, enjoying every moment of the twenty-second ordeal. The scattering bystanders particularly amused him. The sound of sirens ruined his high and he fell back against the wall and sat for a few seconds.

"Fifty grand baby," he yelled.

He scooped up the three spent shells and packed them away with the rest of his gear. The sirens were louder now, but feeling bulletproof, he took his time. Leaving the turret like a tourist leaving a hotel, he walked out, looked around, and headed for the top of the hill. His only concern was beating the search helicopter that would soon be circling the area looking for him.

Luke was already spending his money as he slapped one foot in front of the other going down the steep gradient on the other side of the hill. He slowed approaching the bottom, making sure no one was near.

From one hundred feet up the slope, he had a full view of the back of the stores and parking lot where he had left his car. A twenty-four-hour hamburger shop, a drug store and convenience store kept the lot active. His car would never come under suspicion. He sat for a moment and watched for anything unusual, but he felt safe.

The car, which he had backed in for easy access to the trunk, was only fifteen feet from the edge of the woods. He glanced around once and then broke at a fast pace for the car. He had the trunk rigged with an automatic opener so with one push of the key ring button, it popped open.

Confident that no one was watching, he threw the bag in and sat on the ground. In an instant, his boots were off. He pulled his pant legs out of his socks and yanked them down straight. He rubbed his hands together quickly, peeling the silicone rubber off in pieces into a small bag.

With one more nonchalant look around the lot, he opened the door and got in. The people who walked near the stores never gave him a second look. Little did they know the chaos that he had caused on the other side of the hill.

The next part of his plan was a quick stop at a nearby lake where he would deposit the gun and its shell casings. His boots would be filled with rocks and sunk. His clothes would be burned when he was able to find a suitable location.

All was going perfectly according to plan, and in a few hours he would be drinking Jack Daniel's from the bottle at the upstate cabin. No one would ever know he had left there.

He was feeling cocky, but knew better than to speed. A trivial stop by the police could ruin his well designed plans. He kept both hands on the wheel, and even signaled when changing lanes.

Feeling more comfortable as he got miles away, he flipped on the radio while he dreamed of his fifty large. He glanced in his rear view mirror and looked back at the road ahead. It took a few seconds for the silhouette in the mirror to register. He looked again as his dream turned into a nightmare.

A patrol car approached him quickly. Luke's first instinct was to look at the speedometer, but he wasn't over the limit. He clutched the wheel tightly, praying that the car would pass. It didn't. With lights now flashing, the car was right up on Luke's tail.

He remained calm – he had to, his life depended on it. He slowed the car and pulled to the side. He knew that there was nothing in the passenger compartment that would raise immediate suspicion. There was of course the nine-millimeter handgun, but that was hidden in a cut in the seat and was almost invisible. But the trunk was a different matter.

Luke had to make a decision. If the cop was just pulling him over for a burned out light bulb, he could probably just get off with a warning and no harm done. But if the cop wanted to start snooping around, Luke's life was over. His only alternative made his perfect plan a bit more complicated, but it was the only way. He would have to kill the officer, leave the scene and pray that no one witnessed it. There weren't many cars passing and there were steep embankments on both sides. The nearest house was a quarter mile in the distance.

He watched and waited while the officer sat in his car looking at a clipboard.

C'mon.

In a split second, the squad car backed up violently. The officer swung his door open with his gun drawn, pointing it at Luke through the space between the door and the body of the car.

"Step out of the vehicle."

Luke dropped the car into gear only to stop short when the flashing lights of more patrol cars approached from ahead. There was still a way out – there had to be. He started turning the wheel but his options ran out. The thumping sounds of a police helicopter directly above put the final nail in his coffin.

What the fuck?

He leaned forward, looking up through the windshield. Spinning the tires in desperation, he took the car down the embankment, only to wedge a large concrete slab under it. The tires still spun, but they were lifted off the ground. He jumped out, his pistol in his belt, and ran for the houses, but he knew there was no way out.

The wind from the chopper kicked up dirt, blinding him and almost knocking him down. An officer yelled to him over the loudspeaker.

"Lie flat on the ground with your hands above your head."

He stopped running and turned toward the approaching officers. The helicopter backed away. Luke could hear a dog barking. The K9 unit had arrived.

Eight officers, all with guns drawn, approached. They took small steps toward him while yelling for him to drop to the ground, but he wasn't going back to jail. He moved his jacket revealing the pistol.

"Gun! Gun!" the officers yelled.

"Don't do it Luke, it's over."

"How the fuck do you know my name?"

"Doesn't matter."

Luke took one look around, and in a quick motion yanked the gun from his belt. Eight guns fired simultaneously, dropping him to his knees.

He held tight to the gun at his side. His vision blurred...sounds echoed. He felt cold.

"How?" was the last word he muttered as his body convulsed and his face slammed hard into the dirt.

Chapter Fifteen

It was lunchtime twenty-four hours after Ben's burial. The family gathered in the great room. Claire flipped through the TV channels.

"Can't you just settle on one station?" Wes asked.

"It's called channel surfing Dad. You have more channels here with the satellite than we have at home. Just want to see them all."

Jill and Jessica sat on the floor, coloring with the four children.

"Claire, do us all a favor and put the cartoons back on. They're acting like angels right now and I'm not up for any running around," Jill said.

Claire complied and threw the remote down. She looked at her watch, as did Wes at the same time.

"Howie, you got three hours before your flight. We leave here soon. You all packed?" Wes asked.

"Yeah, I'm ready."

Betty answered the phone in the kitchen. "Howie, it's for you. Detective from New York."

Howie jumped up and met her near the kitchen.

"Hello?" he listened for a moment. "You're kidding – no way," he looked at Claire and pointed at the phone mouthing Dracken's name. "Wow! Really!"

The room sat riveted as Howie paced and listened in disbelief.

"What happened?" Claire said loudly. Howie just put his finger up for her to have patience.

"Okay, I'll go up and go online for the details...me? I'll be back tonight. Okay thanks."

He stood in the middle of the room.

"You're not going to believe this."

"They caught Luke?" Claire asked excitedly.

"Better – they killed him."

"Beautiful," Wes said.

"Wait, it gets better, Wes. You're gonna be thrilled. They killed him chasing him down after he killed Dracken." Howie jumped in the air and screamed at the top of his lungs, "Yeah baby."

"Oh! Ya just gotta love that," Wayne said.

"Lemme go upstairs on the computer and print the story from our local paper. I'll make copies. This must be the front page." Howie's footsteps boomed through the house as he charged up the stairs. Jill followed him up.

"That's the happiest I ever seen him," Wes said.

"You feel better Claire? Knowin' that they're gone," Wayne asked her.

"Ya know, I do feel a bit safer, but then again I never really thought of them as a threat to me or the kids for some reason. I guess I should be happy, but two more people are dead. I don't know."

"Those are two men who deserved to be dead," Betty said firmly. "After what they put us all through."

Wes stood up and looked up toward the balcony. He could hear Howie still screaming in joy. "That is good news," he mumbled. "Good news indeed."

"Hey Mom, you want to take a ride out to see him?" Claire asked.

"You go ahead, dear. I'm not really up to it; matter of fact, Wayne, if you would, bring me my tank."

"You okay Mother?" Wes asked.

"Just need a little oxygen. I'll be fine," she said, slipping the mask over her face.

"Hey Howie," Wes yelled up. "Make those copies and bring 'em down. You can read it on the way to the airport. We should get a move on."

Howie came down carrying two bags and laid them near the front door. "I'm ready."

Wayne helped Betty to her feet. She pulled the mask down around her neck. Howie stood waiting as she approached him.

"I'm so sorry Howie. You've lost a good friend for life."

She put her arms around his neck and pulled him down, kissing him on the cheek.

A line had formed behind her, and one by one they said goodbye. Jill and Jessica hugged him together as they cried. Wayne was next. He grabbed Howie and they swayed slightly.

"I'm gonna miss you, man," he said, slapping him on the back.

"Me too, Wayne."

As Wayne moved to the side, Claire stood, her head down and arms folded. She looked up shyly and then back down as she stepped forward. He guided his hands over her head from front to back, finally resting them on her shoulder.

"I'm only a phone call away," he said.

She nodded.

"You'll make it out here and the kids will do fine. You can come visit me anytime – you can afford it. Remember you're rich now."

Claire looked shocked for an instant.

"I didn't mean that..."

"No, I know. I just didn't think...call me about the money stuff when you get the chance," she said.

"Okay...look, I'll call you tonight when I get home."

They hugged one more time before Howie went to the children to say goodbye. Claire went into a kind of fog.

Howie gave his final wave as he and Wes went out the front door. There was complete silence as the echo of the door slamming faded. Slowly they took their seats, and Claire once again picked up the remote and surfed the channels. But now she wasn't bored as before. She played with the remote to hide her thoughts – thoughts of independence. She wanted to smack herself in the forehead as she had a revelation thanks to Howie's enlightenment. Ben had left her well off. Between the selling of the house, the savings and now the insurance money, she didn't have to live right there. She could buy her own place in Rapid City. It wasn't a huge city, but there were people – lots of people. And schools filled with lots of children. Everyone would be happy. She would be close by and there would be that buffer zone that all families should have. Claire jumped as Wayne sat down next to her.

"Did you tell Howie to get some packing boxes for the house before we get there?" he asked.

"I don't really think that he's going to have the time. I'll call the neighbors to scavenge for some."

Jill came up behind her and dropped a piece of paper over her head. It floated back and forth before falling into her lap.

"There's your story. Here Wayne, one for you."

Claire took the page and started reading but had trouble concentrating. Her mind was more on the idea of living off the ranch. She would be keeping her promise to Ben by moving to South Dakota, but how would Betty take it? She would need the right words.

Howie arrived early to an empty office on Wednesday morning. Coming up to his desk, he slowed in amazement at the stacks of neatly placed piles of papers that he needed to go through. With the back of his hand, he nudged a pile aside far enough to place his coffee.

"Where do I start?"

He shuffled some papers into bigger stacks, trying to avoid the inevitable – looking over the partition to Ben's side. He sat and leaned back in his chair, waiting for his computer to boot up.

God, Ben, I'm sorry.

He stood up and held his breath. Ben's desk looked just as it did on the last day that he was there. There were no piles of papers - no mess. There were just the pictures of Claire and the kids and some brochures. In the middle of Ben's blotter stood a greeting card, about ten inches tall. Howie picked it up. It was a hand drawn picture of a sunrise over mountains. Inscribed on the bottom were the words, "Ben, we will always remember you. Good luck on your trip through the mountains of the West. You were our friend, our colleague, our brother."

Tears poured down Howie's face as he opened the card to see the signatures of everyone in the office. Sitting back down, he leaned forward, putting his forehead on the edge of his desk. Tears, falling straight to the ground made a tiny puddle. His head shot up when the sound of talking came from the office lobby. He leaned his head back and sniffled, feeling around in his top drawer for a tissue. Two brokers walked past his aisle.

"Hey Howie, good to see you're back," one said. They didn't stop. They could see that he wasn't ready to talk.

By the time the majority of his coworkers came in, Howie had Ben's desk cleared into a box. There wasn't much - just the pictures, some bills and a few knick-knacks. The company forms and brochures were left for the next broker who would occupy that desk. Ben's client book now sat on Howie's desk.

"Howie, you want to come in for a second?" the assistant manager said.

Howie closed the door behind him.

"You feeling okay now?"

"Yeah, I'm all right."

"How's Ben's family doing?"

"As good as can be expected. His wife will be back in a couple days to pack up and move out West."

"Good, good. Listen, I guess you already figured that you were going to get Ben's book. You're a good broker - maybe take a few less chances and get a little more conservative. His clients will expect that - well, hell, I don't have to tell you. You already know most of them. It'll be a big bump in commissions for you. Sad way to get it, but I know you'll do the right thing for those people. Well, that's all I got - go to work."

"Thanks Mike, I appreciate it."

Howie stopped short as he came back to his desk. Someone had left a newspaper with the sports section face up. He stared at it for a second, then looked at Ben's book and then down to Ben's picture with the kids, which looked up at him from the box on the floor.

He slid the box under his desk and picked up the paper and the phone at the same time. He started to dial then stopped. Leaning back just far enough to see Ben's picture, he pursed his lips and laid the phone back in the cradle.

Automatic doors swung open. Claire pushed a cart with one suitcase through. She looked through the crowd as she walked, followed by Wayne and Jessica. An overhead speaker announced flight arrivals, barely discernable over the noise of the crowded terminal.

"Claire, over here," Howie called, waving and fighting his way through the people.

She waved back and pushed the cart along faster until they met.

"Its good to see you," she said as they embraced.

Wayne and Jessica waited behind her. Howie, still holding on to Claire, reached his hand out to Wayne. Letting her go, he reeled Wayne in. "Glad to have you guys around again. I was getting a little lonely." He then kissed Jessica on the cheek.

"You? Lonely? I doubt it," Claire said. "I'm sure there was some young thing to talk to."

"How you feeling Claire?" he asked.

Howie pointed toward the door and they started walking.

"I'm doing better, but I'm not looking forward to packing up the house."

"Oh I have to warn you – I brought Ben's truck. I didn't know how much stuff you had," he said, looking at Wayne's cart, which had three suitcases on it.

Claire made a face. "I'll have to get used to it. I've decided to drive that in South Dakota. You'll sell my car for me, Howie?"

"Sure, how much you want?"

Now outside, they stopped and waited for a traffic light to change to get to the parking garage. Jet engines roared above them as planes shot up into the evening sky.

"Well, find out what it's worth and just sell it."

"Okay. So Jesse, how was the flight?"

"It was okay. A little bumpy but okay."

Claire walked a bit slower as the truck came into sight. Expecting the truck to be in the shape that Ben kept it in, she was surprised to see the color dull with dust and bird droppings.

"You could've got it washed you know," Claire said.

"Yeah, in my spare time. What do you think I've been doing the past few days? I had paper work and phone calls that kept me busy late every night."

Wayne and Howie packed the suitcases into the rear as the women hopped into the back seat. As Howie backed out of the spot, Claire began crying.

"What's the matter?" Howie said, halting the truck. He jumped out and opened her door.

She looked up at him with tear filled eyes. "It just reminds me so much of him."

"You wanna take a taxi?" Wayne asked.

"No...no. I'll be all right. Just give me a second."

Within five minutes the truck, with its windows open, drove away.

"How were the kids when you left?"

"Oh God, they cried and that made me cry and then Jill's kids cried. It was a nightmare and poor Jill is still living it... and will be for a week. I hope her and Betty can handle it."

"They'll do fine," Jessica said.

"Don't tell me they'll do fine. I'd rather worry about them constantly. The only consolation in leaving them is that they'll be on my mind and maybe I won't cry over Ben as much."

"Well, with Wayne and Jes stayin' with you, that'll keep your mind occupied. And you can always call out to Betty and Wes and talk to the kids."

"I don't think I can afford any more long distance after the last few days. We spoke for how many hours the past few nights – and you called from my house."

"Well it's closer to work..."

"I know. I'm kidding, Howie," Claire said.

"Hey, how much time do we have to pack the place up?" Wayne asked. "I mean when are the movers coming?"

"Monday morning, first thing. We got the weekend. That's it. And by the way, the garage is filled with boxes. I mentioned to Gail that we needed them and all the neighbors brought some."

"They must want me out fast," Claire joked. "Oh yeah, Howie, tell me about the real estate agent again."

"I told you, she was there and I explained everything. She looked around again – you
know – to refresh herself. We'll give her a key when we leave and you'll sign power of attorney to me. When she sells it, I'll go to the closing and sign the papers."

Claire was silent upon approaching the house. One light was lit in the living room. Howie pulled in next to her car. He glanced over at Wayne. They didn't need to say a word – they both knew that Claire would be in tears within minutes of being inside.

Claire quietly walked from the truck up the stairs. Howie held the door open for her.

"Howie, it stinks in here. What the hell went on?"

"Well, one of the guys at work had a kid and he handed out cigars. I only had a few puffs and that was two days ago. I thought the smell would be long gone."

"Well you were wrong," she said loudly.

Wayne and Jessica came in, each carrying a suitcase.

"What's going on?" Wayne asked, wondering why Claire had raised her voice. "And what's that smell?" He and Jessica both sniffed the air and cringed.

"Howie smoked a cigar in here. Talk about being dumb as a stump," Claire said.

Howie sported a dumb smirk.

"Howie, I'm sorry."

"No, no, you're right. But Ben used to say that to me sometimes – the dumb as stump thing."

"Yeah, that's where I got it."

She disappeared into the hallway to the bedroom.

"Nice job, Howie," Wayne whispered. "You plan this? She ain't upset, she's just pissed."

The three looked at each other and laughed.

"Guess that it worked okay. Let's get the windows opened."

Howie tapped on Claire's door and stuck his head in. He watched as she flew around the room, picking up pictures into her arms.

"Howie, do me a favor. Run to the garage and grab some boxes."

"You're going to start packing now?"

She leered at him, still not thrilled with his cigar. He shut the door and quickly headed back to the living room. Jessica was rummaging through the refrigerator.

"Don't plan on eating any time soon," Howie said. "She's hell bent on moving out now."

"But we're starving," she said.

"Well, I've been ordered to get boxes. Why don't you go in and ask what she wants to eat."

Claire had taken her shoes off, so Howie didn't hear her come up behind him.

"Just order out," she said. "I don't care what you get."

Howie jumped in surprise and ran down the stairs to the garage.

"You really that mad about the cigar?" Jessica asked.

"No, I just want to pack the place up and get back to the kids."

She sat on the couch. "I just looked into their room and it made me miss them really bad. And the idea that I can't be near Ben..."

Howie had just come in from the garage with three boxes, but upon hearing Claire crying he quietly turned and tried to sneak back into the garage. Unfortunately, the metal door had never been oiled and it squeaked just loud enough for Claire to hear.

"Get up here, Howie. I know you're there."

He climbed the stairs holding the boxes in front of him and then backed down the hallway to the bedroom without having to make eye contact.

"Look, none of us wants to do this. I want to pack it and move it and get back to them as fast as I can."

Howie listened from down the hall.

"I still know you're there, Howie."

"Damn," he said, coming back into the room.

"You heard what I said?"

"Yeah."

"I want to try to put blinders on and just concentrate on getting out of here."

"Claire, can we order food now? We're starving," Jessica said.

"Sure, I'm sorry. Howie get the menus."

He handed menus to Wayne and Jessica.

"Now how does this work? You just call and they bring cooked food?" Jessica asked.

Howie laughed. "Yeah, that's how this works."

"Now hold on there, Howie. We don't know from this," Wayne said. "Out West, if you don't cook, you don't eat." He thought for a second. "You know Howie, you didn't look so smart back at our place when you asked how we held the bull down to milk it."

Jessica, who was drinking a glass of water in the kitchen, started to choke and spit the water over the counter. "You're making fun of us, and you thought you could milk a bull?"

"Okay, lets stick to the matter at hand – just decide what you want," Howie said.

Half an hour later the doorbell rang. Wayne and Jessica answered the door with the excitement of school children.

"Its here," she yelled, ripping open the bag. Within minutes the house was overcome with the smell of Chinese food.

"This is unreal," Wayne said. "You just call and in minutes there's food at the door."

Jessica looked at Claire sadly. "I guess you're going to miss this a lot, huh?"

"No Jessica, I'm not going to miss this at all...because I'm not going to be living on the ranch."

Claire got up and took her plate into the kitchen. The others just stopped chewing and looked at each other.

"Claire...Claire sweetheart. What does that mean?" Wayne asked.

"It simply means that I will move out there, but I'm going to live in Rapid City."

"You tell Betty this?" Howie asked. "Mainly because she's gonna blame me."

"Look, I really don't want to talk about it now. I just want to get as much done tonight as possible." She picked up a list of things she needed to get done.

"I'll pack my bedroom and the kids' room. You guys just throw everything small enough to fit into a box and mark what's in it. The kitchen and Ben's office will take the most time."

"I'll take the office," Howie said, running down the stairs.

The phone rang; Claire answered. "Hello...oh, hi Gail. We're back. C'mon over. Okay whenever."

She swung the front door open and unlocked the storm door. Howie came back up from downstairs, and before reaching the top, threw a handful of cartons toward Wayne and Jessica. "There's newspapers in the one box to wrap the glasses."

Claire sat on a small chair in the children's room just to take one last look at the peaceful, cozy space before she tore it apart. With the sounds of boxes falling and dishes clanking in the kitchen, it was hard to reminisce. She got up and pulled out a drawer and dumped it upside down into a box. She leaned her weight on the clothing until it was flat, then grabbed another drawer.

The sound of Gail's voice drew her back out to the living room. She waved to Paul who stood behind his wife while the two women embraced.

"How was everything around here while we were gone? Guess that Dracken story went over big, huh?"

"Its all everyone around here is talking about. I mean we met out in the street and talked about the details. I tell you though, it's brought the neighbors together," Gail said.

"Well at least something good came of it. Oh, you remember Wayne, over there in the kitchen, and that's Ben's sister, Jessica.

We're packing it all up fast. I can't stand to be here... you know, the memories and I got the kids waiting out there."

"Can we help?" Paul asked.

"Oh, thanks Paul, but not tonight. But if you want, tomorrow would be great."

It was well after midnight when they finally called it quits. The smell of Magic Marker used to identify the contents of the cartons was still prevalent. They all held drinks as they sat on the couch, exhausted. Jessica nursed a large paper cut on her thumb.

Boxes were piled five feet high in front of the living room window. Claire stared at them as she went over in her mind what needed to be done the next day.

"We got a lot done. By this time tomorrow, we should have all the little stuff packed. We probably have more time than we need."

"Claire, I don't mean to pry but...you're going to move to Rapid City?" Jessica asked.

"Yup, I'm going to take all my furniture and move it into a house there. This way I'm not in the middle of nowhere and I'm keeping my promise to Ben."

"I knew we were storin' all this in one of the barns but I didn't know where it was goin' from there. Now I know. But does Betty?" Wayne asked.

Claire stood up without answering his question. "I'm going to bed – see you all in the morning."

Claire sat on the living room floor, carefully wrapping Hummels from a curio cabinet. It was eight o'clock and she had already quietly packed three boxes. Howie was still asleep in the guestroom; his loud snoring finally coming to an end as the phone rang.

"Hello?" Claire said.

"Hi Claire, it's Detective Brent. How are you?"

"I'm fine. Doin' better I guess. We're just here packing up. I was going to come and see you before I left just to say goodbye. I have to pass by you on my way to a bank on Monday. You'll be there?"

"I should be. Call me and let me know what time and I'll make sure. Oh and by the way, when are you heading back out there?"

"I have a flight for Monday afternoon if I can get it all done by then. Whatever's left to do, Howie can manage for me."

Brent paused for a moment. "Actually, I'd like to speak to Howie. Is he staying there?"

"Howie, yeah he's here. Let me wake him." She tapped on his door and pushed it open. "Howie? You awake?"

"Barely, why? What time is it?"

"Phone for you." She laid the phone on his chest and walked out without closing the door.

"Hello?" he said, wiping his eyes.

"Howie, Detective Brent here."

Howie's eyes opened wide and he sprang up.

"Hey, how are you? What's up?" he asked, peeking into the living room and closing the door.

"We need to speak to you about something."

"Yeah, okay, what about?"

"I'll talk to you about it when I see you. I know you're helping Claire get ready over there so why don't you stop in say Tuesday morning early – say around eight."

Howie swallowed hard. "Level with me. Am I in trouble here?"

"We're not sure. Come in and we'll talk." Howie hung up the phone and fell back into the bed.

"What'd he want?" Claire asked.

"Oh...just about some old speeding tickets. Maybe they'll give me a break."

Claire was slow to respond. "Okay...you getting up now? Because I have to leave for a while."

He sat back up. "Where you off to?"

"I'm picking up the death certificates at the funeral home."

"You want me to go with you?"

"No, I want you to help them finish. Plus, I miss the kids, but I like the idea that I can hop around town for a little by myself without having to drag them in and out of the car."

Claire crept up the inside stairs of the funeral home. Her legs trembled slightly as she came to the last step. The office door was open, but there was no secretary. She walked in. "Hello," she called and then approached the funeral director's door. Startled as it pulled open, she stepped back.

"Oh, I'm sorry," the director said. "Come in, come in. Mrs. Pearce, am I right?"

"Yes. That's right."

"You called for your husband's death certificates." He flipped through files on his desk as Claire stood in fear of what she was about to read.

"Here they are." He handed the manila envelope to her and could see the fright in her eyes. "Are you all right? Would you like to sit for a moment? Some water, perhaps?"

"No, I'm okay. I'm just afraid to read how he died." She looked down at the floor. "Was it the fire that killed him or what?" She started to open the envelope. "You know, maybe I'll do this later. Thank you for your time."

"Good day, Mrs. Pearce. If I can be of assistance, please let me know."

Claire sat in her car over looking a small baseball field. The envelope sat on her lap. She lifted the flap that was tucked inside the envelope, and without looking down, pulled out the stack of certificates.

Please God don't let it be the fire.

She read past the name and address and all the small print and technical jargon and after a minute finally found the cause of death box.

"Broken neck," she mouthed. "Thank God." She shuffled the copies of the certificates. "I guess thank God – but he's still dead."

* * * * * *

By dinnertime the house no longer looked like a home. The shelves and cabinets were all bare and nails stuck out from the walls where pictures once hung. The dining room chairs were upside down on the table and the space underneath was crammed with boxes. Claire walked the entire house, checking every drawer. Howie, Wayne and Jessica sat on the couch and watched as she inspected.

"Everything up to snuff?" Wayne asked.

"Yeah, we did pretty good. We're ready for Monday morning, no problem."

"Claire, about the going away party next door. Do we have to go to that?" Howie asked.

"No, no reason. They can see you anytime. I'll just go for an hour or so. Matter of fact, I better get into the shower real quick." She went to turn the corner, but grabbed the wall with one hand and pulled herself back. "Howie, you okay? You a little sad?"

"I'm okay. Go ahead and get ready. You're going to be late."

Claire walked inside but returned immediately.

"Here, I didn't want to give these to you this morning but I figured you might want to read them." She handed each a copy of Ben's death certificate and dropped the manila envelope on the coffee table. "Howie, you said you need two copies for the accounts at your place, right?"

"Yeah."

"Okay, find a place when you're done where they won't get lost in this mess."

She walked away as the three started reading.

The sound of a diesel engine revving woke Claire early Monday morning. She looked around at the bare room knowing that it had been her last night there. She sat in the bed and listened as the truck engine continued. She heard talking outside and peeked out the window. A large green moving van was attempting to back into the driveway. Howie was already outside yelling directions to the driver.

Claire hadn't undressed from the night before, so she just slipped on her shoes and put on a sweater. Wayne and Jessica stood on the front stoop, the storm door wide open.

"Well, I guess this is it," Claire said.

The engine finally shut off. The driver came around the truck carrying a clipboard. "Who's Claire Pearce?" he asked in a heavy Russian accent.

"That's me."

"Sign here, here, and here."

She scribbled her name on the sheets and pulled out the copies, which she took inside. Two more men came from the cab and swung open the back doors to the truck, pulling down two hand trucks. They slid out a long metal ramp from under the body and, just like that, they were ready to go. Howie opened the garage door, exposing a wall of boxes all taped shut and labeled.

"We'll start loading the boxes. You guys get the furniture," Howie said to one of the men who pointed to the boss.

"They don't speak no English, just me. But I heard you," the boss said.

"Good; they want to get on the road as fast as possible. You know that they're following you in that blue truck right?"

"Yes, I understand that." He looked at Wayne. "We will be driving very fast and for many hours," he said before walking past and going inside.

"You could've got someone that speaks English, Howie," Jessica said.

"You want English, you pay double. You gonna be able to keep up with these guys on the road?"

"Doesn't really matter. We get there when we get there," Wayne said.

"Yeah I know, but you might not want to let these clowns out of your sight. Then again Claire's only paying half here. They get the rest out there."

Claire came out carrying her purse and wearing a blue baseball cap with her long blonde hair tucked behind her ears.

"You don't need me for a little while, right? I have to go to two more banks and stop at the police station, and I want to say goodbye to my boss."

"You're wearing a baseball cap?" Wayne asked.

"Well, I don't have time to shower and I'm certainly not showering with these guys in the house."

She walked in between the truck and the fence down the driveway. Howie followed.

"What's at the police station?"

"I was going right past it, so I figured I'd say bye to the detectives. Why? Howie? Something you're not telling me?"

"No, nothing. See you later."

Claire walked to the front desk of the station house. "Like to see Detective Brent please. Tell him Claire Pearce."

The desk sergeant made the call and directed her to go on back. Brent and Casey met her halfway down the hall. Brent reached out his hand.

"How are you Claire?"

Casey stood behind Brent, a cast covering his right arm.

"I'm fine – how are you feeling?" she asked Casey.

"I'm healing pretty good. No major problems. C'mon back. Coffee?"

"No thanks, I really can't stay more than a few minutes, but I would like to ask you about what happened – that's if you don't mind," she said to Casey.

They sat in Brent's cubicle.

"You mean about the accident?"

She nodded.

"Well first of all, I'm very sorry for what happened to Ben," Casey continued.

"I don't blame you for what happened. It was his crazy idea that got us all into this," she said.

"I am glad that you feel that way. I am also sorry that I have no recollection of anything hours before or after the accident. I'm told that's not unusual," Casey said, taking a sip of coffee.

"Nothing at all?"

"I'm sorry. I wish I could tell you something, but it's just not there – like it never happened."

"Okay, then tell me this. Why did you want to talk to Howie? Is there something that I don't know? He said something about old speeding tickets?"

"Yeah, don't worry, we'll help him out the best we can...with his tickets," Brent said.

"Okay." She still felt that they were leaving something out, but she had more on her mind. "Well, thanks for all your help. If you're ever in South Dakota, drop in."

"We'll be sure to," Brent said.

Claire pulled up to the house. The movers were just coming down the front stairs with her dresser. She cringed, watching the sides bump against the railing.

"Don't scratch that," she called out.

Howie, upon hearing her voice, came to the front door. He watched her eyes as she walked up the driveway, not once looking away.

"Howie, what's wrong with you? You're starting to give me the creeps."

"Nothing, nothing, why?"

The two movers heaved her dresser onto the truck as she walked by. Her eyes opened wide as the light breeze blew the smell of their sweaty bodies in her direction. She pinched her nose and climbed the stairs. Howie waited right inside.

"Okay Howie, I don't know what's going on and I don't care. They just said that they would help you with your tickets." She made quotation signs in the air with her fingers.

"We're blowin' through this," Wayne said. "They don't need us, and now that you're back, I think we'll just take off. I don't see the reason to follow these guys."

"Yeah, Wayne, go. Leave now and you'll be there by tomorrow night. Ben's truck all packed?"

"Yup, it's ready to go."

"So take off, man. We got it from here," Howie said.

"Jessica," he yelled. "Let's go."

Howie and Claire walked them outside.

"Well buddy, I guess this is it for a while," Wayne said to Howie. "You really have to come out."

"Yeah, maybe I'll get out there."

Howie extended his hand. Wayne swung his arm around until their hands met with a loud clap. They pulled each other in for a final hug before Howie turned to Jessica. "Bye Jesse, it was good to see you."

"Same here, Howie."

They both hugged Claire and jumped into the truck.

"See you tomorrow, Claire," Wayne yelled, pulling away.

Howie and Claire stood in the street waving as the truck drove out of sight. By two o'clock, the movers were finished. Claire handed the boss a wad of cash and waited for a receipt.

"We get the rest before we unpack the truck."

"No problem. Just get it out there safe," Claire said.

She carried a paper bag while following the truck down the driveway. As it drove away, she added the bag to a small pile of garbage in the street. She crossed her arms as she walked back up.

"Well, I'm going to make my flight at least. You want me to take a cab?"

"Course not. I'll take you."

"Okay, I just want to walk through the house for a bit before we go."

The living room was bare. Lighter shades of carpet outlined where the couch and cabinets once stood; deep indentations marked the legs. Claire kneeled and rubbed the carpet where the front of the couch had ended.

"Wow, look how dirty the carpet is here, where everyone's feet went. I guess over time you just don't notice it," she said.

She crawled to the wall and put her face close to the floor.

"What are you looking for?"

"Ben used to fall asleep sometimes with his head leaning back. Look, here I found one." She pinched something in her fingers. "Put your hand out." She dropped a blonde hair into his palm. "One of Ben's."

Howie stared at it.

"C'mon Howie, I wanna go out back."

The condition of the backyard resembled the living room. Where children's swings and plastic sandbox once stood, there was now an outline in the grass and holes in the dirt.

"This is what I'll miss the most. Ben out here with them, playing."

Howie stood behind her.

"Howie, you haven't said much since I got back. I'm going to ask you for last time, and I hate to pry, but are you gambling again? Ben mentioned a couple times that maybe there was a problem."

"No, I've got that under control. Look, everything's fine."

"Okay Howie, okay. Let's go in. I want to see the kids' room one more time."

They stood in the children's room, the stars still on the ceiling.

"It's so empty...I will miss it...but right now it's no longer a home. It's just a house – an empty house. Let's go. I can't wait to see my kids."

Claire and Howie stood face to face. People toting suitcases rushed past them on all sides at the busy airport terminal.

"Howie, promise me that you'll come out and visit."

"Sure, and you can come here too."

"When the kids get older it'll be easier."

"Yeah."

"Howie, never forget Ben. He loved you and I know you felt the same about him."

Howie's eyes filled with tears.

"I'm sorry Howie. I didn't mean to get you upset."

"Its okay. I'll never forget him...you better go."

"Yeah, I have to get searched for an hour," she said, holding back tears herself.

He kissed her on the cheek and turned her, giving her a slight nudge toward the gate. He watched as she disappeared through the doors.

* * * * * *

Howie dialed his cell phone from the airport parking lot. His heart raced as he waited.

"Sixth precinct, Sergeant Tully."

"Yes, can I speak to Detective Brent please."

"Hold for a minute."

"Brent here."

"Hi Detective, it's Howie. Listen, Claire's on her plane and I don't wanna go through another night thinking about this. You got time now?"

"Sure, how long will you be?"

"Twenty minutes, tops."

"See you then."

Having finished at the police station, Howie returned to Ben's house. He sat with his back against the living room wall. His body trembled. He raised a beer bottle to his lips, steadying it with both hands. Tears poured down his cheeks. He pushed his palm into his eye, wiping it to the side. He lifted the near empty bottle to the light and swished it around before placing it on the floor next to the other four empties.

"Ben...Ben, as usual, I'm comin to you for help. What do I do here? Looks like I'm in a no-win situation."

The house was cool, but his hair and T-shirt were soaked with sweat. A small brown paper bag lay next to him. He ran his hand over it, feeling the shape of the hard object within. He reached back to the other side and popped open another beer.

Chapter Sixteen

Back in South Dakota, Wes pulled his truck up in front of the house. Claire bolted towards the front door and burst in.

"Hi everyone," she yelled, running up the stairs.

She slowed as she got to the room where the children slept. Gently pushing the door open, she tiptoed in and stood for a moment, waiting for her eyes to adjust to the nightlight.

Sarah was asleep on her stomach in the crib. "My angel." Claire reached over the rail and stroked her hair while watching her breathe. Michael, sleeping in the bed adjacent, coughed and rolled over. Claire walked around and knelt, putting her face within inches of his. He breathed heavily through his mouth. She pulled his blanket up over his shoulders. Not wanting to leave the room, she sat on his bed, tempted to wake them and take them downstairs.

"You know what guys? I'll come get you early. As long as I know you're near and safe."

She kissed Michael and backed up, stepping on something soft. She bent down and picked up an article of dark clothing but couldn't make it out in the dim light. Out in the hallway, she inspected the piece.

Ski mask?

She carried it downstairs where Betty waited to greet her.

"How are you dear?"

"I'm good Mom. How were the kids since I spoke to you last?"

"Absolute angels."

Jill walked up from behind. "I wouldn't say absolute."

"Hi Jill. Thanks so much for taking them – thanks to both of you. I never would've gotten everything done with them under foot."

Wes came in from the back, carrying split logs for the fire.

"Come dear, tell us how everything went," Betty said, taking Claire by the arm to bathe by the warm fire.

"Wes said you spoke to Wayne?"

"Oh...they just called to say they're done for tonight. I think she said they're in Ohio. They should make it back by late tomorrow night."

Claire yawned, sparking a chain reaction. "God, I'm really tired."

"Well tell us quick what happened," Jill said.

"Not much more than we expected. We packed. I went to the banks. I said goodbye to the neighbors. I quit my job, but they knew that was coming..." She stopped talking for a second and stared into the fire.

"Claire? Something wrong?" Betty asked.

"I don't know. Howie was acting really strange. Real paranoid, and the detectives wanted to talk to him about speeding tickets but...I'm not sure I believed that. Oh well, whatever."

"I wouldn't worry about Howie, dear, he'll be okay."

Claire stood up. "Yeah I hope so. Maybe I'll give him a quick call before I go to bed." Just then she realized that she was still holding the hat that she had found upstairs. She stretched and flipped it inside out.

"Mom, who does this belong to? I found it on the floor next to the kids' beds."

"Lemme see that," Wes said, taking it from her. "Looks like one of Wayne's."

"But Wayne hasn't been here in days," Claire said.

"It probably fell out of a wash basket or something," Betty said.

"Probably...okay, let me say goodnight. We've got lots of time to talk tomorrow...and forever after that I guess."

Wes was the last to kiss her goodnight.

"Would you like me to take you to see Ben with the kids in the morning?"

"Yeah, Dad, I'd like that very much. I really miss him."

"We all do, sweetheart. Get some rest."

The crowing of the roosters had Claire awake early. She felt around for her slippers, and at the same time struggled to get her robe on. She walked toward the door, still having one arm caught in the sleeve.

Sarah was already standing in her crib when Claire walked in. Her eyes lit up upon seeing her mother, and she threw her little arms open repeating, "Mommy, Mommy, Mommy." Claire scooped her out of the crib and danced her around the room, keeping an eye on Michael to see if their laughter would wake him.

"Let's get your brother up."

Claire knelt next to Sarah and together they tickled Michael lightly under the chin until his eyes opened wide. "Mommy," he screamed and then began to cry at the top of his lungs. Sarah not to be outdone cried louder without knowing why. Seeing the joy on their faces and feeling so needed started Claire crying as well. She hugged them, smearing the tears until all of their faces were soaked.

"Tell you what. Let's get dressed and have breakfast. Then we can go out and play with the animals. How about that?"

The crying quickly turned to laughter as the two children, with Claire's help, fought to get dressed. Claire heard a sniffle come from behind her. She turned and covered her mouth in disbelief.

"Oh my God! How long have you been there?"

Betty, Wes and Jill poured into the room, all in tears.

"We had to watch the reunion, dear," Betty said. "I hope you don't mind."

"No, it's okay, Mom."

"We're going to go out and play with the animals."

Betty looked at Wes. "You know, Claire, it's a bit chilly out yet. Maybe you should take a ride with Wes first and then get them later."

"Ah no, I can dress them warm enough."

"Um, Claire? I really need to talk to you about something," Wes said. "I think we should go out for a ride...alone."

Claire stood up. "Sounds serious, Dad."

"Very serious."

"Something wrong with the kids? Is that what Howie wasn't telling me?" Claire asked in a nervous tone.

"No, no," they all yelled at her.

"It's actually a good thing," he said. "Let's go."

"Well can we eat first at least?"

"You know Dad, maybe better she get something in her stomach," Jill said.

"All right. Let's eat."

At the breakfast table, Claire looked back and forth at Betty, Wes and Jill.

"No one wants to look me in the eye. What is this big secret?"

She took a bite of a muffin while waiting for a reply.

Jill laughed. "It's a big secret."

Claire chewed slowly, with a slight smile while she looked at them curiously. Inside, her stomach churned.

Oh God, she's saying it's a big secret. I hope they didn't build me a house here or something. Can they build a house in a couple weeks?

"All right, Wes, let's go. Let's get this over with." She bent down and stuck her head between the children, kissing them both. "I'll be back in a little while. Then we'll go to see the animals."

Both children gave a look of distrust.

"Don't worry, I won't be gone long – I promise. I'm just going for a ride with Grandpa."

In the great room, she put on a denim jacket and called to Betty. "Mom, can you call Howie quick and let him know I'm okay? I forgot to call him last night." She came back to the table. "I'm afraid if I call him now, we'll start a long conversation."

"Okay dear," Betty replied.

"Now you gonna tell me what this is about, Dad?" she asked as they drove toward Ben's grave.

"Nope."

"No? Well when then? Did you build me a house or something like that?"

"Ah, you guessed it," he said, but she didn't know if he was telling the truth or not.

"Okay, I'll just sit here quiet and you'll let me know."

She kept her eye constantly toward the horizon, expecting to see some type of construction but none appeared. She wasn't really expecting to head in the direction of the grave, but Wes made a beeline for it.

Pulling up to the gravesite, Claire looked around, still having no idea what awaited her.

"Okay, hop out," Wes said.

"Okay, I'll play along," she said, stepping out.

Wes stayed inside and winked.

"What's that for? And aren't you getting out?"

"Nope, just you."

Now she was more confused than ever. She closed the door and crossed her arms. She looked around as she walked in front of the truck toward the grave.

"Dad, what am I looking for?"

"Just keep walkin."

As soon as she was far enough away, Wes put the truck into reverse. Claire turned in surprise and took two steps toward him but it was too late. She threw her arms in the air as she watched him drive away.

"What the???"

The sound of his engine waned; another grew louder from the opposite direction. She turned, now a little afraid. She backed up, still with her arms crossed and her hair blowing slightly in the cool breeze.

A black pickup truck came closer and at high speed. She could only make out the white cowboy hat of the lone occupant.

With blurred vision and a headache, Howie awoke, still in the living room where he had passed out the night before. Having no blanket, his body shivered, as he lay curled up on the cold floor. He attempted to straighten his stiff joints while he moaned from the horrific hangover. Fourteen beer bottles were lined up against the wall next to him. He pushed his tongue out of his mouth continuously until his saliva again flowed and lubricated it. He raised his left arm to his face to see his watch.

"Ah shit, eight-thirty."

He picked up his cell phone and dialed.

"Brenda? It's Howie."

"Howie...are you coming in today?"

"Yes dear. I'll be there but it'll be a little while. I have to run home and get some clothes. Actually, I may be here for a while." He stood up and staggered. "Not sure if I'm ready to drive yet."

"Are you okay, Howie? Sounds like you drank too much."

"Yeah...yeah Brenda, way too much. Give me a couple hours, I'll be there."

Facing the living room window, he squinted as the sunlight came through, magnifying the pain in his throbbing head. Shielding his eyes, he walked toward the window and peeked out, but there was nothing unusual.

At the kitchen sink, he doused his face with cold water. He ripped off a paper towel and wrapped it around some of the remaining ice cubes from the freezer. Walking back into the living room, he realized that he wasn't ready, mentally or physically, to drive.

Coming back into the living room, he tried not to think about the night before. Sitting in an empty house with no television or radio, and drinking until blacking out, had to be a sign of a mental breakdown.

* * * * * *

Claire walked toward the approaching truck. The silhouette of the driver was becoming clearer.

"Wayne? Why would Wayne be out here? Wait – Wayne's in Ohio," she yelled.

The truck stopped thirty feet in front of her.

"Ben?"

She ran full speed for three steps and then stopped short. Ben, now growing a full beard and mustache, opened the door and got out. Again she ran and stopped.

"Its me Claire," he said, walking toward her.

She began to back up. He stopped. "Now take it easy and I'll explain."

"Am I dreaming?" Her heart rate sped uncontrollably.

"It's really me."

Not knowing whether to believe or not, she exploded toward him, wrapping her arms around him and knocking him to the ground.

"Oh my God, it's really you." She touched his face and head, wanting desperately to believe.

Claire became incoherent and repeated soft slaps to the face wouldn't bring her around. Ben lifted her from under her arms and dragged her backwards to the truck, sitting her up against the front tire.

"Ben, is it really you? Is it really you?" She repeated.

Ben reached into the truck and pulled out a small plastic first aid kit. "They told me I'd need this."

She hadn't totally fainted yet but her eyes were beginning to glass over as she mouthed Ben's name. He broke open a small vial and stuck it under her nose. Her head jerked away from the smelling salts, but he kept it under her nose until she came around. She stared at him as he knelt next to her, running his fingers through her hair. Tears streamed down his cheeks.

"I'm so sorry Claire...to have put you and the children through this. Can you ever forgive me?"

"I don't get it, Ben... what's happening?" Let me look at you," she said, attempting to stand.

She pulled him closer and looked into his eyes. She kissed him on the lips and then pulled her head back four times until she believed that it was actually him. She then squeezed him tight and kissed him passionately, moaning with joy. But the joy only lasted for a few seconds as a multitude of questions exploded through her mind.

"Wait a minute," she said, stepping back, still a bit wobbly. She wiped tears from her face. "I saw your body...your dead body in the morgue. There was this huge hole in your head right there." She pointed to his forehead.

Ben took a step towards her.

"Stop," she yelled. "How long have you been alive?"

"Well over thirty years now."

"You're going to joke now?" she came towards him, he retreated.

"I knew this was going too good at first," he muttered.

Once within striking distance, she smacked him on the chest, the sound scaring a flock of birds into the air.

"Claire let me explain."

"Explain what? You let me think you were dead...you were dead...I saw you dead."

"That wasn't me...in the morgue. Well it was me, but I was drugged and in a freezer for a while. They made me up to look dead."

"That's great, that's just great. So you let me believe it was you. I picked out a casket and then went to not one but two funerals. I cried so much my eyes burned like someone put a match out in them."

"Claire, can you please be mad at me later? I just want to hold you, please. I'm begging."

She wanted to stay mad, but his pathetic pleading broke her down.

"Ohhh, come here. I don't understand but I'm happy. You're not leaving again, are you?"

"No, we're together for good."

"Oh my God, the kids. You gotta see the kids."

"I have seen them. But I wore a ski mask – the one you found last night. Mom told me about it. I didn't want them to know it was me."

"I knew Betty hesitated too much when I asked her about that hat. Wait a minute...who knew you were alive? Am I the only one who didn't know?" She backed away again.

Afraid of taking another beating, Ben stepped back toward the truck.

"Look, get in and I'll explain everything from beginning to end."

She just stood and stared at him.

"It's really me." He motioned for her to come closer.

She walked over meekly, kicking up rocks and acting nonchalant until she got close.

"What's with the beard?"

"Can't let anyone recognize me. Like it?"

"It's okay," she said, getting closer and falling into his arms and crying.

"It's gonna be all right. We're a family again."

She cried harder – harder than when she had been told he was dead. Fearful that she would pass out, he led her to the door.

"Let's sit inside and I'll tell you the whole story."

She nodded as he helped her into the truck on the driver's side. She slid over but stayed close.

"Where do I start?"

There was a box of tissues on the dashboard; he had come prepared. She wiped her eyes and nose and managed the words, "Start from the beginning."

"Well if I stayed in New York, I was a dead man. There was no way around it. Either Dracken or Luke would have killed me – we have Howie to thank for Luke."

"Howie? What do you mean?"

"Howie was the one who told Luke."

Claire covered her mouth and gasped. Ben nodded.

"The detectives found out when they got hold of the other attorney, Dan Perry. When he swore up and down that he didn't tell Luke, they looked at Howie. I had told them that he had seen Luke at the Motor Vehicle where my lawyer's office is. Turns out that Howie met him somewhere else but told me about motor vehicle so I would connect him to meeting my attorney – so I'd automatically blame the attorney.

"But why? He's our best friend."

"He didn't do it to hurt us. He thought we'd leave town as soon as we thought Luke knew. You're not going to believe why."

"Well tell me," she said.

"He was gambling again. He owed Victor Dracken's associates money from gambling losses. My will was the perfect way to get Dracken killed. He figured with Dracken dead, his empire would collapse along with the gambling debt. Howie promised to give Luke the account number for killing Dracken. Howie planned to turn Luke in after he killed Dracken and not give him a penny of my money." He shook his head and laughed. "That nut even called the junkyard where Connie and Luke worked and made believe he was Dan Perry with that fake voice gadget. That way Connie would call me to say that Luke knew and we'd leave town. You following this?"

She nodded slowly. "Yeah but..."

"This obviously wasn't that well thought out but he was desperate. Oh, by the way, he told the detectives the whole story last night and thinks he's going to be arrested, maybe today."

"Is he? I mean if I understand this right, he kinda hired a hitman himself," she said.

"No, they won't arrest him. I told them to let him stew over night though. They're going to tell him I'm alive but that wasn't part of the plan. I didn't want him to think that I died because of him."

"Wait a second. Why wasn't I told, and who knew you were alive?"

"You couldn't know. Your grief had to be genuine. If you knew, how would you cry? My mother was the only one who knew because they were afraid of her heart giving out. She knew even before the accident – well the faked accident."

"But she cried."

"She cried because of the pain you and the others were in – and she couldn't help you. Surprised that didn't stop her heart."

Ben stared out the window and tried to hold back tears.

"I'm so sorry for what I put you and everyone through." He pulled her close and kissed her forehead.

They wept together for a few minutes and after soaking a few tissues, Ben continued.

"Ok, where was I? Oh yeah, Dad and Jill found out soon as you left for New York. Wayne and Jessica don't know yet – not 'til they get back."

They sat quietly for a few minutes. Ben could see that Claire was running through the time-line of what had had happened.

"You know what else is weird? When I sang to Michael, I could feel you there – your spirit."

"I was there, Claire. I felt all your pain. I cried more than you did thinking about what you were going through."

She held him tight and then pointed at the grave.

"I can't believe that I talked into an empty grave, thinking you were there."

"It's not empty," he said with a smile.

"It's not? Then who's buried there?"

"Harry."

"Harry the homeless guy? From around your building? You're kidding: this just gets weirder and weirder."

"He was such a nice guy, I figured he'd like it here. He said he always wanted to come out this way. And as for weird, you ain't heard nothin' yet."

Claire clutched tightly to Ben's arm and rested her chin on his shoulder.

"What I'm about to tell you can't be repeated. Gail can't know, and she can't know I'm alive either." Ben took a deep breath. "The cops knew where Luke was all the time. They let him kill Dracken."

Claire's eyes opened wide in astonishment. He nodded.

"Yup, they couldn't get Dracken on anything, so they let him die. They figured they could get Luke off the street at the same time. Killing him was just a bonus."

"God, I can't believe that. Isn't that kind of illegal?" Claire asked in utter disbelief.

"Yeah but sometimes they do what they have to do. Twenty years from now this'll break as a major story when one of the cops spills the story for money or something."

"Wow, this is unreal," she said.

"Hey, let me call the detective, see if they told Howie yet. I can't wait to talk to him. He's gonna be pissed that I let him wait overnight thinking about going to jail but he'll get over it."

"You know Ben, he was actin' really weird since the detective asked to see him. I mean a lot of things are adding up now."

"Lemme call. Let's see if the cell phone works out here. We should be close enough – yeah we got a signal."

He dialed, and after many strange beeps and tones, Casey picked up the phone.

"Hey detective, how's those bones mending?"

Claire smacked herself on the leg, realizing that Casey hadn't really been hurt.

"Hey Ben. We had some trouble trackin' Howie. He didn't go to work and wasn't home. We're going to take a ride to your house first, then to his."

"Shit, I hope he's okay. Let me know when you find him."

"Will do."

Ben snapped the phone shut.

"What's wrong?"

"They don't know where he is. Huh, that's strange."

"Hope he doesn't snap," she said.

"Yeah...well they're going out looking for him. They'll call as soon as they find him."

They sat in silence as the cool breeze blew through the cab.

"This the first time that the silence feels good," she said. "Because I'm not alone."

She took one more tissue and blew her nose.

"Ben? What now? I mean are you still going to be a broker out here?"

He shook his head. "There's more to the story." A huge smile came across his face. "Well, you know that million dollar reward on Dracken's head?"

"You mean?"

"Uh-huh. It's ours. The FBI handled that. We couldn't take the life insurance money because I wasn't really dead, but it looks like it on every file and the FBI handled that too. We are rich – and out here a million dollars is stinkin' rich."

"We're rich, we're rich. That sounds nice," she said.

"I'm going to have to have some cosmetic surgery though, and I'll probably have to keep the beard."

"Where are we going to live?"

"Well, I was thinking somewhere outside Rapid City. Most of the folk around here don't get there too much. Odds are, I won't ever be seen."

"It's amazing – one minute I've got a dead husband and now I've got a million bucks and a whole new life." She then had a revelation. "My god, we can travel. No more worrying about your clients."

"Oh, one more thing. My name has changed."

"Oh no."

"Sorry, Mrs. Gordon."

"Gordon?"

"I'm now Art Gordon and you're Mrs. Gordon."

"How boring is that. Couldn't they have picked a livelier name?"

"That's what they didn't want and I picked it." He looked at her, waiting for her to recognize the name.

She shrugged her shoulders. "What? I'm supposed to know that name?"

"Remember all the Wild Wild West shows I made you watch?"

"Yeah?"

"Artemus Gordon – one of the main characters."

Claire's eyes lit up. "Oh yeah, I remember. God, that's funny."

They sat quietly again.

"Ben, let's get the kids. I can't wait anymore."

"Okay, but you have to stop calling me Ben."

Howie pulled the door at Ben's house shut and checked to make sure it was locked. He held the handrail tightly, taking one step at time. He held the brown paper bag up high across his forehead, shading his eyes from the bright sun. His head pounded with every step.

Holding his keychain close to his face, he found the button to unlock the doors. The car chirped as the alarm turned off. He got in, throwing the paper bag onto the passenger seat. The view out the windshield was foggy. He rubbed the inside but realized that it was his vision that was impaired. The view out the back was worse – Brent and Casey rolled down the street toward him.

"Hey Case, hit the siren, let's scare the crap out of him."

Casey flipped the switch for the siren on and off once quickly, causing a loud burping sound. Howie, in a panic, turned the key and fired the engine. Flooring the gas, he spun the front tires until they gripped and sped the car down the road.

Casey and Brent looked at each other and followed.

"Whata we do now? I don't want to chase him."

"I don't know. What's protocol for pursuing a man that you're about to tell that you're not going to arrest him?"

Coming up to an intersection, they looked both ways.

"There he goes. Way down that block." Brent pointed while Casey tried to look past his head. They turned in Howie's direction, but didn't speed after him.

"Call him on his cell."

"Way ahead of you," he said, flipping through notes, looking for Howie's number.

"Got it, dialing." He waited. "No answer."

They came out to a busy road and looked both ways.

"Well, pick a direction," Casey said.

Brent pointed right. They crept along, looking into the parking lots of the strip-mall-lined road.

"Wait, hold it. Pull in."

Brent pointed into a parking lot. Casey turned in. Howie's car was parked headfirst against a fence that divided two parking lots. Light exhaust smoke still puffed from the pipes. Casey sped towards it, stopping twenty feet behind.

"You see him?"

The detectives stepped out leaving the doors wide open. Both had their weapons drawn fearful that Howie would snap with the idea of being arrested for causing his best friend's death.

"Howie?" Brent called, nearing the driver's door from the rear.

"Howie... no, don't. Ben's still alive," Casey yelled into the car.

Howie was slumped across the front seats holding a gun to his head. He looked up at Casey.

"I killed him – I was the cause of Ben's death," Howie said crying.

"Ben is still alive. Put down the gun and we'll prove it," Brent yelled.

Howie raised his head up higher. "How could he be alive? I saw his body. You're lying," he screamed through the closed window.

Brent and Casey kept their guns trained on Howie.

"It was all staged, Howie. We couldn't tell you. The only reason we're telling you now is to save your life. He's in South Dakota with his family. Put the gun down and we'll call him. You can talk to him," Casey pleaded.

Howie pushed the silver 9mm weapon hard to his temple. "I killed him... I killed him. I saw him dead. You're lying," he yelled.

"No, here, wait..."

Howie let out loud scream. He squeezed the trigger. Both detectives dropped their weapons to their sides.

Chickens flew out of the way as Ben kicked up dust, spinning the tires on the approach to the back of the house. Betty and Wes waited at the back door, holding the children from running into his path. Skidding the truck to a halt, Ben flung open the door and kneeled with arms extended. The two children hesitated for a second, not sure if the bearded man was really their missing father.

"Daddy?" Michael said. He then began repeating it over and over faster and faster while stamping his feet in a dance. "Daddy...daddy...daddy?"

He ran to Ben's arms. Sarah followed, letting out a shrill scream.

"Daddy's back," Claire yelled.

Ben rolled around the ground as they giggled. Claire stood over them, wiping away tears in her elation. Betty, Wes, and Jill all stood two steps outside the back door. Claire, finally able to take her eyes off the happy trio on the ground, caught Betty's eye.

"Oh Mom, he's back, he's back," she yelled, running to them and forming a huddle.

Betty's eyes watered as she put her arms on Claire's shoulders and faced her. "Claire, I'm so sorry that I couldn't tell you, but it was the only way, dear."

"I understand, Mom."

"She kept it from me too – didn't know she was such a sneak," Wes said.

Michael pulled on Ben's hand to get up. "Daddy, let's go see the animals."

"Yeah, the animals," Sarah said.

"No no, not now," Claire said. "We'll have plenty of time for that – and I mean plenty. Bring them in."

The women filed inside. Wes held the door while Ben herded the overjoyed children inside. Wes placed his hand on his son's back. "God, it's good to have you back. Can't wait to see the faces on Wayne and Jessica."

Betty held the phone up in the air. "Ben it's for you." She looked at Claire. "We have to be careful who we let Ben speak to. Remember, he's dead."

"Who is it?"

"Detective Brent. Such a nice fellow."

Claire watched Ben's face light up. "You're going to let me talk to that goof? Really?"

"Yeah we had to chase him and then he tried to kill himself but the idiot forgot to load the gun – oh wait..." Brent said.

Ben could hear Howie explaining something in the background.

"I meant the guy that he got the gun from forgot to or didn't mention the gun had no bullets."

Brent handed his cell phone to Howie who had relinquished his firearm to Casey.

"Hello?" Howie said.

"Boooooooooo. This is the ghost of Ben Pearce."

"Ben... is that really you?" Howie asked in amazement.

"Its me. Sorry we couldn't tell you but..."

Howie broke down in deep sobs now realizing that his friend was still alive. "You let me think you were dead? You got any idea what I've been through?"

"What *you've* been through? You started this whole thing."

There was silence for a second.

"I never meant..." Howie started.

"I know, I know. Don't worry. Just hop a plane and get out here as soon as you can. I wanna give you a beatin." Ben said, starting to cry himself.

Howie nodded his head but couldn't get any words out. Brent gently removed the phone from Howie's hand.

"Ben? Its Brent. We'll take care of him now. We'll stick him on a plane."

"Ok," Ben said in a whisper. Tell... tell him to call me in a little while or from the plane."

Ben hung up the phone and turned. The family waited for Howie's reaction.

"They told Howie that I'm alive and he's headin out here."

The family huddled around him – the tears flowed freely. Ben Pearce once again had the perfect life.

Ken Myler lives on Long Island, New York. He is an avid boater who enjoys navigating the Great South Bay but his passion for hiking and cycling draw him to the unexplored arches and spires of the American West. His admiration of nature is surpassed only by his love for animals.

He is an admitted daydreamer having a wandering mind rivaling that of the fictitious character – Walter Mitty. Many of his stories have been maturing secretly since childhood and only recently did he put them to paper. Discovering the calming affects of Native American flute music, he uses it to focus on the many twists and turns that he writes into his stories.

Printed in the United States
66397LVS00001B/88-192